THE BESTSELLING ECSTASY SERIES
by Janelle Taylor

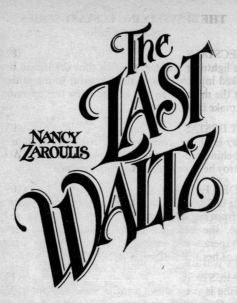

The LAST WALTZ

NANCY ZAROULIS

ZEBRA BOOKS

KENSINGTON PUBLISHING CORP.

ZEBRA BOOKS

are published by

Kensington Publishing Corp.
475 Park Avenue South
New York, NY 10016

First printing: June 1986

Printed in the United States of America

For Jerry

Acknowledgments

For their help, my thanks to the kind and painstaking staff of the Boston Athenaeum, the Boston Public Library, and the Massachusetts Historical Society; and to Thomas N. Brown, Antonio Carrara, Morris J. Karnovsky, Timothy Sullivan, Alexandra Zaroulis, Katherine Zaroulis, and particularly to Gerald J. Sullivan, my best reader.

Part I

One

There is no family so secure that scandal cannot touch it. Every family is vulnerable in some way, and not the finest brownstone mansion or the largest fortune—not even the most ancient lineage—can protect a family from scandal's hot, foul breath.

Ethel January understood this, even if her children did not. She was always, as long as I knew her, exquisitely sensitive to other people's opinion—or at least to the opinion of those whom she considered qualified by birth or fortune to deliver judgment.

Thus it must have terrified her to learn, the week before her eldest son Curtis' wedding in May of 1870, that there was brewing beneath her own roof a scandal which would, if it became public, not only destroy Curtis' alliance with the Parker wealth but also ruin the matrimonial chances of all her other children as well.

There were in fact two scandals. I do not know what she would have done had she learned of them both: probably, being a January by marriage and a Cunningham by birth, she would have dealt with the second as

11

swiftly—and as ruthlessly—as she did with the first.

The rising sun, that bright dawn, would have slanted down the long, straight streets of the New Land lined with close-massed dwellings of brick and brownstone—the Back Bay, as it came to be known. Here and there it would have glistened on a limestone facade or a fanciful, iron-framed oriel window or illuminated the ugly vacant lots that awaited their turn to be built upon; but mainly it shone on sober, dark-hued town houses, evidence of the city's wealth, testimony to her citizens' fondness for the new architectural styles of the Second Empire lately imported from Paris and erected on the filled land which twenty years previously had been a festering mud flat, the tidal basin of the Charles.

Within those houses, that morning, slept the men who ruled the city. Beside them, their wives; in other rooms, their children, their indigent sisters or sisters-in-law, their aging parents—for the men of Boston were family men above all, and any one of them, even the wealthiest, would have been disgraced had he refused to offer a home to a needy relation.

In the high, narrow brownstone that her husband Asa had built on Marlborough Street in the spring and summer of '68, Ethel January lay beside him and went over once again the details of the ceremony planned for the following week: every seating arrangement, every bouquet, every recipe of every item on the menu. These were properly the concern of the bride's family, of course, but the January reputation was at stake as well, and she felt her responsibility very heavily. So it must have been an unpleasant interruption to hear the soft knock at her bedroom door.

With great caution Mrs. January slid from beneath the silk comforter, threw her wrapper around her shoulders, and went barefooted to open the door. It was the cook. She had come to announce disaster, of course. Good news could be contained for a convenient moment, but disaster needed to be told at once. And needed to be dealt with discreetly, silently, so as not to awaken Asa. Mrs. January stepped into the hall and closed the door behind her before she spoke.

"Yes, Margaret? What is it?"

In the pale illumination given by the skylight into the stairwell she noted traces of tears on the cook's thin red face, she saw the chilblained hands twisting nervously before the woman's starched white coverall.

But Margaret could not—would not—enlighten her; she asked Mrs. January to come below stairs to see another of the servants, the cause of the trouble, the new little Swiss maid, Hannelore, who had been with the family for less than a year. Mrs. January had hesitated to hire her, for the girl was extremely pretty; but in the end, lacking other candidates, she had taken her on and had every day since that time expected the summons which had come to her now.

In the kitchen Hannelore sat weeping at the scrubbed deal table. Her fair hair streamed down around her rosy face; her wide blue eyes were red and swollen from her tears.

"Well?" said Mrs. January. "What is it?"

"Oh, ma'am, oh, ma'am—please—"

"Stop this at once, Hannelore, and tell me what is

13

the matter."

"I—I—no, please—"

It was cold in the kitchen, and Mrs. January had only her thin wrapper over her nightdress. Her annoyance mounted; she turned to the cook for enlightenment.

"She's caught it," said Margaret. She patted her abdomen. "Here. She's four months' gone at least."

Hannelore burst out with a fresh fit of tears. "Oh, ma'am—"

"Is that so, Hannelore? Are you—are you in the family way?"

"He said I'd come to no harm, ma'am, he said no one would know—"

"Who? Who was it did this to you?"

"Oh, ma'am—it was Mr. Curtis, ma'am, Mr. Curtis said—"

"*Mr. Curtis?*" Mrs. January's shoulders slumped as if she staggered under a heavy blow. "Mr. Curtis? What do you mean?"

"It was him, ma'am, and he said—"

"Never mind what he said! You stupid, foolish girl—never mind that! Are you accusing *my son* of—of— Stop your bawling! Stop it at once!" She whirled on Cook and the kitchen maid, aware of their undisguised interest in the proceedings. "Get on with your work—breakfast as usual! Stop your gawking! Hannelore, go up to your room and do not leave until I give you permission."

It seemed that the girl hardly had the strength to rise, but at last she obeyed and disappeared, still weeping, up the back stairs to her attic dormitory.

Mrs. January went at once to her son's room—her

eldest son, her pride and joy, whose betrothal to Grace Parker had brought such happiness to them all. She had four younger children, but Curtis was her favorite. She could hardly comprehend the news which the maid had just given her.

He was asleep. Roughly she shook him awake. She told him of Hannelore's condition and demanded to know if it were so—and, worse, if he had caused it.

"Mother, I want to explain—"

"Explain! Explain! What is there to explain except your—your utter irresponsibility! Do you know the consequences if this news gets out? Do you think Ezekiel Parker will allow his daughter to marry you if he hears of this?"

And so on: an unpleasant scene. Mrs. January was shocked, but she need not have been, for Curtis was only human, after all, and humans are notoriously unpredictable. I have lived long enough now not to be surprised at any behavior: I have lived with people of wealth and social standing and I have known, too, people of humbler means; and if I have learned anything it is that we are all alike under the skin, we are all subject to the same desires, the same hungers and compulsions. There is no limit to human behavior either bad or good, and the man who saves your life in the morning will take it at night if he is desperate enough, and you need not be surprised either way, for that is our nature, good and bad together, inextricably intertwined.

In the end Mrs. January said that she would dismiss the girl at once and perhaps they could avoid a scandal. Curtis did not quarrel with the need to dismiss her, but he begged his mother to wait until he could go downtown to see an officer of the bank and get some money for her so that she would not starve. Mrs. January agreed; but when he returned at midmorning Hannelore had gone—had been sent away after all. He was furious. He tore out of the house and started off on foot to look for her, but in half an hour he was back. He had no idea where she might have gone, he knew no one who could give him information. He even went to Margaret, and to the maids, to ask them if they might know. But they could—or would—tell him nothing.

It had been, thought Mrs. January, a narrow escape. And then, not a week later, Isabel, her middle child, tried—and failed—to elope with Lawrence Cushing, and for a time scandal hovered close again.

Isabel had met him the previous summer at Nahant, north of Boston, where she had gone with her family for their annual flight from the city's heat. Nahant was fashionable then, in the years just after the Southern Rebellion, and the January family, in their dignified way, were as fashionable as any in Boston.

One morning about a week after their introduction she had awakened at first light—fully awake, as if someone had called her. She got up at once. Quickly she put on a loose summer smock and morocco slippers and, as silent as a thief, she let herself out of the house. The birds were just beginning to sing, the dew lay heavy on the grass; the sea, beyond the cliffs, stretched to the horizon like a sheet of pearly silk.

Answering that mysterious call, she made her way to the bluffs above Perkins' Cove, a favorite swimming spot despite its pebbly beach. The sun was just coming up as she reached the line of scraggly, wind-whipped shrubs that clung to the land's edge. She looked down: and there, far below, she saw him.

He stood knee-deep in the water; his golden hair gleamed in the first rays of the sun, his body was wet and glistening. A strand of seaweed had caught on his shoulder but he did not bother to throw it off. He was naked. To her, he must have looked like the god of the sea suddenly come to life: primitive and powerful, beautiful beyond any beauty she had ever seen. Breathless, enchanted, she watched him as he plunged in. He swam with hard, sure strokes, his arms flashing in the sun, his long legs propelling him through the surf, then standing again, shaking the drops from his face, his body like the body of an ancient statue, finely muscled, perfectly proportioned, his skin if you stroked it as smooth as Grecian marble.

Again and again he dived, and stood, and dived again. She could not look away; she watched, trembling, her heart in turmoil, until the sun was high and he at last was done and came to fetch his clothing by the water's edge. And then, almost too late, she awakened from her enchantment and fled before she was discovered and— worse—disgraced.

She told no one of that morning until, years later, she told me; but it was then that she began to love him, it was then that her passion for him was aroused and never left her.

She met him again in the winter, at the Mayburys' on New Year's Eve. While Curtis proposed marriage to

Grace that night, in the Mayburys' conservatory, Isabel danced with Lawrence Cushing: she gazed into those brilliant eyes, as helpless as a rabbit who encounters a hypnotic snake, and fell in love with him all over again. Cushing was a marvelous dancer; he whirled her around and around until she nearly fainted in his arms, he literally swept her off her feet. She could not erase from her mind the vision of that young sea god swimming at sunrise at Nahant. And now here she was, in his arms, dancing, dancing— Dear heaven, how she adored him!

He called the next day—New Year's Day—and the day after that, and the day after that. . . . But many young men called on Isabel, and Mrs. January, preoccupied with the news of Curtis and Grace, paid no particular heed to Cushing. And so all that winter and spring Isabel and Cushing kept their secret; Isabel was mad for him, she had taken leave of her senses. She would have done anything for him, anything he asked her to do.

And all unsuspecting of the disaster that lurked, Mrs. January and Mrs. Parker plotted Curtis' and Grace's wedding; they were like two generals—allies, but from not entirely friendly nations—planning a final drive to victory. Since Grace was an only child, she acted diplomatically to cement the relationship between the two families by asking Isabel to be her maid of honor. And Isabel, preoccupied by her infatuation with Cushing, caught up in the busy round of lunches and teas and dinners and dances that were the lot of the new debutante, had said yes in the winter, when she was asked, without ever thinking that by May, when the ceremony was held, she would not be there, she would be

18

far away in the West with Lawrence Cushing.

Poor Isabel! What had she imagined? A Boston brownstone standing isolated on the vast prairie, with squaws for servants?

But Cushing betrayed her. By April he knew that he was in serious trouble. His debts were being called in— gambling debts, cockfighting, his mistress' husband becoming suspicious. He could have left on his own, of course. But he asked Isabel to go with him. And she agreed.

"Why?" I asked Curtis once.

He shrugged. "I don't know, Marian. She was my sister, we grew up together in the same house, but she was like a stranger to me. He must have bewitched her. She was always so sensible, so coolheaded—"

"Love changes that."

"So they say."

"And why did he ask her to go? Why did he bother with her at all?"

"She may have amused him. She was pretty, she came of good family, she had money. Perhaps he thought that he could marry her, stay in Boston, lead a respectable life. And then when it all closed in on him, perhaps he was amused at the thought of thumbing his nose at Boston society. As if to say to them all—all the people who were after him—'You see how unimportant you are if Isabel January will give you up to go with me!'

"In any case, none of us noticed what she and Cushing were up to. We were all too busy with our wedding plans, Grace's and mine. I remember once thinking that Isabel looked—well, sparkling. As if a light had been turned on inside her somehow. I'd never seen her look that way before, but I thought it was just the general excitement of her debutante year." He paused, pulling at his cigar, then holding it away from him and contemplating its thick, pale, ashy tip. "He came from good family, you know. Cushing. He'd been ruined by living abroad all his childhood. His father died shortly after Lawrence was born. His mother carted him off to Europe, to England, and she didn't come back until it was time for him to go to Harvard. He was a classmate of Leighton's."

"Yes," I said. Leighton was the next youngest after Curtis; then came Isabel; then Elinor and Ned.

"He was very clever, of course. Devious."

Other men might have said "a bounder" or "a cad."

"She'd have been better off if she'd never met him," he went on.

"Would she?" I said.

My question startled him. "Of course. Of course she would! He brought her nothing but pain, and humiliation—"

"And joy," I said. "He brought her great joy, once. Few of us ever have such happiness."

He stood up, then, and began to pace the Turkey carpet as if the mention of happiness unnerved him more than any talk of sorrow: a tall, spare, kindly-looking man with close-cut gray hair and thoughtful brown eyes. He is handsome in the way of one of Charles Dana Gibson's men, but stronger-looking, not so pretty. "You don't understand, Marian. You don't know—"

Ah, but I did, for Isabel had told me: how she loved him, how he seemed to love her, how he schemed for moments alone with her so that against all the rules of etiquette he could embrace her, how she would have been compromised if anyone had learned of their behavior and yet how she acquiesced, she could not help herself.

Once, desperate, she had allowed him to spirit her away from an evening of charades at a house party. They had fled to an upstairs sitting room; for an hour they were alone. He kissed her as no man kisses a woman to whom he is not betrothed—and not even then. He kissed her and kissed her—she had never dreamed that men could behave so; her girlhood had been sheltered, she was ignorant of men, ignorant of love. She stood before him trembling, nearly sobbbing, overwhelmed by emotions that she could not even name, and all the while he caressed her and murmured sweet, false promise.

"I remember that night," said Curtis, "that night when she was to go away with him, and of course none of us knew, none of us had the faintest notion. It was the night before the wedding, when just the two families had come together for a dinner. It was supposed to have been given at Aunt Reed's, but then it was changed to our house, I don't remember why, and that must have upset them, forcing them to change their plans. And at about ten-thirty, after we had finished dinner and more people had come in and the house was pretty well full, Mother came looking for me and found me with Cousin Sam Swift, who was enlightening me about the Parker genealogy, and her face was—not panicked, not that, she was in control, but there was a kind of tightness around her mouth and a look in her eyes, and I knew something was wrong. She led me out into the hall. 'I can't find

Isabel,' she said.

"'What do you mean, you can't find her?' I said.

"'Just that. She isn't here.'

"I remember that I was not alarmed—only annoyed that my evening might be spoiled by some prank of Isabel's. People were coming out into the hall. Mother seemed to expect me to do something—to produce Isabel—and to do it quietly so that no one would know that anything had happened.

"'Go back to the party,' I said. 'I'll look for her.'

"I used the back stairs, of course, but I was simply repeating what Mother had done herself. Isabel wasn't anywhere in the rooms upstairs. I even went up to the attic, to the servants' rooms. I stood and held a candle and called her name. For one terrible moment I thought that Hannelore might answer me. But of course she had gone. I wanted to throw myself down on one of those wretched beds and just forget it all, just go to sleep. I remember thinking how low the ceiling was; I could hear rain pounding directly above my head. Cramped and low—I'd never seen the servants' rooms before. Then I went down again all the way to the kitchen. I asked Cook and the others if they'd seen Isabel. By that time I was beginning to be alarmed myself and I didn't care if they thought my request was odd. But they hadn't seen her. Just then the scullery girl took a load of trash out to the back areaway. The rain was flooding a bit, she said—a regular cloudburst. I don't know why it occurred to me to look for Isabel outside on such a night but I opened the back door and stood for a moment looking out. The fence at the back alley—a high, wooden paling—was perhaps twenty feet away. I couldn't see it. Pitch-black. Pouring rain. I looked out—and then I saw a kind of movement not even definite enough to be a blur. Just a sense of something there. I closed the door behind me and stood sheltered a bit by the overhang. I was in my good clothes, you understand, and reluctant to ruin them—a light brown Prince Albert, I remember, and a silk waistcoat. But I knew that someone was there. I didn't think at first that it was Isabel. I thought that it might be a prowler. We'd had burglaries nearby, and the watch never went into the alleyway. Finally I called. 'Who's there?' I said. I could hear the noise of the party from the floor above. I called again, a little louder. 'Who's there?' Still I had no answer, but I knew then that I was not alone. I stepped out into the yard. At once I was soaked—dripping. I made my way to the fence and there I found her. I don't know how long she'd been standing there waiting for him. I didn't say a word. I just led her into the house and up the back stairs to her room. I was afraid to leave her alone, but fortunately one of the servants had seen us and had sent for Mother.

"'Go—quickly—change your clothes and go down to say good night to them,' she said to me when she came. 'They are just leaving. Tell them—if they ask—tell them that Isabel has been suddenly indisposed and I am with her, tell them anything you like, but go!'

"Isabel stood in the middle of the room, not moving a muscle. There was a dark wet stain on the rug all around her from her soaking dress. Her eyes were open, but she didn't seem to see us. She didn't say a word. And then, just as I was going out, her face seemed to crumple. She opened her mouth, wide, as if she were going to let out a shriek that would be heard on the Common, but no sound came. I'd never seen a person in such agony, and yet she was completely silent."

"So," I said. "He jilted her."

"Yes."

"Why?"

"I don't know—I never knew. Things got too hot for him, probably, and he just went without her."

"And the next day," I said, "you were married?"

"Yes. The ceremony went off remarkably smoothly. Isabel performed her part just as we had rehearsed it. And then Grace and I went away, we went to England, and we didn't return until after—" He stopped, embarrassed, and I took pity on him and said what he could not.

"After Nahant," I said.

"Yes."

Where Isabel went to mend her broken heart; and where she broke mine.

Two

Nahant: where Boston families fled the summer's heat and the sun sparkled on the sea and the air blew fresh bloom into pale cheeks. I think of them as certain species of birds, migrating every year to that small seaside enclave, entrance to which was as restricted as entrance to, say, the Saturday Club, or the Porcellian. The Januarys had a house on the bluffs. Every morning Mr. January, with his fellows, took the steamer across the harbor to Boston; every evening he returned. His wife and children stayed at Nahant and had the full benefit of the air. It was marvelously restorative: every June, it seemed, a number of the refugee colony arrived from Boston pale and weakened from the rigors of the winter's social schedule; and every September they returned home strong and healthy once again. Many cures were effected at Nahant, not the least of them the mending of the ravages of an unhappy love affair.

That summer of 1870 was the first that I had spent at Nahant, for our family was not the social equal of the Januarys and the other Boston families who summered there. We were not in fact a Boston family at all; we had lived for most of my life in Somerset Falls, a small town west of Springfield, where my father had been a teacher of mathematics at a boys' academy.

My brother George, two years younger than I, was the favorite of both my parents. He was a dear boy, bright and kind, and never a torment to me in the way of many younger brothers. We had happy childhoods, George and I: happier than those of the children of the rich whom I have known since. I never minded that my mother and father loved him best; it seemed natural that they should, since I was only a girl.

In the summer of my thirteenth birthday, when General Lee was defeated at Gettysburg, and thousands rioted in New York against conscription, my father announced that he was going to the war. My mother was appalled.

"They need men who can march and shoot," she said. "You'll only be a hindrance." I saw tears in her eyes and I thought that they must be tears of anger; sorrow, to a woman of my mother's disposition, seemed an emotion as foreign as patriotism.

But my father was determined to go, and so he did; and he endured longer than anyone thought he could. We were the ones, my mother said later, who had difficulty enduring, for the academy paid no salary to a teacher who did not teach, and the army paid irregularly and very little at that. By the beginning of '64 we were in a bad way for money, and so, one bright and bitter day, my mother announced that we were going away for the duration. A distant—and wealthy—connection in Boston, she said, had offered her a position as paid companion to his invalid wife. The salary was not large, but with our savings she thought we would manage; and there were better prospects in the city for George than could be found in a small country town. Both he and I could finish our schooling and see a bit of the world beyond the Berkshires.

We lived in two rooms in Pembroke Street in the South End. It was not a fashionable address, but it was a perfectly respectable one. The houses were swell-front red brick, like those which eventually lined the streets built on the New Land in the Back Bay; but the area never caught on as the place where the rich and fashionable wanted to live, and so it was left to people like us.

We heard regularly from my father; we enjoyed the excitement of city life; our landlady was a kind, pleasant woman frequently generous with stray molasses cookies and peppermint drops; and so we were not unhappy.

Nevertheless we looked forward to the day when my father would come home to us again. I remember how my mother, on hearing of the surrender at Appomattox, clapped her hands and rushed to embrace us as she exclaimed, over and over again, "Oh, now he will come home! Now at last he will come home!" Despite her frequent outbursts at him, I think that she loved him very much in her way; and I am sure that she was tired of supporting us, constantly worrying about money.

Five days later he was dead of dysentery. The news came to us early on a Saturday morning. The boy who delivered the telegraphed message would not stop to answer questions; he thrust the folded slip of paper into my hand and turned and ran down the stairs. From the streets I heard the sound of church bells, but for a while I was so engrossed in our own trouble that I neglected to ask why they tolled. Late in the day, when my mother, exhausted from weeping, had fallen asleep with George sitting beside her holding her hand, I crept downstairs and out to the dusky street to have a breath of air. The landlady sat on the front stoop, dipping snuff; her normally cheerful expression had been replaced by one of deepest gloom, and I wondered, in the instant before I spoke to her, why she mourned a man she had never met.

"So he's gone," she said. "Sit, child, and keep me company. A terrible, terrible thing. Shot in the back of the head. Terrible."

I was numb from my grief; her words did not at once make sense. I heard the church bells, still tolling as they had earlier in the day.

"And your pa, too. Gone forever. Poor, poor man."

She patted my arm. I remember very clearly my confusion at her words. Who else had died?

And then she told me, and I had new reason to weep.

In the days that followed, the city of Boston, like the rest of the country, was convulsed with grief over President Lincoln's murder. On the Sunday, every church was filled with mourners; black bunting was displayed on the fronts of Union houses, and staunch Union men wore black armbands and wept openly in the streets. And so our private sorrow was subsumed in the larger, public mourning for the martyred President, and for months afterward, if suddenly I burst into tears at any place, at any time, I had no need to be embarrassed or to explain my visible grief, for everyone wept at odd times then, mourning Father Abraham, and they simply assumed that I mourned him too.

We buried my father in Somerset Falls and then we returned to the city, where now, it seemed, we must stay. I finished my schooling the following year and secured a place as governess to a family in Mount Vernon Street; my brother George, who had hoped to attend Harvard as our father had done, went instead in the spring of '66 to the offices of the merchant trading house of Peele & Lothrop as a junior clerk.

And so we survived for several years. My mother lost her place when her invalid charge died; unable to secure another, she took up painting china. For a while she seemed in a fair way to make a success, sometimes selling as many as a dozen floral-emblazoned pieces a week, but then business fell off and she was left with a large inventory.

Still, with my wages and George's together we were able to live. Our savings, of course, had long since vanished, but my mother was optimistic nevertheless. "George will rise like a shot, once they see how smart and quick he is," she said. "He'll be a partner before you know it. And as for you—"

She did not need to say more: for me, the obvious thing was to find a husband. Needless to say, none appeared. Worse, as '66 became '67 and then '68, George failed to achieve any promotion at Peele & Lothrop's. In the winter of '69-'70 he fell ill with pleurisy; although he recovered from it in a few weeks, he was left with a nagging cough that racked him night and day and seemed to melt the flesh from his bones.

And then, in the summer of 1870, we went, quite unexpectedly, to the seaside: my mother, my brother George, and I.

'It was a case of threatened disaster turning into a chance at good fortune—or so my mother said. I had my doubts, but I was never able to oppose her when she was set on having her way. And certainly the disaster was imminent enough: George, gaunt and white, was very nearly exhausted from his cough, and although the doctor faithfully prescribed a variety of tonics which George faithfully took, by June he had grown worse.

"Sea air," said the doctor, "would do wonders."

My mother excoriated him when he was gone. "Where does he think we'll get the money for a voyage," she cried, "or even for a month at a hotel?"

Her humor was not improved, that day, by the news that I had lost my position to a Frenchwoman, my employers having decided that my little charges had got from me all that was to be had in the way of elementary learning, the rudiments of music and drawing, et cetera.

"Well," said my mother. "It never rains but it pours. George is ill, you have lost your place—what next?"

She sat in a chair by the window to get the last of the light. We had had our supper (and meager enough it had been: an egg apiece, bread, and tea) and then George had gone to sleep as he so frequently did even before dark. He was visibly weaker; if he did not improve he would no longer be able to work. And then how would we survive?

"I will go to the Intelligence Bureau tomorrow," I said. "I'll find something."

"There are a dozen women for every place," said my mother. Her voice held a bitter tone directed not at me, as I well knew, but at the brutal fate reserved to women who had no man to support them.

I made no reply, for there was none to make. Suddenly she held out her hand and beckoned me from where I sat in the shadowed interior of the room. "Come here, Marian. No, face the light. I look at you every day but I never really see you. What a pity you are so plain! Sometimes men are willing to overlook a plain face if a woman has a good figure, but you're as flat as a tombstone."

Calmly, without embarrassment, I let her examine me and deliver her judgment on me, knowing that these analyses of my person, which she made from time to time, were simply part of her continuing attempts to help us to survive.

"Look at you," she said. "Such a beanpole you are— and *why* did you inherit your father's hair?"—for my hair was red like his, and my skin very pale, so that although I was perfectly healthy people often thought I was ill.

"If you had a fortune your looks wouldn't matter," said my mother. "You'd have your pick of a dozen men. But as it is—"

I did not make the obvious retort, which was that she herself was no great beauty. She was forty-three years old, shorter and plumper than I; her brown hair showed traces of gray, her high-colored face had begun to show lines, her jaw had begun to sag. Her one great asset was her vitality, a bravado if you will, that made you think her far more attractive than she was. Her bright hazel eyes stared at me without watering, and I knew that behind them her busy brain was plotting some new means to extricate us from our poverty.

And then from the next room we heard the sound of my brother's cough: deep and wet and seemingly endless although in fact it probably lasted for no more than two or three minutes. Fleeting terror crossed my mother's face; and then, forcing herself to composure, she said, "Go and see to him. And let me think."

A week later we were in Nahant, guests of the Talcott family of Beacon Street. To this day, I do not know how my mother secured our invitation or how she arranged with George's employers to give him two months' leave. We traveled up by the cars one sunny afternoon; we were met at the station in Lynn by the Talcotts' runabout.

"You see," said my mother triumphantly as she settled herself on the soft black leather cushions, "people are really very kind. Even wealthy people." She lowered her voice in deference to the coachman. "Now let me warn you once again: the Talcotts know nothing of George's condition, and unless you cough excessively, George, they never will. Naturally I couldn't tell them about it or we'd never have been invited."

She put her hand on my arm. She wore her old gray gloves, heavily darned, for they were her best pair.

"There will be a large assortment of young men here, Marian. Some stay the summer, some come and go. Because we are the Talcotts' guests we will be invited to a number of affairs, I am sure." She gave me a little pat to emphasize her words. "From the moment we arrive until

32

the moment we leave, Marian, you will have opportunities to meet people. So be on your best behavior, be as charming as you know how—but not witty, men don't like wit—and perhaps we will have a double reason to celebrate when we go back to the city. If you can't catch a husband here, I don't know where you can."

Poor Mother! Our poverty drove her to such indelicate, unladylike bluntness; most women did not need to speak so plainly to their marriageable daughters, although all women everywhere worked toward that same goal. Even now, in these modern times when girls routinely go to college and we all may soon have the vote, women want nothing better for their daughters than a good match.

In any case, my mother left me in no doubt, that day, of her hopes for me; and as we rolled out onto the Neck, and felt the fresh wind in our faces, and saw the endless sea before us, shifting and sparkling in the sun, my delight was tempered by anxiety, by the uneasy knowledge that my so-called holiday was to be no holiday at all, but a time of serious work.

In recent years Nahant has fallen out of fashion, overtaken by showier places like Newport and Bar Harbor; but then, in 1870, it was still the favorite resort of moneyed Boston. The summer cottages were modest, even humble, by Newport standards, but they seemed grand enough to us then, strung out on either side of the long, curving Neck, high on the bluffs, each with its piazza and a stretch of lawn.

The Talcotts were a kindly couple, unassuming despite their wealth, eager to make us feel at home. Mrs. Talcott must have spoken a word for me in the right quarters, because within a few days of our arrival I was presented with a gratifying number of invitations for teas and picnics and evening parties and all the other activities with which the young crowd passed the time. I had not, of course, "come out," and in fact it was widely known that I had been employed as the Chadwicks' governess. Probably, therefore, I did not receive as many invitations as I might have. But there were more than enough to make me happy; and on the whole people were very civil, much less conscious, I think, of any difference in caste or class than people nowadays. George, too, had his share of the fun. He improved rapidly, as much, I think, from being relieved of his clerical duties as from the restorative powers of the sea air. It gladdened our hearts, Mother's and mine, to see him coming back; what a dear boy he was, and how we loved him!

Whenever I set off on one of my outings my mother would spend an anxious half hour with me beforehand, doing her best to make me presentable: a new arrangement of my recalcitrant hair, a brooch positioned just so to hide the frayed edges of my collar, a silk rose, acquired from some unknown source, pinned at my belt or precariously thrust above my ear. I stood awkwardly before her, tall, reedy, red-haired—how she worked over me, and how disappointing were the results! For I was not only not beautiful; I was awkward, I had no style, I had no idea how to make the most of myself. Since then I have seen girls as plain as I make the best match of the season, but they had an assurance that I lacked. I have it now, but it was a long time coming; and now, of course, I do not need it.

When I returned, my mother would question me about what I had done and whom I had met. I tolerated her interrogations as best I could, understanding the reason for them, but it soon became obvious to me if not to her that, while the flowers of Boston society were perfectly willing politely to include me in their social affairs, I would never be accepted as one of their own. And why should I have been? I was a visitor, nothing more; when autumn came we would return to Pembroke Street and they to Marlborough and Beacon and Mount Vernon streets, and once again we would be creatures of different worlds as foreign to each other as Hottentots and Frenchmen. And so after a while I gave up any hope of succeeding at the task my mother had set for me, and I began to enjoy myself.

On the Januarys' piazza, that summer, Isabel lay on a wicker chaise longue and watched the gulls circle and scream and dive, dipping past the edge of the cliffs and rising again, soaring free. From below came the sound of the waves slamming onto the rocks: there was no beach there, only a drop fifty feet and more onto jagged outcroppings surrounded by dark, white-flecked swells. There was a way down, if you knew it; once, when she was ten or eleven, Leighton had showed her and dared her to try. She had taken the dare and she had almost succeeded when suddenly, seeing how far below the edge of the cliff she was, how near to the waves which hurled themselves onto the slimy rocks and then, with a frightening, sucking sound, slithered off again, seeing that she was in very real danger of slipping, dropping into that icy sea, she had panicked and called for help and Leighton had panicked too and had run to get the hired man, and together they had rescued her.

Although the incident had terrified her, it had had another, more positive result: it had given her, for the first time, some power over Leighton. He had been forced to ask her not to tell, for if their parents had discovered the escapade Isabel would not have been the only one punished. She had seen at once the possibilities of blackmail, but she had taken pity on his miserable, sunburned face, his lanky frame slumped dejectedly on the great boulder cropping up from the lawn. She had gotten over her fear quickly enough; but she was angry— with him, with herself more—and so she had made him wait a good long thirty seconds and more before she gave her promise. For years, whenever she thought of the incident, she had remembered that about it: the intoxicating sense of powe:, the knowledge that she had held, so to speak, his fate in her hands.

But that had happened long ago and she did not think of it now. She lay like an invalid and seemed not to improve despite her mother's anxious care, despite Dr. Mifflin's prescriptions for loose lacing and long walks and glasses of sarsaparilla or raspberry vinegar served with sugar and water and ice.

Dr. Mifflin, in fact, had diagnosed her condition correctly as an *affaire de coeur* but he had not divulged this information to Mrs. January nor indeed to Isabel herself. He was an old man who knew a passable amount of medicine and a great deal about human nature. She will heal herself, he thought; time is what she needs, and distraction. When next he saw his granddaughter Pussie, a sprightly "bud" who had come out with Isabel the previous year and who was, he knew, one of her closest friends, he suggested that all the girls in their set get up some kind of informal party and see to it that Isabel attended.

"She was invited to the picnic last week at Dungeon Rock," replied his granddaughter, "and she wouldn't come. And she hasn't been bathing all summer."

But Pussie obeyed him, and the next week Isabel received an invitation to an "afternoon" at the Mifflins'. Pussie delivered it herself, although she did not stop to call, and Elinor, interrupting her chess match with Ned, took it to her elder sister, who seemed to have become a permanent fixture on the piazza.

It was just past sunset. Above the rooftops of Lynn the western sky still glowed pink; overhead the stars shone more brightly every moment as darkness came on. The day had been very hot, even here by the shore. Now a little breeze stirred the honeysuckle which entwined the trellis; both the vine and its support had been badly damaged in a hurricane the previous September, but it was a strong, healthy plant and it bloomed exuberantly now, with so heavy and sweet a fragrance that here on the piazza one hardly noticed the strong salt smell of the sea. Lights had appeared in the houses strung out sparsely along the cliff; the shadowed corner near the honeysuckle was nearly dark. A strange, white-winged moth worried at the blossoms, thrusting its long, slender, slightly bent proboscis deep into the heart of each flower, seeking the honey, sucking it, alighting on another and thrusting and sucking again.

"Isabel?"

"Look at that moth. It has been working for the past half hour, and still it has not had its fill." Coming from

37

the dusk, her voice sounded strange, disembodied.

Elinor shuddered, not looking. "This came for you. Pussie Mifflin delivered it but she couldn't come in."

"What is it?" Isabel did not look at her sister. Her eyes held to the insect; she was fascinated by its restless labor, in and out, in and out. Nothing else, in the past weeks, had so caught her interest; certainly no human activity.

"I don't know. An invitation, probably."

"Open it and see."

Elinor sighed, impatient to return to the chess. She had been repeatedly admonished by her mother to "do" for Isabel, but Isabel had had no commands for her, nothing that she wanted done. Only to be left alone, it seemed. They had no idea what was wrong. The Januarys were a healthy crowd, unlikely subjects for the declines which often struck other less fortunate clans. Elinor had become accustomed to seeing their mother, at odd moments, standing by the window staring at Isabel recumbent on the chaise; Mrs. January's face bore a worried look, naturally enough, but also an expression of hurt, as if Isabel, by stubbornly refusing to show more definite symptoms, were somehow trying to rebuke them all for some unknown offense.

Elinor opened the envelope and moved to the light coming from the dining room window. "It's an afternoon at the Mifflins'," she said. "Next Wednesday."

Isabel made no reply, and so after a moment Elinor put the folded paper back into its envelope and dropped it into her sister's lap. Startled out of her preoccupation with the moth, Isabel looked up. For a moment, in the dusky light, their eyes met. They were five years apart:

too far for intimacy in their childhood, and even further apart now since the previous winter, when Isabel had formally entered the grown-up world. Unlike many of her acquaintances, Elinor did not look forward to making her debut. Isabel's life seemed very vain—excessively frivolous, Elinor thought. She herself was a serious girl who took very much to heart the lessons learned at Sunday school, the sermons preached by the Reverend Mr. Eldridge. Like many youngsters, Elinor was naive, and very literal: she could not understand why there seemed so great a gap between what she heard at church and what she saw all around her. She was particularly fond of the parable of the rich man getting into heaven, but she had not yet found the courage to discuss it with any of her family.

"Will you go?" she said.

The moth still labored: in and out, in and out—but more slowly now, heavy, nearly satiated.

"No," said Isabel.

In the end, however, she decided to attend after all. Mrs. January was vastly relieved, but consideration of her mother's feelings had played no part in Isabel's decision. She had stopped thinking of her parents' feelings on the night she had promised Lawrence Cushing that she would go away with him. Her reason for getting up from her chaise and going into the world again was simpler, and rather more selfish: despite her best intentions to languish there, possibly for the rest of her life, she had, to her surprise, recently entered upon the first step to her recovery: she had begun to be bored.

And so she went; and there I met her.

Three

At the Mifflins' the lawns and gardens swept down to the cliffs and everyone wore white or the palest of pastels and the linen-draped tables on the piazza held the makings of a sumptuous tea: peach ice cream and ladyfingers and minted lemonade punch and tiny thin sandwiches with exotic fillings.

For a long time afterward I used to dream of that place: once again I saw the slender figures of young women moving sinuously, gracefully, like underwater weeds; I saw the grape arbor and the rose garden and the target set for archery; I saw the vivid green lawn blooming with the women's frilly parasols like overblown peonies scattered across the grass, and the spare figures of the men in white flannels dancing attendance; I heard the sound of laughter rising over the dull, constant pounding of the surf against the rocks far below the cliffs, and the sharp *click* of croquet mallets against the wooden balls. Since then I have seen paintings of such scenes: golden moments of a happy summer afternoon captured forever in oils on canvas. But the paintings are not so vivid as my

dream, or so revealing: no artist has captured the
tensions, the conflicts, the little underlying rivalries
which always ebb and flow on such occasions like fast-
moving, treacherous undercurrents.

I watch the participants in my dream: I see Pussie
Mifflin, perspiring in pink and white stripes, coming to
greet George and me with what seems to be genuine
pleasure. I never hear her words. Always, dreaming, my
attention is distracted by George pulling at my sleeve,
pointing to a sleek white yacht sailing out of the harbor.
How he would have loved to be with her! His face is open,
young and happy and beginning to glow with health
again. He speaks, in my dream, just as he did that day.

"Will you be all right for a while, Marian? I'm going to
say hello to some of the fellows."

He bounds off, and the young men greet him warmly.
He is much quicker at making friends than I am, less shy,
less awkward—but why not? His task this summer is
simpler than mine: he has only to recover his health,
while I must, according to my mother, make arrangements for my life.

This is an anxious time in my dream. George's turning
away from me. Once in a while I awaken then, and I have
heard my voice echoing in my ears and I know that I have
cried out to him to come back, to stay safe with me.

But of course he did not. He went to speak to them, to
the flower of Boston's young manhood: Arthur Train,
and Pussie's brother Henry, and Reginald Rice, and
Harold Hopkinson, and Avery Kittredge, and Oliver
Townsend—all of them and more were there that
afternoon.

Meanwhile Pussie, like the good hostess she was, deposited me with half a dozen girls who had arranged themselves prettily in the shade of a large tulip tree midway across the lawn. They greeted me cordially enough before returning to their gossip; and so, comfortably aware that I was not unwelcome, I relaxed a bit and turned my attention to the little vignettes all around. At a long, open stretch of lawn, six or seven young ladies holding bows and arrows waited like latter-day Dianas to have their turn at the bull's-eye, waiting to pose gracefully, classically, before their admiring onlookers. A mixed group played croquet; another, in the little white gazebo, gathered around a young woman who strummed a guitar, sending our way from time to time snatches of popular ballads.

I looked for George and found him heading toward the piazza, to the tables of food; but then I heard a shout go up from the archery green, and then my neighbor spoke to me and I lost track of him.

"Look at that," she said. "Isabel hit the bull's-eye. Some people have all the luck. Too bad the photographer has gone." (For there had been a group portrait taken, as I learned; George and I had missed it.) She was a thin little blonde, expensively dressed; her pale, sharp face and wispy hair and ragged, bitten fingernails did not match the opulence of her costume, heavy lace-trimmed ecru grosgrain silk, pearls around her throat and a cluster pearl ring on her little finger. I knew who she was: Alice Redfield, of the Pinckney Street Redfields—an old family, and one in which, people said, each succeeding generation became more eccentric. "You'd think some of that talent would run in the family but I've never even hit the target, let alone the center ring."

And, seeing my puzzlement, she added: "Isabel and I are second cousins, didn't you know?"

The connection as it turned out, was not quite so close, but it was enough for Miss Redfield to give me ten minutes' gossip about the Januarys. Curtis, of course, was widely admired for having made the match with Miss Parker; Leighton, the second eldest, was widely if surreptitiously admired for being a bit of a rake but a decent, jolly young man all the same; the two youngest, Elinor and Ned, were children still and so too young to be gossiped about; and then of course there was Isabel, the middle one, whose coming out the previous year had been surprisingly modest and whose behavior for the past several weeks had been simply surprising. They had all been puzzled when, immediately after her brother Curtis' marriage to Miss Parker and her money, she had withdrawn completely from the social round and had literally not been seen from that day to this—"Not even to Class Day, mind, and it was my brother John's graduation this year, and Mother so proud." Miss Redfield paused, giving me a speculative glance. "You worked for the Chadwicks, didn't you? I've never met a girl who worked. Never met one socially, I mean—like this." She looked away, across the lawn to the water. "That's all right," she said. "I don't mind." She gestured to where George stood with several of the young men. "Is that your brother? Pussie said you had a brother."

"Yes," I said. I waved to him, but he was looking toward the archers, he did not see me.

"If you'll introduce me to him later on," said my new friend, "I'll introduce you to mine when he comes back from his Grand Tour. Sometime in the winter, he said—I don't know exactly when."

"Yes," I said. "All right." I was, in truth, not paying strict attention to what she said. I had followed George's glance and I saw now that Isabel had left the archery field and had walked to the edge of the cliff where she stood, her back to us, looking out to sea. Despite the stiff breeze which whipped her skirts and caused her to lower her parasol, she stood as firm and straight as if she had been planted in the ground. After a moment we saw Pussie hurry to her and speak to her, anxiously leaning in, a protective arm around Isabel's shoulders.

"They say it was because of a young man," said Miss Redfield.

"What was?" Pussie had left Isabel's side; she was striding purposefully across the lawn, beckoning her friends to her as she went.

"Her—ah—decline."

Now Pussie had stopped to talk to her brother; after a moment he loped away to a cluster of the young men. My companion, distracted at last from her confidences, jumped to her feet and pulled me up with her.

"Come on," she said. "Let's see what Pussie's up to now."

The party had begun to divide into two groups, male and female; only Isabel remained apart, still standing at the far edge of the lawn where jagged rocks protruded from the ground, announcing the drop to the slimy, seaweed-covered rocks below where the water surged and boiled and hissed like a witch's cauldron. It was just past four o'clock. The shadows had lengthened across the green and gold lawn, and the sea had taken on the faintly purple iridescence which comes at the end of the day.

Suddenly Pussie clapped her hands; coming from those soft, plump little palms, the sound was startlingly loud.

"Attention!" she cried. "All hear this! We are going to have an exhibition! A contest—games of skill! The gentlemen will entertain us! A race first—across the lawn!"

The young men's faces bore the amused, slightly patronizing look which gentlemen often assumed upon hearing women's thoughts; but here and there—on Arthur Train's face, on Reggie Rice's—we saw a flicker of genuine interest.

"On foot?" drawled someone. "Why not ponies?"

"Potato sack!" called someone else.

"Feet tied together—hop like rabbits!"

"Crawl!"

"What, and stain my whites?"

There was laughter then, and a pause while they conferred among themselves. I saw George with them; I was glad that he was included in their fun.

"All right!" called Harold Hopkinson. "Here it is! A gymnastic tableau first, and then—"

"Don't tell!" cried several of the others.

All around me the young women murmured delightedly. Isabel had joined us at last; she sat next to Pussie, her face shaded by her parasol. I sat close enough to see how tightly she gripped its handle, but I had no time to wonder why, for the men had begun their exhibition and I wanted to watch to see how George did.

As smoothly as if they had rehearsed, a dozen or so youths, George among them, strung out in formation; others leaped nimbly to their shoulders and still more on top of them, until in only a moment a triumphant pyramid rose. They held it for our applause, and then the pyramid dissolved and they formed twin rows in a handstand. George and two or three others stood back, unable to perform that feat or the next two; but he looked happy enough, and so I watched the performance and did not worry about him.

The gymnastic exhibition done and our applause graciously acknowledged, Harold signaled to a few of his fellows to come forward.

"Ladies!" he cried. "Your indulgence, please! In order for us to perform our next feat of skill and daring it will be necessary for you to accompany us to a point—ah— there on the lawn." He waved his arm toward the wide expanse of green which ended abruptly at the edge of the cliff.

We hesitated, glancing at one another for reassurance. Without waiting, Harold led his little band at a run toward the edge of the cliff; and after a moment we rose and followed, necessarily a little slow in our confining costumes. Pussie, urged on by the beginning of alarm, managed to take the lead, but we soon caught up with her.

"Harold!" she panted. "What are you going to do? I don't think—"

He grinned at her, mocking her apprehension. They stood at the unprotected edge. Far below, the waves slapped against the rocks. Stretching up and down the coast were the summer houses of their friends and families, each with its frontage onto the sea. The cliff line ran unevenly, jutting out, rising and falling; here and there it was broken by fissures, some with caves underneath.

"A long jump—across there." He pointed to a place where the cliff split to a width of perhaps six feet.

Someone gripped my arm, and I heard Alice Redfield's voice in my ear. "Look," she said. "Look at the drop."

She pulled me with her to the edge, but after one glance I drew back, dizzy and faintly sick.

"Do you think—it looks very dangerous, Harold," said Pussie, still breathing hard.

"So it is. That is why only six of us will attempt it."

"But—"

"Come on, Pussie. It was your idea to get up a competition. Just this one thing more and then we'll come back and play like good boys."

Pussie glanced around at us as if looking for help. But no one said anything, and so, with a fatalistic little shrug, she retreated to stand beside Isabel while Harold got his troops into line.

"Are you ready?" he cried. "Ladies and gentlemen—the long jump. Go!"

Oliver Townsend went first: thirty feet back, a good running start, suddenly exploding, pushing himself up to sprawl splay-legged in the air, hanging above the crevasse for a heart-stopping moment before thudding safely down on the opposite side, his body crumpling a little, well in from the edge, from the murderous rocks below.

A shocked little sigh of relief went out from the rest of us. He had gone from safety to danger to safety again so quickly that we had hardly had time to be afraid for him; but now, with the second man, we knew what we should see and we feared to see anything else—any misjudgment, a slip, a loose stone underfoot throwing off balance. But the second man, too, got across, and then the third and the fourth. After each successful jump came a burst of applause, too heartfelt to be called polite.

Pussie looked around at us as if to say, "It will be all right. Harold knows his men, he picked only the best. They are simply showing off, like ten-year-olds, and they are young men, after all. One could call them boys still. Look how they enjoy this madness!" Applause again: Willie Putnam safe across. And now the last: Henry Mifflin, tall and thin, loosely put together as if he did not have a muscle in his body, languid, hardly seeming to have the energy to work himself up to this exertion—Ah! Done!

"Thank goodness that's over with," muttered Alice. Relief flowed through us all as Pussie, smiling, led us to congratulate them.

"Wait!" The voice was eager, supplicating, so high that it might have been a girl's. He separated himself from the others and began to trot down the edge of the cliff to the starting point. "May I try?" He stood with his feet apart, hands clenched at his sides.

"*No*—" I started to run to him, but Alice held me back.

"Wait," she said. "It will be all right. They won't let him."

"Sorry, George," called Harold. "Jump's over."

· "Please! I can do it!" He was like a small child begging to join his older brothers.

Moments of great crisis stay with us forever. I look at this small notebook before me, my handwriting in black ink on the white paper, and I see beyond it, back in time, to that afternoon in Nahant, to all of us standing at the edge of the cliffs like participants in some monstrous *tableau vivant:* and who will call out the correct answer, who will tell us what we were?

He stood perhaps forty feet across the crevasse, crouching, ready to run.

"George!" called Harold. "Come back, we'll do another stunt if you like—" He shaded his eyes with both hands and peered across the gaping split at the lawn's edge. "Come back! Walk there—around the end!" And, to the others, quietly: "When he comes up, get him— hold him. Carry him back to the house if necessary."

"Miss January!" cried George. And now I bolted forward, I ran to the edge of the split, I started to call to him but he ignored me. "Miss January! Will you give me permission?"

I glanced around at Isabel. She stood a little apart, watching him as we were all watching him; her face showed not fear, not apprehension, but a calculating look, as if she were appraising some item for sale in a shop. She was not afraid for him as all the rest of us were afraid; and I was slow to understand that. Perhaps if I had been quicker—perhaps if I had seen the danger in her attitude, the danger for him—

"Miss January! Please!"

Was it possible that the breeze died, that the soaring

49

gulls hung motionless in the air, that time itself stopped? It seemed so: for a moment, for an eternity.

And then she nodded; and, in case he could not see, she called back to him.

"Yes!" she cried, and her face was no longer calm, it was suddenly alive, laughing, her eyes sparkling. "Yes! Go on! Go on!"

I was aware of sudden movement around me: Harold and some of the others rushing to prevent him. They lacked running distance to jump across from our side, and so they needed to run to the end of the split, running therefore at a tangent to George's straight aim, losing precious seconds.

George had made an awkward, stumbling start, his face contorted with his effort, his feet flying out at odd angles as he propelled himself forward to the place where he must jump.

And there, just before the edge, he gathered himself; he lifted himself into the air; and then he jumped— hurled his body across the expanse above the rocks and the surging sea below.

His feet missed the edge, but his hands and his head struck, and for a moment he seemed to hang in the air, feet dangling, seeking purchase. His hands scrabbled at loose rocks and tufts of grass. Little puffs of dust floated out where the grass came loose. His hands clawed and clung and found no purchase. He made no sound. It seemed impossible that he should hang on so long suspended without a firm grip.

"Quick!" cried Arthur Train. He threw himself down at the edge, Henry Mifflin holding him from behind, and grabbed for George's hands. "Quick—*here*—"

One hand found George, and slipped away, and found him again—and then Arthur lost balance too, and Henry was not strong enough to hold him and for a moment it seemed that they would all go down together. And then someone else threw himself onto Henry and held him fast; and Henry held Arthur.

And then suddenly George's hands slipped and without a word he was gone.

And all around us shone the bright day: the sun and the sparkling sea, the gulls dipping and soaring, the air tangy with the smell of brine and seaweed and myriad life thrown up to rot on the shore, the buoy's bell clanging in the harbor, the late afternoon ferry coming in to dock, the beautiful young people gathered on Pussie Mifflin's lawn, frozen for an endless moment by the horror of what they had seen.

And his body below, bent and crumpled on the rocks, huge fractured boulders which would lie exposed until high tide, when, if he were still there, the sea would come and take him and float him out and bury him without ceremony, without mourners.

I stood at the edge of the cliff and looked down. Behind me, someone had begun to scream. I could see George's body, his head at an odd angle. There was no blood. The screaming went on, and now someone had begun to cry.

I looked around. Behind me, another body lay: Letty Monroe, who had fainted. A sudden commotion had begun: several of the men running back across the lawn to get help, the girls fluttering around Letty, reviving her.

Isabel had not moved. She stood like one in a trance, perfectly still, her gaze turned inward, blind to the commotion all around her. We were perhaps twenty feet apart. Suddenly I wanted to speak to her, to confront her.

Later that day, later that summer, there would often be times when I felt so weakened by grief, by remorse, that I could not move, could not stand or walk; but just then I felt steady and strong. And so I went to her. I walked to her and put myself before her and stared at her until she was forced to see me.

Still she said nothing; she simply stared at me with the question in her eyes: who was he? Even in my anguish I could not help but notice the way she looked—like a warrior princess, I thought. Her penetrating dark blue eyes gazed out at me from beneath her dark, straight brows; they nearly belied the sweetheart shape of her face, the luscious creamy texture of her perfect skin. At last I felt compelled to speak.

"Did you know him?" I said.

"No."

I heard voices behind us: a rescue party from the house. She held my gaze and I held hers; but neither of us could speak more, and so we stood like dumb combatants for what seemed an eternity. She would not yield, she would not turn away. Alice Redfield came to me at last. And as she put her arm around me, and tried to lead me away, and murmured words of comfort—what? I cannot remember—I saw then in Isabel's face the knowledge of who I was and who he had been. I saw that: but no remorse. And so I allowed myself to be taken away, helped into the carriage, accompanied back to the Talcotts'; and somehow—somehow!—I needed to find the words to tell my mother what had happened to her beloved son, her only boy.

The Januarys came to the funeral but not Isabel. And so I did not see her again until the fall.

Four

"You must go to them," said my mother, "and ask them for help."

I had heard many harsh and bitter words from her in the weeks just past, but never had I heard her speak like this, in the deadly quiet tone of defeat.

We sat together that afternoon in our little front room and watched the rain stream down the windows. It was a Sunday in mid-October. We had not been to church that morning because we had no money for the collection plate, and, further, my mother had declared that our mourning, dyed and patched and shabby, was no longer suitable to wear to the house of the Lord. "We will read our verses," she said, "and say our prayers, but we will no longer disgrace ourselves by appearing at public worship dressed like beggars."

And so we had had our private service, and a cup of tea and half a plain roll each, and now we sat together and watched the rain. We lacked the energy to do any kind of handiwork, and we were too distracted to read. My mother was not strict about Sunday: she had always allowed us to play, George and me, or do our lessons or read our storybooks. But since George's death there had seemed no purpose to anything: certainly not to make the effort to knit a pair of stockings on a rainy Sunday afternoon.

"You must go to them," she said again. "We cannot survive if we do not have help from somewhere."

What she said was true, for we neither of us had had work since our precipitous return from Nahant in midsummer. The closet was filled with unsold, flower-painted plates, and I had worn holes in my only pair of black shoes walking the city to look for paid employment. I could not even find a place as a shopgirl, for there were far more applicants than openings, and those with experience were preferred for the few available positions. And in any case young women in mourning were not supposed to hunt for work; people were affronted by such seeming lack of delicate feeling. We had sold what salable things we had—a few bits of jewelry, some books, even some of our clothing—and had fallen so far behind in our rent that our landlady, kind as she was, had been forced to give us notice.

The room was growing dark, but we always waited until the last possible moment to light the lamp, or even a candle, since kerosene and candles were as dear as everything else. Now, however, my mother rose heavily from her chair and lit the lamp on the table in the center of the room. She did not sit again; rather, she stayed standing to give herself the advantage over me.

And now, in the light, she must have seen something in my face which led her to exclaim, with a hint of her former spirit: "What choice do we have, Marian? We will be in the street by the end of the month! I would go myself, but I do not trust myself to remain calm. If I should see *her*—"

Her voice quavered, her eyes brimmed over, and she began again that harsh and painful sobbing whose sound had filled my ears since the moment I had had to tell her the news of George's death.

I went to her; I put my arms around her and held her close. Her head came just to my shoulder.

"Go to them," she said. Her voice was muffled against the cheap black cloth of my dress. "This is on their heads—on *hers*."

And so, the next morning, I found myself limping down Arlington Street toward Marlborough. I was lame because I had trod on a sharp stone which had bruised my foot through the hole in my shoe. The day had dawned cloudy, but now, at ten o'clock, the sun had broken through the overcast and begun to dry the puddled, muddy streets. Lacking carfare, I had walked from our rooms in the South End; ordinarily I did not mind walking, but I had had no breakfast because we had no food, and my stomach ached now on its ration of black tea.

On my right lay the Public Garden. The leaves of the tall beech and elm trees shone golden and russet and purple in the warming sun; late dahlias bloomed along the walkways, and the water of the lagoon sparkled in the distance.

When I reached the corner of Marlborough, I stopped for a moment to steady myself. My head felt light, and my

knees had begun to tremble. I realized that I had not
thought precisely what I would say to Mrs. January. I
needed to work out some reasonably coherent speech lest
I become tongue-tied or, worse, begin to cry. I berated
myself for having agreed to see her. Why should they
help me? My mother, I thought, was mistaken: they
would feel no obligation to us, we were nothing to them.

And then I thought of George: of his bright, eager face,
of his hopes for the future, his pleasure in being invited
to the Mifflins' party. Tears filled my eyes so that I could
not see, but I strangled my sobs. I had too much pride to
be seen weeping in the streets, and so I wiped my tears
away and took a deep breath and walked on to find
number 63.

The door was opened by a pleasant young maid. In the
manner of her kind, she knew that I was not paying a
social call—not at that hour of the morning—and so she
treated me to a moment's intense scrutiny while she tried
to place me. The fact that I had no card was heavily
against me, for everyone—even dressmakers looking for
work, even callers for charity—had cards. At last,
perhaps taking pity on me, she invited me to wait in the
vestibule while she went to consult her mistress. I had a
bad moment when I realized that Mrs. January might not
be at home and that I might need to confront, say, Isabel;
but in a moment the maid was back with instructions to
follow her upstairs.

I did not, in that first visit, notice the details of the
house's decor, although later I came to know it all by
heart and even, for a time, to think of it as my home; but I
had an impression of dark-patterned walls and dark

gleaming wood and shining glass and metal and deep, rich carpets underfoot. As we ascended I caught the pungent odor of floor wax; from behind a closed door I heard someone practicing scales on a piano. It was a homely, reassuring sound: like the multiplication tables, scales are universal levelers.

I lost this momentary confidence, however, when I entered Mrs. January's small sitting room and found her, not alone as I had hoped, but with a plump, hard-faced woman of perhaps fifty-five who greeted me coolly, no smile, no outstretched hand. Mrs. January introduced her as her sister-in-law, Mrs. Roberts Reed. I was identified only as "Miss Childs," but from the way that Mrs. Reed stared at me I imagined that she knew who I was.

Mrs. January offered me a chair and a cup of coffee and a tight, well-bred smile. She was a pleasant-faced woman of middle height whose most striking characteristic was her air of unassailable smugness: she gave you no hint that disaster could strike at her or hers, although at this time, in October of 1870, disaster had in recent months only just missed two of her children. I have since seen that quality in many people of old family: money has less to do with it, I think, than the sense of permanence, the sense that one's family had been in this small corner of the world since its beginnings, and that all the rest of us are here on sufferance.

"How is your mother, Miss Childs? Well, I hope."

I don't know what I had expected her to say: probably just that, or something equally innocuous. I was aware of Mrs. Reed, whose tightly laced corsets creaked a bit as she shifted her bulk in her chair; and it was she—her unlooked-for presence, her intruding, as I saw it, upon my little time to have an audience with Mrs. January—it was she who prompted my reply. I had no idea that I would say what I did: the words simply tumbled out of my mouth without any thought of mine to guide them.

"My mother is very poorly, thank you. She cannot recover from her—from our—loss. And we have no money at all."

For a moment Mrs. January dropped her well-bred air and I saw that I had touched some deeper part of her, however briefly. Then her expression of *politesse* descended again over her face like the thick, smooth glaze on a Lalique bowl. She glanced at Mrs. Reed, who had commenced a curious kind of rumbling deep in her throat like a human steam engine. "Lottie, I think perhaps you—"

But Mrs. Reed ignored her. "Tell me, Miss Childs, where do you live?" she said.

I glanced at her but I did not answer, for I knew that I must not be deflected from the purpose of my visit. But her question hung in the air, and so after a moment, not looking at me, Mrs. January said: "She lives in the South End, Lottie. On Pembroke Street."

"Just the two of you now?" said Mrs. Reed, speaking again to me; and again I did not answer. I felt my face flush under her scrutiny; I wished that I had the courage to ask for a private audience with Mrs. January, but such boldness was beyond me.

"Never mind," said Mrs. Reed. "Abby Mifflin told me all about it—how Pussie plagued her to be allowed to

59

have her party, and how things got out of hand. You were there, weren't you? Yes. Stupidity, that's what it was— stupidity, and thoughtlessness, and those jackanapes wanting to show off."

"Young men—" began Mrs. January.

"Young men always want to show off, that's right, Ethel. It was the same when we were young, if you remember. They want to show off, and they don't stop to consider the consequences until it's too late. Well, miss. What's done is done. You need some way to live now that he's gone. I daresay I can find some sewing for you. You governessed for the Chadwicks? I don't know of an open place, but perhaps by spring— But that's no help to you now, is it? You look to be a sensible young woman, not flighty like some of them. When I was at Isabel's coming-out last year I thought how giddy a lot of 'em are. Silly. Giggling all the time. They're involved in serious business, but they don't seem to know it. Catching a husband and then living with him for the rest of your life isn't something to play at. Boston girls aren't as bad that way as New York girls, but all the same they're giddy enough to make your head spin. Well, miss." She broke off to stare at me again. She seemed to expect some reply, but I could think of nothing to say to such a speech. Even my plea to Mrs. January had vanished from my mind.

Mrs. Reed lived to be nearly ninety, and for years before she died we were good friends, despite our inauspicious meeting. Although she nested, as it were, at the very heart of Boston society, her house in Mount Vernon Street being a gathering place for all the best people (as well as some not admitted elsewhere, like certain theatrical people—like Senator Sumner, for that matter), she herself was not a Bostonian or even a New Englander. She had been born in Albany; she had met and married Mrs. January's brother, Edward Cunningham, and then survived him to marry Roberts Reed. New England family ties being what they are, she would have been thought of as Ethel January's sister-in-law had she gone through five husbands after Cunningham. Perhaps it was the fact that we were both outsiders that drew us together: I don't know. But in any case it was she, that day, who became my ally. Had my fate been left to Mrs. January to decide I would have been given a small sum of money—conscience money—and sent on my way, conveniently disposed of. But Mrs. Reed became my advocate; even as I sat with them that morning she persuaded Mrs. January to take me on, to give me some sort of regular employment in the household. And so I was able to return to my mother a short while later with good news: they would help us through this bad time, they would not let us starve.

My mother was not so pleased as I had expected. "They'll make a servant out of you," she said. "That's not what I wanted. I wanted them to give no more than what they owe."

But of course we had no choice; and so, each day, I walked to Marlborough Street and let myself in at the front and went to Mrs. January in her sitting room to learn what work she had for me that day: fine sewing, or letter writing, or accompanying Elinor to her riding lessons, or, occasionally, helping Mrs. January through one of her luncheon parties.

61

"Blood money," said my mother. With the onset of cold weather she had taken to her bed; she lay with an old woolen shawl around her shoulders and a tattered nightcap on her head and stared up at me with accusing eyes. "I told you to ask for help, not to become a member of their family. How can you go there each day, how can you live among them as you do?"

Had I been able to speak truthfully to her I would have replied that the January household was a far more pleasant place to spend my days than our two barren rooms in Pembroke Street; as it was, I muttered some evasion and escaped to the butcher's to get a piece of cheap meat to boil for supper.

My mother was not alone in resenting my presence at number 63 Marlborough. One morning some weeks after my first visit I went as usual to report to Mrs. January in her second-floor sitting room. The door was always closed, and always, of course, I knocked. But this day the door was slightly ajar; as I lifted my hand I heard voices from within. And so I stood suspended for a moment, my hand raised; I had not meant to eavesdrop, but one cannot overhear one's name in conversation and close one's ears. I recognized Mrs. January's voice, of course; and I knew the other, too, although I had heard it only a few times. But once I had heard it give an order that caused my brother's death, and so I could never forget it, I would have known it anywhere from among a thousand.

". . . ask her to leave, Mother. I find it intolerable to have her constantly underfoot. It is dreadfully embarrassing."

"I felt that we should help them. Under the circumstances."

"Circumstances! What circumstances? An accident—"

"Yes. An accident. But if you had not—ah—encouraged the boy to make the jump—"

"Encouraged! I simply gave him permission to do something that he was obviously going to do in any case."

"Your Aunt Reed felt most strongly, Isabel, that we should give her—"

"Aunt Reed! What has she to do with this? What right has she to interfere? Let her take Miss Childs if she wishes! But I cannot bear to have her here any longer! She is a constant reminder of—of—"

"Isabel—"

Before I could gather my wits to escape she had rushed out into the hall, nearly toppling me as she went. For an instant she stopped, as startled as I; her eyes were wide with alarm, her mouth open to emit a cry which strangled in her throat.

Then she recognized me. Her face composed itself; she drew a deep breath and steadied herself against the balustrade.

Many times, in later years, I saw her behave so: suddenly discomposed, she had an almost miraculous ability to recover, to regain control. Even in my own discomfiture I remember a small, grudging feeling of admiration. I knew that I had no such ability; I had been as badly startled as she, but I remained so, gaping, blushing, unable to think of anything to say that would not further embarrass us both. Even though I was half a head taller, and at least a year older, I was plainly at the disadvantage.

I was, I suppose, waiting for her to say the first word. But she did not; she simply stared at me for a long moment more, transmitting her dislike very plainly in her glance, and then she turned and went upstairs to her room.

I felt her contempt more keenly than if she had spoken it. I stood quite still, collecting my scattered wits, until she had disappeared into the upper reaches of her house, and then I went in to Mrs. January to receive my instructions for the day.

With the self-discipline which sustained women of her class, she greeted me calmly as she always did. She must know that I encountered Isabel just now, I thought; she must suspect that I overheard them. But her face gave no hint of it. Like so many women, she survived her life by refusing to admit many things in it that cried out for recognition. She sat in the pale light of the winter's morning, her hands busy with a piece of beadwork, her eyes calm as they met mine, her voice cordial if not overwarm.

She asked me, that day, to finish addressing the invitations to her New Year's party three weeks hence. "And then, after lunch, I want you to go with Elinor on her Sunday school visit. She was to have gone with Mrs. Malory and her daughter, but both of them are down with pleurisy and won't be well for days. And these people must be seen to, they are in a very bad way."

The Januarys attended the Emmanuel Church in

Newbury Street, a fashionable Episcopalian church heavily populated by the city's wealthier class. Frequently, on Sundays, small knots of poor people gathered to watch their betters alight from their carriages and disappear behind the heavy, carved wooden doors into the Gothic splendor (never seen by the onlookers) of the interior. Occasionally there would be a catcall or a derisive whistle; but for the most part the crowd was silent, hungrily watching, thinking God knows what as they followed with their eyes the parade of silks and velvets and gold-knobbed canes.

And so, that afternoon, Elinor and I made our way to the North End into the warren of streets surrounding the Old North Church. The North End today has become a largely Italian neighborhood, but in those days it housed poor Americans struggling to withstand the onrushing waves of immigrant Irish.

It was a raw day, threatening snow; the streets were slushy underfoot as we made our way through the Haymarket, past butchers' stalls, and greengrocers', and rough-looking men standing beside open braziers selling roasted chestnuts and potatoes. Ragged street urchins called to us as we went, trying to cadge a penny or two; traffic was heavy and we needed to look sharp to avoid colliding not only with the children but with draymen's horses and scurrying delivery boys. I wished that we had accepted Mrs. January's offer of the carriage, but Elinor had not wanted it. "No," she said, "the streets there are too narrow, and besides, it is not fitting to make a charity call except on foot."

She was not an easy person: not then, not ever. She

was only fourteen, and so hardly in a position to dictate
to anyone, but even at that age, so young, she seemed to
have looked about her, to have examined with a critical
eye the world into which she had been born—a world of
money and social position, and their concomitant self-
satisfaction and arrogance—and already she seemed to
have found it wanting. She did not say so directly, of
course: she was only a child still, and helpless as children
are to change the circumstances of their lives.

She was a pretty child with light brown hair and dark
brown eyes. Her thin, fine-featured face wore a
meditative expression; she was a serious little person,
and although she smiled frequently enough, and seemed
not unhappy, you knew at once that she was one of those
who was not content simply to live her life but must, to
her own torment and perhaps that of others, ponder the
meaning of what we do here, what we are. Even at
fourteen this was obviously what she was; such qualities
are born into a person, they do not suddenly blossom in
middle age.

By the time we reached our destination, a tenement in
Salem Street, I was panting and sore from lugging the
heavy basket of foodstuffs which was the offering—or
penance—that we took with us. Elinor had wanted to
carry it partway, but she was thin—frail, even—and after
she had taken it for half a block she had needed to put it
down to rest. And so I had carried it, and I lugged it up
three flights and into the dark, fetid room where the
objects of our charity lay. They were Americans: poor,
dogged by bad luck, hardly able to survive—but
Americans all the same, from Vermont, they said, and

wanting to go back as soon as they had money for the fare. A mother and three young children: there was no sign of a man, and neither Elinor nor I had the courage to inquire if one existed.

We did not stay long. Elinor made a gracious little speech, no less sincere for having been memorized beforehand; and I was only too glad to escape, since the scene before me was a vivid reminder of what my mother and I might have suffered had we not found help from Elinor's family.

When we came out into the streets again we found that snow had begun to fall, and by the time we were halfway back to Marlborough Street our cloaks were white with it. I did not mind: snow is a clean cover over the filth and ugliness of the city, it transforms even the chaos of the Haymarket into a scene of fairy-tale beauty. The chestnut sellers' fires burned more brightly through the thickening white fall; from the interiors of the little shops in the market building the lights gleamed a cheery invitation into the darkening afternoon. The racket of sound had begun to be muffled by the snow; soon, if it continued, everything would lie buried under the smooth, smothering blanket, and for a while, at least, until it melted or until it turned ugly and gray with soot, we would dwell in a painter's landscape, a magical landscape where any adventure might happen.

We went carefully, picking our way through the slushy muck underfoot, holding on to each other for support. And then, as we paused to allow a delivery wagon to pass, Elinor turned to me and said abruptly: "I was very sorry about your brother."

I was taken unawares, and so I had no immediate reply, but she must have seen some response in my face which embolded her to continue.

"Isabel is very proud," she said. "I have never known her to admit an error, although she makes errors like all the rest of us. But she will not say so."

The way clear, we crossed the street. Elinor still clung to my arm. The snow came thicker now, and the wind buffeted us.

"Did you know that she has a suitor?" she said, raising her voice against the wind.

"No," I said.

"I think she will marry him. He's going to be very rich. Not as rich as Curtis' wife, but rich enough. She is very pleased with him, I think. When I asked her if she would marry him she wouldn't say yes or no, so I imagine he hadn't asked her yet. Probably he will at the holidays. It's so silly, isn't it? Girls having to wait for men to ask them. Avery Kittredge is his name. He's always polite to me, but I have the sense that he doesn't really see me. Have you ever felt that about someone? He has called almost every evening for the past month. Lots of times, of course, Isabel isn't in, so he sits and talks to Mother and Father. I think they'd be glad if he married Isabel simply so that they wouldn't have to spend so much time with him. Isabel has a very full calendar. She is invited everywhere. I should think she would be happy to be done with it—to be married so that she could get some rest."

I had not expected to like any of them when I accepted Mrs. January's offer of employment in the household. Had not expected to—had not wanted to, in fact. I had meant to keep my distance from these people whose daughter had, even inadvertently, so cruelly wounded my mother and me. But now, trudging through the snow with this small, earnest, confiding young person, I felt the beginnings of affection for her. It was not, after all, her fault that she was Isabel's younger sister. I sensed that she needed a confidante and that for whatever reason she had chosen me. Perhaps, that afternoon, she would have confided in anyone; I didn't know. But after I delivered her safely home, and then spent an extravagant penny on the horsecars to save myself further exposure to the storm as I went home, I found that I had a new sense of contentment in my heart: a sense of having found, however temporarily, a friend. Even in so unlikely a place as the January household.

Five

You could not have said that Avery Kittredge was the dullest man in the world, for dullness, like beauty, is often in the eye—or the ear—of the beholder; but certainly he was not one of the more sparkling additions to any hostess' affair. He was a tall, stout young man whose broad, square face looked impassively out onto the world without the slightest betrayal of what he thought about what he saw. He was not stupid: in his father's office he dealt with mortgages and insurances and stocks and bonds with considerable skill, and it was only years later, when he was outmaneuvered by the machinations of a Western cabal, that he proved to be inadequate to his task of increasing his family's wealth. But he had a certain slowness in his speech, as much from inbred caution as from shyness, and a deceptive attitude of seeming not to understand much of the banter and wit flying past him, that made you think of him as one of nature's solitaries, destined never to bask in the glow— or the glare—of society.

Did he want to? I don't know. I think only of the

disaster of his match with Isabel January, who dragged him with her, willy-nilly, to the pinnacle of that glittering world and then (as he saw it) betrayed him when he could no longer support her ambitions.

But in the beginning he loved her, mismatch though it was. For all his caution, and his shrewdness, and his hardheaded business sense, he was as much a victim of his heart's desires as any of the rest of us.

As for Isabel, she never loved him, not for a moment. She married him for the worst of reasons: to save her damaged pride.

I met him early one evening shortly before Christmas, that year, when I had stayed past my usual time to help Elinor finish a beaded purse that she was working for her mother. The maid was just admitting him as I was coming down into the front hall. He had been invited that evening to a small dinner which Isabel had been allowed—even encouraged—to give for a dozen of her friends; since he had not at that date formally proposed marriage to her (although he showed every sign of being about to do so), it is probable that Mrs. January was moved by more than ordinary good manners to allow Isabel to include him.

Mrs. January, who had accompanied me downstairs, introduced us. I had a bad moment when I recognized him as one of the young men who had attended Pussie Mifflin's garden party; but he, apparently, did not remember me. He gave me an impassive stare; as I went out I felt as though I had been given no more notice than if I had been the carved rosewood side chair in the hall. Not that I minded: I did not expect, or want, a warm reception from Isabel's friends. And so I was greatly surprised once, years later, when he reminded me of that night.

"I remember very well," he said. "You were in mourning, of course; and I remember how your black dress made your hair seem even redder than it is. And you were very thin, and taller than most girls I knew, so that it was not so much of an effort to speak to you. You looked very tired, as if you lived under difficult conditions, which I suppose you did. I would have spoken to you of your brother, but it hardly seemed the appropriate thing. And I was nervous enough, God knows, at the prospect of Isabel's party that night; I didn't feel competent to say a tactful word to you, and perhaps have it not be tactful at all, and perhaps have you—I don't know, start to cry, perhaps."

When I arrived home I told my mother what I had done that day, for she always demanded a strict accounting; and then, acknowledging the risk, I told her about Avery Kittredge and about the family's expectations that he would soon ask Isabel to be his wife.

My mother lay so still, not responding, that although she stared at me I thought that she had not heard. She was propped up on pillows in her bed, a shawl around her shoulders; she spent her days so, for coal was very dear and I did not light our stove until I arrived home each evening. Finally she said, "Is he rich?"

"I don't know. I imagine he has enough."

She nodded. Her accusing eyes followed me as I moved around the room. "So," she said, "that is her reward for sending your brother to his death. A husband."

"Oh, Mother—"

"A husband. A fine house of her own, a carriage, a place in the world—"

"Her marriage has nothing to do with—with what happened to George."

"She should have been drummed out of decent society. Every door in Boston should be slammed in her face. And you come to tell me that she is to marry this young man! When you, Marian—yes, I will say it!— when you have nothing, thanks to her. Nothing! Except her family's charity. Where is your young man? Where is your house, your carriage? Don't look at me! I *will* say it! I will get up tomorrow and put on what poor shabby clothing I have and I will walk the streets and I will say it to everyone I see! That young woman has ruined our lives, and she has no right to a happy life of her own!"

She continued in this way for some time longer, and then, having cried for a while, she fell asleep. In the days that followed she did not mention Isabel again; certainly I did not. I understood my mother's jealousy, but I did not share it, and I wanted no more tirades.

We had no Christmas that year, my mother and I, although Mrs. January very kindly gave us a small ham, and I found a discarded pine bough in the street which I carried home and laid across the top of the glass-fronted bookcase. But at the Januarys' they celebrated extravagantly both Christmas and New Year's, for Avery had spoken to Mr. January at last and had been given permission to ask his question of Isabel. Of course all his trouble would have been for nothing if she had said no, but she accepted him, and everyone congratulated him

73

and told him what a lucky fellow he was to have got her.

"We will announce the engagement on New Year's Eve," said Mrs. January. "I've already invited half a hundred people, and now we'll just do some invitations for the family. They won't mind being asked at the last minute, and they would mind very much indeed if they were left out."

And so I spent the afternoon addressing still more cards, and by the time I had finished with them I had nearly half a hundred again, for the Januarys and the Cunninghams were large clans, and you could not invite one cousin and leave out another.

It was almost four o'clock when I copied the last address: nearly twilight and time for me to go. I had stayed past dark on a few occasions, but I was afraid to walk home then and I could not afford to take the horsecars every time. Mrs. January might have offered to pay my fare, of course, but she did not and I would not ask. I put the envelopes in two neat piles on her small, spindly-legged desk and straightened suddenly as a muscle in my back went into a painful cramp. I would have rubbed it, but I could not reach it through the thick whalebone and muslin of my corset. And so I stood at attention for a moment like a soldier, willing the pain to go away, and thus I must have looked rather intimidating to the little boy who just at that instant came hurtling through the door.

"Mother! See what I bought—"

He pulled himself up short, nearly dropping the apparatus which he carried. I knew who he was, although I imagined that he did not know me: Ned, the youngest

January, ten years old.

"I beg your pardon," he said. "I was looking for my mother."

"She has gone to make calls," I said. I held out my hand. "I am Marian Childs, and you must be Ned."

Carefully he set his treasure on the table before he shook hands with me. Now that he had recovered from his surprise he seemed a remarkably self-contained little fellow, well drilled in good manners. He was a thin boy with pale, almost translucent skin and soft, straight brown hair that fell over his high forehead. Even at ten, so young, his face had striking intelligence: or perhaps intuition is a better word, for intelligent people, very often, know a great deal about this thing or that, but they fail to understand what is going on around them. Ned always knew what all of us thought and felt and did; it was part of his talent, his gift.

But he was like other children in that he was shy with new adults, and so, to put him at ease, I said: "What did you buy? May I see it?"

"It is Elinor's Christmas present." He lifted it from the table and held it for my approval: a stereopticon. "And I bought six views: Venice, and the Alps, and the Coliseum—here. Look. Aren't they wizzer?"

I took it from him to examine it: a small wooden viewer with an attachment to hold a pair of picture cards. When you looked through the lens the picture was not flat, as pictures are, but three-dimensional as in life. Elinor loved it; she bought new views whenever she had the money. Often enough, of course, she did not: she saved what little she had for her charities, denying herself the ribbons and lace collars and boxes of bonbons with which her friends indulged themselves.

It occurred to me, that afternoon, that this was an unusually sophisticated and elegant present for a ten-year-old boy to choose, and so as I looked at it I was able to say, quite honestly, that I thought it "wizzer" indeed and that Elinor was a lucky girl to have so thoughtful and generous a brother.

After that pleasant introduction, Ned and I were good friends from that day on. I did not see much of him, for he was an active, popular boy, busy after school with his friends; but from time to time we would meet, coming or going, and always he had a pleasant word for me, and once in a while he stopped to talk, to give me his news.

Even my mother's behavior, some days later, did not put him off, but, as I said, he was a child of unusual understanding.

To my surprise, Mrs. January asked me to attend the New Year's Eve party for which I had addressed so many invitations. "You need a little recreation," she said, not unkindly; and then, so as to preserve our respective positions, she added: "And besides, you can help to keep track of the servants. I will be busy all evening in the receiving line, I won't be able to oversee them. You can do that for me, if you will."

I hesitated. I was not—am not—overproud, but her invitation carried overtones of condescension which even I could not help but hear. And then, too, I knew that my mother would be furious; she would not want me there under any circumstances. Finally I said that I would come if I could, that it would depend on my mother's condition. Mrs. January nodded briskly and turned to other matters; long since, she had stopped inquiring about my mother's health, and I have sometimes wondered if she knew through some extra-sensory means the degree of my mother's hatred for her and all her family. Certainly, after that evening, there was nothing to sense; my mother laid it out plain for all to see and hear.

I walked home that afternoon feeling happier than I had in many months, I did not know why. Perhaps it was the onset of a new year, which, whatever it might bring, could surely not be as bad as the one which had just passed, or perhaps it was simply the thought of that evening's party at the Januarys' to which I might go if I pleased and watch Isabel's friends congratulate her. I did not mind, no matter what my mother might say: it would be an evening out, a bright spot in my dun-colored life.

I found her as I generally did, lying in the rumpled bed, her shawl draped over her shoulders, staring at me accusingly. Her expression darkened when I told her that I might return to the Januarys' later in the evening.

"You are their employee," she said. "Now you want to hobnob with them. They are simply using you, Marian. If you think that they will accept you as one of them you are mistaken."

"I do not think that, Mother. But if I can be of help—"

"Help!" She spat it out. "Yes, go and help them. Leave me here alone. Go on— You are getting above yourself, my girl, and you will have a rude awakening. You will see—when they have no further use for you they will toss you aside and pretend that they never knew you.

And if you think that you will find a husband there you are very much mistaken. No one in that circle would ever marry you. You are simply hired help to them—nothing more."

She turned away from me then; she refused the cup of beef tea which I offered her; she refused to acknowledge anything I said. I sat alone in the front room for a time, wondering what to do; finally, after one last futile attempt to break through her anger, I put on my coat and hat and went out. It was a selfish thing to do, perhaps, but I was young, after all, and I had had little enough enjoyment in my life. What harm could come from my going to an evening party at the Januarys'? I thought as I hurried to the end of the street to find a hack—an unaccustomed luxury that, I thought, I had earned.

When I arrived the house was already filled with guests; Mrs. January, at her post in the hall, greeted me with a look of relief. "Just look in on the kitchen," she whispered. "I warned Cook about not letting the ices melt, but I'm afraid she'll forget, there's so much to do." In the basement I found the cook, a thin, red-faced woman, well in charge. "Don't worry about me, Miss Childs," she said with some annoyance; "it's those girls serving you need to look after. Someone will drop a tray yet, with this crush."

And, indeed, it seemed that all of Boston's many-branched best families had come out this night to welcome 1871 with the Januarys. The double parlors and the dining room were impassable with a crowd of finely dressed ladies and gentlemen, young and old, most of them having known each other since childhood and so

78

able to talk freely, the women not having to wait for introductions to the men as they did at less familiar gatherings.

They say that Boston people are cold, and so they often are, but only with strangers. With each other they are as warm as any people on earth. Some of them, this night, even spoke warmly to me; they knew of my position in the household, they knew that Mrs. January had befriended me. Despite my shabby black dress, so at odds with their finery, despite what I am sure was my rather awkward air, still they were friendly to me, and I was grateful for it. Even Isabel spoke cordially; perhaps, I thought, she did not want to break her stride. She stood with her mother for a time before going to circulate among the guests; she wore pale pink embroidered silk, with tiny sleeves and a heart-shaped neckline; the skirt was pulled up behind into the fashionable new bustle with a small train. Around her throat she wore a gold, enameled locket; in her upswept hair she wore white camellias. Her eyes sparkled, her full cheeks were flushed, her hands fluttered from her hair to her necklace to her embroidered bodice in a self-conscious way which, even then, I knew to be unlike her. Avery Kittredge was at her side most of the time. He hovered over her protectively; Isabel was short but slightly plump, in the fashion of the day, but Avery's bulk made her seem positively fragile. They were the picture of young happiness. Had it not been for the nervous movement of those hands, I would have thought that she was triumphant, as all young women are upon the announcement of their impending marriage; but the hands betrayed her. I wondered if anyone else noticed them.

Although I saw a familiar face now and then, I was, as I had been at Pussie Mifflin's, mainly an observer. I saw Miss Mifflin in a crowd of her friends, and she smiled at me and seemed to remember who I was, but I did not try to join them. Soon the orchestra began to play and the floor was cleared for dancing. I retreated to the back hallway where, standing near the door, I could watch without being seen. *One* two three, *one* two three— around and around they went, two by two, the women expertly managing their heavy skirts, their trains; the men expertly guiding them. *One* two three, *one* two three—my foot tapped to the rhythm, my head nodded in time as I watched them go. How well they all danced— even Avery Kittredge, big and bulky as he was, glided around the floor with the assurance given by years of dancing classes at Papanti's.

I felt a tap on my shoulder and turned to see Ned looking up at me.

"Would you like to dance?" he said.

"What—in front of all these people?"

"No, right here in the back hall. No one will notice us."

"I'm afraid I'm not a very good dancer, Ned."

"I'm not either. I haven't started at Papanti's yet. But we could try—come on."

And so, feeling slightly foolish, I let him awkwardly put his arm partway around my waist and we stepped off. His head hardly reached my shoulder, and his arm was hardly long enough to circle me, but his bright smile gave me confidence and soon we were doing well enough. *One* two three, *one* two three, just the two of us alone in the back hallway going round and round to the infectious rhythm of the music. I looked down on his silky brown head and smiled at him as he lifted his bright little face to grin at me triumphantly.

"You see?" he said. "Easy as anything."

"I'll tell your mother that you don't need to go to Papanti's after all," I said, laughing. I could not remember when I had felt so happy.

One two three, *one* two three—and then the music stopped and he released me with a quaint little bow. "Thank you," he said. "I'll go and find the others now"—meaning his brood of young cousins. I went to the kitchen then, to see that all was well—which it was—and then I returned to watch the dancing again. Go on, I thought, dance all you please; I too have had my turn.

At last the music stopped and it was time for supper. I stood near the table in the dining room, watching to see that the maids hired for the occasion placed and served the food correctly. By and by I felt a presence at my side and I turned to see a short, stout, florid man with twinkling blue eyes and a gold tooth gleaming through his lips when he smiled.

"Damned eager, ain't they?" he remarked, grinning. He was slightly shorter than I; I could see his shining bald pate as he turned his head from side to side so as not to miss any of the entertainment provided by the crowd.

Despite his language he was undoubtedly a gentleman; and despite the convention that unmarried ladies did not speak to men to whom they had not been introduced, I was happy to reply. I knew what he meant: the guests were consuming the food so quickly that the servants hardly had time to replenish it, and I wondered what Mr. January would have to say about his grocer's bill when his wife presented it to him.

"Mrs. January's cook does very well," I replied, smiling at him.

"Freeloaders, the lot of 'em. They didn't eat all day, I'll wager, knowing they'd be fed well here." He seemed to swell like a strutting gobbler as he spoke; he smiled relentlessly, displaying his tooth, his goodwill. At last he offered his hand. "Samuel Swift," he said, chuckling. "Ethel's second cousin on her mother's side. I know who you are. Lottie Reed told me about you. Ethel's lucky to have you. Isabel's too busy with her own affairs to help, and Ethel has much too much to do."

Cousin Sam Swift, who was to become my friend, had all of the good qualities of his kind and very few of the bad. He was connected to all of the best families but, like many such, he had been born without a great fortune. On his own he had made it, and now, at fifty, he had been free to retire and indulge his passions: the cultivation of orchids and the study of Yankee genealogy. He was obsessed by these two things, and sometimes he overburdened his companions with details of his studies, but I for one never minded listening to him because I knew that he had a very kind heart and a generous nature.

We were interrupted just then by the sound of an altercation at the door. All through the rooms I was aware of voices fading, conversations trailing to an end, faces turned toward the reception hall. People gathered round and craned their necks to see; they shushed each other so as to be able to hear. It was impossible to distinguish words; we heard only the angry tones of the voices, Mrs. January's overpowered by another.

"Come on," said my companion. Unceremoniously he seized my elbow and propelled me through the crowd. As we made our way the voices got louder and louder.

Suddenly, in the midst of the crush and before we reached a place where we could see, I recognized the second voice. I felt my stomach drop; I felt my face burn until it must have matched my hair. "No—please—" I wrenched my arm from Samuel Swift's firm grip. I wanted to turn and run—to disappear; and yet I could not, I had to stay and watch. I was aware of his stare, his attention momentarily deflected from the commotion. O God, I thought, let me be dreaming—a nightmare could have been no worse than what was with me now.

Suddenly a figure broke free from the little knot of people in the foyer and burst into the parlor. She did not see me: her gaze swept the room, not resting anywhere, and then swept back again because she did not find what she sought. She had lost her bonnet, and her hair sprang wildly from her head like that of some crazed Medusa— and indeed she had turned many of her audience to stone, not least me. The buttons at the neck of her black dress were open, as if she had needed to gasp for air; and as her shawl slid down I saw that her sleeve was torn.

"Where is he?" she cried. "Where is my boy?" And, having no answer, she cried again: "Where is he? You took him! Now give him back!" She whirled to face

Isabel, who stood frozen behind her. "You took him! *You*—" And then her eye fell on Ned, who had been crouching on the stairs. She stared at him for a moment, immobile, and then with a great cry she bounded up the stairs and leaped upon him and seized his arm. "Here he is!" she cried. "Here—"

And now at last someone came to stop her. Mr. January, his jaw set hard in anger, followed her up and put his hand around her wrist and twisted it. She showed no sign of pain; her face kept its wild expression. She and Mr. January struggled together precariously balanced until it seemed that both of them, and Ned, too, would tumble down to the feet of the throng gathered in the hall.

She stood for a moment glaring at us all. I wanted to turn away, for I was terrified that she would see me—recognize me and speak to me, identify me as her daughter—but if she knew me she gave no sign. Then, with a kind of exaggerated, theatrical dignity, she gave up, she let go Ned's arm. Mr. January released her. As she descended he stood watching her go. The crowd parted to make way; she walked through, her head high, her hand clutching her trailing shawl. The butler opened the door for her; she passed through into the night and he closed it behind her.

There was a moment of appalled silence and then I heard people's voices buzzing up around me. I felt my knees give way, but before I could sink to the floor I had a hand at my elbow to support me.

"Steady," said Samuel Swift. "Just a step, now—over here—" And he guided me through the crowd to a chair and sat me down and peered into my face. "Don't move," he said—an unnecessary caution, for I could not have risen to save my soul. "I'll just get a glass of punch for you, you'll be right in no time."

All around me the guests stood in little groups of twos and threes, recovering from their shock. I saw Mrs. January signal to the orchestra, and in the next moment strains of music floated over the room like soothing balm on an angry burn. Snatches of conversation penetrated my daze. "A madwoman?" "How did she get in?" "What did she say—'You took my boy'?"

I was aware of someone crouching at my side. I turned to see Curtis, his kind face tense with worry. I knew, I don't know how, that his concern was for me, not for his sister, whose party had been so rudely disrupted.

"All right now?" he said. He reached for my hand and held it tight. "Can I get you something to drink?"

"Yes," I said in answer to his first question; and, "No, thank you—Mr. Swift is doing that."

Dear Curtis! Even when his bride, Grace, joined us; even when Samuel Swift returned with a cup of punch; even when Isabel and her mother passed by with only a glance in my direction as if by ignoring me they could obliterate the entire incident—still he stayed by me, he fended off those few guests who knew that the intruder was my mother (most, blessedly, did not); and when, finally, I felt well enough to stand, he called for the January carriage to take me home and promised to look in on me—on us—the next day before he began his round of New Year's calls.

And so I missed the high point of the evening—the

announcement of Isabel's engagement—and I returned to our dreary little rooms. They were dark and empty. I had not expected to find my mother there, although I had no notion of where she might be. Oddly enough, I was not concerned for her safety. She had committed an unpardonable act; whether it had been inspired by temporary madness or whether possibly it had been a calculated thing I did not try to fathom. Nor did I wait up for her. I lay down on the bed fully dressed and within a moment I slept. When I awoke the next morning—New Year's Day, 1871—I awoke to a gray, cold day, an unlit fire, an empty larder, and solitude. She had not returned.

A short time later Curtis arrived as he had promised, bringing with him a basket of food. He spoke, at first, in a hushed voice, as one speaks in a home where someone is ill; but as he saw my expression he spoke more freely.

"She isn't here?" he said.

"No."

"Was she, last night?"

"No. Not since I came back."

He considered; and then he smiled at me. "Well then," he said, "come home with me—to Mother's, I mean."

"But—" If she returned and found me gone—particularly if I had gone to the Januarys'—it would be, I knew, the final unforgivable act in her eyes. "I should be here when she returns."

"If she does. Do you have any idea where—"

"No."

"No friends, no family?"

"No."

"I will go to the police," said Curtis. "I will tell them

that she is—ah—temporarily deranged. They are very good, they have many ways of finding people, sources of information—if she is in the city we will know it. Leave a note here in case she comes back."

And so I did; I put a few things into a satchel; I stopped downstairs to have a word with our landlady; and then I climbed into the trap waiting at the curb and Curtis climbed up beside me and we drove away. I did not stop to consider the consequences of my going with him; I knew only that I could not bear to stay alone and that, whatever the January household offered, it would be more than what I had.

Six

My arrival at the Januarys' that bleak New Year's Day
was perhaps not so unwelcome as it might have been,
simply because they had no time or energy to spare to
consider me. Hardly having recovered from the festivities of the evening before, they were, that day, preparing
for the steady stream of callers who annually made their
appearance to welcome each new year. The remains of
the party had been cleared away, the furniture put back
in place, the wilting bouquets replaced with fresh ones.
Mrs. January greeted me civilly enough and directed me
to put my valise in her room for the moment—"I'll have
Mary make up the extra bed in Elinor's room until we can
settle you for good. And Marian—just look in on Ned,
will you, and make sure he's properly combed his hair?
People will start to call soon, and I want him to be
presentable."

Curtis spoke a kind word to me before he went to
collect his wife, and Elinor shyly welcomed me, so I felt
less ill at ease than I might have. I did as Mrs. January
instructed and delivered Ned to the parlor neatly washed

and brushed; I helped the downstairs maid to set out the punch cups and bowls of nuts and bonbons; I carried coats and cloaks and hats upstairs when the crush in the downstairs hall became too great.

And when that day was done, and the next, and the next, I found that I had settled in and that Curtis' invitation had been an act of charity for his mother as well as for me, for she badly needed help, and certainly she got none from Isabel, in whose behalf she labored.

The wedding: how it ruled our lives! Not six months previously they had gone through such a ceremony, but that had been different, that had been for their son and the burden of the work had fallen on the mother of his bride. Now Mrs. January was the mother of the bride, and so it was she who must oversee the business, it was she who was responsible for the success of the affair.

Her first crisis came not long after New Year's. She sat by the fire in her sitting room one snowy afternoon and looked up at me with anguished eyes. She held out to me a list of names—a hundred, at least—written in an unfamiliar hand.

"This has just come," she said. "The Kittredge people to whom invitations are to be sent."

I took it from her and glanced at it. I recognized only a few of the names.

"It is impossible," she said. "Out of the question. Mrs. Kittredge knows perfectly well that you cannot have Mrs. Roberts Reed and the Bartlett clan together at the same affair. The Bartletts had close ties to Secessia, they have family in Virginia still—and Mr. Reed, in the year before he died, was a founding member of the Union Club."

89

Even I, lacking intimate knowledge of the details of their lives, understood the significance of what she said: the Union Club (the "Sambo Club," as it was cruelly known) had been formed in 1863 by men who had quit the Somerset when the Confederate sympathies there became too oppressive. We were now nearly six years away from Appomattox, but feelings ran high still, and more than one gentleman had been cut dead in the sreet by another of equal social standing whose views on the late war had not softened.

"Yes," I said, "it would be very awkward."

"Awkward! It would be a disaster! Isabel will never forgive me if her wedding does not go smoothly, and yet what am I to do? This woman wants invitations sent to these people; how can I refuse her?"

"Perhaps you could speak to Mrs. Reed," I said, "and ask her, for Isabel's sake—"

"You don't know her, Marian. She is a woman of strong principle. She insists on having Senator Sumner to dine."

She might have said "the Devil," for Senator Sumner had been banished from Boston tables years before on account of his outspoken abolitionism. Only a few families—the Lodges, the Adamses—continued to receive him, and severely jeopardized their own social standing by doing so.

"Then perhaps you should speak to Mrs. Kittredge," I said, "and ask her to modify her list."

She threw me a startled glance, as if I had uttered some impertinence; I was in fact only trying to be helpful, although I had, I admit, little sympathy for her troubles.

Having just passed through some months of real difficulties, I was hardly prepared to commiserate with hers, which seemed so trivial.

In the end, after some days of agonizing, she threw up her hands and instructed me to address invitations to all the names on the Kittredge list. "If they spoil Isabel's wedding they'll have only themselves to blame," she said. "And, knowing Isabel, she'll not let them forget it."

She did not, in fact, and for years afterward her relations with her in-laws were soured by the memory of her wedding reception, at which there developed two hostile factions, with a few flustered peacemakers scurrying back and forth between.

I saw little of Isabel that winter, despite my now constant presence in the household. She was caught up in a whirlwind of activities, some routine, some given in her honor. If I passed her in the hallway or encountered her at table she greeted me civilly enough with none of the hostility she had previously shown; on the other hand she was hardly friendly. I did not mind; I was content to help Mrs. January as I could and to play companion to Elinor and Ned when necessary. Leighton was cheerful and friendly when he was at home, which was seldom; and Curtis always spoke a kind word to me during his frequent visits.

One afternoon about a month after my arrival he took me aside in the downstairs parlor. His face was troubled; I knew before he spoke that he had bad news.

"They have found your mother," he said. I waited for the inevitable: in the river, perhaps, or dead of exposure in the streets.

"In Hartford."

"Hartford!" I needed a moment to comprehend it. "Why? With whom?"

"With a family named Trout. Do you know them?" I did not; had never heard of them.

"For the moment she does not know—ah—that she has been discovered. I told my friend in the police to be discreet. We simply wanted to know that she is alive and well, I said; we did not necessarily want to make contact. I will leave that up to you."

I made a show of considering, but it was a show only for his benefit: I had known all along that unless she was in need, unless she was sick or starving, I would be content for the time at least to let her go her way. She had, after all, been the one to leave; and I could get along without her well enough.

"No," I said. "Don't—don't have anyone speak to her. She will know where to find me if she needs me."

Grace came to fetch him then, and soon they had gone. Since returning from their wedding journey they had lived in a charming little house around the corner in Clarendon Street; it had been given to them, fully furnished, by Grace's father. Like most New Englanders, Mr. Parker was thrifty to a fault; I had once heard Mrs. January comment on the shabby state of Mrs. Parker's wardrobe, and the Parker hospitality, such as it was, was notoriously thin. But he doted on his daughter—his only child—and so he had presented Curtis with the keys to the house and waved aside any attempt at thanks.

I had not seen it, but one afternoon not long afterward when Isabel announced that she had an unwonted gap in her schedule and was going to fill the time by calling on her sister-in-law, Elinor suggested that we accompany her. I could hardly believe that Isabel wanted me along, but she made no objection and so, shortly after three o'clock, she and Elinor and I set off.

Mr. Parker had done well by his daughter and her husband: the house was a small panel-brick affair, nicely decorated in the newly fashionable Eastlake style, with heavily patterned wallpaper and furniture modeled entirely on squares and rectangles. A coal fire murmured and hissed in the grate; the tea table was well filled with sandwiches and cakes, plates of toast, and little pots of jelly and butter. We passed a pleasant hour, for Grace was a cordial, unassuming young woman despite the wealth which might have made her unbearably haughty. She even included me in their talk and tried to make me feel at home. This she could not do, of course, but I was grateful for her effort. She was very plain—thin and sallow, with no flair for dress—but she had a good heart; and so we passed a pleasant afternoon, and as the clock rang half after four Isabel announced that it was time to go. She stood before the gilt-framed mirror over the fireplace to adjust the angle of her hat. Her diamond ring sparkled in the light as she moved her hands. Grace watched her admiringly. "That hat just suits you," she said. "They were all the rage in London last summer, those little flat ones. Mother won't give up her bonnets; she says that they have years of good wear in them. But I like these new ones. Mrs. Elwood Cushing says she's going to give me two of hers when she leaves next week. She doesn't have room for them in her trunk, she says, and she doesn't want to throw them away."

Isabel continued calmly to tuck in the wisps of hair around her face. The flush on her cheeks might have been caused by her nearness to the fire or by the reflection of the pink material of her bodice. Her hands were steady; her eyes did not waver from her reflection. I note these things in retrospect; at the time I had no notion that they were remarkable.

Finally Isabel spoke. "Where is she going?" she said.

Just then we heard the front door slam: Curtis, home from his law office.

"England," said Grace. "She has friends there. And her son, of course. They lived there for years when he was a boy, and now it seems that he wants to settle there for good."

Isabel turned to face her, every hair in place, chin high, eyes shining, lips curved into a pleasant, impersonal smile. She leaned in to receive Grace's kiss on her cheek. "I am late," she said. "Mrs. Willard is having a musicale at seven o'clock, and she hates to have people wander in after the program starts."

Grace laughed. "I'd wander in as late as possible if I were you. She always insists on giving her daughter the greatest share of the program, and if that girl can sing I can fly."

Curtis, looking in, provided a little diversion then, so that Grace did not notice when Isabel dropped her gloves. When she did not move at once to retrieve them I leaned down and picked them up and gave them to her. She stared at me in a startled way as I put them into her hands, as if she had never seen me before, as if she did not know who I was.

The moment passed. We said good-bye to Curtis and Grace and stepped out into the darkening afternoon. It had begun to rain: a cold drizzle, the air so raw that the breath from the passing horses steamed up like thick fog. I felt Elinor slip her arm through mine. She was shivering, and I was glad that we had only a moment's walk to the January house.

"Did you hear what Grace said?" she asked as we started off. "About Mrs. Cushing? Do you suppose, if I asked her—or if Mother asked her—that she'd give me some of her things for the church collection? It would be better than throwing them away."

"That would be an impossibly forward thing to do," snapped Isabel. She had set a fast pace, and we were hurrying to keep up with her. "You can't just go and ask someone—"

Suddenly she stopped and stared at her younger sister. "Yes!" she said, so loudly that to my chagrin a passing man turned to look at us. Women seldom went about unattended by a man—any man, even a servant—and it was only because we were three together, and the distance so short, that Mrs. January had consented to allow us to go on foot instead of being driven. "Yes," said Isabel again, "of course she'd give you some of her things. Why not? Come on—we'll go right now and ask her. She lives on West Cedar Street. We can be there in fifteen minutes."

She was in torment, of course, although she needed to keep it hidden. Years later, when she told me of that evening—when she told me everything—I remembered the peculiar harshness of her voice, the intensity of her stare as we stood under the street lamp in the raw, misty evening. We were two doors from her home; now she was proposing to walk another half mile, at least, to call on a woman whom she hardly knew to ask her for a donation of cast-off clothing for a church charity—an organization in which Isabel had never shown the slightest interest before that day.

Elinor stared at her, shivering, mystified; I hung back, hardly able to restrain her and yet unwilling to see Elinor catch cold tramping through the night. And besides, Isabel had said herself that she had an early engagement that evening, she needed time to dress, to take a quick bite before she went out.

But Isabel was pigheaded, stubborn, and insistent on her own way always.

"I think I would have gone mad that night," she said, "if I had not spoken to Mrs. Cushing. I needed so badly to find out about him—to learn where he had gone. I had no idea. Nothing. I'd not had a word from him since that night months before—"

Lawrence Cushing.

And she was engaged to marry Avery Kittredge.

I suppose that there will come a day—a century from now? two centuries?—when women are as free as men to act forthrightly, instead of needing always to resort to subterfuge. Already I see it in my daughter Diana: instead of waiting for invitations, she invites whom she pleases to dinner, to share our seats at Symphony, the theater. But Diana is a free spirit; even today, most young women do not behave so. And Isabel, who was so stubborn, so intent on having her way, nevertheless always contrived to get it strictly according to convention.

Looking back, I can see that it was as if, having already committed one nearly disastrous breach of conduct, she had determined to behave thenceforth with the utmost propriety. And so she could not have said to Elinor and me that night, "I want to visit Mrs. Cushing to inquire about her son." She needed the excuse of the clothing for charity, no matter how improbable that excuse sounded.

We had no defense against her will, and so, instead of the warmth and comfort of the January house, we had instead the long walk up Beacon Street, past the Public Garden (a dangerous place to be when darkness fell), down Charles Street to Chestnut, up Chestnut to West Cedar. After a few half-hearted protests we did not speak, Elinor and I; she was only fourteen and so had a small waist cincher, but I wore full corsets and my breath came shallow and hard as we hurried along, and my heart pounded and I thought that I must faint if I could not free myself and draw a deep breath into my constricted lungs. When finally we arrived at number 16, I stood panting on the steps as Isabel rapped the brass lion's-head knocker; I hoped that the servant would take a moment to answer, to give me time to recover.

To my surprise, Mrs. Cushing herself opened the door. She hardly knew Isabel, and she had never met Elinor and me; but she was well schooled in the manners of her class, after all, and so she promptly invited us in, and helped us hang our sodden waterproofs on the hall tree, and ushered us into her pretty parlor to warm ourselves by the fire.

"I was feeling sorry for myself because no one has called all day," she said, "and now you have saved me from total despair."

She was a small woman whose improbable golden hair and somewhat flamboyant dress were commonly attributed to her long years of living abroad. Her friends defended her: "Europeans—even the English—are different," they said. "It is a wonder that she has been corrupted so little. Her décolletage is a trifle extreme, perhaps, the colors of her dresses a trifle bold—and her hair? Her hair is its natural color: look at her son."

When finally I met him, that son, I saw that the color of his glowing golden crown was exactly like his mother's. And his face, too, resembled hers: but the strong, angular features, the slanting cheekbones and long jaw did not suit a woman, although they gave to him his peculiar, compelling attraction. And the eyes: brilliant blue, sometimes almost green, slightly slanted— a Slavic face, a Russian face, at odds with his New England name. They say that his father was dull and dim; he died when Lawrence was an infant and left no trace on his son's character or on his appearance.

Mrs. Cushing settled us on plush seats near the fire and poured more water into the teapot. She was without servants, she explained, because her all-purpose girl had needed to leave the week before in order to take a new place being held for her, and it hardly seemed worthwhile, she said, to hire someone for only two or three weeks. (We learned later that she had not had servants since the previous summer, since shortly after her son left the

city; like many people of the best families, she was
perpetually short of money. She had lived abroad so long,
I think, partly in a futile attempt to economize.)

She spoke then of servants in general; of several
amusing visits she had paid to the Intelligence Office
downtown to hire new ones; of a friend of hers who
refused to hire anyone under thirty years of age; and so
on. She carried on very well; her talk flowed without
pause, her hands occupied themselves in serving us, her
smile flashed back and forth between us as her brilliant
eyes took us in. It must have been obvious to her that
there was some purpose to our visit other than simple
friendliness, since Isabel was hardly her friend and
Elinor and I did not know her at all; but since she had no
idea what it was she floated for a while from topic to
topic, hoping to light on the right one.

"You know of course that I leave next week for
London," she said.

"And you are giving away—" began Elinor eagerly;
but her older sister silenced her with a look.

"Will you stay with friends there," said Isabel, "or
family, perhaps?"

"My son," said Mrs. Cushing. "He has been there
nearly six months now, and he wants me to join him."
She laughed. "Mothers dote on their sons, do they not?
As you will discover, all three of you, when you have sons
of your own. How is your brother Curtis? Grace seemed
very well when I saw her, and of course she was a
splendid match for him."

"Yes," said Isabel. I saw that she had ignored her tea;
her full cup sat before her, growing cold.

"We all want the best for our children," said Mrs. Cushing. "And since I have only one, all my hopes rest on him—although he is hardly a child any longer, he was twenty-three last August. He was, I believe, a classmate of your brother Leighton's. There was some talk of their joining in a business venture a year or so ago, but nothing came of it, I don't know why. But now Lawrence has determined to settle in London, whether permanently I can't say, but he wants me with him, the dear boy, and of course I will go. I wouldn't be surprised if he had his heart set on marrying a title"—and here she uttered a coy little laugh—"but what good it will do him I don't know. They aren't transferable, are they? To the one marrying in, I mean. And of course a title doesn't guarantee a fortune, does it? Still, it might be interesting to have a title as a daughter-in-law. On the other hand, I don't care if he never marries. We have such good times together, he and I, that I shall be quite jealous of his wife."

"Every word she spoke," Isabel told me, years later, "was like a knife through my heart, and yet I would not have stopped her, I needed to hear her out, to hear everything about him that she wanted to tell."

Certainly, that afternoon at Mrs. Cushing's, Isabel betrayed none of the emotion to which she later confessed. She sat calmly among us, neglecting to eat and drink but otherwise seemingly at ease, and nodded and smiled and never once even mentioned his name to spur our hostess' volubility. Not that Mrs. Cushing needed prompting: once started on the topic of her son, she went on about him for some minutes more; and then, recollecting her duties as a hostess, she began once again to cast about to see what purpose our visit had. Elinor seized her chance. In a tentative voice that grew stronger as she saw the receptivity in Mrs. Cushing's face, she spoke of her "people," as she called them, and of the charitable activities of the Church, and if Mrs. Cushing would care to donate some of her castoffs . . . ?

Mrs. Cushing seemed relieved to have discovered at last why we had so unexpectedly descended on her. She laughed and reached out to pat Elinor's hand.

"How old are you, child? Fourteen? And already so grown up that you busy yourself in such work? Of course you may have my things—take whatever you like. Or better yet, don't take anything today. I will make up a collection tomorrow. Send your coachman around late in the afternoon to pick them up."

Elinor beamed; she even dared to sneak a triumphant glance at Isabel. I was happy for her, for I had grown very fond of her; and, ignorant as I was of the real purpose of Isabel's call on Mrs. Cushing, I was grateful to her for her indulging her younger sister's dearest wish.

Soon we took our leave; and, plunged once again into preparations for Isabel's wedding, I might have forgotten about our call on Mrs. Cushing. I never saw her again; she remained in England until her death some years later.

But an incident which occurred a month or so later brought her forcibly to mind again, and her son even more.

One blustery afternoon in March, after a week of bitter weather during which all the household had battled coughs and sneezes and running fevers, Elinor insisted upon going to a meeting of the Poor Relief Society. "Let her go," said Mrs. January at last. "She seemed well enough this morning. Just make sure that she wears her flannels, and warn her that I want her home by three."

And so Elinor went off to her meeting; and Ned was at school; and Isabel (so I thought) had recovered sufficiently to attend a luncheon. Shortly after two we heard the front bell; the maid opened it to discover the Reverend Mr. Eldridge himself, Elinor in his arms. She had fainted, he said. Mrs. January, rising from her sickbed, leaned over the balustrade and called to him to bring her upstairs if he could. He was a tall, muscular man of perhaps fifty; Elinor's weight was nothing to him. Rapidly he ascended the stairs and then the next flight, following Mrs. January as she led him to Elinor's room. I was there, for I had continued to share it with her at her request. Mrs. January demanded the smelling salts, but they were not to be found. "Isabel may have taken them," she said to me. "Look on her chifforobe— hurry!"

I caught only a glimpse of Elinor's pale face as I hurried out. Mr. Eldridge had gently lowered her into her bed; she looked limp and very nearly lifeless.

Intent on my mission, I ran to Isabel's room. The door was closed, but no matter, I thought; she had gone out. I pushed it open; I was halfway into the room before I realized that she was there.

She had uttered a startled little cry at my entrance; and then—so slowly did my senses react—I realized that I had heard something else: a little crash, a small sound of shattering glass.

She sat by the window which looked out onto Marlborough Street. Her face was wet with tears. For a moment—a fraction of a moment—our eyes met. And then I saw more than tears; I saw her sorrowing heart reflected on that lovely face, her sorrowing breaking heart. Never had I seen such anguish. I felt as though it struck me. At her feet lay what had fallen from her hands when I burst in upon her: a photograph in a glass case, broken now, its shards scattered on the floor.

At once she reached to retrieve it, but her finger grazed a piece of the glass and with a little cry of pain she started up, holding the injured hand in the other, blood suddenly dripping down the front of her pale brown skirt.

In that moment I had crossed the room and bent to pick up the photograph. She let go her bloody hand and reached to snatch it from me, but not before I saw the face. It was distorted by the fragments of glass which remained in the frame; for a moment I thought that I looked at someone whom I had met not long ago—yes, Mrs. Cushing—but then I realized that it was the face not of a woman but a man: a young man, yet curiously odd-looking, as if he had lived and known far more in his young life than most men his age. He had light hair; strong, angular features; high cheekbones; pale eyes which even in those dull sepia tones seemed to catch and concentrate the light; a full, sensuous mouth which seemed about to speak.

And say what? Words that had beguiled her, had nearly destroyed her? Words that she could not forget but that would (so she thought) never be spoken again?

But I knew nothing of him then; and I had no time to consider who he was or what he was to Isabel. I did not even stop to see about her injury; I saw the bottle of salts on the chifforobe and without a word of explanation I took it and hurried back to Elinor. Tending to her for the rest of the that day and the next, and tending to Mrs. January as well, occupied my thoughts so that it was not until I encountered Isabel one morning at the breakfast table (an unusual occurrence in those days, for she usually slept late) and saw the bandage on her hand that I remembered the nature of her injury and the way in which she had received it.

We were still on an awkward footing, she and I, and so by the way she avoided my eyes I knew that she would not welcome questions. Perhaps, I thought, she told them that she hurt herself in some other way.

And so, by default, I became party to her secret. And, more, I had a card to use against her if I chose. Curiously enough, I did not want to. The wound caused by George's death had grown a scar, it was no longer open and bleeding; had the incident happened six months previously, in the fall, I might still have been angry enough to want to hurt her as she had, however unintentionally, hurt my mother and me; but now I did not. Let it pass, I thought, and see what comes of it. One day I came upon one of the maids trying to sponge the blood from Isabel's skirt, but she could not get it clean and so the skirt was discarded.

Spring drew on; the day of the wedding approached. All of our energies were devoted to that; we had no time, no thought for anything else. I was as caught up in it as if I had truly been a member of the family, for there were a thousand details to be attended to; Mrs. January could not have managed alone, and Isabel was no help because she was the star of the production, so to speak, on stage all the time. She had no time to assist those of us who were managing the show backstage.

On her wedding day we rose at dawn to make ready. I was busy with the cook, and with tending to Elinor, and with myriad details of checking off lists and dealing with last-minute arrivals of flowers and messages of goodwill and overseeing the maids, and so I did not see Isabel until midmorning when, summoned by Mrs. January, I went to her room to view her in her wedding gown. It was a symphony of white lace and silk and embroidered pearls, more splendid than any gown I had ever seen, and for a moment I was so overcome with admiration for it that I did not look at her, I looked only at what she wore.

And then my eyes found her face, and what I saw there was so stark a contrast to the splendor of her dress that I remember still my feeling of shock—what was wrong?

She said nothing. Her lovely eyes looked out at me with an expression of blank despair. I saw no joy, no anticipation of the great event; I did not see even ordinary prenuptial apprehension. No: this was something else, something frightening—like a trapped animal, I thought, and yet even more than that. Anguish, I thought: she is in very great pain, she agonizes over—what?

I had seen her so once before, on the day that I surprised her in her room, the day that she cut her finger on the broken glass of the photograph of the young man—who?

The moment passed; Elinor and Grace came in; we proceeded with the events of the day. I had no time to reflect on what I had seen.

Later, when it was over and Isabel and Avery were in England on their wedding journey, Mrs. Roberts Reed chastised me for overworking.

"You've worn yourself out," she said disapprovingly. "You look peaked. I will speak to Ethel. She should have Dr. Slocomb prescribe a tonic for you. But then, you will be going to Nahant with them next week, won't you? The sea air will revive you."

She did not at once realize her tactlessness, and I, already fond of her, was loath to point it out. Nahant was the last place in the world that I wanted to go: it would be a long time, I thought, before I could bear to see those cottages again, the lawns stretching to the cliffs . . .

But she saw in my face the effect of her remark and at once—for she was a blunt, honest woman—she apologized. "That was stupid of me, Marian. How could I—I didn't stop to think. I'm very sorry."

It was one of the few times that I have ever seen her discomposed; usually she was self-confident to a fault, sailing blithely through the reefs and shallows of her life with no thought of foundering.

"How is—have you news of your mother?" she said then. "You said only that she was in Hartford."

"As far as I know," I said, thankful that my voice was steady. "I have not heard from her, no. I can only assume that I will if—if there is some need."

She studied me for a moment, her eyes alive in her thickset, homely face. "Stay with me," she said then. "Of course you don't want to go to Nahant. Stay with me, and next month come with me to Newport. Then in the fall you can rejoin Ethel if you want. I know she's become fond of you. And Elinor and Ned think of you as one of the family. You will be all right here until—"

I waited, knowing what she would say.

"—until you marry," she went on. "As of course

you will."

I was reminded for a moment of my mother's efforts, a year or so ago, to make of me an attractive prospect for some likely young man.

"Indeed you will, Marian. If I have to—well, never mind." She studied me for a moment. I know what passed through her mind: had I been a beauty, my lack of a fortune or good family would not have mattered, for many wealthy men were happy to have a beautiful wife, no matter her antecedents or her poverty. But I was plain: not precisely homely, but plain. I was several inches taller than most women, and very thin; and my red hair, which would perhaps have been an asset to a pretty woman, served only to call attention to my undeniable lack of good looks.

I glanced away from her, but I held the image of her in my mind's eye. She was far plainer than I, and if she had succeeded in marrying not once but twice, then surely I too might find at least one man willing to give me his name.

Suddenly she spoke. "Have you ever been in love, Marian?"

The question startled me. I felt myself blush as I looked at her. "I—no, not—"

"It can be very painful. Sometimes it can nearly kill you. If you—*when* you find your young man whom you will marry, try not to love him too much. It is better so; you protect yourself from being hurt. Men are different, you see. They have much to occupy their time—they are overburdened, many of them. But women have nothing. They have only men. Even when children start to come, and you are busy from dawn till dark with feedings and sniffles and changing their linen—even then, the focus, the center of your life, is the man. But you must always remember that you are not the center of his. Protect yourself against being hurt, my dear. You are young, you have much to learn. But you will never learn anything more valuable than that."

She paused; she looked down at the stubby fingers clasped in her lap. I could not imagine what had prompted such an outburst. Had she, once, been unhappily in love? I knew that what she said was true: girls thought of nothing but men, of love, of marriage. What else had they to think about? They knew nothing, had no occupation—it was as if men were the ones who were truly alive, truly living in the world; and women were the audience, the onlookers, never quite participating.

And when some women tried to break the mold, to live larger lives, they were denounced as freaks, monstrosities—flying in the face of nature.

Finally, feeling the need to reply, I said, in an attempt to lighten our tone: "Do you tell this to every young woman you know?"

She snorted. "Hardly. It would be a waste of breath. And I have little enough of that with these stays." She winced as she shifted her weight in her chair. "But I like you, Marian. And I want to see you happily settled. And you've no one to look out for you, after all. So. Take my advice for what it's worth from the mouth of an old woman, and come upstairs with me now"—we were in the parlor—"and we will find Ethel and tell her of your change in plans for the summer."

And so I stayed with Mrs. Reed that June, and

luxuriated in the comfort of her Mount Vernon Street establishment, and regained my strength in the quiet of the deserted city, the hot streets cooling at night in breezes from the river, the blinds of the houses drawn all day against the sun. Everyone went away in summer; there were no social engagements to prepare for, no schedules to be kept. At the end of the month we went to Newport: not then, in 1871, what it would later become, but very like Nahant, a quiet seaside retreat for gentlefolk who thought it bad taste—bad breeding—to display their wealth and so lived a simple, almost spartan life. Newport had a higher intellectual tone than Nahant: Professor Longfellow had a cottage there, and Professor Agassiz, and Mrs. Julia Ward Howe. They accepted me as Mrs. Reed's companion and so, although no marriageable young man turned up (nor had I expected one), I passed a pleasant summer with her there and returned to the city renewed and refreshed and ready to take up my duties in the January household once again.

I had expected an easy time of it—or at least a less frantic one—but two weeks into September a message came that the wife of Mr. January's older brother—considerably older, as it turned out—had died. They had both been in poor health for months and so had not attended Isabel's wedding.

Mrs. January was not particularly saddened by the loss but she was, I saw, somewhat apprehensive about its consequences.

"Asa will want him to come to stay with us," she said. "And where will we put him? And what will we do with him?"

She did not reply to her own questions, but the answer

to the second, at least, was obvious; and so, not a week later, I found myself with a new set of duties: tending to Uncle James January.

He was almost twenty years older than his brother—half brother, more correctly, since their father had lost three wives to childbed, producing a son each. He was past seventy: a frail, white-haired man with a long, thin face and delicate, mottled, blue-veined hands. His voice was soft and thin and kind, and his blue eyes sparkled with interest when Mrs. January announced to him that I was to be his attendant.

"Better than that dog-faced nurse I've had," he chuckled, holding out his hand to me. I had expected to see a man overcome by grief—he had, after all, just lost his wife—but he showed no sign of sadness. Later, when we knew each other well, he told me that he had been glad to see her die because she had suffered so much—far more than he. "And her death brought home to me the fact that I don't have much longer here myself. So I resolved not to mourn. She didn't want me to grieve for her, and so while I miss her I haven't been sad. I'll be with her soon in any case. And meanwhile"—he patted my hand—"I have you."

Two days after Uncle James's arrival Isabel and Avery returned from their journey abroad. They went directly to the Kittredges' on Commonwealth Avenue, where they would live until their own house, being built in Exeter Street, was finished. They came to dine the next evening, along with Curtis and Grace. At Mrs. January's request, I joined them. "Give Uncle James his supper and then come down to us," she said. "And make sure that Cook does the blancmange properly—help her if you can.

I don't care if she takes offense. She wasted a dozen eggs last week, and if she can't do better than that I'll have to let her go. Although where I would find a replacement I couldn't say. No one wants to work for a living any more."

She looked tired, I thought—strained and tense. She might have been expected to be happy, at her daughter's return, but instead she seemed almost distraught. And now, seeing her, I realized that she had not been herself since the family's return from Nahant. The funeral, I thought, and the strain of accommodating Uncle James have worn her out.

And so I said that I would keep a close eye on Cook and, after settling Uncle James, I put on my black silk—a hand-me-down from a January cousin—and went downstairs to greet Isabel.

They were all in the parlor, sipping sherry, waiting for dinner to be announced. Even Elinor, I saw, held a glass, although I saw her drink from it only once and then grimace at the taste. It was, at first glance, the perfect family gathering: the proud father and mother, the new young in-laws, the children thriving.

But then, as we sat down to dinner, I noticed that Isabel too seemed ill at ease, even as her mother. She bloomed with good health. Her cheeks were rosy; her luxuriant hair, arranged in a new way with frizzy curls across her forehead, shone under the gas lamps; the skin of her shoulders and bosom, more exposed now as befitted a married woman, glowed like satin. And yet . . .

I said hardly a word to her beyond greeting. But I watched her: I was curious to see how her new situation suited her.

She and Avery, in deference to their newlywed state, were seated side by side; he seemed to take pleasure in the arrangement, glancing at her frequently, seeing to it that she was promptly served, deferring to her in conversation. She, on the other hand, hardly seemed aware of him. She never once looked at him; she directed her remarks to others (but not of course to me): she might have been on her own, so to speak. Only her rings—the diamond, the gold band—showed that she had an attachment. The man at her side might have been a stranger, and she, not having been introduced, very properly not speaking to him. But she laughed and chattered and regaled us with stories of their trip, and joked with Curtis, and teased Leighton about his frequent escapes to New York (where lived, it seemed, a young lady who had caught his eye), and chaffed her father into unaccustomed good humor.

But then, during a lull, she gave it all away, to me at least, for she raised her eyes to find mine watching her, and for a moment our gaze held. I do not know what she saw in my eyes, but I will never forget what I saw in hers: bewilderment, and pain, and a kind of frantic signaling of which she may not even have been aware.

As I had seen her on the day that I discovered her with the photograph of the young man who so resembled Mrs. Cushing.

As I had seen her on the morning of her wedding.

And then she looked away and the moment passed.

And I was left with the knowledge that we had two unhappy women: both Isabel and her mother, I thought, were hiding some trouble from the rest of us.

Seven

"Good," said Uncle James, "but not good enough. Ha!" His long, thin fingers fluttered over the board and then seized his knight and hopscotched it to knock out my badly protected queen. He grinned at me. "You haven't the instinct to win, Marian. This is a game of war—of conquest. Women can't play it. Although I must say you're a fair opponent. Most women wouldn't even try, but you've kept me going for fifteen minutes."

It was a dreary winter afternoon. We sat in his room, warming ourselves before the fire. The maid had drawn the heavy drapes against the day; we had had our tea (and Uncle James his "nip," as he called it) and now, with the conclusion of our game, he waved his hand at the board and told me to put it away. "No—not another," he said. He settled himself more comfortably in his morris chair and submitted while I pulled his cashmere shawl around his shoulders. He wore a dark green velvet lounge jacket and flannel trousers, and soft, fur-lined slippers on his feet. He had made a remarkable recovery since his arrival; it was, he said with a wink in my direction, the result of the devoted attention he had received.

Despite the difference in our ages, our stations in life, I had grown fond of him. He was not an easy patient: like many men successful in business, he had been accustomed to giving orders in his household as well as in his office, and he was loath now to change positions and submit to other people's wills. But though he railed at the doctor, and even at Mr. and Mrs. January, refusing to listen to their advice, he did not object to me; under my care he had rapidly improved, and for the past two weeks he had risen from his bed each afternoon to spend a few hours in his chair by the fire. At first he had Ned help him to dress, since of course I could not perform such a task; but then he grew strong enough to dress himself—a feat which he announced with some pride.

We sat now comfortably together, I ready to do his bidding, he ready to do mine. I thought that perhaps he might ask me to read to him from the *Transcript*, which had just come, but he seemed content to chat. We often talked, he and I; he knew of how I had come to the Januarys', and the story of my early life, and of my father's death, my mother's flight—even of my brother George and how he had died. I knew less of him: he seemed to prefer to hear me, for all that I had so little to tell. He began, this day, to talk of school—early school, and how I remembered learning my letters and numbers—but then we were interrupted by a knock on the door.

It was the upstairs maid, saying that Mrs. January wanted to see me.

"Yes—all right, tell her that I will be down directly."

Uncle James threw me a skeptical glance. "I shall protest," he said, with what I hoped was mock annoyance. "This is my time with you. She shouldn't interfere."

"She may not be well—" I began, and then, embarrassed, I could not think how to continue, for Mrs. January was most certainly not well; her condition, however, was not one that I could discuss with him. Both she and Isabel, it seemed, were in the family way, and while Uncle James had spoken frequently, and with high anticipation, of Isabel's condition—he looked forward, he said, to the new generation—we had not mentioned Mrs. January's identical state. It seemed unnatural— shameful—for a woman of her age to be with child. I had, one day, overheard Grace's opinion of her mother-in-law ("Disgraceful," she had said; "I can't bear to speak of it to anyone") and I heartily agreed. Of course I had no idea how women came to be in the family way but, however it happened, it seemed properly to be the province of young women. A woman about to be a grandmother should not herself be producing yet another child.

I found Mrs. January in the front hall, dressed to go out. "Hurry," she said. "Get your things. You'll need your overshoes, it's sloppy underfoot. I have the carriage, but still you don't want to get your feet wet. I've just had a note from Avery. Isabel has—well, they've had the doctor but of course I must go to her. Come along."

I knew of course that many women suffered miscarriages; even today, in this enlightened new century, many women insisted on wearing tight laces for far too long, and they lose their babies in consequence. I supported

115

the Sensible Dress League for years, and despite their failure I think that they were right.

As we hurried out to the carriage Mrs. January gave no hint that she was in the same delicate condition as her daughter. She climbed in more rapidly than I, and when we arrived at Isabel's she scurried up the front steps as if she were a maiden of seventeen.

We found Isabel upstairs in her room—hers and Avery's—with her in-laws as well as her husband in attendance. Under calmer circumstances Mrs. January might have instructed me to wait in the receiving room, but she said nothing and so I trailed along behind and tried to make myself as inconspicuous as possible.

Isabel lay in bed, propped up on pillows, looking more irritated than ill.

"I'm quite all right, Mother," she said shortly. "It was nothing. You should be concerned for yourself. Avery shouldn't have sent for you, there was no need—"

He hovered over her protectively, if such a large and bulky man could be said to hover. Despite their respective positions—he on his feet, she lying invalid—it was clear that she was the dominant force; he hung on her words, on the slightest movement of her eyes.

But of course she was very precious to him: she carried his child, his heir. He could get legitimate succession no other way.

We stayed for perhaps half an hour, until Mrs. January had assured herself that Isabel was truly all right. I said nothing, of course, and no one said anything to me. As Mrs. January prepared to take her leave I saw Avery lean down to Isabel and say a word or two close to her ear. She

ignored him and so he spoke again, this time putting his
hand on her shoulder. She refused to look at him; she
looked down, she looked away, and after a moment, in a
surprisingly violent gesture, she shook him off.

His smooth, square face bore no resentment—no
expression at all. The moment passed; we said good-bye
and went home.

I was glad for Mrs. January's sake that her daughter
was well, for she had, that winter, other troubles to worry
about: her own condition, of course, and Uncle James,
and above all Leighton. He was spending more and more
time away from home, away from the city, in fact: a
young woman in New York was exerting an increasing
pull on his heartstrings, and while he freely admitted
going to visit her, he was less forthcoming on the
subject—all-important to the Januarys—of her family.

"I have no idea who they are," said Mrs. January,
exasperated. "I mentioned their name to three people
last week, and no one had ever heard of them."

"Have they any money?" said Mrs. Reed, casting an
appraising eye up and down Mrs. January's thickening
figure.

"I don't know. They must have something—Leighton
is no fool, he would never court a girl with no money."

Mrs. Reed smiled at this. "Love," she said. "You can't
argue with love, Ethel. When do you suppose we'll meet
her?"

"I have no idea. I suppose it will have to be after—
after I am well again."

"Yes," said Mrs. Reed; quickly she changed the
subject. Despite her lecture on the hazards of falling in

love, she was as reluctant as every other married woman to discuss the workings of women's bodies with those most in need of the information. I have myself been at pains to tell Diana more than she wants to know about such things: we live in our bodies all our lives, and I cannot see why we should be ignorant of their functions.

As the winter passed, both Mrs. January and Isabel retired increasingly from society until at last they kept company only with their closest family. It was unseemly then for women to show themselves when they were obviously with child, and for that matter it still is. I saw a good deal of Isabel during that winter, for she came to call two or three times a week and Mrs. January, with me in attendance, went as often to her. Isabel was unfailingly polite to me, but distant—I knew perfectly well that she wished me gone and that, being forced to suffer my presence, she was simply putting up with me as best she could.

She was, after all, a snob: not in matters of money or of family, but on a more personal level. If she found you amusing, or if you could help her in some way, there was no better friend than she. But while some people are unfailingly polite to everyone, Isabel was not. And if I make her sound unpleasant I do her an injustice, for no one was more charming when she chose, and to bask in that light was reward enough for me, as for so many others, to forget her previous coolness. She had a warmth—a kind of tangible vitality—that transmitted itself to you and made you feel that you were as charming as she was.

It was this quality, I think, that made her success: she

collected people the way others collect paintings, or jewels, or (like Samuel Swift) rare tropical flowers. And people were always happy to be hers: if you were regularly invited to Isabel's you occupied a social place in that universe—that small, hermetic world of Boston society.

Some people, of course, did not care. Her sister, Elinor, for instance. And Farnsworth Bowditch. "She is a leech," he said. "A parasite. What does she do in this world?"

He was working at the time; he squinted and grimaced at me and paced back and forth before the easel, while I sat shivering in the chilly air of his studio, unable to move lest I spoil my portrait.

"What does any woman do?" I retorted. "She gives people pleasure—she entertains them by bringing them together."

"Stuff and nonsense, Marian. She exploits them, pure and simple."

As you do, I thought; but I said nothing, for Bowditch's exploitation was that of the artist. He laid bare his subjects' souls on his canvases, he exploited them in order to reveal them. When finally he finished my portrait, and I paid him for it and took it home with me and put it over the mantel in my front parlor, I had then to face the prospect of looking at myself every day— myself as Bowditch had revealed me: a woman seated, dressed in a gray gown with a green silk shawl draped over one shoulder. Her dark red hair was piled high, revealing a long white neck. Her hands were slim, gracefully arranged; her face was lifted, just a little, as if she were listening for something. A voice? A favorite refrain? Her large gray eyes looked out from her thin face with an expression of—no, not sympathy, but expectance, perhaps: she knew that you had an interesting story to tell and she was happy to hear it.

It was not a bad portrait; over the years I have come to like it very much.

In any case, our friendship, Isabel's and mine, had not yet begun in that winter, and so for her mother's sake we maintained our facade of politeness but never broke through to anything more. But as I observed her, as I could not help but do, I was reminded again and again of the way in which she had shrugged off Avery's hand. For she did not seem what she should have been—not, at least, to my inexperienced eye. She should be happy, I thought; she has had one great adventure—marriage— and she is about to have another. These are every woman's twin aspirations, now as then. And she was wellborn, beautiful, rich—why her look of discontent, why the nervous picking of the pleated ruffle at the neck of her dress, the snappish tone to her voice?

And then suddenly I had something else to concern me and Isabel's state of mind no longer seemed so important.

One night, sleeping fitfully, I started up in my bed thinking that someone had called my name. Elinor, whose room I still shared, was sleeping peacefully; I listened for a moment more and then I pulled on my wrapper and, heedless of the cold on my bare feet, took the night candle and slipped out into the hall. The house was silent; moonlight streamed through the leaded skylight in the roof. I padded along to Uncle James's room and cautiously opened the door. He too lay quiet in his bed. I went to his side and bent over him; I could see the gentle rise and fall of his chest as he breathed.

As I came into the hall I stopped again to listen. I felt like an intruder—a wakeful invader of this household of slumberers. And then I heard a sound, and then another, and I realized that I had not been mistaken. They seemed to come from Ned's room.

I went so quickly that the rush of air nearly extinguished my candle. I found him thrashing in his bed. I held the light steady as I stared down at him. Blood streamed from his nose; his cheeks and chin were covered with it, and his pillowcase and sheets; his eyes were panicked; he moaned and choked and twisted. Why did he not wipe the blood away, I wondered, or at least pinch his nose to stop the flow?

And then I saw that he could not, for his hands were tied to the bedposts; he lay spread-eagled like a victim tied for sacrifice. *"Ned—"*

Nearly panicked now myself, I set the candle on the night table. Rapidly I began to free him. His bonds were strong: lengths of torn sheet, knotted so tight that at first I thought that I would never be able to loosen them. My fingernails broke as I tore at the fabric. It would not give. I took my handkerchief from the pocket of my wrapper and held it to his nose. Mute, terrified, he stared up at me, his tears mingling with his blood, his mouth open in a wordless cry of anguish and humiliation.

I too was speechless; I could think of nothing to say to him, and so, silent in that silent house, the only sound his choking sobs, I set to work again to free his hands. At last the knots came loose. He pulled down his arms and flexed his fingers. I gave him my handkerchief; as he pressed it to his nose he turned away from me. I heard him sniffle; then he coughed, but still he said nothing. I sat on the edge of the bed and put my hand on his shoulder; when he made no response I reached out and began to brush back the long silky brown hair that had fallen across his face.

"Ned?"

No answer.

"Ned, look at me."

No answer.

"Ned. Please."

Suddenly, all in a rush, he came to me; heedless of the blood, he flung himself upon me and I took him in my arms and cradled his head against my breasts as I crooned to him and rocked him and comforted him as if he had been a child of three or four instead of a great boy of nearly twelve. He clung to me; he put his arms around me and buried his face against me; his body was tense and rigid. After a moment I heard him sob again. Good, I thought; let it come, let it calm him.

We stayed so for a long while. I heard the clock downstairs chime three, and then the quarter hour. Gradually I felt his tension ease.

"Marian?" He spoke without moving, his voice muffled.

"Yes."

"You mustn't tell."

"I won't."

"Father did it."

122

"Yes."

"He said—he said it was for my own good."

At the Chadwicks', where I had governessed, I had heard the doctor speak to Mrs. Chadwick of the dangers of allowing her boy to "abuse himself," as the doctor put it. I had no idea what that meant, but it must have been something very bad, for Mrs. Chadwick cried all day and night after the doctor left and held long consultations with her husband before summoning the doctor to the house again to tell him I knew not what, for of course I was not party to the conversation. But as far as I know she did not act as Mr. January had done; even though I did not spend the nights at the Chadwicks' house, I would have heard, one way or another, of such a drastic thing.

"Marian, I wasn't doing anything wrong. Honestly I wasn't—"

"Hush. I know you weren't. I know."

"He didn't tell me why. He just said—he said I'd go insane if he didn't do this. Why did he say that, Marian? What did he mean?"

He pulled away from me then; he faced me, his eyes imploring me to give him an answer that I did not have. His face was a bloody mess still, but the flow had stopped. My wrapper and nightdress were smeared and stained, and even in the midst of trying to think what to say to him I wondered fleetingly how I would clean them without discovery. (In the end I did not even try; I bundled them into an old portmanteau and threw it onto a neighbor's trash in the back alley.)

"I don't know," I said at last. "What were you—what did you do that made him—"

Even in the faint light given by the candle, now nearly gone, I could see color on his face that had nothing to do with his bloody nose. "He came in when I was sleeping," he said slowly. "And he—he—" His face worked; he wrenched away from me and threw himself face down onto the bed with such force that I feared he would begin to bleed again.

"Ned . . ." I put my hand on his shoulder. He responded to my touch and with almost equal force he flung himself against me again and held fast as if he were drowning and I his safe harbor.

We stayed so all the night. At dawn I tied his hands again before I stole back to my room. I did not see him that day: we were busy, both of us, with our usual tasks, he with school and sport, I dividing my time between Uncle James and Mrs. January. Mr. January brought two business associates to dinner, but I did not see them, for I shared a tray with Uncle James. I was happy not to be with them. I could not have spoken normally to Mr. January; somehow, I was sure, I would have betrayed both myself and Ned. In the evening I accompanied Elinor to a dance at Papanti's, and then, returning home, I took a glass of hot milk to Mrs. January and spent a half hour with her before I retired. Elinor was asleep. Although I had had little rest the night before, I was not tired. I wore only light stays, so I needed no help to undress; I put on my nightclothes, including a clean wrapper which I had taken, as I was allowed to do, from the surplus clothing stored next to the servants' rooms. It was late—nearly midnight. The house was quiet, everyone asleep. Except Ned? I slipped out into the hall and retraced my steps of the night before. I found him wide-eyed, bound again but calm, no panic. He even managed to smile at me in his trusting, childlike way.

"I thought you'd come," he said.

"Of course. Do you think that I could sleep, knowing that you are like this?"

I untied him; I sat with him for a while before returning to my room. And in the morning, before any of the family were astir, I awakened early as I always did and stole back to him and tied him again. And the next night, and the next—we became conspirators, the two of us. We never discussed it: never said a word about what we did. It was understood that I would go to him, night and morning, for as long as he needed me. I could not believe that Mr. January would continue Ned's punishment for very long, but when summer came and the family decamped to Nahant and still it went on, I made my excuses to Mrs. Reed and said that Nahant was no longer a place of painful memories for me, and that because Uncle James needed me I would go there with the Januarys.

Of course that was not true. I felt my tears well up as we rumbled across the Neck and proceeded toward East Point, past the Talcotts' house, past the Mifflin place to the Januarys'. But Ned's need for me—and Uncle James's too—was more important than any unhappy memories, and so I dried my eyes and smiled at my companions and resolved not to be defeated by my memories.

Mr. January and his wife had a sorrow of their own that summer, for in early May their last child was born, very weak, and within a few days it died. It was a girl. Elinor wept, I remember; she tried to hold the baby after it died, but they would not let her.

Two weeks after Isabel's child was born. They named her Charlotte Elizabeth. She was an ugly baby, but healthy and strong; and so Elinor had a new little creature to love, after all, even if she needed to go out every day to see it instead of having it in the house with her.

"Isn't she sweet!" Elinor would say, cuddling Charlotte, kissing her fat cheeks and her downy little head.

And Isabel would watch them, a sour look on her face. "I'd trade her sweetness for looks," she would say. "I don't relish the prospect of marrying off a plain girl, I can tell you. Ah well, perhaps she'll have style."

Eight

It was on a night in November 1872 that Leighton was prepared to announce his engagement to Caroline Fairbanks. We had, that week, endured the suspense of the presidential election: Grant or Greeley, it made no matter to me, but of course the men were always concerned. I used to hear them: Mr. January and Leighton, and Curtis when he visited, talked about the "whiskey ring," and the Crédit Mobilier, and Oakes Ames. It meant nothing to me then: still doesn't. Greeley went mad and died three weeks after the election, so perhaps it was as well that Grant was re-elected. On the other hand, perhaps it would have made no difference had Greeley won.

I remember that it was a cold, windy night, a Saturday, and Leighton for once was at home instead of in New York. His activities, however, had been severely limited, because an epidemic had swept through the equine population and there was not a horse to be had in all of Boston. He had planned that day to drive to Milton to see a racehorse owned by a friend, but instead he had taken

Ned to the tailor's for a fitting of a new woolen jacket. At seven o'clock we sat down to dinner. Uncle James had come to the table that evening, as he had begun to do on his good days; he insisted that I sit next to him. Leighton waited until after we had finished our third course—a baked ham—to smile expansively around the table and lift his wineglass and clear his throat so that we would know that he had some announcement to make. I glanced at Mrs. January and saw from her expression that she knew what he would say.

"You have no doubt wondered at my frequent absences in New York—" he began; and stopped to listen. Faintly we heard the sound of bells; and then, in an unaccustomed rush, the maid threw open the door. "Please, sir," she said to Mr. January, "there's a gentleman wanting you, he said it's urgent and he doesn't have a card."

And so Leighton was left holding his glass, his announcement unspoken, and we began the nightmare vigil of the Great Fire.

All night the city burned, and all the next day: all the downtown was gone, the commercial districts, and why the fire did not leapfrog the Common and attack Beacon Hill and then the Back Bay no one knew. We heard later that the glowing sky over Boston was seen in New Hampshire and Rhode Island; near midnight, when we were watching from the upstairs windows, the light was bright enough to read by.

Mr. January and Leighton left at once; like so many others, they had securities deposited in the banks and insurance offices that were going up in flames. At one point during the night, we heard later, Major Higginson stood armed with a shotgun to guard against looting, not by the crowd of rowdy drunks who roamed the streets but by a mob of his customers who feared—rightly so, it turned out—for the safety of their certificates.

We watched all night. Even Uncle James stayed up, more enlivened than I had ever seen him. He showed no concern for what he might lose. "Let 'em burn," he said. "All those pieces of paper—I won't need 'em in the time I've got left." And he laughed at Mrs. January's horrified reaction.

Ned disappeared for a while that night, and so we were diverted from the fire watch to search for him. Mrs. January even sent me outside, thinking that he might have slipped out into the crowd which thronged the normally quiet streets; the Public Garden and the Common, usually deserted at night save for footpads and thugs, were alive with people, all watching, all waiting to hear of the progress of the fire. There was little traffic because the horses were all down—a fact that impeded the battle against the flames, of course, because the steam engines could not be brought in. The wind blew sparks and fragments of burned paper—bank notes and stock certificates—across the Common to where we stood. Householders had directed their servants to wet down the roofs, and so atop every house you could see two or three people sloshing buckets, no doubt with resulting leaks in the servants' quarters in the attics. Most of the houses had gone dark because the authorities had shut off the gas for fear of explosion. Here and there a flickering, old-fashioned light showed at a window:

candles, or kerosene lamps.

I did not find Ned, but as I was retracing my steps to the January house I heard my name—"Miss Marian!"— and I turned to see Mrs. Roberts Reed's coachman. He had run all the way from Mount Vernon Street; he leaned against a lamppost to steady himself as he panted out his message: "Master Ned's with us. Mrs. Reed sent me to tell you."

He came home on Sunday, paler than usual, tired as we all were from the long vigil, but oddly exhilarated, too. He had climbed to Mrs. Reed's roof to watch the fire, and since her house was near the top of Beacon Hill he had had a front-row seat, so to speak, at the spectacle. I am sure that he did not once think of the possible loss to his father's fortune, for he was never very much concerned with money; rather, as I learned, he was entranced by the awesome power of the fire, the spectacle of it, its effect on his emotions. He pulled a sheaf of papers from inside his jacket and held it out to me.

"Here," he said shyly. "This is for you."

"Why, Ned," I said, "what is this?" We were alone in the parlor; the others had collapsed in their beds, Mr. January and Leighton still downtown. I looked at the scrawled sheets:

> The mighty flames devour the hoard
> Of gold and paper, wealth
> Gone by the board
> This night of fire,
> This night of dire
> Catastrophe.

Burn! Light up the sky!
And dwindle down, by and by,
To glowing embers
And then—die.

"I wrote it for you," he said. "If you like it I'll write others. I wanted to give you something—something special."

Not for the first time I thought of how, through the mysterious working of fate, this boy had been given to me to love in place of that dearly beloved brother whom I had lost. And I had loved him: had saved him from his father's harsh punishment, had been a friend to him as no blood relative could have been. (The punishment had stopped upon the family's return from Nahant, but still I often went to visit with him at dawn, and we talked for a while before the day began.)

I was deeply touched; I understood that this was, indeed, the most valuable thing he could have given me: a part of himself. "This is wonderful, Ned—splendid! I had no idea you were a poet."

"I'm not—yet." He grinned at me mischievously. "But when I am I'll dedicate every book to you."

And he did: that one slim volume.

Nine

The winter passed, and then the spring. Boston recovered from the Great Fire and rebuilt the business district only to see many men who had survived the fire of '72 go down in the panic of '73. The Januarys suffered less than others, but still there was a general cutting back, little entertaining, no new clothes. Leighton's wedding, which took place in June, conveniently occurred three months before the crash, and so the festivities were not marred by the knowledge that half the men present were ruined, no longer able to afford a place in the rather more gaudy ranks of New York society. When the crash came, in September, Carrie's father killed himself. This unhappy event elicited a sour comment from Mr. January. "Soft," he said. "Those New York men are all soft—no backbone to 'em. He could have weathered it if he'd kept his wits. Look at James here—he saw it coming."

To everyone's surprise, Uncle James, who supposedly had retired from the business world, had seen the onset of the crash and in July had sold many of his holdings and advised his brother Asa to do the same. With their profits they had bought shares in Agassiz's copper mines in Michigan: a foolish move, many said, but one that proved almost miraculously farsighted.

That winter was peaceful, but in the spring we had new trouble, for the time for Elinor's debut was drawing near and she dreaded it as if it were her execution.

One afternoon, while Uncle James took his nap and I sat in the back parlor reading the new issue of the *Atlantic,* I heard the sound of angry voices. They came from within the house—from upstairs. What trouble now? By the time I had thrown open the parlor door and run up the first flight I could identify them: Elinor and her mother. Up the second flight—and then I paused. Trouble there might be, but I had no right to interfere; I must wait until I was called.

Suddenly the door to Elinor's room—and mine—burst open and she came running out, calling my name. I ran the last few steps. "Elinor! What—"

"Tell her," she cried. "Tell Mother about the Poor Relief meeting—she doesn't believe me!"

I saw Mrs. January's bewildered face in the doorway, and at the rear of the hall I saw the maid pause to stare.

"The Poor Relief! What—"

Mrs. January, too, had become aware of the maid's presence. "Come in here," she said, suddenly irritated. "We needn't disturb the household."

We stood awkwardly in the center of the room. Elinor's tearstained face was blotched and red; in her hand she clutched a sodden handkerchief. She glared defiantly at her mother; she was always delicate and thin—frail, even—but she had a soul of white-hot iron.

"The problem is my schedule," she said. Her voice was unsteady but quite loud: a kind of bravado that I have myself often used. "It seems that a number of well-meaning people have arranged affairs for me—luncheons, teas, dances—because in May I am to make my debut and all of these functions are necessary, it seems, if I am to be properly introduced to society. And of course the world would end if I were not introduced to society, that is the most important thing in my life just now, isn't it? None of you would ever be able to show your faces in Boston again if I did not go through that stupid ritual—"

"Be quiet!" said her mother. "I will not listen to this nonsense any longer. Your future—your entire life—depends on these few months when you will come out into the world—*our* world—and begin to find your place in it. And this luncheon tomorrow, tiresome as it may seem, is an important occasion for you." She turned to me. "Mrs. Bartley Fitts gives the best dances in Boston, and if she likes a girl there's no end of what she'll do for her in the way of introductions. And she gives these luncheons, every year, for the girls who are coming out so that she may look them over—yes, I speak frankly—and see whether they measure up."

"I will not miss the Poor Relief meeting," Elinor burst out. "Mr. Jaeckel is coming all the way from London to talk about his work there. I will never again have a chance to hear such a famous man. He is an inspiration, they say. He has recognized the entire system of charitable assistance in the East End, he directs hundreds of workers in his almshouses—oh, Marian, explain to Mother that I must meet this man, I've looked forward to it for months!"

I was by this time more than a little uncomfortable. I thought that it was unfair of them to expect me to resolve their dispute: no matter with whom I sided, the other would be angry. To preserve my status in the household, such as it was, I should of course ally myself with Mrs. January; but I loved Elinor and I wanted to see her happy. In the end, of course, she might be happiest meeting an eligible young man at one of Mrs. Bartley Fitts's evenings; but she did not think so now, and there seemed to be no way to convince her.

"I think that you have explained it quite well enough," I said. "Perhaps there is another day that you could go to Mrs. Fitts's—"

"She has had three luncheons today," said Mrs. January with an air of having settled the argument. "This is the last. And you"—turning to her recalcitrant daughter—"will go to it. Now I will leave you to think about your behavior. A little time with your conscience will do you no harm. Come, Marian, and help me deal with Miss Merriman. She's been impossibly slow with the alterations I gave to her two weeks ago."

And so, willy-nilly, the decision was made without my help. As I followed Mrs. January out of the room I caught Elinor's glance. Her expression hurt me. She looked abandoned—betrayed. I wanted to speak to her but there was no time; Mrs. January, indignant, swept me out before I could think what to say. I consoled myself with the thought that perhaps the luncheon would be enjoyable and that she would not therefore object so much to missing the chance to meet Mr. Jaeckel. As it turned out, however, it was an unpleasant affair—or at least she reported that it was—and when she returned home that afternoon she went to our room and cried herself to sleep.

As the spring came on and the date of her debut came ever nearer, she became increasingly morose and withdrawn; despite the fact that she and I shared a room, she hardly spoke to me. Several times I tried to talk to her, to make amends, but she would not respond. Give it time, I thought, she will come to me again.

And then one day, a week before her coming-out party, I found Elinor in our room leaning over the washbasin. She was vomiting—retching again and again with a harsh, painful noise that sounded as though she would tear out her intestines. In an instant I was at her side, holding her head. She was too weak to rebuff me; again and again her stomach disgorged its contents until it had no more, and then still she retched, gagging, helpless.

The doctor, hastily summoned, could find nothing wrong. "She has never been particularly—ah—robust," he said, resting his hands on his paunch, "but I see no signs of illness. Let her rest for a day or two. Light diet. This sedative. No visitors—no activity. Her coming-out is when? Next week? Well. We shall see."

Mrs. January was dismayed. "We have two hundred people coming," she said—hardly news to me since I had addressed the invitations. "Surely we cannot be expected to cancel it now."

"Wait and see," he said, annoyed. He had no children;

he and his wife had never confronted the problems of bringing daughters out into society and then marrying them off.

In the end the party was held as planned, and Elinor was properly launched. But for all the week before she took no solid food and she vomited what little liquid she managed to swallow. Her frail body seemed to waste away even more; her eyes had a haunted look, as if she knew some dreadful secret which she feared to tell. The dressmaker needed to alter her dress three times and still it did not fit correctly.

"I don't understand it," said Mrs. January. "This should be the happiest time of her life. Why does she take on so?"

"A good nerve tonic—" began Mrs. Reed, who had stopped for supper.

"Nerve tonic my foot," sniffed Mrs. January. "Asa said she needs a proper spanking, and I must say I think he's right. She is simply being stubborn."

Stubborn she certainly was. She still refused to make up her quarrel with me. Even as I held her head over the bowl while she vomited, even as I hovered nearby while the dressmaker fussed and tucked and pinned, even as I carried bowls of broth to her room and sat beside her as she sipped—still she spoke only a word or two, and those hardly civil.

Isabel, big with child again, tried one day to reason with Elinor. "Of course it's a bore," she said. "Simply put up with it. Everyone does. You might find that you enjoy it. What is so terrible about going to a few parties and having people make a fuss over you because you are a pretty young girl coming out into society? Do you want to spend your life with a basket on your arm, running up and down every tenement in the city?"

Elinor stared at her, her big eyes burning in her tense pale face. Isabel did not look healthy herself. Her eyes were dull, shadowed underneath; her face was puffy, her trim figure thick and clumsy. She panted a little as she spoke, and I saw beads of perspiration at the line of her front curls. This was her third pregnancy in three years, a son—Arthur William—having been born to her the previous summer.

It was a warm afternoon in May, two days before Elinor's debut. We were in Mrs. January's sitting room. Through the open windows a breeze blew in to us the scent of young trees in bloom, fresh-baked bread from a neighboring kitchen, the sour odor of the river. The walls of the room were papered in a pattern of pale pink cabbage roses, and a rosy light was reflected from outside as well, from the bright sun on the row of red brick houses to the rear. I felt suddenly restless, confined. On such a day, I thought, we should be outdoors—strolling in the Public Garden, perhaps, admiring the newly laid beds of spring flowers, tulips and pansies and fragrant hyacinth. But neither Isabel nor Elinor was in condition to walk, this day, and so we sat inside and they chafed at each other and I listened.

"I don't know," said Elinor at last. "Certainly I don't want to spend my life as you are now."

Even when spoken quietly, as they were, such words can wound. Isabel's face took on an angry flush; she started to reply and then checked herself. Elinor's words hung in the air; no breeze could blow them away.

"You are a foolish girl," said Isabel at last. And, having been hurt, and wanting to hurt someone in return, she threw a vindictive glance in my direction. "Marian, here, would give anything to be in your place, wouldn't you, Marian?"

"I don't—" and then I caught myself. I paused; and then: "It will be a very good party." I stifled any sharper retort: one did not speak unkindly to women in Isabel's condition. One did what one could to make things easy for them—to cause them no worry, to help them in every way . . .

Help them! But I did not know—how could I? What I did to Isabel that night might have brought her death— yes, even that—but I did not know, I had no way of knowing.

Because the day had been so warm, I walked out before dinner, about six o'clock, and turned toward the Public Garden to seek a little breeze. It was still quite bright, the sun not yet gone down, and so I felt safe enough. I wanted to be alone, to get away from that unhappy household and find a moment's peace. I walked down Marlborough Street, its brownstone house fronts ruddy in the light of the setting sun, here and there a carriage delivering a lady late from her afternoon calls, an occasional gentleman walking home from downtown.

Deep in thought, I did not hear the man's footsteps behind me until he was almost at my heels. Before I could steel myself against an unwelcome familiarity I heard the voice:

"Miss Childs?"

Rashly I glanced around. He was at my side; I could not escape him unless I ran, and in my full skirts and corsets I could hardly have outrun him in any case. I had neglected to bring a parasol, and my small, flat hat did not allow me to hide my face.

"Miss Childs, forgive me, I did not mean to startle you."

He was tall and blond, with brilliant blue eyes and a harshly handsome face that seemed oddly familiar to me, although I was certain that I had never met him.

"It is Miss Childs, is it not? Miss Marian Childs?" He gave me no time to reply. "My name is Lawrence Cushing. I am acquainted with the January family—"

I gaped at him so that he must have thought me a fool. Now, indeed, I recognized him: once I had seen his face in a photograph, the glass shattered on the floor, cutting Isabel, making her bleed. And once I had met his mother, whom he so resembled.

"I beg your pardon for speaking to you like this. Come, may I walk with you?" (For I had stopped, feeling suddenly too weak to go on; now, slowly, I proceeded, and since I did not order him away he walked with me.) "I had no other way," he went on, "to—to do what I must."

I felt vague alarm then, but short of turning my back on him I did not know what to do to stop him. In any event he gave me no choice, and after a moment his urgency transferred itself to me and I heard him out, stifling my uneasy doubts.

"You are, I am told, a friend of the Januarys' daughter," he said.

"Elinor? Yes, but—"

140

"No—no, the elder daughter. Mrs.—ah—Mrs. Avery Kittredge."

Now it comes, I thought; I knew no way to stop it.

"Never mind—I am told that you know her. I would beg you to do me a service. I know that it is perhaps an—ah—unusual request. Please—listen to me. I have come all the way from London just to see her. I have friends here. I have made inquiries about her. I understand that she is—ah—"

I felt the hot blush rise to my cheeks. Surely he would not ask me to discuss Isabel's condition!

"She is not able to go out into society just now," he went on. "I beg your pardon, I do not want to be indelicate. But I must see her. Do you understand me? I must—I cannot live another day without a word with her!"

We came to Arlington Street; we crossed and entered the green and gold garden where twilight hovered waiting to descend.

"Mr. Cushing, whatever it is that you want—"

"Your help. Only that."

"But I cannot—"

"Just give her this." He took out an envelope. I did not move to take it. We kept on walking.

"Just give this to her," he said. "Please. I beg you."

We halted on a winding path by the lagoon, its surface undisturbed by the swan boats, which were not introduced until later in the decade. In his pleading he had put his hand under my elbow; now he took it away and we faced each other. As tall as I was, I needed to look up to him. It struck me that his speech and his

141

appearance were at odds: his speech pleading and almost humble, his face and form that of a supremely self-assured, almost devil-may-care young man about town.

"But—I am not her close friend. There are many others you could ask—why me?"

"Many others, yes—but my position in Boston is extremely delicate, I cannot let my presence here be generally known."

So, I thought, my original suspicion had been correct: he wanted me for something underhanded, something improper—else why so secret?

"Do this for me," he went on. "Do this kindness to a stranger."

The sun had gone; shadows crept across the lawns. At last the breeze I had sought came up, and I shivered slightly. To do what he asked was wrong—I knew that it was wrong. And yet . . . and yet . . .

I looked away from him; I could not think while I met his eyes. Perhaps it was nothing, after all; perhaps she would simply read it and throw it into the fire.

Almost imperceptibly I nodded. An odd look of triumph flooded his face. Such men, I thought, are accustomed to having their way with women; I doubted that I was his most difficult case. I took the envelope and put it into my small beaded bag: a final gesture of surrender. We turned and began to walk again. He saw me to the Arlington Street gate and there we parted.

Isabel had planned to stay at the Januarys' for dinner, where Avery would join her, and so when I returned I found her resting where I had left her, in her mother's sitting room. She was alone—a fact that I took as a sign of fate.

We were hardly good friends at that time—our friendship came later—and so she regarded me with mild curiosity as I went in and closed the door behind me. I had no idea how to begin tactfully, and so I simply plunged in, feeling the need to hurry lest someone interrupt us.

"I met—I was out walking just now and I met a—a gentleman who gave me this." I fished for the envelope; I found it and handed it to her. She took it and stared at it. After a long moment she looked up at me again. Her face was frozen; she might have been carved from stone.

"Mrs. Cushing's son," I said. "You remember—the lady we went to visit."

I was trespassing, and we both knew it. Through no fault of my own I had been made party to her secret, and now she would dislike me even more than before.

Suddenly, startling me, she heaved herself up from the chaise where she lay. "Not a word!" she said. Her voice was soft but charged with feeling. "Not a word of this to anyone, do you hear?"

"Of course not, but—"

"Go! Go away! How dare you—*go!*"

I was terrified that she would harm herself. I knew that women in her delicate condition must be gently treated, not disturbed—ah, what had I done?

"I didn't mean to upset you, but he insisted—"

"Go! At once!"

I obeyed her. I left the room and pulled the door shut behind me and leaned against it, listening for sounds of disaster. After a moment I heard not the cry for help that

I half expected but sounds of sobbing, low and desolate, all the more unnerving for that.

What should I do? I had no idea. Call for Mrs. January? Elinor? Elinor, at least, was in no condition to help anyone. I stood irresolute, listening. After a time the sobbing stopped and I heard nothing. Cautiously I opened the door. Isabel lay on the chaise, her hand over her eyes, the other hand clutching the letter.

"Isabel?"

She made no reply, but I saw her bosom rise and fall with her breathing so that I knew at least that she was alive. I withdrew; I shut the door. Say nothing, I thought. Pretend it never happened.

Dinner that night was a difficult affair, what with Elinor's hostility and the secret that, however unwillingly, Isabel and I shared, that lay between us like a time bomb. And when would it explode?

This is what he wrote; years later, at the end of her life, she showed it to me:

My Dearest Isabel,

Please believe that I never wanted to hurt you.

What I did four years ago I did in your best interest. Taking you with me would have done you far greater harm than leaving you behind. I understand the sacrifice that you were willing to make for me, and I will love you for it always.

I beg you to write to me—a few words only, to let me know that you do not think of me unkindly. The above address will reach me.

Know that my feelings for you are what they always were: I love you more than my life.

Lawrence

That day had been very warm, and the next was warmer still: muggy, uncomfortable, summer heat coming too soon after the long cold months just past. At dawn on the day of Elinor's party we had a thunderstorm but it did not clear the air. The clouds hung heavy all day, darkening the house, dampening our spirits. Mrs. January was calm and almost fatalistic: there was a very real question as to whether Elinor would get through the evening, but Dr. Slocomb had not expressly forbidden her, and so we went ahead. "Everyone's dress will be ruined if it storms tonight," said Mrs. January. "Wouldn't you know we'd have this weather, after all these fine days? Ah, well. I only hope that Elinor holds up. The weather is beyond me."

Elinor spent the day in her room. She cried for a while in the morning, but toward noon she became calm. She lay wide-eyed on her bed, quiet, seemingly tranquil. When the time came to dress she allowed her mother and me to lace her; she showed no enthusiasm, but she did not argue, she did not resist. Her dress was of white shot silk, with short puffed sleeves; the overskirt, pulled back to form a bustle decorated with pink satin bows, revealed a pink ninon underskirt. Above the rich fabric of her costume her face looked as though she were marching to the gallows. All evening she hardly smiled; and afterward, when the guests had gone, she cried for a long time before she fell asleep.

In June, shortly after Elinor's party, Isabel gave birth prematurely to a stillborn infant. Of course we could not have blamed Elinor directly. But the question lingered and nagged: had her behavior had that disastrous effect on Isabel? Or—and this was something that only Isabel and I knew—was it that other, that interloper from her past?

Ten

They gilded the State House dome that summer, and so we returned from Nahant to find a glittering, gaudy landmark that seemed out of keeping with its tasteful underpinnings. Moreover, some people resented spending money for such show during a time of severe depression. The country still had not recovered from the panic of the previous year; beggars roamed the streets, bankrupts killed themselves every day. From the security of the White House, President Grant issued statements of optimism which no one even pretended to believe. I do not understand the national economy: never have, never will. I know only that innocent people are hurt through the machinations of a few greedy men.

"Take me to see it before I die," said Uncle James one mild day in late September.

I stared at him, shocked, not sure I had heard correctly. He seemed no different: he sat easily in his chair, his eyes as bright as always, his expression as alert, no tremor to his hands or slurring of his speech.

He smiled at my dismay. "Yes," he said. "Soon, now,

I'll be gone. You'll have to find other ways to occupy your time. As I'm sure you will. You are a resourceful girl—clever and good and— Well. You'll be all right. I couldn't go in peace if I thought you wouldn't. Now. Have Ethel call the carriage, and you and Ned and I will drive up Beacon Street to have a look at what they've done to Mr. Bulfinch's dome."

A week later he was dead. He went peacefully in the night, no pain, no fear: his face was as calm as if he were still sleeping, his hands lying loosely on the coverlet.

I did not cry then, that morning. In his kindly way he had prepared me for his departure, and so I was able to suspend my grief and take comfort from his easy death. My tears came later, when they read his will.

We sat in the library while Mr. Quimby broke the seal and unfolded the stiff, crackling pages. He began to read, naming various small bequests to second and third cousins, great-nieces and -nephews, who had appeared as if by magic, propelled by their anticipation. I looked around as the lawyer's voice droned on. Even the most genteel people in the world cannot conceal their greed: certainly these people could not. Uncle James must have been very rich indeed, I thought, to have brought out so many distant connections: there were at least twenty-five people in the room. Then came larger amounts to Asa January and his children. I saw an odd expression on his face and Isabel's, but I did not immediately understand it.

I was aware that Mr. Quimby had stopped reading, and for a moment I thought that he had finished; I looked to Mrs. January to give us the signal to rise and go into

148

the dining room where luncheon would be served.

But I was mistaken; there was one final bequest: "To my faithful friend, Marian Childs, in recognition of her devoted kindness to me in the last days of my life, I leave the remainder of my estate."

Shocked silence: for a long moment no one spoke. I could not believe what he had said, that dry, gray-faced lawyer who spoke of vast fortunes as easily as I spoke of a week's pin money. I was overwhelmed. I tried to respond, but I could only manage a quavering word or two before I began to weep.

At last there was a little commotion across the room: a small woman, one of the distant relatives, whose voice penetrated my tears.

"Outrageous!" she snapped. "Who is this—this stranger that she should receive so great a gift? She is nothing! She schemed to get it, she enticed him to change his will—I shall contest it! It is not fair!"

"That's right," said someone else. "This is fraud—outright chicanery."

Mr. Quimby cleared his throat nervously at this threat of mutiny, but it was Curtis who spoke. "Since Uncle James provided for everyone in his will, it is, as I am sure Mr. Quimby will tell you, perfectly legal. You can contest it all the same, of course—if you can find a lawyer to take your case—but you will be wasting time and money both. And of course it would be a nasty scandal."

They sat silent, glaring at him and at me as well. I dried my eyes; I sat silent under their anger, feeling as though I had committed some misdeed. At last Mr. January took my hand and squeezed it for emphasis while he spoke.

"You will need advice, my dear," he said. "Even a fortune as great as this needs careful attention or it will disappear overnight."

"You have earned it, every penny," said Curtis. I saw Isabel throw him a warning glance.

"So she has," rumbled Mrs. Reed. She heaved herself out of her chair and shuffled to my side to embrace me. "So she has. And now she can have a proper wardrobe, and perhaps a carriage of her own, and a house, perhaps, or one of the new French flats—"

"All in good time," said Mrs. January. "She will need a while to accustom herself to her new situation. And then we shall see." She smiled at me in a determined way; she was too proud to let me see her disappointment.

Isabel said nothing. She surveyed us coolly as if she were watching a play. She looked very handsome even in her unadorned mourning. She had retained a little plumpness from her pregnancies, but it suited her. She was just then, in the fall of 1874, beginning what was to be her lifelong occupation—the scaling of the social heights, with all its attendant expense. Avery made a comfortable income and had a considerable amount coming to him in trust, but she must have wanted very much a generous slice of Uncle James's pie.

Well: she didn't get it. And perhaps, in the end, it was as well she didn't, for she would only have spent it to enrich grocers and florists and wine merchants, and the manufacturers of gold and silver mementos which she would have distributed as favors instead of the more modest items which she was forced to buy. Her success never came from the lavishness of her parties, although once or twice, at Newport, she came within striking distance of the Mesdames Vanderbilt and Astor; rather, she succeeded because of her cleverness, her talent for bringing the right people together, for creating a kind of chemistry that people found enticing.

Had I known of her ambition, that autumn, I might have been more cautious when, sometime after the New Year, she made her first overtures to me in a not very subtle way.

"We are having a musicale on Sunday evening," she said. "Come along if you can—and you, too, Elinor. You ought to get out more"—this to Elinor—"and don't tell me you don't want to. You can't spend your life in solitude, it isn't natural."

She had stopped for a cup of tea one afternoon. Mrs. January was out making calls, so Elinor and I entertained her.

"I do not spend my life in 'solitude,' as you put it," said Elinor. She sat gingerly on the edge of her chair, as if any moment she would spring up and run away from us. Her hair straggled around her painfully thin face; her fingernails were ragged and none too clean; there was a spot of grease on her gray serge skirt, and her shoes were scuffed and soiled with mud.

Isabel, always immaculate, looked at her younger sister with distaste. "Don't you have anyone to do for you?" she said. "Really, Elinor, you should pay more attention to your grooming. People don't like to see—"

"Don't tell me about people!" Elinor sprang up with such suddenness that she nearly upset the low table on which rested the tea tray. "Don't you ever dare to tell me

151

about people! You know nothing about them! You know only stupid, silly women and stupid, boring men who have nothing better to do with their time than congregate like a flock of sheep! In your house, in your friends' houses—like sheep! Always the same faces, always the same gossip—I know what every one of them will say before they say it, and sometimes I say it first, to mimic them, and they don't even know!" She stood over Isabel during her outburst, leaning down to her in a threatening way, her hands clenched at her sides, her body tense with fury. Isabel was so shocked that she had no reply; she simply tilted back her well-coiffed head and stared at Elinor, openmouthed, incredulous; and so it was left to me to play the peacemaker.

"I don't think that we have a right to judge—" I began; but I got no further, for then she turned on me.

"*You* don't think! *You*— No. You don't. That is obvious from the way in which you have taken hold of your new fortune." She took a few steps to the fire and held out her hands to it. When she spoke again her voice was calmer but infinitely more bitter. "Do you know how Uncle James got it, all that money?" She turned to face me, squinting slightly, for she was shortsighted. Soon after this time she began to wear spectacles, forbidden by her mother until then because a girl in spectacles could never hope for a proposal of marriage. She needed a pair of No. 17, as it turned out, so she must have seen dimly indeed.

Her question was not rhetorical; she expected an answer.

"No," I said.

"He never told you?"

"No."

She gave me a grim little smile. "Then I will tell you now. I think that you should know."

"Elinor—" began Isabel; but she saw that Elinor was not to be stopped.

"From the cotton manufacture," said Elinor. "He had shares in all the largest corporations. Do you know what they called him? The operatives, I mean. They called him Bloody Jim, because he was so ruthlessly opposed to the ten-hour day. He is known in every factory in New England, and hated more than any other corporation man. He used to hire blacklegs by the hundreds to take the places of workers who protested. And once he had an organizer so badly beaten by his thugs that the man nearly died. They were nothing to him, those people. Just a means to get money. I think he died because the legislature has just passed a ten-hour bill for women and children. I think that killed him. It is blood money that you have, Marian—never forget it."

At the time her words, extreme as they were, meant little to me. I had no idea what the textile factories were.

I knew only that I was rich; and therefore I was free. Or so I thought.

153

Eleven

I went alone to Isabel's musicale the following Sunday evening. Elinor had stopped speaking to me altogether, and she instructed the maids to move her things to Isabel's former room.

I was deeply concerned about her, for she was obviously a soul in torment, but I did not know how to help her. Looking back, I understand that no one could have helped her: she found her own way, in time, and we none of us had anything to do with it. I missed her and I would gladly have been her friend again; but I was, perhaps selfishly, caught up in the excitement of my new life and so I waited for her to make peace with me. That she never did is one of the sorrows that I have carried with me ever since; and whenever I have been criticized for being too willing to patch over a misunderstanding, too quick to offer the olive branch, I think of Elinor and of how I might have helped her had I been less self-absorbed.

In the days following the news of my inheritance I realized that I was a difficult person and I struggled to come to terms with my new self. No longer was I dependent on the Januarys for food and shelter: I could buy and sell them if I wished, for Uncle James's fortune had been far greater than Asa January's. No longer did I need to feel humbly grateful for every morsel of food that passed my lips: I could pay them for my keep, and this, in fact, I immediately arranged to do. Mrs. January was not ashamed to accept my offer: in her shrewd Yankee way she knew exactly what my presence in the household cost them, and she was perfectly willing to have me make it up.

On the other hand, no amount of money could buy me what they had and what I so obviously lacked: family, social connections, that supportive network of interlocking friends and relations that gave to them their firm sense of place in our little corner of the world. My new fortune could buy material things—clothing and jewels and a carriage, a house if I wanted it; but why would I, without a family to inhabit it?

And so I moved with caution, those first few weeks: I ordered several dresses from the dressmaker; I bought a few small pieces of jewelry, including a brooch of seed pearls and gold filigree which I had long coveted; I began to make regular payments for my board; and I waited. I was, I felt, on the threshold of my new existence, but I wanted to enter cautiously. I did not want to rush in and possibly awaken to find that I had only dreamed it.

The guests at Isabel's that night were a cross section of Boston's best, with a few visitors from foreign parts— New York, Philadelphia—to add interest. I had a new dress for the occasion—gray silk, with the new straighter skirt and heavy ecru lace at the neck and wrists—and whether because I looked unwontedly fashionable or because news of my sudden wealth had got about, I found myself spoken to by people who formerly would never even have acknowledged my existence by so much as a cool nod. Cousin Sam Swift, who had helped me on that terrible New Year's Eve at the Januarys' when my mother made her appearance, now took me around on his arm to introduce me; he offered to fetch me in his carriage the next day so that I could visit his greenhouse and see his collection of orchids. As it happened I could not go; but I was flattered nonetheless, and I did not mind his reason for inviting me—that I was now, suddenly, someone new.

Isabel, radiant in violet brocade, insisted that I sit beside her during the programme; and later, introducing me, she kept my arm tucked in hers in a reassuring way. For it was to be a long time before I was comfortable in this world which heretofore I had only glimpsed—in which I had been only tolerated, not welcomed. Eventually, of course, when I knew everyone, I came secretly to share Elinor's opinion of them; but at the time I was flattered and grateful and totally indiscriminate in allowing myself to be taken up.

The music, that evening, was provided by an immigrant Italian violinist. He was extraordinarily handsome: a tall, dark, mournful-looking man with great fiery black eyes, a prominent nose, and a wide, expressive mouth. He had a young woman to accompany him on the piano: she too was dark and handsome, but with little sense of the drama that every performer must

have. They played for perhaps forty-five minutes: a
sonata by Schumann, love songs by Franz Liszt, themes
from some of the operas, very much in vogue, of
Giuseppe Verdi. The man, whose name was Signor
Ristori, lost himself to the music as if he and his
instrument were one; he bent and crouched and swayed
as he fiddled until I thought he must topple over at each
climax of the music, but he never did. He was simply
giving expression to his talent, and therefore, poor as he
was, he was more fortunate than anyone else in the room.

When we were introduced Signor Ristori held my
hand for a moment and gazed at me from his deep-set
eyes. "*Elegantissima*," he murmured; "*onoratissimo*." I
had never met such a specimen of masculinity; New
England men were sticks compared to this exotic
Mediterranean. Despite my momentary discomposure, I
noticed that the collar of his frilled shirt was frayed and
that the material of his black coat was shiny with hard
wear. Isabel told me later that she paid him five dollars
for his time, and a dollar to his partner. "But I've made
him fashionable, Marian—no one would have dreamed of
having an Italian before I did it. Several people warned
me, in fact, that I was simply letting myself open to a
huge burglary—that he would come in and see what we
have and go back to his friends with a complete report,
including the most likely entrance and exit to the house.
But I thought he had an honest face, and so far I'm right.
He's played at a dozen houses since he came to me, and
not one has had so much as a teaspoon missing."

Perhaps it was the music, which was as good as
anything I ever heard afterward, or perhaps it was simply

the fact of a pleasant evening spent in hospitable company, but I slept deeply and long that night and awakened more refreshed than I could remember. Even Elinor's cold presence, passing me in the hall before breakfast, could not dull my sense of pleasant anticipation.

At breakfast we were joined only by Ned, Elinor having eaten early in the kitchen with the maids. Ned was nearly fifteen now, growing fast, the first shadow of a beard on his face, his voice deepening, his tall, well-formed body putting on weight. He ate rapidly and excused himself at once, not daring to be late for his classes at the Latin School; but only a moment after he left at a half run he was back again, an embarrassed expression on his face. He held out a card to me. "Ferris has asked her to wait in the hall," he said. "I told him I'd bring this to you." He looked deeply troubled, as if he were apologizing to me—for what, I could not imagine.

I looked at the card, which was in poor taste: overlarge, with a hand-painted purple pansy in the lower left corner and Gothic lettering announcing "Mrs. Burton Barringham."

I glanced up at Ned, puzzled. "Who—?"

"Your mother," he said quietly, in the way of someone making the announcement of a death, perhaps, or the failure of a promising investment.

I stared up at him, unable to speak. I felt a hot blush stain my face.

Mr. and Mrs. January were instantly on the alert. "I will see her if you wish," said Mr. January. He was a man of ordinary size, with no great distinction to his

appearance, but he had the air of authority that money
and position confer, and I was sure that he could have
made short work of my mother now as he had done once
before in much more trying circumstances.

As I rose from my seat, my beefsteak and eggs half
eaten on my plate, Mrs. January put out her hand to
detain me. "Let him," she said. "He can say that you are
not here. You do not have to see her if you do not want."

"No," I said. I was grateful for their attempts to help
me; I was also aware that they wanted at all costs to avoid
any trouble, any possibility of scandal. "I will see her. Go
on, Ned—don't be late."

The dining room was at the rear of the hall, and my
mother awaited me at the front, so we had a moment to
observe each other as I went to her. The light was dim, for
the skylight at the top of the stairs shed little enough light
on a sunny day, and this was a dark, mild morning in
March, the sky threatening rain. The Januarys never lit
the gas in the hall until evening; like all people
accustomed to generations of secure wealth, they were
very careful with their spending.

My mother waited until I was at her side before she
spoke. She appraised me with a satisfied look; and only
then, after rather too long a hesitation, did she produce
the expected cry of delight, the standard, rather stagy
embrace for the long-lost child. "Marian!" she cried;
then her arms were around me; then she drew back to
look at me again; then another embrace, and so on.

With some difficulty I extricated myself and led her
into the drawing room. It was dark and cold, for the maid
had not yet drawn the drapes or laid a new fire. I pulled

aside the heavy window coverings. At the curb I saw a hack, a passenger inside, the driver slumbering with his head drooped on his shoulder. I turned to face her, careful to keep a distance between us. I did not ask her to sit down.

"Well, daughter," she said, "you are one of the family here, aren't you?"

In the drab light she looked like an apparition—as indeed she seemed to be, appearing without warning after all this time. But her costume was very definitely of this world: she wore purple, as if to match the pansy on her card—an odd, heavy, shiny material that caught what little light there was. Her small, tilted hat was purple too; around her shoulders was a long black fur piece; crystal earbobs, far too large to be diamonds, dangled from her ears as she talked. They glittered and twinkled in the pale light, so that together with the shine of her costume and the sparkle of her bright eyes, the flash of her very white teeth (her own?), she was altogether a dazzling figure. It was an improbable getup for an early morning call, but then my mother was an improbable woman, much changed now from the frantic wreck who had so shocked the Januarys in this same house more than four years before.

She examined me as closely as she had once done when she had sent me off, that summer at Nahant, to catch a husband.

"You look very well," she said. "You never were a particular stunner, that's certain, but you look good enough. That way of doing your hair suits you. And your dress is nicely made. You do look a bit thin. Are you sure you aren't lacing too tightly? I lace myself too small, I know I do, but I don't have to worry about myself the way you young women do. My childbearing days are over, there's nothing I can do to my insides that hasn't already happened to them. And besides, Bert likes a small waist. He says I look like a girl. And I don't mind telling you that that's important, because he's a good five years younger than I am, and I need to keep myself up to the mark. I know I should have told you, Marian, but it all happened so fast, he was pressing me to set the date, and I thought, Why not? I deserve a little happiness after all these years—oh, I won't tell you what I've suffered since I saw you! But I knew you were safe here—never mind how, I have my friends too, and they kept me informed—and I made up my mind to come to see you as soon as ever I could. And then when I heard about the money—"

She stopped abruptly, conscious of her slip. Her eyes shifted to the window behind me, and I saw her embarrassment change to alarm. I turned to see what had caused it.

A man was just stepping out of the cab. He threw a word to the dozing driver; in three steps he was across the little front walk and up the brownstone stairs and at the door. We heard the bell ring and then ring again. The bay window protruded just by the entrance, so that as he stood waiting he was not more than ten feet from me, separated by a pane of glass.

He was a stocky man in his mid-forties. From the top of his brown beaver to the tips of his high brown boots, he was as gaudy as my mother, albeit considerably less shiny. His long, fawn-colored frock coat was unbuttoned to reveal a yellow brocade vest and a full green cravat. He wore a stickpin which was equal in size to my mother's earbobs but whose stone was turquoise. His gloves, not worn but held carelessly in his large hand, were lemon yellow. He slapped them impatiently against his green-trousered leg while he waited for the door to be opened to him. As he turned to look about, I saw his luxuriant brown mustache and his small, close-set eyes; the mustache amused me but the eyes did not. They met mine; we stared at each other for a moment through the window, and then he, recovering more quickly than I, made a little bow accompanied by a grin almost obscured by the hair on his lip.

Ferris opened the door then, and he came in. I glanced at my mother. She looked very anxious, but she attempted a smile. I wondered what the Januarys were thinking. Ferris knocked; at my summons he entered. "Mr. Barringham, miss." He oozed disdain; I have never known a servant who was not at heart more arrogant than his employers.

"Yes," I said. "Show him in."

"I asked him to wait," said my mother hurriedly, "but I imagine he was too eager—"

But then he was upon us, and she could say no more. He came in holding his hat, and I saw that his hair was luxuriant on his face only, for his head was nearly bald. I put out my hand, and he took it and held it. "Well, Marian," he said. "Well, well, well."

"Bert, I was just telling Marian—"

"Let me tell her," he said. "We have much to talk about, the three of us. Yes, indeed."

At that point I withdrew my hand, since he obviously was not about to release it. All during the interview with my mother I had had a sense of unease; I had not been able to silence the inner voice that told me, with brutal honesty, that she had come not because she loved me but because I was not now what I had been before. I was different: I was rich. And now this man was proof that I had been right to be on my guard.

And so we stood, an awkward trio, while they revealed to me the purpose of their visit: not in so many words, of course, they were stupid but not that stupid—but so clearly that by the end of the interview I knew what they were about.

"We are staying at the Revere House," said my mother. "And we want to let a house as soon as possible. And of course you must come to us, Marian. We have been apart for far too long, and it was my fault, I know that it was, but now we can be together, just the three of us—"

"Until you marry, of course," interjected her husband. He put his arm around her shoulders in an offensively familiar way; in another man it would have been a gesture of affection, but here it was an affront. "We'll find a husband for her, eh, Lucilla?" He grinned at me; his teeth were small and crooked and dark. "And meanwhile—"

"There's no hurry," said my mother. "You have plenty of time, Marian. You can have your pick of men, now that— Well. You are in a different position now, you can afford to wait—"

Floundering, she glanced at him for direction. I did not

know whether to laugh or cry. They were so eager, so anxious in their greed, that they were hardly worthy of my anger; and yet I was too deeply hurt to laugh them off as I would have done had they been strangers seeking to lay hands on my money.

My money: and so it would remain. I felt righteous anger stiffen my spine as I found my voice at last. In one step I was at the marble mantel where hung the bellpull. I jerked it so hard that I thought it must tear loose; and even before I had let it go Ferris was in the room.

"You may show Mr. and Mrs. Barringham out, Ferris," I said. My voice sounded strange: high and tight. My throat was constricted; I felt tears sting my eyes, but I was determined not to let them fall.

My mother refused to go at first. She protested; she rushed to me and tried to embrace me, but I pushed her off. "Marian—no, listen to me—you must see that we have only your best interests at heart—" And then I saw Mr. January at the door, his wife hovering behind, and then, miraculously, I saw Curtis, who had stopped while walking downtown to deliver some small thing from Grace to his mother and had been apprised of the intruders.

He hustled them out, he and his father both, and then he returned to say a reassuring word to me. He found me in his mother's arms, weeping at last. I think, now, that I wept not only on account of the unpleasant interview just past but for all the years before. I wept for my brother, and for my mother's flight, and for my years of poverty-stricken solitude, and for the need for human affection which had been pent up in me all this time, and now it all came out, and so they let me cry, and so I did; and felt better for it, oddly renewed.

"She will come again," said Curtis that evening. "Her husband will force her, even if she does not want to."

We sat in the drawing room: Mr. and Mrs. January, Curtis and I. The rain which had threatened all day had begun to fall at dusk; it poured in wind-driven sheets, beating against the glass, turning those streets still unpaved into treacherous swamps. Curtis was soaked and sniffling, drying his boots against the fire.

"What can I do?" I said.

"You do not want to go to them?"

"Of course not. But where—"

"Here with us, my dear." Mrs. January, like so many others, had grown markedly warmer to me since my inheritance. And I was grateful to her: she might have been jealous, she might have borne ill will toward me. Money makes many friends, few of them true, but I trusted her. "You have become a daughter to us, Marian. You are welcome to stay as long as you please. I will tell you now what I never did before, that bringing you to us was one of the best things that Curtis ever did." She gave him a loving, maternal smile, unwontedly warm.

"I inquired today about the husband," said Mr. January. He, too, had been soaked upon his return home; he sat with a blanket over his knees, a glass of hot whiskey and lemon at his side. "Wilson Fisher said that a man answering to that description had been fortune-hunting at Saratoga Springs two summers ago. He'd almost snared a woman from Rochester, a widow with a nice inheritance, when she found him out for what he was and sent him packing."

"They will come back," said Curtis again. "You should—ah—prepare some kind of defense against them."

"What kind of defense can there be against such people?" said Mrs. January. "I'm sorry, Marian—I know she is your mother, but I cannot help but think that you are well rid of her."

I did not disagree: in all honesty, how could I? And I observed this in myself and understood what it meant: that I was with them, now—with the Januarys. That I was no longer waiting for my mother, for she had come back, ending my wait: and I knew that I did not want her.

"You must be sure that she stays away," said Mr. January. "If she thinks that there is any money to be had—or, worse, if *he* thinks so—they will give you no peace. Curtis, what should she do?"

Despite his years of experience, he deferred to his son with increasing frequency: not so much a sign of age as of shrewd respect for Curtis' knowledge of the law.

"She should be prepared to offer a bribe," said Curtis, so promptly that I knew he must have considered the question before this moment. "A payment—perhaps a lump sum, perhaps a series of smaller amounts—to ensure that they stay away."

"Blackmail," breathed Mrs. January. "Curtis—how can you suggest such a thing to Marian?"

"Extortion, more nearly," said her husband. "But you may be right, Curtis. Some people are so much trouble they're well rid of with a little payoff. But not too much, mind. You don't want to encourage them to come back for more."

Curtis glanced quizzically at me. "Well, Marian?"

I realized that my hands were clasped so tightly in my lap that my fingers ached. I flexed them; I looked at the three of them looking at me, waiting for me to make my decision. I knew what it meant: an irrevocable break with my mother, my only family.

"Yes," I said: and so it was done. Curtis drew up a proper legal document, and when they next appeared, as they did two days later, Ferris was instructed not to admit them but to direct them to Curtis' office in State Street.

"They were deuced cool about it," he said later. "That fellow didn't bat an eyelash. Just took the agreement and read it through and put his name to it as quick as you please. They must have expected something of the sort. I don't think you'll see them again."

And so, as easily as that, I was rid of them. It was my first lesson in the power of money: I had learned that it can buy freedom and peace of mind.

Later—years later—I learned that freedom and peace of mind are beyond price, and that the people of wealth whom I knew were as subject to the miseries of mind and body as all the world's poor.

But that was a long time afterward; and meanwhile I felt that I had struck a fair bargain, and the price of my freedom seemed small indeed.

I never saw her again.

Twelve

We had a mild, damp spring that year, day after day of misty gray skies, the sun occasionally burning through. The Charles took on the color of pewter; the red brick and brownstone of the new Back Bay, so vibrantly warm and rich in the sun's glow, seemed as drab as the muddy streets marking off the blocks; the new trees planted to make us more like Paris came slowly, reluctantly into bloom, hardly green at all. The Public Garden, assiduously tended by municipal groundsmen, was an oasis of color for a week or so after the new plants had been set out from the hothouses; and then they too faded in the unending gloom.

The weather matched the climate in the January household, for the family was growing increasingly concerned about Elinor, and the gloomy skies without simply mirrored the atmosphere within. For Elinor, having "come out" against her will, now seemed determined to go back in. She refused all invitations and issued none of her own; she insisted on continuing her work for the Poor Relief, she declined to participate in her Sewing Circle. Even Isabel, who had little patience with groups of silly women devoid of men to sharpen their wits, was critical of her sister on this last point.

"I don't blame you for not wanting to go to some of the parties, or to the dances at Papanti's," she said to Elinor, "but don't give up your Sewing Circle. That's a group of friends you'll have all your life, and they won't forgive you if you snub them."

"I told them what I thought of their charity," said Elinor. "Spoiled, stupid girls—what do they know about sewing for the poor?"

It was a Boston custom, as rigid as a code of law, that each year's crop of debutantes formed their own Sewing Circle, meeting weekly at the homes of the members. After a luncheon that would have fed a poor family for a week, the Sewing Circle sewed, very slowly, items of clothing to be donated to deserving individuals; and while they sewed they gossiped. For most of the year just past, said Isabel, her Circle had chewed over the revelations of the Beecher-Tilton trial in New York. The Boston *Transcript*, which was the only newspaper allowed in the homes of most of them, had ignored the trial completely, presumably on the grounds of good taste, but the other papers had published full accounts of the testimony. Smuggled-in copies of the choicer issues, laughed Isabel, were read to tatters at the meetings.

But Elinor would not be moved, and at last Isabel gave up. "She will come to her senses eventually," she said; "I only hope that it won't be too late." And then, with an oddly brisk, businesslike air, she put Elinor and her recalcitrance aside for the moment and turned to more pressing matters: the party that she was planning to celebrate her fourth wedding anniversary. "What about it, Marian? Shall I invite Mr. Harding? He'd dearly love to have a chance to see you again."

She had caught me off guard, and for a moment I did not know how to reply. Or, rather, I did not know how to say no, for Alfred Harding had become an embarrassment to me, and, lacking Isabel's dexterity, I did not know how to rid myself of him. He had appeared at one of Isabel's big crushes in the winter: a tall, dark, exceedingly beautiful youth, at least two years younger than I, who firmly attached himself to me that night and gave every indication of refusing to be dislodged. He had called on me the following day and the day after that; he had invited me to go ice skating (which I did) and to go to the theater (which I did not); he had sent flowers and had (so I learned later) told all of his friends that he was infatuated with me.

Never having been the object of a young man's attentions, I hardly knew how to respond. If I had been attracted to him I might have allowed him to court me; perhaps I would have married him. But he was too obvious; I did not trust him. Perhaps his only fault was that he had appeared too soon after all Boston learned that I had inherited Uncle James's money: a cleverer fortune hunter would have waited awhile. I tried, politely, to discourage him but he would not be put off; he even followed me to Nahant, that summer, and made any social occasion there a torment for me for fear that once again I would turn away from a pleasant impersonal conversation to find him panting at my side, eager to monopolize me. Although the world prizes beauty in a woman above all else, those of us who were born without it have this advantage: we are unaccustomed to having suitors right and left, and we can pause, therefore, when one appears, to consider why he has come. Alfred Harding's motive, I thought, was my wealth.

"Leave him out," I said then. "He has become tiresome." I spoke with what I hoped was an air of nonchalance, but Isabel understood.

She laughed. "He has been devoted to you," she said. "You need to be careful, now that you are such a prize. Never mind. We will find someone more suitable for you, and Mr. Harding can take himself elsewhere."

And so Alfred Harding did not attend her anniversary party, although several other pleasant, eligible young men did; none of them seemed promising, however, and so I counseled myself to be content, to wait, to drift along what had become a pleasant current and let the future take care of itself. With Isabel as my sponsor, as it were, I had more than enough invitations to keep me busy.

It occurred to me from time to time to wonder why she had taken me under her wing; but I thought that perhaps time had healed our mutual wounds and that she had at last simply become fond of me. Because of Elinor's stubbornness, Isabel had lost the chance to launch a sister; I was her substitute, I thought. Isabel took me on afternoon drives, she invited me to her receptions and musicales, to a grand ball which she held at the home of her parents-in-law on Commonwealth Avenue (since Isabel's house in Exeter Street was too small for such an affair). I was happy to be taken up. A single woman, then as now, needed more than money to find a place in the world. She needed sponsors—connections—the means to be introduced. Isabel was mine. I was glad that she had become my friend. We believe what we want to believe in this life, after all. And so, as the months passed, I was as welcome everywhere as Isabel herself; where she went, there went I, and for the time being I wanted nothing more.

She had her own struggle all this time, of course—a battle with her stubborn heart which she could not confess to anyone. I had seen it when I gave Cushing's letter to her; now it flared up again, on a brisk autumn afternoon when we had returned from a drive to Longwood to visit Cousin Sam and inspect his greenhouses. He was prouder of his orchids than some people are of their children: he told us their origins, their characteristics, their habits of propagation—he was truly a connoisseur, obsessed as all connoisseurs are and eager to impart his knowledge.

"Orchids!" laughed Isabel as we drove away. "They're a vulgar flower, don't you think? Too showy. Give me a nice white rose. But there—I suppose it's better to walk through a greenhouse than to sit in his library and listen to his lectures on genealogy. He can trace us all back to the Middle Ages, and with the slightest encouragement he will."

We arrived at Exeter Street just past four, and I agreed to stay for a cup of tea before continuing on to the Januarys'. When we entered the hall we saw a card in the silver card holder. "Bother," said Isabel. "Who is this? People know that I'm never at home on Tuesdays."

Having removed her gloves, she picked up the card to see the name. I paused, waiting for her to tell me who the caller was.

She stood perfectly still, holding the card, staring at it as if she had been mesmerized. Then she looked up at me, shaking her head slightly as if to clear it. The afternoon had darkened and the gas had been turned on; in the light from the jets on the wall I saw that her face had gone pale. Her eyes looked dark—fathomless. She held the card so tightly that it bent and crumpled between her fingers.

The maid hurried to explain: "I told him you weren't in, ma'am, but he said he was an old friend and you wouldn't mind if he waited. I'm sorry if I shouldn't have let him—"

"No," said Isabel. "No—it's all right." She turned to me. "I must excuse myself, Marian. Take the carriage, it's getting dark. I'll call around tomorrow, or send a note."

Having been dismissed so abruptly, I was naturally curious to know why. Who had come? And why was I not to meet him? As I went out into the chilly autumn twilight and climbed once again into the carriage, I glanced back at the house; but the draperies at the windows were drawn against the coming night and I could learn no more from the house than I had from Isabel herself.

It was Cushing, of course. That was the first time she had seen him since before Curtis' wedding—before the night that he deserted her. Since then she had heard from him once, so far as I knew: he had smuggled a letter to her and had used me to do it. Now here he was again, demanding to see her. She wept, that day, at the end of their meeting; and she wept again, decades later, when she recalled it.

She did not knock before she opened the door to the drawing room. She had hoped to catch him by surprise, but it was never possible to do that. He was a man who lived by his wits, who was always on the alert. At the instant he heard the click of the latch he was poised like a panther, while she had to enter the room and compose herself; and so from the beginning she was at a disadvantage.

If she had been able to draw a deep breath she might have been more at ease, but her corsets prevented her; and so she suffered the heavy, smothering beat of her heart and fought to get air into her constricted lungs and felt the blood rush to her face even as she held out her hand in an automatic gesture of courtesy.

Courtesy! To this man who had betrayed her! Who might have ruined her, had their escapade been known! She had fought every day of her life to put him out of her mind, she had done the only things she knew to forget him—she had married, had borne children, had begun to build a life in society—and yet now, confronting him, she knew how futile all her effort had been. All her life was a sham, a lie: she cared nothing for it.

She beheld him: and he— Well. One never knew, with Lawrence Cushing.

He took her hand and kissed it, first the back of it, and then the soft, plump palm, and then the inside of the wrist. Neither of them said a word. What could she say to him that she would not in the next moment regret? And what could he say to her that would make up for all her years of suffering, of longing for him day and night, week after week, month after month? On the day of her marriage she had wept for him, and that night as well, and when she brought her children into the world—ah, how she wished they were his children, his flesh and blood mingled with her own!

And then he put his arms around her and held her close, and even through the cruel cage of her stays she felt his light, lithe body, so different from Avery's bulk. He pressed his face against her neck and kissed her there; his mouth was warm, it moved against her skin, his arms held her fast. He did not act on impulse; he moved deliberately, and as warm as he was, his heart and his mind were cool.

She did not embrace him in return. Her arms hung at her sides, her mouth did not seek his, her body stayed rigid. And so, after a moment, he stopped. He put her gently, deliberately away from him; he held her at arms' length and gave her a searching look as if he would read her mind.

There was nothing to read: her mind, at that moment, held only the simplest impressions. I am here, she thought, in my own house, in my drawing room with the patterned paper on the walls, the carved sofa by the fire, the marble-topped table in the center of the Aubusson carpet. It is late afternoon, dusk: soon the servants will bring tea, my husband will return from his office, we will dress for dinner. Dining in or out? She could not remember. What date, what day of the week? She did not know. All the world for her, this moment, was concentrated in his eyes—even in the dim light of the gas jets by the fire they were so blue, so brilliant that she was nearly blinded by them and yet she could not look away.

Then at last he spoke; but instead of breaking the spell he intensified it: his voice drew her deeper in to him, further away from her life.

"You had my letter," he said. "Not even one word would you send me. Did you read it? Did you read what I wrote to you?"

She shuddered; she could not speak.

"I am sorry that you did not wait for me." He spoke softly, speaking as a lover speaks and yet more cruelly than any lover, casting up to her her misdeeds. "If you had waited, we could be together now." She did not think of the injustice of what he said; she concentrated on the sound of his voice, its tone, its timbre. It was just as she remembered it: she had not forgotten. "I am here for only a day or two," he said. "But I came straight to you, I could not stay away. When I learned that you had married, I thought that I would never come to you again. Let her go, I said to myself, she is yours no longer. But I had to see you. I could not rest, I could not live another day without seeing you."

Every woman on earth longs to hear such a speech. Even as her reason tells her that it is a lie, her heart believes it. Isabel's heart had been broken by this man; it was not yet mended—never would be. How could she withstand him?

At last she found her voice. She could not remember all the angry, bitter, despairing words that she had hurled at him over the years. It was her broken heart that spoke now: she was without guile, without defense. "I waited for you that night," she said. "It rained and rained—do you remember? For a long time afterward I was ill. I wanted to die."

"But you went on living."

"Yes."

"And you married."

"What choice did I have?" Her mind had begun to clear. She heard her voice come stronger. "I had no word from you—nothing until four years had passed. Four years!"

"I had no way—I dared not write to you, I feared that any letter I wrote at the time would be discovered and you, perhaps, in difficulty because of it, compromised—"

"Compromised!" She withdrew; she walked to the fire, she felt its heat on her hands and face—nothing compared to the heat inside her. "I would have given my life for a word from you, and you feared that I would be compromised!" She turned to look at him. She wanted to see him wounded as she had been wounded, she wanted to see his eyes dimmed with pain, his face working to hold back his tears. But she saw only that powerful, oddly primitive countenance that haunted her all her waking hours and in her sleep as well.

"Isabel—" He approached her, but now she drew back.

"No! Do not touch me again."

"Will you forgive me?"

"Why? To ease your conscience?"

"To let me see that you do not hate me."

"What difference does it make whether I hate you or not?"

"To me it makes all the difference in the world."

For a moment she yielded: she believed him. But she was a January, after all, and despite the anguished cry of her heart she could not help but hear the cool, clear voice of reason from her mind. She composed herself; she remembered who she was.

"You are mistaken," she said. "It is not important. Nothing, between us, is important. You should not have come."

"Perhaps. But I wanted— Well. Simply to see you, I suppose."

To see her! Only that, and nothing more! If he had loved her he would have asked her to go away with him. Even now, encumbered as she was with family, with position, with a place in the world—if he had loved her, he would have begged her to go with him, and the world be damned.

And she would have gone. She told me so, years later, at the time she told me so much. "I would have done it, Marian," she said. "I would have gone if he had asked me, even then."

But he did not: and so his visit was in a way another kind of rebuff.

She gathered up her pride and clasped it to her like a sable cloak: and it warmed her and gave her confidence.

"You should not have come," she said again.

"I wanted—"

"You should not have come. We have nothing to say to each other."

178

"You could say that you forgive me. Then I could go in peace."

She stood silent. She was a small woman but, like Queen Victoria, equally small, she was capable of great dignity. She clung to the certainty of her life; she reminded herself that this man offered her nothing.

"Just please go," she said. "Go however you will, in peace or not, but go."

He held out his hand, but she did not take it.

"Very well." Before she was aware of what he was about, he had swiftly kissed her cheek. Then he turned and left the room. She realized that even though he was simply obeying her request she was bitterly disappointed with him for having done so.

And then something inside her broke again—her heart? her will?—and, suddenly weak, she sank down onto the carved, plush sofa and abandoned herself to her tears. Bitter, bitter tears—more painful than any that she had wept before.

Avery found her so, half an hour later. He was horrified: what had happened? Was she in pain? Did she want the doctor?

Yes, she wanted to say, yes, I am in agony, but no doctor can assuage it, for I must live my life with you while the man I love has gone away from me again.

But she greeted him instead with the excuse that she had a headache—that universal female euphemism covering every imaginable ailment, both physical and spiritual—and shortly left him to dress for dinner. They were dining in, she remembered, with six guests.

Thirteen

I did not see her for some days. Then one afternoon she called on me. She made no mention of our last parting, of her mysterious visitor; she seemed her usual brisk, efficient self. She had come to ask a favor of me, the granting of which, as she said, might amuse me. "Signor Ristori needs an accompanist," she said. "His sister, whom you saw last winter, has broken her arm. I told him I'd speak to you. Would you accompany him for one evening only, at my Monday musicale? He says that he has sent to New York for a cousin to come, but she won't arrive in time."

I was appalled at her suggestion. "Isabel, I can't play well enough—"

"Of course you can. You sight-read beautifully. I've heard you do it."

"No."

She threw me a calculating look. How she loved to manipulate people! "He badly needs the money I'll pay him. If you won't help, he'll miss the engagement. His repertoire is all duet, he needs the piano."

I thought of Signor Ristori's fine eyes, his gentle, courteous demeanor. Clearly he was a worthwhile person, deserving of help; it would be unfair to deprive him of an evening's pay simply on account of any qualms I might have about public performance.

"All right," I said. "But just this once."

Isabel smiled at me in a satisfied way. She was never happier than when she had arranged something: anything.

And so, the following Monday afternoon, I set out to rehearse with him at the elder Mrs. Kittredge's on Commonwealth Avenue near Dartmouth Street, for this was to be a large affair, too large for Isabel's place, and her mother-in-law was always generous about lending her own rather more spacious quarters. It was a mild, hazy day in early November. I had walked instead of taking the carriage: cold weather would soon settle in for the duration of the winter, and I wanted to enjoy the sun and the fresh air while I could. The streets were filled with vehicles, but there were few pedestrians; men were the walkers in Boston, and at this hour they were not yet done with their work in their offices downtown.

The sky was milky blue, the sun strong enough to warm me. I wore a new lambskin jacket of pale gray and a decidedly French hat of jade green. The dressmaker, Miss Merriman, had become ecstatic when she first draped the skin around me, before she cut the pattern: "With your eyes, Miss Childs, and your skin, that gray is perfect!" I had looked at myself in the long pier glass: standing in my chemise and petticoats, the lambskin covering my shoulders, my hair disarranged, I resembled nothing so much as a scarecrow.

"Wonderful!" said Miss Merriman. "I know that the fashion is toward plumpness, but you have a style all your own. And if you'd just let me put a little padding there, at the bust, and over the hipline, it'd give you a much nicer silhouette. It wouldn't take much—"

But I wanted no padding; corsets were bad enough.

At last I came to the Kittredge house. It was an imposing affair of brownstone, Gothic or medieval in style, with a high, pointed gable and an arched, recessed entrance. The butler let me in. "Mrs. Kittredge is not at home, miss," he said (meaning the elder), "but she instructed me to tell you to ring for whatever you need."

My partner awaited me. He stood at the french doors at the rear of the long double drawing room and looked out across the back garden, brown now in the dead of the year, and through the empty house lot opposite which fronted on Marlborough Street. It was a somewhat dreary prospect even on so pleasant a day; if I had paid all this money for a house, I thought, I would want a better view.

He turned to greet me, his hands outstretched. In two steps he had crossed the shining parquet floor and clasped my hands in his. *"Deliziosa,"* he said. *"Come è bella—e gentile da soccorrermi."* He did not smile; his face was serious—somber, even—and he stared at me in a melancholy way from eyes that were deep-set, black, opaque: unreadable.

"Good," he said, pressing my hands as if he would transmit some of his musical ability to me; "good good good. Now. To work!"

He released me and picked up his violin and bow from

where they lay atop the mahogany piano. I removed my gloves and my hat, and then my jacket, underneath which I wore a white waist and a skirt of pale gray. I sat at the keyboard and flexed my fingers. Several pages of music were propped on the rack: Schumann, Mendelssohn. Signor Ristori nodded at me; we began. My fingers were stiff and slow; he understood this and paced himself accordingly.

The second time went better; the third, better still. We must have presented a strange sight for any curious onlooker, an ill-matched pair attempting to make music to an empty room, Signor Ristori tapping his worn black boot on the shining parquet floor, encouraging me, giving me confidence.

As the light began to fade we went on, more sure of ourselves, of each other; the music filled the empty room. Signor Ristori, with his shabby clothing, his hand-to-mouth existence, might have been a prince as he played: it was the music that made him so, his ability to produce it that made him seem a noble being, a natural aristocrat despite his humble circumstances.

We came to the end; we played the last notes—a lingering, mournful trio of half and three-quarter beats on the violin, the pulsing notes of the piano underneath. Their sound hung in the air after we had stopped. I sat with my hands in my lap like a docile student. Signor Ristori remained standing in position, his violin tucked under his chin, his bow resting soundless on the strings. He gazed into the middle distance: what did he see that gave so sorrowful an expression to his face?

Suddenly, still clutching his instrument, he turned

and bent down to me and with his free arm he embraced me and pulled me up to him and held me so close that I could hear the frantic beating of his heart. *"Mia cara,"* he murmured. *"O mia dolcissima signora! Ah, quanto la desidero! Quanto la bramo!"* And then he kissed me: a long, long endless time when his strong, warm mouth covered mine and took my breath and made me helpless even as it set my blood raging. I was too shocked to protest—too shocked even to realize fully what was happening.

At last he released me. "Apology," he said. "I am so sorry, *signora.* I was—how to say, I don't know. You not be angry. I cannot help. I am—I am—"

To my dismay, he had begun to cry. Of course I knew that Latins were very different from our cool and self-contained New England stock, but I had no idea how different. Oddly, I was not offended by his embrace. I understood it. He was not trying to ravish me: he was trying to assuage some private grief by reaching out to another: sometimes only human touch can help us, while all the words in the world leave us still alone, still in need.

And so, after he had regained his composure, we parted friends; and we gave that night what everyone said was a not unprofessional performance.

"There," said Isabel later. "You have done your good deed for the month. Poor man—he really does need the money."

I had not told her of Signor Ristori's momentary indiscretion; I felt that had I done so I would have betrayed a confidence and, worse, possibly jeopardized his future engagements. His cousin arrived from New

York soon after, and so I did not accompany him again; but I heard him play several times more that winter, and when he saw me in the audience he would smile at me in his melancholy way and offer a small bow, no more than a nod, and I would respond. He was a decent man, I thought: I bore him no ill will. He had succumbed for a moment to his need, and I had been there to fill it. That was all.

He had, in fact, taught me a lesson: showing so unashamedly his own solitude, he had heightened my awareness of my own.

We were at the turn of the year: 1875 was giving way to 1876. I was twenty-five years old. I had no family—no blood tie save that which I had severed; I had no friends save the Januarys and Mrs. Roberts Reed. I had a good deal of money, but I was without prospect of a husband.

Although I did not know it, Isabel had already begun to hunt for one for me.

Fourteen

"Perseus Motley!" exclaimed Mrs. Roberts Reed. She studied me for a moment, her small eyes inscrutable in her plump face. "Isn't he a bit dry, Marian?"

"Perhaps," I said. I smiled at her; I did not mind her bluntness. "But that's better than wet behind the ears, isn't it? He seems very steady."

"I know his mother—known her for years. Of course the Motleys are one of the best families—one of the very best, unquestionably—but still . . ."

I understood: she thought that I could do better.

But at that time—we were talking on an afternoon in February of the following year, the Centennial year—I was not so sure. After the episode with Alfred Harding, I had begun to realize that finding a suitable husband might take more effort than I had imagined. I did not want a showy, fashionable young man who would love me for a time and then, having run through my fortune, perhaps love me no more. Nor did I want a lesser light whose only credential would be his devotion to me (and my money), who would lack the family connections that

186

I lacked myself.

No: I wanted someone safe and steady, someone who would give me what I had never had—a sure position in the world.

And certainly Perseus Motley could give me that. His pedigree was one of the oldest and best in New England, but the family's fortune had run down, their luck had run out, and in the wake of the Panic of '73 they had lost what little money they had left. Perseus and his aged mother were the last of them.

"You can't do better than a Motley," chuckled Cousin Sam Swift. "True, they aren't what they were a hundred years ago, or even fifty, but the blood is there. And you'll see it in your children, Marian, mark my word if you don't."

I met him at Isabel's on New Year's Eve. She brought him to me with an air of triumph.

"Marian, this is Perseus Motley. He has wanted very much to be introduced to you, and I promised him that tonight he should."

He bowed slightly over my hand. "Miss Childs."

Isabel had told me nothing about him, and so I was free to judge him objectively in those first moments of our meeting. He was slightly taller than I, with wiry brown hair slicked back over his long head; his pointed features were as neat and precise as the knot on his neckcloth, his eyes and mouth very narrow. Wire-rimmed spectacles perched on his beaky nose. He was perhaps thirty. He might have been the senior clerk in a merchant trading house; he gave the impression of always measuring, always calculating figures in his head. Despite his rather fussy manners and a habit of tilting his head to one side like a curious bird while he listened to what you had to say, I did not dislike him.

We chatted for a while that evening, and when it came time to go in to supper he asked me to be his partner. Despite the fact that he was not a handsome man, or a particularly charming one (or even, as I had learned, one with a good deal of money), he had an oddly pompous air, as if he felt that he conferred a great favor upon you by speaking to you. Such an attitude came, no doubt, from being a fond mama's only son, and even more from knowing that he was the scion of one of the most ancient Boston families.

Even so, I liked him better than the flashier, younger men whom I had met—certainly I liked him better than I liked Alfred Harding—and so when he called the next afternoon I was not unhappy to see him among the crush of visitors in the January drawing room. We had time for only a word or two; he asked me to go to a lecture the following evening at the Lowell Institute. And so I did; and after that he asked me to go to a recital, and to go sleighing on the Brighton Road, and to a reception in Cambridge given for a noted scholar from that other Cambridge across the Atlantic.

In other words, he had begun to court me. I understood that, and I allowed him to do it. I did not mind. I submitted myself to what I thought was my fate; and if Isabel had nudged fate along, if she had indulged in a bit of matchmaking—well, that was fate too.

Later—years later, after Perseus had died, and Cushing, too, and she and I had come together again after long years of separation, I put the question to her: knowing what Perseus was, why had she presented him to me as a candidate for marriage?

She was an old woman then, and she spoke with the bleak, blunt honesty that often the young cannot bear to show.

"Because I hated you," she said simply.

Although I knew in that instant that it was true, I was too shocked to reply.

"Why should I not have?" she went on. "You were free, and rich—you had Uncle James's fortune! More money than I ever dreamed of having! And you were free to spend it as you wished. While I—I was tied to a man I did not love. Even then I knew it. I was miserable, all the more so because I had no money at all, Avery had forbidden me to entertain for the rest of the winter, he had even threatened to cut off my dressmaker's allowance. What was I to do? I was helpless. He had had reversals, he said, and I suppose it was true, many people lost their money in the panic and never got it back. And there you were, as rich as Croesus and at liberty to do as you would."

And all the while, trapped as she was, threatened with having to give up the only pleasure in her life—her entertaining—and forced to submit to her husband's demands, to lie with him in their marriage bed and suffer him to take her whenever he pleased, all the while, every day and night of her life, her soul rebelled. She did not love him. She loved that other—that slim golden sea god whom she had watched once at dawn when she was only a girl, when she did not know what love meant. She had

loved him since that moment; she could not stop loving
him. And he was—so she thought—forever lost to her.

I knew little of that in the winter of '76. I knew only
that Perseus Motley offered me a place in the world and
that he seemed to be a man who would be a good husband
to me. He did not drink or smoke or gamble; he did not
run with a wild pack of friends; he was not unintelligent;
he approved—so he often said—of my quiet way of life.
"You have been careful with your fortune, Marian," he
said approvingly; and I was sure that he would not turn
spendthrift once I was his wife.

And so, when he proposed marriage to me one cold
February night as we returned home in a hack from an
evening at Mrs. Reed's, I accepted him. In the moment
that he spoke, there flashed before my mind's eye the
memory of Signor Ristori's embrace; and as I accepted,
as I said that I would be his wife, I prepared myself for a
similar embrace from Perseus.

But he made no move; he simply held my gloved hand,
pressing it a bit, half turned toward me in the cramped
space of the carriage. It was dark; I saw his pale, thin face
only faintly. I could not make out his expression behind
the glittering, twin discs of his spectacles. His dry voice
sounded as though he were making a business transaction—as, indeed, he was. He should have spoken first to a
male relative or protector, but I had none; and, besides,
as he pointed out to me in his precise, logical way, we
were neither of us children, we had lived in the world for
a while and we presumably knew what we were about.

And so I banished all thought of Signor Ristori and his
Mediterranean temperament, and I consented to become

Mrs. Perseus Motley.

The day of our wedding dawned clear and cool. At midday the guests began to arrive, and at promptly one o'clock, in the January drawing room, the Reverend Mr. Eldridge performed the ceremony. I remembered, later, that it was his hands, and not mine or Perseus', that trembled as we said our vows; that it was Mrs. January who shed the obligatory tear, and not Perseus or I; that it was Cousin Sam Swift, later, and not Perseus who drank too much champagne and needed to be quieted by the soberer members of the party. Even Perseus' nuptial kiss was oddly insubstantial: a fleeting brush of his lips on mine, lighter than the touch of a moth wing.

We went to the Hotel Brunswick on our wedding night. Our suite faced onto Boylston Street. It was not yet dark when we arrived; I went to the windows and looked out at the early evening traffic five stories below. The day had been cool and windy, and now the breeze blowing into the room carried with it the familiar smell of the streets, the familiar sound of human voices, horses' hooves and iron-rimmed wheels on the cobblestones.

The room was shadowed, for we had not turned up the gas. I heard Perseus moving behind me. I thought that he might come to me, might even embrace me, but he did not; and so, after a moment, I turned to find him.

He was sitting in a small chair beside the fireplace, watching me. As my eyes adjusted to the darkness I saw his face: unsmiling—somber.

I hesitated. I had no idea what to say to him. He was my husband now: what did one say to a husband?

A bottle of champagne stood in a cooler beside the

marble-topped table in the center of the room. "Would you—shall we have some champagne?" I said. I loosened the buttons of my moiré bodice; my fingers were steady, not trembling as I had feared they would be.

"Let it chill a bit," he said. "They should have brought it cold. I felt it; it's not right yet."

And so, lacking an invitation to approach him, I remained standing by the window. I had no idea what to do. No one had ever told me what—if anything—happened between husband and wife, what mysterious thing joined them, mated them, made them truly one. Some women said to their daughters, on the eve of their weddings, "Submit. Let him do as he will. Endure. Do not complain." But no one had said even that to me. I did not know that there was anything to submit to, I had no idea what I must endure.

At last, because I was tired, and because I felt oddly in the wrong, as if there were something that I must do but could not, not knowing what it was—at last I moved into the room and sat opposite him. The light reflected from the street gave enough to see by; I saw that he was staring at me in a peculiarly hostile way, and suddenly I was alarmed. What was wrong?

"Perseus—"

He held up his hand as if to ward me off. "No. Let me speak. Let me explain to you how we will live, you and I. I want you to understand. I have thought about it a great deal."

He leaned forward in his chair as he spoke, but he did not try to touch me, to take my hand.

I stared at him, growing more apprehensive by the minute.

"Men and women," he said, "when they marry, when they sleep side by side, perform a—a physical act which is called the act of procreation. It has other names as well, but I will not offend you by repeating them. It is, quite simply, an act whereby the man joins his body to the woman's and enters into her. It is horribly degrading— animalistic. It is also quite painful for the wife, as I need hardly tell you. Many men, I understand, grow to enjoy it—why, I cannot imagine—but no woman does. How could she? It is a revolting, disgusting performance. I have decided that I will not inflict it on you—on us. Do you understand what I am saying to you, Marian?"

I did not, but I nodded, slowly, because I knew that he expected me to do so.

"You are—you are the very highest type of woman," he went on. "I would not have married you if I did not think so. And I refuse, absolutely, to subject you to that act which so many men insist upon. If I may say so, you should consider yourself fortunate. Many women, I am sure, would give anything to be spared such humiliation."

His eyes were steady on mine, his voice calm and self-assured. I did not understand what he described to me— how could I?—but I believed that he spoke sincerely: of behavior such as I could not imagine, of horrors of which I had never known—was that what Isabel had suffered? Curtis' wife? Mrs. January? My own mother? How could good and decent people perform such acts and arise each day and face the world? Why did not someone protest, put a stop to it?

And yet men and women both seemed to survive it and even to live happily together. How? I didn't know: couldn't imagine.

We sat in darkness. From beyond the open windows came the sounds of the nighttime city, all the myriad life, all the thousands of souls living, breathing, blood flowing warm through their veins, while we sat apart, each of us alone.

Later, after I had lived with him, after I had seen his diaries following his death and knew for the first time what he was, I understood his speech to me that night. For Perseus was a wanderer on this earth, an outsider, a stranger all his life to the ways of ordinary folk. The idea of physical contact with another human being nauseated him: to have exposed his private parts to a woman, to have put himself deep into the soft, dark moistness of a woman's body as he had heard men talk of doing—no. He was incapable of doing that. And so of course he was driven to do what he did, he was compelled to spend his life trying to prevent the world from doing—or even thinking about—what he could not.

After a while, that night, I rose and went to the dressing room and took off my new clothing with the help of a maid, provided by the management, to unlace me; I put on my new nightdress and peignoir and went to the bedroom beyond and lay down on the wide, soft bed. I felt a tear slide down onto the pillow, and then another. I did not know why I wept. I knew only that something was very wrong and that somehow it was my fault. After I had cried for a while I fell into a fitful sleep, waking from time to time to find myself still alone.

And so, like many another woman but for very different reasons, I spent a miserably unhappy wedding night.

Part II

One

"But of course you must buy it!" said Isabel. She sat with me in my carriage looking eagerly at the brownstone house on the water side of Beacon Street which had recently come on the market.

"How can you say that?" I protested, laughing. "You haven't seen the interior."

"I don't need to. You can do anything you want inside. It's the location and the house itself that you can't change."

She was right, of course. For the three years since my marriage to Perseus we had been living in a rented house on Joy Street at the top of Beacon Hill. From time to time I had looked at houses to buy, but I had seen nothing that appealed to me. Further, the impermanence of rented quarters seemed appropriate to our marriage: it was not, of course, a marriage at all, but an arrangement of convenience. For a long time after that disastrous wedding night I had struggled with myself over what I should do: leave him, have the marriage annulled, and begin again to search for a husband who would give me a life? Or stay, make a secure and comfortable life for myself sheltered by Uncle James's money and the name and position that Perseus had given me?

In the end the question resolved itself, for the longer I hesitated the more accustomed I became to our life together, and at last I knew that I would remain Mrs. Perseus Motley.

Isabel's enthusiasm about the Beacon Street house, that day, mirrored my own; and so I bought it. I furnished it in a variety of styles: dark, heavily carved Renaissance pieces in the front parlor; Louis XVI, lighter and more delicate, in the rooms to the rear that overlooked the river; luxurious overstuffed Turkish ottomans and chairs in my upstairs sitting room. In that house, whenever it pleased me, I entertained; several times every week I attended others' entertainments; and so we went on, month after month, year after year, and to the world we were a couple as happy as any other, and far less unhappy than many.

Some time after our move to Beacon Street—which is to say, around the turn of the decade—Perseus found an interest that took him away for hours at a time, sometimes from morning until night. Since he was not a sporting man, and not a man to spend long hours at his club, I thought perhaps that he might have taken up some occupation. Certainly we did not need the money, but too much free time can demoralize anyone; perhaps, I thought, he has discovered a vocation so late in life.

When I asked him he gave me an evasive answer: "Some people have got up a Society that interests me," he said; but he would not say more, and I did not want to press him. We lived in a strange, uncommunicative equilibrium, Perseus and I: we went our separate ways; occasionally we appeared together at some social function but more often I went alone, or with Curtis and Grace or Isabel and Avery.

In the winter of '82, Isabel discovered that she was again with child. She had already begun her assault on society, and another accouchement—not to mention the long months of enforced solitude preceding it—was an unwelcome prospect. The child, a boy, was born at the end of August; he was her fourth, another daughter, Victoria, having come in the fall of '77. A few days later I paid her a visit. She was half sitting up in bed; she wore an embroidered green silk bed-jacket, and her hair was freshly coiffed. Strewn over the bedclothing and spilling down onto the floor were sheets of paper filled with names and addresses: on the table beside her were pen and a pot of ink and a stack of fresh notepaper.

"What is this?" I exclaimed as I kissed her. "Have you taken paid employment as an amanuensis?"

"Almost," she laughed. She was pale, perspiring; the room was very warm, and no breeze came from the open windows. "These are friends of Aunt Reed's. I am writing a note to each one of them to ask them to attend an evening of *tableaux vivants*. It is for Major Higginson's orchestra. Aunt Reed herself will make a speech after the *tableaux* encouraging people to attend this season's concerts."

In the previous year, Major Henry Lee Higginson had achieved his dream and had given to the city the Boston Symphony Orchestra. Despite his generosity, however, he and his musicians did not have universal goodwill. Some people had been offended, it was said, by the choice of selections: the nine symphonies of Beethoven had been given to universal acclaim, but new music had been introduced also, a symphony by Johannes Brahms, whose dissonances and loud crashings and mournful bleatings had caused many people to walk out in the middle of the performance. So Major Higginson needed friends: he needed people like Isabel and Mrs. Reed to help his orchestra to survive.

I tried not to show my skepticism. Despite the frequent musical evenings which she arranged at her home, Isabel was not a music lover. For her, music was a means to an end rather than an end in itself.

We chatted for a while, that day, and I was allowed to put my head into the nursery to see Mason, as he was to be named—a fine, pink little speck, as healthy as her older three. After a time Isabel seemed to tire, and I gathered myself to go; just as I was on the point of leaving, however, Avery came in and insisted that I stay.

"Don't see enough of you, Marian," he puffed (for he, like Isabel, had put on weight, and in the manner of Boston men he had just walked the mile and more from his office downtown). "Stay and tell me how you are. What is that?" he said to Isabel, meaning her writing materials. When she told him his face dropped down into a look of disapproval. "Stuff and nonsense," he said abruptly. "There are a dozen women at least who could write invitations for Mrs. Reed. What do you want to trouble yourself for?"

She gazed up at him, calm, unrepentant. "Because it

interests me," she said.

"Interests you!" He seemed to have forgotten his remarks to me—indeed, to my embarrassment he seemed to have forgotten my presence altogether. He nodded his head toward the closed door of the nursery, from whence we heard the first faint cries of hunger from the new arrival. In addition to his two daughters, he had two sons now to carry on his name, to continue the family line, and—not least—to occupy his wife's attention. Most Boston men, Avery Kittredge included, were of the opinion that motherhood and domesticity were a woman's highest—her only—calling; no woman needed more than a husband and children to make her happy.

We heard a soft tap; before Isabel could answer, the nurse had come in carrying the infant. Reluctantly, with a look of annoyance, Isabel swept aside her papers and took her child. It was the signal for Avery and me to leave, and so we did. He shook my hand at the front door. "Good of you to come, Marian. How's Perseus?"

"Well enough." I assumed this; I did not know it. Certainly this was not the time to speak of Perseus' increasing involvement with his Society, whatever it was.

Avery seemed oddly at loose ends—reluctant to see me go. "I saw Ned today—passed him in the street and he looked right through me. When I stopped him he said he'd been thinking of a line with five beats to a rhyme with 'power.' I was glad I was by myself so that no one else could hear him say it. Have you seen him lately?"

I had not: not for weeks.

"Ask him to tea. Put some sense into his head. You and

he were always good friends, and he'll listen to you before he will to me or his father."

And so, promising that I would, I made my way home with more than usual to occupy my thoughts. Poor Avery! Disappointed not only in his wife but in her younger brother as well.

It was common knowledge up and down State Street that Ned January was—well, not precisely a slacker, but certainly not a "comer." Since his graduation from Harvard the year before he had, as expected, entered his father's firm at a very junior level and begun to learn the business. He went to the offices of January & Co. a reasonable number of hours each week: he performed his duties efficiently, if not altogether happily; he was intelligent enough, without question, to do anything he wanted. Nevertheless he lacked enthusiasm—that rapacious desire to multiply money that characterized the Boston man of affairs. All around him, in copper, in railroads, in insurance, in cotton and wool and leather— even, like the Ameses, in shovels—Boston men were giving the New York crowd a good run. But Ned January, apparently, was not to be one of them.

It was known he was fond—too fond—of amateur theatricals and, worse, that he lived too much at the Tavern Club, an "artistic" set made up largely of young men under thirty. Most damaging of all was the fact that more than once Ned had given readings of his poems, at my house among others. He had acquired, I imagined, a reputation for being frivolous; and who would trust such a man—a man who wrote poetry—with truly important things such as matters of business, of multiplying money?

Despite the concern for him in certain quarters, Ned himself seemed more or less untroubled by his situation. I saw him a few days after Avery's request, when he came to visit me in the late afternoon on his way home from his father's office. He stretched his long legs comfortably before my fire and smiled at me—the same smile of the boy who had been my friend long ago at the Januarys'. He was a tall young man—taller than Curtis, and more muscular, for he had been an excellent athlete at college. He was handsome like Curtis, too, and very much resembled him, with his wide brow and regular nose and chin and fine, deep-set eyes. But Ned's eyes, if you looked closely, were different from Curtis'. They seemed to see more, and to show a mind more reflective, more meditative upon what they saw.

He seemed, in fact, to possess a kind of sixth sense; even now, as we sat companionably together, he seemed to know what I was about, and he forestalled my questions with a laugh and a shrug. "Don't worry about me, Marian. I'm doing very well. Don't tell anyone, but I'm finishing a four-part thing—an ode to the seasons. I'll try to have it published if I think it's good enough."

And here, surely, was evidence that he was not frivolous—that he even had, perhaps, aspirations to become another Longfellow. Such hopes might be farfetched, but they were not to be laughed at or condemned as mere foolishness.

I abandoned my plans to interrogate him, therefore, or

to lecture to him of the benefits of more mundane kinds of work, and I let the conversation drift where it would. His eye fell on a small bronze statue of a dying stag.

"Is that new?"

"Yes."

"Someone give it to you?"

"No. I bought it."

My answer interested him. "I didn't know you were a patroness of the arts."

"I am not. From time to time I see something that I like and I buy it."

"Perseus like it?"

"I don't know. He didn't say."

He made no response to this at first; and then, quietly, with infinite compassion, he said, "Is there anything I can do for you, Marian?"

I had no idea how to answer him. "Do for me? I don't—what do you mean, Ned?"

"I mean, you look as though something is troubling you."

"Really? Mrs. Terrill told me only yesterday that I look very well."

"Oh, you do—you do. But all the same— Well. We are good friends, are we not? If ever you need help in any way, I hope you'll come to me."

It is unnerving to be offered help when we are not conscious that we need it. But Ned had that poet's instinct for ferreting out truth, and I realize now, as I did not then, that he saw my situation more clearly than I did myself, and felt compelled, because of our friendship, to begin to help me to see a way out of it.

The *tableaux vivants* for Major Higginson's orchestra took place on an evening in October at the home of Mrs. Roberts Reed in Mount Vernon Street. Many people came; a capacity audience balanced cautiously on the small gilt chairs closely arranged in rows the length of her double drawing room. Seventeen ladies—debutantes and young matrons both—and four young men had been selected to perform scenes taken from Greek mythology. Despite her recent confinement, Isabel was among the performers; she had tried to recruit me also, but I had declined.

"But why, Marian?" she had protested. "You look ever so much more classical than I do—you are tall and graceful, and I don't think the color of your hair matters a bit. Surely there must have been a redheaded Greek once in a while—or you could wear a wig."

But I refused her; in this modern-day Athens there might be other women with hair the color of mine, but in the ancient city I was sure there were not, and I did not care to wear a wig. And besides, as I pointed out to her, she would do better to choose women upon whom she wanted to confer a favor: the cachet of appearing in these *tableaux* would put the participants nicely in her debt.

The printed program announced the scenes: Apollo with his love surrounded by the nine muses; Athena in armor springing from the head of Zeus; Jason with his golden fleece, and so on.

It is one of the charms of amateur theatricals— perhaps the greatest one—that we see our friends taking risks that we ourselves would not dare. On this evening the ladies whom we watched were risking more than

207

usual, for classical drapery often reveals more than it covers up, and these young women, ordinarily swathed from top to tie in layer upon layer of fabric, showed to us all, this night, that they were, some of them, formed as exquisitely as any Praxiteles marble. The men, too, revealed more than some people cared to see; I heard more than one murmur of disapproval as Apollo, his legs encased in what looked like dancer's tights, lounged amidst his bevy of beauties. After each scene a makeshift curtain was drawn while the next was arranged, and during these intervals we in the audience shifted uneasily on our spindly chairs and chatted back and forth—for since this was a quasi-civic function it was entirely a Boston crowd, and it had the air of a family gathering: everyone knew everyone else, they had known each other always. As the curtain was drawn (to warm applause) on the fourth scene (Demeter and Dionysus, portrayed by Isabel and a young man whom I did not know), I caught a glimpse of Avery. He was seated across the room with his parents, and so it was impossible for me to speak to him or even to catch his eye; but I was unnerved by the sour expression on his face, his unenthusiastic clapping, and I remembered his displeasure with Isabel for helping Mrs. Reed to organize the evening.

Afterward, when the *tableaux* were done and Mrs. Reed had made a graceful little speech asking her guests to patronize the orchestra during the coming season, the servants removed the chairs and the audience mixed and flowed as people do at a reception. Twice I tried to get to Avery, to speak to him—perhaps to deflect his annoyance at Isabel, if it seemed necessary—but I was prevented; people came up to speak to me and I could not maneuver myself away, and then, when I was free and looked around for him, he was not there—nor Isabel either.

"He's taken her home," said Mrs. Reed when I inquired. "I don't think he approved of our little effort. I told Ethel when they married that he looked a bit stodgy, but Isabel would have him, there was no stopping her. Well! If he fusses at her enough she'll have to give up socializing, poor dear—although I know she'd not like that, she'd wither away if she couldn't go to her parties. And she's just come out of confinement, she needs a bit of fun to take her out of herself."

I turned away from her with a sense of unease. It was unlike Isabel to leave so early; Avery must have insisted on it. Someone came up to speak to me then, and so my thoughts were momentarily distracted; but later, as my carriage trundled me home—down to the lowlands, as it were, from the Olympian heights of Beacon Hill—I thought of her again, and of him. What had he said to her? Or she to him?

Years later, when she had made me her confidante, she made particular mention of that night. "It was then," she said, "that he became for me not my husband but my enemy. He was trying to hurt me—to destroy me, to break me to fit a mold of his making. I never forgave him for that night."

They had, as I suspected, left Mrs. Reed's at Avery's insistence. As their coachman guided the horses down the steep slope of Mount Vernon Street, its slippery cobblestones made more treacherous this night by a pounding, blinding rain, Avery glanced at his wife's profile. She had seemed happy this evening—happier than he had seen her for months—and consequently he was annoyed with her. She never looked so for him, at home alone: it was only company that made her so—the presence of other people, the prospect of fast-flying conversation, testing her wits against theirs. Avery did not do well in such situations; he knew that he was not unintelligent, but he lacked the nimble mind required for repartee.

She did not speak to him or even seem to notice him. He wondered if she recalled his warning to her: that after this affair there would be no more—that he expected her to devote herself to him, their family, to the properly domestic concerns of every wife.

He cleared his throat, preparing to speak, but another glance at her face prevented him. She stared unseeing at the rain through the small side window of the carriage: she was physically beside him, but her thoughts were far away. He felt that if he spoke to her he would cause her to return against her will.

He felt hurt—offended. Why did she avoid him? Why was she not content? What drove her—compelled her always to seek amusement with other people? It was not natural, he thought: his wife was not a normal woman. And therefore it was his duty as a husband to teach her how to behave—yes, even now, when they had been married for more than a decade, with four children, a good house, a place in the world. Even now, he thought, she needed restraint and guidance.

They arrived to find the wet nurse feeding the baby. Despite the common use of substitutes, Avery thought that a woman should nurse her own child. His mother agreed with him and had frequently said so at each new arrival. He looked at his son's dark, downy skull. The child needs his mother, he thought. She should spend her time with him—with all of them. She has no notion of what her proper responsibilities are.

With an abrupt "Good night" he left the nurse and followed Isabel into their bedroom. She was undressing. Her little maid, who had just come down from Halifax a month or so previously, was laboring at the long row of tiny buttons down the back of Isabel's low-cut green bodice: the fourth time that evening that she had done so, since she, like the other ladies' maids, had been on duty all evening for the *tableaux*.

Avery watched them struggle: first the bodice, then the skirt, then the bustle, the petticoats, the chemise—and then the corset, a long whalebone-ribbed thing encasing her from bosom to hip, laced so tight that she was like a trussed carcass, as pliant as a block of wood.

They had glanced at him when he came in, but they took no notice of him now. Some men, perhaps, would have felt that they were intruding; they would have retreated, shy of witnessing a ritual so intimate—so thoroughly feminine. But Avery stayed. He watched his wife and her maid as a man who bred horses might have watched his stableboy groom a prize mare. He had no notion that he was intruding. If you asked him, he would have said that he was in his own house, his own bedchamber; he had paid for the floor under his feet, the

211

roof over his head, the clothing that covered his body. And for her clothing too, and for the wages of the maid who helped her into and out of them. Everything within his sight was his, and more beyond.

"Thank you, Elsie," said Isabel when at last she was free and stood wrapped in her soft, comfortable dressing gown. "Just put those away, and then you may go to bed. I'll take down my hair myself."

The maid dipped a curtsy and scurried away, grateful no doubt for an extra half hour's sleep. She slipped past Avery without looking up at him; masters—as opposed to mistresses—were distant, alien beings who were best avoided.

When the girl had gone Isabel sat at her mirror and rapidly began to remove the pins from her hair. She took off the matching switch, which gave the necessary fullness to the back; she brushed down the elaborate arrangement of tiny curls at the front and on top. Her hair was sticky from the pomade which held the curls in place. She paid no more attention to her husband than if he had been a servant: less, for servants needed watching, they needed direction. She was perfectly well aware of his presence: she ignored him deliberately. She was annoyed that he watched her—as if he were appraising me, she thought. She hoped that he would not speak, for then she would need to answer him and she wanted to be silent, to think of the evening just past. A splendid evening, Aunt Reed had said. Such success gave to the people who achieved it a certain standing—an authority. People would come to your next affair on the strength of it. She could invite anyone, now, and they would come to her. And, too, the notion of being a patroness of the arts gave one a certain cachet. Raising support for Major Higginson's musicians had much more éclat than getting up a purse for, say, Elinor's Poor Relief.

Thinking such pleasant thoughts, she had forgotten her husband; but now she looked into the mirror and saw him standing by the bed. He had taken off his jacket and removed his suspenders; he was unbuttoning his trousers, not bothering to turn away from her as he did so.

She paused for a moment, her silver-backed brush held high. She was aware of the sound of the rain beating against the windows. With her heart twisting with pain— she could feel it twisting, hurting her—she remembered a night when she had stood in such a downpour, waiting for Cushing. The rain had beaten on her, crushing her as if she had been a fragile blossom. She had been soaked— cold and wretched, wanting to stand forever in the drowning rain, not wanting to be rescued, not wanting to be taken back to her life to live without him.

But she had lived without him: all these years. And she must continue to do so. And the man in this room was not Cushing. This man was her husband, with all of a husband's rights. She shuddered; she was aware that he was watching her. He stood in his shirttails; he seemed to be waiting for something.

For her: he was waiting for her.

No, she thought. Please. I have just brought a child into the world, I cannot bear another. Not so soon. Not ever again.

The thought startled her, coming so clearly, so simply: never another child.

And therefore: never another submission to him, never another agonizing moment when she must endure what he did to her, the painful, humiliating act whereby he forced himself into her—never! He had no right to subject her to it, to all its consequences: months of illness, months of enforced solitude, the hours of agony to give birth, the danger of death.

He would insist on it to shackle her again: to keep her from society, to make of her a house slave.

I will not, she thought. I will not let him.

She closed her eyes. She heard the rain, she heard the voice in her mind. Never!

And then, as if from a great distance, she heard his voice summoning her. She did not respond. "Isabel," he said again; and when still she did not reply he went to her and put his hand on her shoulder. She started; she tried to shake him off but he held fast.

He was very strong—bigger and stronger than most men, strong enough to overpower almost anyone. She had no defense against him. Suddenly angry, he pulled her roughly to her feet and half lifted, half dragged her to the bed and threw her down. When she tried to escape him he held her wrist so tightly that she carried the mark for days. She cried out then, a little: and as she lay momentarily stunned he came roughly into her and she cried again, louder, so that a nightwalker in the house, overhearing, might have thought that she was being attacked.

As she was: but it was nothing that she could protest.

No judge, no jury would convict Avery Kittredge for what he did; he was acting within his rights, and she had no choice but to submit.

Roughly he came, and hard, his swollen member scraping her dryness, tearing at her, making a searing wound, insistent, thrusting, battering at her, invading her, wreaking destruction.

He sowed his seed in her: but it was not the seed of a child only. It was the seed of bitterness and hate, and of the beginning of her longing for revenge.

Two

That fall Perseus surrendered himself to his obsession.

My first hint of it had come around the time of Mason's birth—that is, in late August. I had met Cousin Sam Swift at a talking party in Chestnut Street, and after the evening's subject had been thoroughly explored—the Emersonian oversoul, as I recall—we were free to gossip among ourselves. Sam himself was a victim of twin obsessions, his orchids and his genealogies, but those were—how shall I say it? Wholesome? Ordinary? Not unexpected in gentlemen of his caste? I sensed as he spoke that he was trying to tell me that Perseus was in the grip of something quite different, although of course at the time I had no idea of what it was or to what lengths—what depths—it would carry him. Nor did Sam: he was simply giving voice, in his blunt and kindly way, to something that he wanted me to know.

"Saw your husband yesterday," he said. He smiled at me, his gold tooth gleaming. "In a bit of a picket on the Common. Did he mention it?"

"No."

"Ah. Well, then, perhaps I shouldn't—but it looked unpleasant there for a moment. You should speak to him, perhaps. He's a bit of an unworldly fellow, isn't he? Doesn't understand people."

"What happened?" I said. I did not want to hear a digression on my husband's shortcomings.

"Well—he saw a couple on the grass and tried to kick them up. And quick as a wink there was a nasty crowd around him, and he only just got away. I was walking right behind him, I was about to speak to him when it happened. He was lucky they didn't set on him—a lot of these foreigners don't know our ways, and they don't take kindly to interference. You might just give him a word to the wise. Couldn't hurt, and it might save him some embarrassment next time."

Later, in his diaries, I read his account of the incident.

At dust, it had been: just at twilight, the hour suspended between daylight and dark when the lights have begun to come on in the houses, the street lights beginning to glow. Perseus was making his way home from the offices of his Society—truly his, now, for he had recently been appointed director. It had been a difficult day with several minor crises and one major one involving a dispute between two powerful (that is to say, wealthy) members of the Board of Trustees. Either man, withdrawing support, would have seriously crippled the Society's work; a good deal of money was needed, and more would be needed in the future. And so he had negotiated all afternoon and into the evening between the warring factions, and now at last he was free to go home.

But such work never leaves a man free: Perseus felt that every waking moment was an opportunity to be seized, and so he was ever on the alert for signs of obscenity or corruption, of a weakening in the morals of his fellow citizens, of assaults on their virtue. An improper chromolithograph in a shop window, a theatrical production whose female members showed an ankle or a glimpse of shoulder, a bookseller who stocked a new novel with suggestive passages—all of these and more cried out for his attention, for suppression, lest their corrupting influence spread. He knew perfectly well that in the matter of shoulders and bosoms exposed he had only to go—for instance—to any evening entertainment patronized by the city's best families and he would see enough flesh to nauseate him. His own wife attended such affairs all the time; he could not prevent her. But he consoled himself with the thought that if the public sector were properly policed the private would take care of itself.

Tired from his worrisome day, hungry for his supper, barely conscious of the familiar, nagging pain behind his eyes which came to him so often that he noticed it only when it was not there, he crossed Tremont Street and stepped onto the Common, into the near darkness cast by the shadows of the tall old elms that lined the walkways. He trod the Long Path. All around him, walking, sitting on benches, reclining on the grass, were people who, like himself, had just been released from their day's work. In this brief time they sought an hour's respite in the park. Some people walked alone, and many more walked two and three together, separate little groups, some men, some women. But many were couples: a man and a woman, a boy and a girl. It was they who drew Perseus' attention.

Some of them sat side by side on the benches that lined the paths; some decorously apart, some very close. Occasionally he saw a man with his arm around the woman or holding her hand. But these, offensive as they were, were not the worst: for behind the benches, among the great elms towering over the greensward, he saw couples sitting on the grass, and some not even sitting, but lying full length, and some of these were so close together that they seemed one.

He felt the pain in his head begin to throb; with every step the impact of his well-shod foot on the ground sent a reverberation up through his body to his head, intensifying the pain so that he clenched his teeth to keep from crying out. The light faded nearly to darkness; he slowed, finally coming to a halt, peering into the gloom.

On the grass lay a man and a woman, their arms clasped around each other; they were, it seemed, kissing—but more than that, surely, for their bodies writhed like snakes, their soft moans—of pain? of pleasure?—were clearly audible.

Perseus stepped off the path and stood over them. They took no notice. He felt his stomach turn over; for a moment he feared that he would vomit and so he clenched his teeth harder still, controlling himself before he dared to speak.

"Get up!" he said; he heard his voice, hoarse and choked, coming painfully from his constricted throat.

They seemed not to have heard.

"Get up!" he said again, more loudly. "This is a public park. I will call the police!"

That word—"police"—seemed to penetrate. The man held still for a moment, and then he lifted himself half off the ground, extricating himself from his companion's embrace, and stared up at Perseus.

"*Polizia?*"

"Yes—the police! Now get up and be off!"

The man looked around. He saw no one in uniform. "*Va' via,*" he said. "*Lasciaci perdere!*" And once again he turned to the woman; she lay on her back, passive, watchful.

"*You* get away! How dare you come here to—to—"

Perseus was aware of a presence—several presences—at his side. It was fully dark now, with only the glimmer of an occasional lamp on a post.

"Trouble, mister?" A pale, thin face underneath a bowler hat tilted up at him: an Irish face, an Irish tongue.

"These people are a public disgrace," Perseus began, "and I insist—"

"They try to rob you?"

"No, but—"

"Then they're not makin' trouble?"

"They are engaging in disorderly, obscene—"

"Why don't you go along then?" The speaker was flanked by several companions; Perseus could not see their faces clearly but he was aware of their threat. The two on the ground made no move; they watched intently, probably, he thought, not understanding a word.

"I cannot tolerate—"

"Go along, mister." His opponents moved, crowding

220

offended by such sights as he had seen tonight.

Down Beacon Street past the Public Garden; across Arlington; on down Beacon to his house. He felt calmer now, soothed by the prospect of action; he felt strong, equal to his task.

I never told him what Cousin Sam had told me—naturally not, we did not have that kind of communication, he and I. And, as I see now, it would have done no good if I had; he was set on his course, nothing now would deflect him, for he had begun what he thought of as his mission. Certainly no word of mine would have stopped him.

In the nighttime, under the cover of the dark, he had begun to walk the streets of the city in neighborhoods well removed from Beacon Street: poor districts, slums where houses and tenements crowded close on each other and the ways were clogged with refuse and lights burned all night in dramshops and gambling places, and women lurked in doorways, poorly clothed against the cold, beckoning, calling to him. From time to time he saw a man like himself: well dressed, prosperous-looking, whose nervous glance betrayed him as an alien.

Many nights he walked until he was exhausted, unable to turn his back on what he saw, unable to put it out of his mind and go home, ranging through the city, discovering its nocturnal life, discovering what it was that he needed to do.

On a bitter night less than a week before Thanksgiving he made his way down a narrow street which led off Scollay Square. The wind tossed him back and forth as if he were a shuttlecock; once, like the women he stalked, him; he took a step backward. "That's it. Just go along." Another step, and then another. The men moved as one, forcing him back onto the path. He could no longer see the two lying on the ground.

They have taken the city, he thought: foreigners, strangers, invaders. Once this Common belonged to us. Now it is a breeding ground for crime—for unspeakable acts.

He thought to make one last protest, but the men stood around him in a tight circle. They did not touch him, did not press in, but he knew that if he moved back toward the couple on the grass they would prevent him—would lay hands on him, perhaps attack him. He was not afraid of the pain they might cause him, but he could not bear the thought of their hands touching his body, even through the protective fabric of his clothes.

He drew himself up. He was not a tall man but he had an intensity that gave him a certain presence. He jerked his chin at the ringleader; he took a step down the path. They understood, and parted to make way. He walked steadily on, not looking back; soon in any case he could not have seen more than the outlines of their dark shapes, the red glowing tips of their cigars.

The night wind cooled his perspiring face. He heard the faint steady thud of his feet hitting the ground; he felt a corresponding beat inside his chest, where his heart was.

A temporary defeat, he thought; he would take a resolution to the City Council: no loitering! He would organize a phalanx of watchmen—vigilantes for public decency. No right-thinking, taxpaying citizen ought to be he needed to shelter in a doorway and catch his breath and burrow more deeply into his fur-lined greatcoat. He thought fleetingly of a warm coal fire and a glass of hot, sweet tea, but that vision did not hold him. Something here led him on: something that perhaps he would find in the dark, in the black, torturous byways down which he scurried.

From time to time he glimpsed his prey: a shawled figure gliding by, or huddled, like himself, in a sheltering alcove. He peered at them, dreading solicitation but driven to go on. He never answered when they spoke: never acknowledged them. They were creatures of the night, of another world. When day came they would retreat, retire, resting themselves against the coming of the dark.

What did they do? If he stopped, if he consented to go with one of them, what would happen to him? He shuddered, not from the cold without but from the fear inside himself. What drove men to them, what did they have to sell that men were so eager to buy?

He did not know: could not bear to know. It had to do with that act of which he had warned his wife on their wedding night. Perhaps it was the same act, he did not know. His mother had cautioned him against it: had, weeping, made him promise that he would never perform it. He had assented blindly, not knowing what it was that he assented to: only that it was something wrong, something foul, something that on his honor he must never do.

He came to a crossway and stopped. Soon he would be near the wharves. He wanted no encounters with drunken sailors. Only last month a respectable gentleman had been accosted there, beaten and robbed and left for dead. The matter had been hushed up to save his family's feelings.

He felt a movement at his side. He turned to see a woman standing next to him. She was small and slight—a child, he thought, she is only a child and quite pretty. She had not yet been soiled and hardened by the horrors of her life.

He started to brush past her and then he stopped, he did not know why. Something in her eyes . . . ?

"How old are you, child?"

"Fifteen, sir."

Fifteen! And even so she lied, she was hardly more than twelve.

"Will you come, sir?"

Her features were delicate, her eyes large and seemingly innocent—what had they seen?

His attention was distracted, then, by a movement in a doorway beyond. She followed his gaze, and when she looked at him again her face was frightened.

"Who is that?" he said.

"He—he brought me here," she said in a voice hardly more than a whisper.

"What do you mean, he brought you?"

"He took me up in Portsmouth and promised me good wages here. But I haven't done so well. He said—he said he'd try me one more week, and then—"

"And then?"

"I don't know, sir. He gives me a place to sleep, he feeds me, but he says I have to bring in my share or he'll let me go."

Her "employer"! As base, as wicked as these women were, surely the men who so exploited them were worse—foul beyond belief!

"Please, sir—"

"Never mind." He hesitated. He could not go with her: the Society had strict rules, and investigators who frequented brothels went in pairs. But the Society was not in his thoughts. He acted alone now, on his own, privately; and he experienced a rush of feeling that he had never experienced before, as if his heart had melted just a little. Why did she move him so? She did, undeniably. He felt pity for her—concern, compassion, any of those things.

He reached for his pocket purse and took out two dollar pieces. "Here," he said. He took her hand and pressed the coins into it. "Take these. Try to keep one for yourself. I will come back when I can. If he harms you, I want you to tell me."

She was too surprised to reply. He left her standing in the dark street holding the coins; then he hurried away before he changed his mind and snatched them back.

Three

Despite my promise to Avery I had seen little of Ned that autumn, and so it was pleasant to go to Thanksgiving dinner at the Januarys' and visit with him. Leighton was, as usual, in New York with his wife's family, but all the others were there: Curtis and Grace, Isabel and Avery and their children, the baby, Mason, asleep upstairs; Elinor, Ned, Mrs. Roberts Reed, Cousin Sam Swift. The children scampered in and out, Charlotte torn between being grown-up and dull, or being a child and enjoying herself. I watched her as she spoke to Ned: he paid close attention to her, and nodded from time to time, and made occasional replies in a respectful way, not like the jolly condescension with which many adults greeted children's remarks.

Cousin Sam followed my gaze. "Charlotte's a regular beanpole," he said. "She'll have her father's height if they don't watch out."

I knew what he meant: tall women were at a disadvantage, since no man wanted a wife who towered over him. Excessive weight might be discounted, of course, if a woman were sufficiently beautiful; but Charlotte would never be that. The child had not even a clever wit to distract people from her physical liabilities: she was slow-spoken, somewhat shy. As Isabel had said to me more than once, a good fortune was Charlotte's only hope; Isabel was, I knew, counting on Avery to provide it.

"Ned is very good with her," I said. "He doesn't tolerate fools among his own friends, since he's so clever himself, but he has endless patience with her."

As I watched the two of them, I was aware that Cousin Sam had turned to look at me.

"D'you know what the word is in State Street?" he said.

"No."

"They say he wants to leave the firm."

Isabel, joining us, had heard his last words. "What—and go on his own?" she said. "How could he?"

"No. I don't think so. He has no taste for it, they say. He wants to leave, period."

"But what will he do? How will he live?"

Sam shrugged. "Perhaps he'll sell some of his poems," he said, smiling to show that he spoke in jest.

"Poems! He can't make a living selling poems."

"True. But perhaps he will have to learn that lesson on his own. Your father was very angry, they say. With Curtis in the law, and Leighton flitting around New York with his heiress—and all good luck to him, he's doin' the right thing but that's no help to Asa—that left Ned to carry on with January & Co."

"And now he doesn't want to. Poor Father!"

"Poor Ned, it looks like. There's plenty of young men glad to have that chance, and your father'll not have difficulty finding 'em. But if Ned goes it'll be for good. Asa won't take him back."

"No. He won't."

Asa January stood across the room, deep in conversation with Avery. He looked old, I thought: tired. He was about sixty-five: not a great age but not young either. Naturally he wanted someone to come along in the firm, preferably one of his sons. His gray hair was brushed carefully over the top of his head to cover his baldness; his face, normally dour and closed, seemed more so today because it had become so heavily lined, the cheeks sunken, the jowls beginning to sag.

Ned, by contrast, radiated health and youth and the joy of life. It was not the least of his charm that he did not exhibit the bored, affected air of so many young men—an attitude especially common, for some reason, among boys who were still at college. Ned had never succumbed to it. He was always polite, of course, and even kind; but, more than that, he had a childlike curiosity about the world and all its wonders that gave him an endearing charm. If you offered him a bit of new information or the tentative phrasing of an idea, he did not put you off with a bored drawl or a smart remark: he was genuinely glad to know what you thought, and he always wanted to know more.

As we sat at table that Thanksgiving Day and submitted to the relentless succession of courses—thick and thin soups, scalloped oysters, roast duck as well as turkey, rice birds and cranberries and salads—I was

aware that Asa January said very little; and, more, that
there lurked behind his black, hard expression a kind of
smoldering rancor, if so chilly a man could be said to
smolder. It seemed that Mrs. January had the same
thought; although she was usually tranquil, I noticed
that now she looked often at her husband in an anxious
way and directed frequent pleasantries to him to which
he seldom replied.

It was Ned himself who sparked the explosion, and I
am not sure that he did not do so on purpose. During a
lull in the talk he leaned forward to speak directly to
Grace, who sat across from him, and said, "I am sorry
about Professor Longfellow."

The poet so beloved by all New England—by all the
world, for that matter—had recently died. Grace, on her
mother's side, had been a distant—very distant—
connection: hardly, I thought, close enough for Ned to
make such a point of it.

But Grace understood him. She had been enormously
proud of that thin thread that linked her, however
tenuously, to genius; she was fond of reading aloud, and
Longfellow's verses had been particular favorites of hers.
"Thank you, Ned," she said, with just the proper amount
of sorrowful tremor in her voice. "We are all the poorer
for his loss."

I felt a twinge of annoyance. Longfellow might have
been a household god in most New England families, but
I always found him boring. To the best of my
recollection, Ned had shared my feelings.

Asa January stared at his son, ready to take up the
unspoken challenge that Ned had offered. "I did not

know you were such an admirer of Professor Longfellow," he said. "But then, it appears that there are a
great many things about you that I did not know." He
looked around the table. I caught Cousin Sam's eye; he
frowned slightly and almost imperceptibly shook his
head. I understood: any attempt to head off the coming
storm would only make worse damage.

"Since you have gone to the trouble of introducing
Professor Longfellow's name," Asa January continued,
"perhaps you would be good enough to recite something
of his work for us."

And now, perhaps, Ned lost his nerve a little. "Father,
I don't think—"

"Yes. A few lines. We are dull, money-grabbing folk
here. We need some nourishment for our spirits as well
as all this food for our bodies."

At this Grace blushed bright red—poor, homely, rich,
barren Grace! "Bodies" was not a word to be used in
polite conversation. She threw an appealing glance to
Curtis, but he chose not to see it.

"You do not wish to recite Professor Longfellow?" Asa
January went on relentlessly. "Very well, then. Let us
hear something of your own. It will be equally as good, I
have no doubt—better!"

If I could have entered his thoughts at that moment I
would, no doubt, have heard something like this: these
faces around the table were his family. For years he had
fed them, and supported them, and made a name for
himself in which they could all take pride. He felt that he,
in turn, had a right to expect certain behavior from them:
no scandal, no disappointment. And by and large they

had done him well: the three eldest had made good marriages, and Elinor—well, Elinor was eccentric, but eccentricity had a long and honorable place in New England. He was not unduly worried about her.

But Ned—ah, what was wrong with the boy? He had always been different from the others: a seemingly normal child who was not normal at all—who indulged in the secret vice; who spent long hours alone, scribbling; and who now, as a young man needing to make his way in the world, spent more time with his so-called artistic cronies than he did attending to his work.

We sat silent. We dared not speak; we hardly dared breathe. Thank heaven, I thought, the children have been taken upstairs. Victoria, at five, would surely have created some disturbance, even if Arthur and Charlotte had remained quiet.

"Well, Ned?"

Ned glanced up at his father and looked away again without reply.

"I am waiting."

Suffocating silence. The creak of the dumbwaiter, delivering the next course, was as loud as an alarm bell.

"Edward Arthur January."

Ned looked up. Their eyes met and held.

He knows what is to happen, I thought, else he could not be so calm. I felt an overpowering sense of dread. Something awful was going to happen, I did not know what, and we must all sit here and wait. There is nothing that we can do to prevent it.

"This young man," said Asa January, addressing us all but looking only at his son, "has announced to me that he does not want to continue his position at January's. He says that he wants to be free—whatever that means. I have always thought that money brings freedom, but perhaps the younger generation sees things differently. And not only does he want to be free. He has a more specific wish than that. He wants to be free in order to make a literary career. A literary career!"

Stop, I thought, please do not do this. Do not shame him—

"And so now he will recite for us. We will be able to hear the wonderful work that has taken him away from the firm, that is more important than earning a living. Go on, Ned, let us hear it."

Silence: no one spoke, no one had any idea of what to say. We were horribly embarrassed, of course, at Asa's outburst, despite the fact that men were allowed considerable latitude in such matters. Many husbands and fathers were tyrants who ruled their households by constant displays of temper; the Januarys were fortunate, and knew that they were, to have Asa, whose anger, while genuine enough on occasion, was not always bubbling just beneath the surface ready to erupt at any moment.

"If you have nothing prepared, write something. Compose a poem for us here—an ode to Thanksgiving." And to his wife: "Ring the bell for Mary. Tell her to bring pen and paper."

Mrs. January stared at him, unable to believe that he meant what he said. Then she picked up the silver and crystal handbell and rang it, sharply, three times, and gave the instruction to the maid, and waited, frozen, until she returned. "Give them to Mr. Ned," she said, and said no more until Mary had left the room. One lived with one's servants as a matter of course, one acted out one's life under their watchful eyes, but some things were too painful for even a servant to see.

Mary closed the door behind her with a solid *thump*. No one spoke. Mrs. January watched her son. Ned sat with his eyes downcast, no expression on his face. Cook will wonder what is wrong, I thought. Mary will tell her that we are in difficulty, but she does not know why.

"Now do as I say," said Asa January. It was as if, confronted by the refusal of this last, youngest offspring to obey him, he was focusing on Ned all the authority, all the iron January will, all the displeasure withheld over the years, anger at one or another of his family, that he had not expressed. We could feel his anger: it permeated the room, battering at us, driving us to seek shelter—where?

Suddenly Ned moved, startling me, startling us all. He pushed back his chair; he stood; and then without a word he turned and left the room.

And after a moment Mrs. January lifted the crystal bell again and summoned Mary to come in; and we finished our Thanksgiving dinner.

Four

The old year went out and the new came in; and it seemed, for a while, that my life would continue as before. It was only a half lie: a shadow of an existence, a dull play in which I was trapped, a captive to my part.

And then, one snowy night, I encountered Otis Whittemore.

I remember that it had been a strange, disquieting day, marred by an unpleasant incident. As I was returning in our little sleigh from an afternoon round of calls I saw a crowd of men and boys at the corner of Boylston and Arlington streets, just by the Garden, and when I saw why they had gathered I ordered the coachman to stop. He pulled as near as he could to the snow-banked curb and promptly, on my order, helped me down. I made my way back to the corner. There, panic-stricken and in great pain, was a poor horse that had gone down: struggle though he might, he could not rise. He had been unhitched from his heavy wagonload, but his shoes were not sharpened properly, and he could not get his footing in the icy, rutted street. The driver, a heavy, stupid-looking man, was beating the animal mercilessly. No one in the crowd moved to stop him.

"Wait!" I cried. I pushed my way through to the front. The horse lay struggling on his side, his dull coat covered with sweat, his eyes wide with panic. *Thwack! Thwack!* Again and again the driver brought down his whip. Its cruel marks ribbed the animal's side. He paid no attention to me, and so I caught his arm as he raised the whip. "No!" I cried. "Wait—don't hit him!"

For a moment I thought that he would turn the whip on me, but then he roughly shook me off and brought it down again on the shuddering animal.

"*Stop!*" I seized the whip and tried to wrest it from his hand but he was too strong for me and I could not. By this time my coachman, fearing for my safety, had come to my aid; I heard guffaws and catcalls from our audience, and I realized that we were badly outnumbered. There was, of course, no policeman to be seen.

"Get away, lady. This here horse is mine, no business of yours."

"He cannot get up, can't you see that? Why do you beat him?"

"He'll get up if I have to kill him! Now go on, lady! He's my property, I'll do with him as I please. *Get* up, you!" And once again he turned on the helpless beast with a fury.

"You *will* not—" Nearly beside myself with pity and terror, I flung myself at him and wrestled his arm down. I heard the jeering voices of the men but I did not care. It seemed to me that somehow I must stop that torture. I was aware that my coachman was grappling with the driver too, and then suddenly I was wrenched free, thrown down, and my coachman dumped unceremoniously beside me. The landscape tilted and righted itself again as I struggled to my feet. The driver towered over us, clenching his whip. "Get away, now," he said, and I heard murder in his voice. "Y' damned interferin' busybody. Get away and don't let me see yer face again!"

My coachman was at my side; I felt his hand under my arm as he turned me away. Tears of helpless rage froze on my face as I stumbled toward my sleigh and I heard another terrible blow fall on the trapped and helpless beast. I felt one with him: we were both prisoners, he and I.

I had taken that year, as I always did, a season's subscription to the Hunnewell lectures. When I arrived home, badly shaken, I looked at my calendar and saw that one of them was to be given that night. I did not want to go. I went directly to my room and ordered tea and had my maid unlace me. I lay on my chaise before the fire, still trembling, still enraged, my hands shaking so I could hardly compose the letter which I wrote to the Society for the Prevention of Cruelty to Animals. It seemed an exercise in futility: what could they do?

I gave up after a time. I drank my tea and nibbled at a slice of pound cake and stared into the dancing flames in the hearth. I felt drained—without the energy even to go down to dinner, much less to dress myself to go out into the bitter night to hear a lecture by someone unknown to me. The image of the downed horse hovered before my eyes; I could not rid myself of him. Poor beast—poor beast! After a while I dozed. When I awoke, half an hour later, I listened for some sound of life in the house but I heard none. I might have been alone, not even a servant to hear me.

I shivered; I pulled myself up from my chaise and went out into the hall. I peered over the banister. From below I heard faint sounds of activity: the maid setting out the dining room for the evening meal. I would, no doubt, dine alone, for Perseus as often as not was late or absent altogether. Afterward I would be alone still, unless I chose to attend a reception at Mrs. Graham's, which I did not care to do, or unless I went to the lecture. That, at least, would have the advantage of putting me among my fellow human beings without requiring me to talk to anyone beyond the usual pleasantries, for while I did not want solitude, neither did I want extended conversation.

And so I went, that night, to hear of the adventures of a man who had lived for a year and more in the frozen wastes of Seward's Folly—Alaska—and who had come now to tell us about it, and to earn, in the bargain, enough money to return.

The hall was crowded when I arrived, but I found a seat at the back of the room between an elderly woman and a large, wheezing man in a fuzzy gray tweed cape. He turned a keen eye on me as I settled myself but he had no chance to speak because in the next moment a gasp exploded from the audience as if from one throat. The speaker had made his entrance onto the platform, but hardly in the usual way, for he had backed onto the stage leading with two hands a recalcitrant, outlandish figure who uttered small cries of apprehension and whose strangely booted feet seemed rooted to the floor, thus compelling its guide to pull it bodily along.

It was surely as weird an apparition as ever confronted a Boston audience, that figure: encased in a brown leather hooded garment with a fringe of fur around the face, the face itself as brown as the hood, a round, wizened, hardly human face, transfixed with terror as it was forced to confront this sea of other faces, all white, all equally transfixed—in fascination, in total disbelief.

"That's Whittemore," rumbled my tweedy neighbor. "Always has a surprise up his sleeve. Ha! No one'll go to sleep this time!" (For there were, alas, occasional dull speakers in the series.)

The lecturer had at last deposited his exotic companion in a chair beside the lectern, and he waited now while a gentleman from the lecture board introduced him: "Professor Otis Whittemore and his companion, a member of the Esquimau people."

A polite applause came from those of the audience who were sufficiently recovered from their shock to pound their hands together. Whittemore acknowledged it with a slight bow; and then, with a reassuring pat on the arm of the creature beside him, he began to speak.

I do not remember what he said exactly, though I know the sense of it because later, many times, he told me of his adventures. Rather, I remember my impression of him as a man: tall and strong and beautiful in a rough, wild, craggy way, even as the land he described. His deep, resonant voice filled the room and held us spellbound; his strong hand seized the lectern and rocked it back and forth; his tanned, windburned face came alive with the excitement of what he had lived, what he wanted to tell us. His audience was composed of staid, safe, irreproachably proper people who never would have dared what he dared: he was an adventurer, a man who challenged life, who took on the world and all its risks and who until now at least had won. He had been in Africa, the program notes said, exploring for the King of the Belgians; and in the East Indies among the headhunters. He seemed outsized—too large, too vital to be comprehended by this audience of dry, careful New Englanders who never risked more than they could comfortably afford to lose, and whose idea of a wilderness adventure was a trip to a hunting lodge in the Adirondacks.

When he had finished what he had to say and had managed to get his Esquimau onto its feet to present it to the audience, he was again rewarded with applause, considerably warmer now.

"One day he won't come back from wherever," said my neighbor. "Boston winter's cold enough for me, let alone goin' to that Godforsaken, freezin'—why, it's Mrs. Motley, isn't it?"

I had half pretended not to hear him, since it is dubious etiquette at best to talk to strange men in a public place. But now I looked at him more closely and I recognized his sharp, shrewd eyes and the canny smile between the mustache and beard that covered the lower part of his face. He was an artist—a painter whose work, a little landscape, I had purchased a month or so ago.

"Farnsworth Bowditch, ma'am. We met at Dresser's Gallery." He gave a sudden grin. "I've been livin' off your fee ever since I got it, I don't mind tellin' you."

"It wasn't so very much," I said, laughing, remember-

239

ing our haggling. "You are a frugal man if you could live on that amount all this time."

"I live well enough," he said. I felt his keen scrutiny; I felt that he was dissecting me, reducing me to planes and lines and masses of color—looking to see how he might get me (or his vision of me) onto canvas. We had by this time begun to make our way out of the crowded hall; glancing about, I saw the faces surrounding us. Many seemed a bit dazed still—not quite recovered from the speaker's revelations. Bowditch turned to me and took my hand. "You must come to see me at my studio," he said. "It's nothing grand but it suits me well enough. I'm having a few people in tomorrow afternoon. Any time after three. One forty-nine Tremont Street. Come along and see for yourself how I do." And, with a friendly nod, he took his departure.

I smiled to myself. Strange, abrupt man! Rough-edged, like his painting: a small square snow scene of the Public Garden. Despite the thick layers of paint seemingly laid on with a palette knife, the canvas had looked a fragile thing, almost translucent: it held a glowing, shimmering whiteness that showed all the beauty of the snowy landscape while intimating one of its dangers—none of the frozen death that snow can bring, nothing of the bleak, barren white wasteland that Otis Whittemore would reveal to us a few weeks later.

The next afternoon, prompted by my curiosity, I set off across the Public Garden and the Common to Bowditch's studio. I have walked that route many hundreds of times over the years, and I never tire of it:

the formal curves of the walkways in the Garden, the miniature suspension bridge over the lagoon, the swan boats in warm weather, ice skaters in cold; and coming out onto the larger, emptier spaces of the Common, seeing the line of red brick houses ascending Beacon Hill to its summit, to Bulfinch's golden dome.

When I arrived at Bowditch's place I found a large and cluttered room filled with a noisy, animated crowd. In the rear, behind a tattered curtain, were his living arrangements: a lumpy bed, a table and chair, a cracked basin and ewer, a small stove. The greater portion of the space was given over to his work: the walls were lined with paintings, and in several places the canvases were stacked eight and ten together on the floor. An easel and a small sitter's platform occupied the center; to one side was a large, round, paint-splattered table, filled now with plates of food and bottles of cheap wine. Someone had brought in a small pot of straggling ivy; it sat forlornly in the midst of the food and drink, looking as out of place as I felt.

For this was a very different crowd from my usual companionship: other artists, and journalists, and women wearing face paint. Bowditch came to greet me; despite his mock ferocity I felt that he was kindly disposed toward me—as well he should be, I thought, since I am one of his few patrons.

"Splendid!" he said. "Hoped you'd come, couldn't be sure—" He crushed my hand in greeting and, without letting go, waded into the crowd, pulling me behind. From time to time he stopped to fling a name at me;

241

sometimes the owner of the name would turn and smile and nod, sometimes not. I was aware that some curious glances were thrown my way: I obviously did not belong here, despite the fact that my money helped to pay what was surely a minuscule rent.

At last we came to a quiet corner where stood perhaps half a dozen people. To my surprise, Ned was among them.

"Marian! What a pleasant surprise! You are expanding your circle of acquaintances, I see."

Bowditch beamed at us. "All the best people, m'boy, all the best. Now here, Mrs. M., is someone you'd like to meet. You heard him last night, you and I together, and now here he is in person, to speak—Mr. Whittemore, Mrs. Motley—the lady has a fine eye, Otis, so be careful, she'll snatch up some of those artifacts of yours before you know."

The man to whom he spoke had been deep in conversation with a fluffy-headed woman standing close by his side; he half turned from her now, as if reluctant to be interrupted but willing to humor Bowditch's insistence.

I had often read, in frivolous novels, of that magical moment when strangers meet. They fall in love on the spot, they feel themselves slipping, careening off the edge, into the abyss . . .

And so it was with me—with both of us. There was an awkward little pause after Bowditch introduced us: Otis Whittemore disentangled himself from his companion and turned, automatically polite, to take my hand. The room was filled with people, but we might have been alone. I heard his voice; I heard mine reply. I felt as though I had suddenly awakened from a long sleep—or perhaps I had fallen into a dream, I did not know. I saw only him, and I knew that I had never seen any man before, that there and then I was given sight, given feeling: given life.

Five

Love is largely wasted on the young, I think: they have not lived long enough to appreciate it.

One needs to have been without love to savor it fully when it comes; one needs to have known the void in one's life, to welcome the lover who comes to fill it.

Otis Whittemore came to me the day after Bowditch's reception. It was a dreary day, raining and cold. He arrived shortly after two, long before calling hours: and it was by this fact as much as anything in his behavior that he revealed himself. He wanted to see me alone; conventional proprieties were not in question, for he was not a conventional man. He was an adventurer, a man who looked at a map and said, "I will go there, I will conquer that." And for him, I suppose, I was as much *terra incognita* as any blank space on a cartographer's chart.

Of course I could have sent him away, I could have said that I was not at home. By admitting him, I revealed as much as he. I rose and put out my hand; he took it and held it for a moment and then raised it to his lips. I felt their pressure on my skin, their soft warmth.

"I was afraid that you would not be at home," he said. "Bowditch says that you are much in demand, you are invited everywhere."

"I am invited, yes. I do not always go."

"But you went to him yesterday."

"Yes."

"You are one of his—ah—patrons."

I laughed then. "I have bought only one thing—there, near the window."

"He is convinced that he is a genius. So you may turn a profit one day."

"I bought it because I liked it. Not for speculation."

"What else do you like?"

I did not understand at first; accustomed as I was to the meaningless pleasantries of Boston gentlemen (Cousin Sam Swift always excepted, of course), I was not prepared to deal with his directness.

"Tell me about yourself," he said.

"Perhaps we should sit—"

"Yes. Of course. Forgive me. I spend most of my life in uncivilized places. When I return I often find that my manners need repair."

We sat, then, facing each other across the fire. I was intensely aware of myself—and even more of him. I felt my rising excitement and I did not know how to control it; worse, I did not want to. Let it come, I thought—oh, let it!

Love, they call it: the poets and singers who celebrate its joys and sorrows. Or perhaps it was only animal passion: how could I love someone I did not know?

We talked for a long time that afternoon, and when we had done and it was time for him to go, he embraced me, and I let him, I did nothing to prevent him, for this was our time, now, and we must take it. I felt his strength; I felt his desire, and I knew that it matched my own. We stood alone in that quiet room, that quiet house, and we might have been alone in the universe: there was only the soft hissing of the fire, the gentle, insistent ticking of the ormolu mantel clock. Only that, and the throbbing heart that pounded in my ears—and it was his heart that I heard, as agitated as my own.

"Tonight I must meet with Mr. Dodd, who has promised to underwrite my next expedition," he said. "But tomorrow—"

"Yes," I said. Not with this man would I be coy, conventionally cool. It was as if we knew that we would have little time, and so from our first moment together we shared an unspoken agreement to seize every chance.

He named a small restaurant off Washington Street, and I agreed to meet him there. Then he went away into the rain and I returned to my chair by the fire. I told the maid that I would receive no other callers; I sent a note to Mrs. Rendell that I was indisposed and would be unable to attend her reception that evening. I wanted to hear no other voice but his; I wanted to be alone to remember every word, every gesture, the feel of his arms around me, his face pressed to my hair.

Madness—yes! I hardly knew him. I might be compromised—ruined, outcast. I did not care. This was my chance, my turn to seize the golden ring. I would not let it pass by.

Six

We had a brilliant season that winter, with more receptions and balls and amateur theatricals than anyone could remember, and sleighing parties and weekend gatherings in the great suburban estates as far away as Manchester and Magnolia on the North Shore, and Milton to the south. Night after night the avenues of the Back Bay resounded with the clatter of carriages; day after day an army of dressmakers paraded in and out of the mansions which lined those same avenues, carrying bolts of cloth and sacks of new dresses and thanking Providence, no doubt, for the sudden upsurge in the city's social life.

In March, Isabel, nearly six months' gone with child, gave a reception for Lady Rathmore. She was the real thing, that lady: distantly connected to the Queen, her blood certifiably blue and gratifyingly ancient. She was to be for two weeks the houseguest of Mrs. Tolland Lyman, whose large new house on Commonwealth Avenue was hardly large enough to accommodate her lady's retinue. When the visit was announced shortly after the New Year, there had been an immediate scramble not only for invitations to meet the lady but for the chance to entertain her.

"Mrs. Lyman will decide who does what," said Isabel. "Somehow I must find a way to convince her that what I will do will be better than anyone else."

I remembered Avery's displeasure at her involvement with Mrs. Reed's *tableaux*. "What does Avery think?" I said.

"Avery!" She dismissed him with a shrug. Despite her apparent blooming health, her face had a worried, distracted expression—no doubt caused, I thought, by her ambition in the matter of Lady Rathmore. "Avery will do as I tell him to do," she said.

"I am glad to hear it. I thought that he was unhappy—"

"*He* is unhappy!" She blazed out at me; she bolted from her chair and walked the length of the room (we were in my front parlor) and back again before she could trust herself to speak calmly. "Marian, look at me."

I did so. She wore a garnet-colored dress of fine merino wool trimmed in black braid and jet buttons; a large bustle protruded behind. Her hair was done in the latest fashion, tight curls on top and a large, twisted coil at the nape of her neck. From a long gold chain on her bosom hung a small watch; gold gleamed at her ears and wrists, and shiny black kid boots shod her small feet. Her face was plump but beautiful still, the wide January brow above the deep-set eyes, the small heart-shaped lower portion set off by her rosebud mouth.

"What do you see?"

"Near perfection." I smiled; to my dismay, her face suddenly went rigid and I saw that she was using all her strength to stay calm, not to burst into tears.

"Isabel!" I sprang up, I rushed to her and took her in my arms. Her head came just to my shoulder. For a moment she rested against me, burying her face against me. I felt that her stiff, corseted body would sag to the floor if I did not support her. "What is it, dearest—what is wrong?"

Her voice came from the depths of my gray cashmere bodice. "Another child!" she said; even so muffled, her voice was so filled with despair that I did not at first know how to reply.

"There," I murmured. "There, there—"

She pulled away from me; her face was hard, dry-eyed, not the trace of a tear upon her porcelain skin.

"It is his fault," she said. "If it were not for his selfishness, I would not be forced to suffer so. I will not be able to go into society for months—*months!*—and it is his fault, he is to blame, and so he will allow me to do as I please until then, I will have a reception every night if I choose and he will not deny me. And when this child is born—"

She turned away, but not before I saw deep color flood her face. "I will not have anóther," she said.

"But how—?"

"There are ways. I don't know what, but there are ways. Pussie told me to ask Dr. Slocomb. He would know, she said."

Pussie Mifflin, at whose garden party my brother had met his death, had married an Englishman—not a title—

who was reputed to be fast-living. She spent much of her time abroad; recently, however, she had been in Boston to see her family for the holidays. Her husband had not accompanied her.

Isabel recovered herself quickly, that day; and shortly afterward other callers came; Pussie herself was the first. She was as pretty, pink and gold and white, as I remembered her; no doubt as a result of living abroad she had a certain indefinable air of sophistication, but she was as friendly as ever and never gave a hint that she thought we, remaining in Boston, existed in a backwater.

"I called around for you," she said to Isabel, settling herself on the sofa by the fire, "and they said you'd come here. I have something for you." She handed Isabel a small parcel. "Go on—open it. Marian might find it interesting too." She smiled at me as if we shared a secret.

Isabel unwrapped it. It was a purple-bound book. "*Confessions*, by Lady X," she read. "Pussie—what on earth? Do you want me to become a devotee of immoral literature?"

"Hardly," laughed Pussie. "But this one will have a special interest for you, I think. It came out in England just before I left. After I read it I went at once to buy a copy for you, since I knew I was coming home."

I watched as Isabel turned the clumps of uncut pages. "What is it about?" she said. "There seems to be a hero called Crawford, but who is Lady X?"

"She is a real person," said Pussie. "The author—who is a man, by the way—simply used that pseudonym, since of course he could not use his real name, but he has

written what is common knowledge all over London. But
Lady X isn't important. Crawford is. His adventures with
Lady X will simply make your hair curl. The point is,
everyone swears that everything in the book is true—
absolutely true. And Crawford is based on someone who
used to live in Boston. He has lived in London since
before I went there. When I met him—oh yes, I know
him—he reminded me that we had met before, right here
in Boston. He knows many of the people I do."

Isabel looked slightly wary, as if she were afraid that
the book would blow up in her face. I remembered that
only half an hour before she had been nearly distraught.

"You may remember him," Pussie went on. "He was
fair-haired—he still is, for that matter—with the most
brilliant blue eyes I've ever seen. Very handsome in a
Byronic way. Well—no—that's too dandified. He's
rougher-looking than that. I think he's the most
devastating man I've ever met. Obviously Lady X agrees
with me, as you will see when you read the book. His
name is Lawrence Cushing. Did you know him?"

There was a moment's silence, during which time the
hiss and crackle of the fire sounded very loud. I hardly
dared look at Isabel; I tried to find some light,
conversational thing to say, but my tongue was so stiff in
my mouth that I would not have been able to speak in any
case. Nor did I dare to pour more tea for any of us lest I
slop the liquid onto the carpet and betray myself in that
way.

At last Isabel replied. "Yes," she said. Her voice was
calm, very soft. "Yes, I believe I met him once or twice."

"I thought it would amuse you to see how a local boy

made good," said Pussie. "Let me know what you think of it." She turned to me. "This is an exquisite house, Marian. When did you buy it? And where did you get that lovely little painting of the Garden?"

Isabel left soon after; and then I met Otis Whittemore, and in the weeks that followed, my life was so overwhelmed by him that I had little enough time even for Isabel. I was more than a little curious about Lady X's *Confessions,* but I hardly dared ask her if she had read it, and she did not volunteer to tell me. She was, I knew, heavily involved in preparations for her reception for Lady Rathmore; and I knew, too (because she made it a point to come by to tell me), the way in which she had managed to secure Mrs. Lyman's permission to entertain that eminent personage.

"It was Cousin Sam's idea," she said, her eyes gleaming with delighted triumph. "Everyone was pestering Mrs. Lyman unmercifully, of course, and why should she choose me over them? But Cousin Sam did a clever thing. He looked up the Lyman tree—she's a Bagwell, and her mother was a Winfield, and his mother was a Wigglesworth—and what do you think? Sam discovered a connection in 1697. A Cunningham married a Winfield! And in the next generation they brought in a Wigglesworth, a brother of one who is in Father's tree. Mrs. Lyman was delighted—or at least she said she was— and at once she gave me the evening."

And so now, on the day before the great day—the day when Lady Rathmore would hold her little court in Isabel's drawing room—I walked around to Exeter Street to help with last-minute preparations. It was a gloomy afternoon in late March, the winter with us still, spring seeming far away. I had had a letter from Otis Whittemore that morning; he would return to Boston in two days, he said (for he was often called away to meet with would-be sponsors). I carried it folded in my reticule; from time to time, as I walked, I took it out and read it over again. I had a stack of his letters locked into my chifferobe; I had brought today's with me because I could not bear to leave it behind, it comforted me to have it near. When I had memorized it I would put it away with the others.

Isabel's stolid downstairs maid admitted me and I went directly upstairs. As I passed the drawing room I saw the men from the florist's arranging tubs of trees and pots of flowering shrubs; the odor of the blossoms—gardenias, mock orange—mingled with the smell of meat and pastries drifting up from the kitchen.

I found Isabel in her room submitting to a final, painstaking fitting of her gown. It was a wonderful thing, that gown: pale blue silk under petit-point lace picked out with pearls across the low-cut bosom and tiny bouquets of silk roses holding back the overskirt over the bustle; it had a three-foot detachable train. But Isabel had been measured for it two months previously, and she had been powerless to control her swelling waistline in the interval. And of course she could not tell Mrs. Denby the reason for her change in measurement. The news would have been all over Boston in twenty-four hours, and Isabel would have been ostracized thenceforth. A woman within three months of childbed did not—could not—go into society.

"If Madam will excuse me," the seamstress was saying as I went in, "there has been at least a two-inch expansion here, and I cannot—"

"You can!" snapped Isabel. "I warned you two months ago to leave extra width in the seams!"

"Yes, madam, and indeed I did, but there has been more expansion in the waist than I calculated—"

She had a sly look, I thought; she must know Isabel's condition, she must have been confronted with this contretremps many times before.

"Then calculate again," said Isabel no less sharply, "and go upstairs and make it right."

She stood in her stockinged feet in front of the tall pier glass in the corner. As Miss Denby unbuttoned the row of tiny pearls at the back, Isabel stood with her eyes shut. She had greeted me when I appeared, but now she waited for the dressmaker to disappear before she spoke to me again.

"I pay that woman twice what she's worth, and still she cannot follow instructions. This is the last, I won't have her again. For the same price, I could have a dress sent from Worth. Here—can you do my laces?"

I helped her as she asked. When I had freed her from her prison she stood for a moment in her chemise and petticoat, rubbing her rib cage, and then she went slowly to her bed and with a low moan she sank down onto it. I pulled a soft woolen coverlet over her. She was pale, with shadows under her eyes and lines of fatigue running down the sides of her mouth.

"Would you like some tea," I said, "or a glass of hot milk—"

"No." She frowned and shook her head, but she did not open her eyes.

"Well then," I said. "Perhaps I should leave you to sleep—"

"No." She turned her head away from me. "Stay with me. Sit here beside me on the bed—that's it." She was silent for a moment; she took my hand and held it between her own, and then, to my embarrassment, she put my hand on her abdomen where it swelled with the child. She pressed it down firmly. "There," she said. "Do you feel that? Do you feel it move?"

I did; and I felt the blood rise to my face, but I did not pull my hand away. A slow, heaving motion had run across her abdomen: and tomorrow night, I thought, she will constrict herself for hours with her corsets, she will crush that tiny creature—

Oh, but they were terrible things, those corsets! I have read that in the time of the Crusades men who went to the Holy Land locked their wives into metal body cages to prevent a bastard being born, and that women so abused went mad, sometimes, from the pain of those devices, or died from flesh scraped raw and then infected by their own wastes. Our corsets were not so bad as that, but they were terrible enough: and all in the name of fashion, feminine beauty intended to attract men so that they in turn might marry us and rule us forever after. Married women wore them, too, of course: to placate our masters? To remind them that we, too, were worthy of their kind attention? Our soft bodies constricted into whalebone cages, our breasts pulled up, our bones crushed, internal organs displaced—I have known of women who broke their ribs in those corsets, I knew of a woman whose womb dropped down outside her body because she was laced so tight that it was forced out of her.

"I went to see Dr. Slocomb," she said, still without opening her eyes; her voice was dry and flat and it startled me because I thought that she had fallen asleep. "He refused to help me. He told me that it was God's will, that I must submit—submit! He said that it was against nature to prevent conception, that only fallen women— women of the streets—tried to do it. I must reconcile myself, he said."

Suddenly her eyes flew open. "But I have found what I wanted after all. A female doctor on Shawmut Avenue recommended to me by Elinor, if you can believe it. She meets many people in the course of her work—people whom you might not want to entertain in your home but who can be useful nevertheless."

This was true. Elinor had found a life of her own, a life very different from ours. She spent her days—and many nights as well—with committees to raise money, with doctors and nurses recruited to minister to the afflicted, with teachers who organized classes in English, and American history, and I know not what. "Yes," I said. "I know."

"This woman—this doctor—has given up her life to them, just as Elinor has. And I went to her to ask her help, just as they do."

"And she gave it—"

"Yes. She was very kind, although I could see that she shared Elinor's opinion of me. They think that I am a silly, frivolous creature because I do not take a vow of poverty, because I lead a life so different from theirs. I don't care. We all of us do what we must. She told me quite honestly that she would charge me a high fee to make up for what her poorer patients could not pay. And of course I was happy to give it. It was a small price to pay for my freedom."

She turned her head away from me then, as if she wanted to sleep, and so after a moment I kissed her and said good-bye.

"No. Wait." Her face contorted as she struggled to sit up. "There—over there in the top drawer of the tall chest," she said. "Do you remember the book that Pussie gave me? It is there. Take it and read it. He is an interesting character. Since you have met him, you will enjoy reading about him."

Her lovely eyes were filled with pain, and her voice was flat—dead. I obeyed her; and then, carrying the book away with me, I left her.

I read it straight through that night, for it was the kind of story that, once begun, cannot be put down. In a way it was anachronistic: in the last century there were young gentlemen of fashion in London, wild and dissolute, who were known as rakehells. That is what the hero—the character supposedly based on Cushing—was in that book. The adventures and misdeeds attributed to him were beyond belief; and equally improbable, in my opinion, was the behavior of the heroine, Lady X, who remained devoted to him from the first page to the last no matter what torments she suffered at his hands.

Perhaps it was true after all: human beings behave in

mysterious ways, and never more so than when they think themselves in love.

The next evening after a light supper by myself—Perseus, as usual, was late—I went upstairs to dress for Isabel's party. In honor of the occasion I wore a new gown, pale gray-green silk trimmed in dark green velvet. I wished that Otis could see me; with a sudden rush of longing I wished that he waited for me downstairs, that he and I would go together to Isabel's, that all during the evening, if I wished, I would need only to turn my head to see him standing across the room, or near me, perhaps, his powerful presence seeming to dwarf all others, his keen eyes surveying the company as if we were some exotic native tribe. I caught sight of myself in the glass. I looked wan—pale, as if I were pining for my love. As I was.

Tomorrow, I thought. He will come back tomorrow. And I turned away from myself and went downstairs.

As I was going out I met Perseus coming in. I stood with my cloak in my hands, ready to have Huldah put it around my shoulders. Something in Perseus' eyes alarmed me; he often seemed preoccupied, but this night his attention was all on me.

"Where are you going?" he said; and this, too, was unusual, for he never asked me what I did or with whom.

"To Isabel's."

"Dressed like that?"

His eyes traveled down me and up again, and I felt a sudden sense of shame that I could not understand. Certainly I was dressed modestly enough by the standards of Isabel's crowd. Like all evening dresses, mine was cut low over the shoulders and bosom but not, I thought, immodestly so.

Suddenly, startling me, his hand flew out as if to touch me—perhaps to strike? Instinctively I flinched and stepped back.

"Look at you," he said. "Like a—like a woman of the streets. Have you no shame? Cover yourself at once. I will not have *my wife* going about at night, alone, dressed like a harlot. Do you understand me? I will not have it!"

Still off balance, trying to deflect his anger, I seized upon one word. "I go alone because you will not come with me. You are invited too—you are welcome to come."

"To do what? To see a roomful of half-dressed women showing themselves to every man in sight? You make me sick, all of you, parading yourselves—"

In the bleak illumination of the gas jets his thin face looked harsh and menacing. I felt a moment of panic. Get out, I told myself; he is dangerous, he will hurt you. And then I remembered whose money had paid for the dress I wore, for the house in which we stood, the servants we employed, the food we ate—for Perseus' clothing, too, for that matter. Uncles James's money and therefore mine. My fear of him dropped away from me, even as Huldah settled my cloak around my shoulders.

In the same moment I had brushed past him and out of the house. Henry and the carriage waited for me at the curb. Not until he had helped me in and we had started on our way did I react to my encounter with Perseus. I had a bad five minutes in the carriage, trembling, fighting my tears, but then it was over and we came to Isabel's. He can do nothing, I thought: he cannot hurt me, he cannot control me. Not even if he discovers Otis Whittemore.

There was a line of carriages all down Exeter Street and around the corner into Commonwealth; coachmen stood in little groups up and down, gossiping in the glow of the sidelights, smoking, undoubtedly sipping from their flasks—for it was only March, we were in winter still and the night was cold and raw. Henry let me off at the door and drove to the end of the line to wait. Before I went in I stood for a moment on the walk looking up at the house. It was brightly illuminated, filled with people, with noise and laughter and light and snatches of music from the orchestra: very different, I thought, from my own, dark and silent and inhabited by Perseus' baleful presence. I remembered what Isabel had said about the female doctor she had visited: that the woman had implied a criticism of those who, like Isabel, devoted themselves to entertaining. What was wrong with it? I wondered. Man was a social animal; it was human nature to crowd around the fire against the dark.

When I ascended the steps and went in I saw that Isabel and Lady Rathmore were receiving in the drawing room rather than the hall: as Isabel explained to me later, this was to protect Lady Rathmore, whose constitution was extremely delicate, against the night air. Certainly she looked delicate: she was a wizened sprite barely five feet tall, thin to the point of emaciation, wrinkled like a prune, her face oddly like a monkey's face: wise and old and brightly curious, with an appealing simian wistfulness.

After I had put my cloak upstairs in the ladies' dressing

room I went down to be presented to her. Isabel stood radiant beside her: was this the weeping, bitter woman whom I had seen the day before? She lives on this, I thought: it is meat and drink to her, it is her life. Avery may try to prevent her but he will not succeed.

Lady Rathmore inspected me closely, tilting up her little face and squinting her small, brown, opaque eyes. As she smiled at me I saw that she was nearly toothless. "Yes," she said, nodding vigorously; "yes, yes, my, yes indeed, very good, very, very—" and before I could say a word she had passed me down the line. I left them; I moved on into the company, I spoke to this one and that. Ordinarily I welcomed evenings out, for they helped to pass the time; but this evening I was impatient. I did not want to exert myself in conversation, I wanted to be alone with my letter from Otis Whittemore. Tomorrow, I thought, he will come. He will be with me. I will see him, I will speak to him, touch him—

"How's Perseus?" said Cousin Sam Swift, approaching me with a fresh glass of champagne. "He don't take to this kind of thing, does he? The Motleys were always like that. Standoffish." He nodded toward Isabel and Lady Rathmore. "I did well by her, didn't I? She asked me to find the connection, and I did. Everything's family, after all. Nothing else matters. Look at 'em all, falling over themselves to meet this ladyship. Any one of 'em's as good as she is—better, in fact—but they'd never believe it. Boston people love the aristocracy, y'know, and the monarchy as well. Odd, ain't it? They led the Revolution a hundred years ago, and it's as if they lost. At heart, they're still British subjects. Well: it don't matter.

When're you coming to see my posies? I've got a new *Leptotes* from Brazil. No one else has it, I'm the only one. Tomorrow?"

I smiled at him. He was impossible to dislike. "Not tomorrow," I said. "But soon. I promise."

He winked at me. "You upset all the laws of nature, m'dear. Laws of nature—the laws of biology—say that women fade as they get older. Just like flowers, don't y'know. You're a renegade. Look at you—blooming! Positively!"

I thought of Perseus' condemnation; I thought of tomorrow, when Otis would come. I glanced toward the receiving line where Isabel stood triumphant, reigning like the Queen herself over this crowd of supplicants.

She has had her moment, here and now, I thought: and soon I will have mine.

Seven

The New England spring is like a fickle lover: warm one day and cold the next, teasing, unpredictable, holding the promise of joy but reluctant to fulfill it.

We New Englanders know our springtime's tricks: we remain inviolate, chaste, unseduced by the vagaries of the weather. It is only outlanders who are bewildered and sometimes enraged by the sudden shift of the wind bringing rain from the east or cold from Canada or, too soon, a blast of southern heat. New Englanders are patient. We wait for summer's more dependable warmth; we know that like a wandering spouse it will always return: hot, moist-handed, demanding the loosening of stays and collars, the drawing of deep breath, surrender to its soft entreaty.

But the spring is treacherous: seductive. And sometimes even New Englanders succumb to its false promise.

Otis and I, that spring, used to meet in out-of-the-way public places; we went often to Bowditch's studio; we took long carriage rides to the country. He came to visit me as often as he dared. But it was not enough: such

263

arrangements never are. When he held me, when he kissed me until I thought that I must die if he let me go, I wanted only to be with him always, to make his life my own. He was like some miraculous drug to which I had become addicted, and always I needed more of him, and more; never could I get enough of him, and to give him up would, I was sure, have brought agonizing death.

The spring came on, warm days followed by cold, periods of steady rain, a final, nasty snow in early April. I was hardly aware of how much time had passed until one day in May, in Bowditch's studio, Bowditch threw a sly glance at Otis and said, "When are you away again, Whittemore? You've overstayed your time a bit, haven't you?"

It was a question which I had never dared ask myself, let alone him. There were several other people in the room, and as it happened they all fell silent just at that moment. Otis took the question matter-of-factly, although he understood, as did I, its true meaning. Bowditch was aware of our friendship and, I think, secretly pleased by it. He had no time for the conventions, and he was genuinely fond of both of us, he wanted to see us happy together.

"No," said Otis. "I was to return to Alaska next month, but my financial backers let me down. I only had enough to send my Esquimau home, poor creature. So now I am entertaining an offer from a publisher who wants an account of my travels."

"That's the way." Bowditch grinned. "Man of letters—much healthier than traipsing about in the tundra or whatever it is."

General conversation resumed then, and Otis turned to me. He smiled. "Well?" he said. "Do you approve?"

He read my reply in my expression—as did everyone else, no doubt, had they cared to look. I did not care, I was beyond caring. I was ready to proclaim myself publicly, if necessary. I loved this man more than I had thought it possible to love anyone, and my love made me reckless.

A few days later we drove out, one sunny afternoon, to visit Cousin Sam Swift in Brookline. Sam had acquired some splendid new specimens, including the Brasilia which he had mentioned to me. "Come for lunch," he said, "and then I'll show you the greenhouses."

I asked him whether I might bring a fellow connoisseur. He was delighted. "Whittemore? The fellow who went to Alaska? By all means—positively!"

While we ate, Otis charmed Cousin Sam with tales of Brazil, where grow some of the most exotic orchids in the world; by the end of an hour, he had convinced Sam to go there himself. Sam winked at me. "Will you come, Marian? We'll make up a party. Think of seeing 'em grow wild!"

His bright eyes gleamed: like all collectors, he was shameless in his greed. Isabel was that way, too, of course—she and all the women like her. They collected people instead of things, but the greed—the lust for possession—was the same.

Later we walked through the greenhouses to see his specimens. Like a proud father, he pointed out his special pets—plants that he had bred himself and matured into bloom.

"Look at this," he said, pointing to a rosy-red specimen. "*Mesophinidium vulcanicum* from the upper Amazon. And this—see that green color—*Oncidium chrysothyrsus*. And this—my prize, the *Dendrobium macranthum* from Manila*." This last was a particularly beautiful flower, rosy, pinkish purple, very large, smelling of sweet rhubarb. It grew in masses in a hanging basket so that I could put my face to it to inhale its strong scent. The greenhouse was ablaze with color, orange-yellow blossoms and cherry red and every variation of pink. I looked at the lush texture of the flowers, the vivid hues; I saw deep into the center of the blossoms, the mysterious hidden heart protected by the extravagant petals.

But I had, in truth, little interest in botany; after a while the names all blurred together in my mind and I stopped hearing what he said. The greenhouse was warm and humid; sunlight filtered through the glass roof; the dirt floor was mostly mud. Planks had been laid for a walk, but my skirts trailed down on either side, so that I needed to hold them up as I went. My dress was a celebration of the season: pale green lawn, with white lace trimming and a hat to match. "You look like a water nymph," Otis whispered to me; I caught the scent of his tobacco as he leaned close, and I felt a faintness which had nothing to do with the oppressive warmth of our surroundings.

The footman came, then, to fetch Cousin Sam to receive an unexpected caller. In his dark blue coat, black satin knickers, and white stockings, the Swift heraldry emblazoned on his breast pocket, he looked like a refugee from the chorus of a comic opera. Cousin Sam's studies of genealogy had led him to one Hugh Bygod, who had lived in the time of Edward II. From Bygod's escutcheon he had devised one of his own: three golden lions rampant on a field of red. He put it everywhere: on his carriage doors, of course; on his best china, his linens, the wall over the library fireplace—even on the finely tooled leather covers of some of his choicer books which he had had rebound.

The moment we were alone Otis swept me into his arms and kissed me as though his hunger for me would never be assuaged. "Come to me," he said. "Come to me—I must see you alone. Come now—we can be at my rooms in half an hour. Be with me—only with me."

I was dizzy—faint from the wine I had drunk, from the heavy fragrance surrounding us, the warmth of the day, the tightness of my lacings—faint, I knew, with love for him. I held his face in my hands and saw love in return. Inexperienced as I was, I knew that he was not playing fast and loose. He cared for me as I did for him, and what he asked of me he did not ask lightly, he was prepared to face whatever came of it. As I was.

We made our escape soon after. Cousin Sam was not as sorry to see us leave as he might have been, since his visitor was a gentleman from the Horticultural Society; they would spend a delightful afternoon together, no doubt, discussing the intricacies of hybridization. Sam took my hand as I went out; he seemed poised to say more than good-bye but he checked himself. We stood for a moment on his wide shady veranda, looking out to the sunny lawn, the gardens marked by well-trimmed yew, the graveled driveway where waited Otis' hired carriage. The gentleman from the Horticultural Society had walked out ahead with Otis; Sam and I stood on the porch, and eager as I was to get away I waited nevertheless. Suddenly, for no reason, I thought of the dreadful night when my mother had invaded the Januarys' party and Sam had kindly taken care of me. Despite his somewhat foolish obsessions—and what obsession is not?—he had a shrewd, compassionate heart.

"Interesting fellow," he said, nodding toward Otis. "Where'd you meet him?"

"At an artist's studio," I said, smiling, teasing him; proper ladies did not frequent such places as a rule.

"Whose?"

"Farnsworth Bowditch."

He sniffed. "Don't know him. Any good?"

"I liked one small thing he did, and so I bought it."

"Good for you. That's what I like, a woman who knows her own mind." He hesitated, seeming about to speak and yet constrained. He peered out to the sunshine, squinting a bit; the day had grown very warm, and I saw a line of moisture cross his upper lip. "Bring him around sometime," he said at last; it was not, I thought, what he had intended. "Does he do portraits? Yes? Been thinkin' of havin' myself done. About time, don't y'know." And still he hung back, my hand in his, reluctant to let me go before he had delivered himself. At last he nerved himself up to a final effort. "Saw Perseus the other day," he said; he lowered his voice but there was no need since the others were far away near the big beech tree in the center of the lawn; they could not possibly have heard us.

I glanced at him, waiting.

"He was full of this Society of his. What's he up to, anyway?"

"I don't know."

"He don't tell you? Hm. Looks as though he's near the edge, if you ask me. How about takin' him away for the summer? Let him rest up a bit, sail, swim—"

The thought of Perseus bathing in the sea brought an involuntary smile to my face; he hated athletic activity of any kind, and certainly he would not have exposed himself to the world in a bathing costume.

"Perhaps," I said. "We were at Bar Harbor last year, and he was very restless, anxious to get home."

"Well. I don't know—seems to me he's all tied up in knots, but some folks thrive on that, I suppose." And he gave my hand a final squeeze and let me go. I caught a glimpse of him as we turned into the road; he stood in the sunshine with his caller, his hand shading his eyes, watching us go.

I never saw him again. As it turned out, we did go away that summer, after all; and when we came back to town he had himself gone away. Inspired by Otis' tales of Brazil, he had managed to annex himself to an expedition led by Professor Bateson; the entire party was massacred by natives as they journeyed up one of the tributaries of the Amazon.

He died in pursuit of what he wanted most in the world; not many people have even that little chance. And so I mourned him, but my sorrow was for myself, because I missed him: he had been kind to me from the start, and he was kind still that last day. He had been trying to alert me somehow to Perseus' condition; he had been trying to say: "He is near some kind of breaking point. Be careful of him."

I see him in my mind's eye, standing in the sun that last day: a warm, golden May day. And it was warm, too, in the carriage that took us across the river to Cambridge: warm with the heat of the day, warm with the heat from our love, Otis' arms clasped tight around me, the carriage rumbling across the bridge and through the traffic in Harvard Square and up Brattle Street to his rooms. I was impatient while he paid the driver, and frightened too lest someone see me, someone who might tell tales, and so longing for him nevertheless that I might have seen my name and his in a headline in the *Transcript* and I would not have cared.

But I did not know what I longed for, I did not know why I was impatient. I knew nothing.

The shades were drawn, the rooms in semidarkness. They were on the top floor of the house, hot from the sun beating on the roof. Our clothing was torture. His fingers fumbled at the buttons of my bodice but he trembled so that he could not manage them, and he laughed a little and said in a choking voice, "You must help me." And so I did; and together, somehow, we released me from the prison of my costume. My stays and my chemise were damp with perspiration, the fine thin cloth clung to my skin, and when finally I stood free, trembling, expectant, my eyes closed to struggle silently for balance, I heard him exclaim at the deep, cruel marks on my body left by the corset. He was on his knees before me. His mouth pressed against me where the lacings had been, over and over he kissed me and kissed me and buried his face against me—ah, and then he suckled at my rigid nipples, he licked my breasts and kissed them softly again and again and I began to melt to him, I felt a maddening aching torment that I had never felt before begin to throb inside me.

And he took me then and laid me down beside him and stroked me and stroked me and I heard the sound of my voice, moaning, crying out to him, in the heat, in the darkened room, and then he knew my secret, he knew that he would have my maidenhead, no man had had it yet, and he came gentler still, and murmured to me as he did, and soothed what he thought were my fears although in truth I had no fear, I trusted him completely, I did not know what was to happen to me.

And I felt a little pain, then, as he came into me, but the pain was nothing, it was eclipsed as he eased himself inside me, into that place that tormented me, and he stroked me there, and filled me, and brought me up to life and held me there for a long exquisite moment before he calmed me and soothed me down again, and I came back to myself and saw that I was there with him in that hot dim room on an afternoon in May when all the world went on about its business and only we two there together to know our love.

I had to leave him, of course: transformed as I was, newly his, I had to rise and dress and go back to that world where I lived alone, without him.

When I got back to Beacon Street a note awaited me. "Mr. Kittredge's man left it not an hour ago, ma'am," said my maid. "He wants you to call round as soon as you can."

I opened it:

5:00 P.M.

Marian—
Isabel's time has come. She wants to see you.

A.K.

I had visited her only two days previously. She had
been tired, of course, exhausted in the final stages of her
pregnancy, but otherwise she had seemed well enough.
The baby was not due for several weeks. What had gone
wrong?

When I arrived I found Mrs. January and Avery's
mother sitting together in the drawing room. The
expressions on their faces told me better than any words
what Isabel's condition was. Mrs. January came to
embrace me.

"Marian dear. She's having a hard time, I'm afraid. Go
up and see if Dr. Slocomb will let you in."

"When did it start?" I said.

"Early this morning. We didn't send for you because
we thought there would be no trouble. But around noon
she started to tire, she is bleeding, and she has no
strength—"

Impossible, I thought. Isabel is the strongest person I
know.

I hurried upstairs, past the little maid weeping in a
corner (and why does she weep, I thought; was Isabel so
kind a mistress?), past Grace and Curtis, to the door of
Isabel's room. I knocked; having no answer, I went in.

"No," said the doctor, glancing around at me. "She is not—"

"She asked for me," I said.

"Mrs. Motley?"

"Yes."

He inspected me. "Yes," he said. "I have met your husband. Mrs. Kittredge asked for you earlier, but I have given her chloroform and she is unconscious now."

I glanced at the still, sheet-covered form on the bed, the swollen abdomen seeming like some monstrous growth upon it. I did not instantly connect the sight with what I had experienced with Otis that afternoon, but of course they followed each other as day follows night, the two were inextricably linked.

"Will she—will she be all right?"

"I am a doctor, Mrs. Motley, not a gypsy fortune-teller. I will do all that I can, and then it is in God's hands, not mine."

I remembered then that this was the man who had refused Isabel's plea for help. He was a tall, thin man, expensively dressed, whose round, rather jolly face belied the life-and-death nature of his business. I looked away from him. The room was dim and hot—much like Otis' room, I thought, but there is no joy here, no love. Not even the fruit of love, I thought. She does not love him, she does not want this child. Perhaps that is why she has no strength, no will to fight.

"I will wait with the others," I said. "Please call me if she comes to." I went out; on my way downstairs I spoke briefly to Curtis and Grace. What would Grace not give to suffer this? I thought. Is no one content with his fate?

273

Must we always, all of us, look for something more?

Avery had come in during my absence. He looked as he always did, solid and stoic, his eyes showing no hint of emotion. He sat now with his mother and his mother-in-law. When I came in he stood up and made as if to seat me, and then he changed his mind. "I want a breath of air," he said. "Walk with me awhile, Marian. We won't be long. If Isabel awakens, we will be here momentarily."

Since he had walked home to Exeter Street from his offices downtown, his excuse was transparent enough; but of course I acquiesced, I was happy to hear whatever he might say.

We went out into the warm May twilight and made our way across Commonwealth Avenue. The Spiritualist Temple at the corner of Newbury—a forbidding Romanesque hulk of rough stone which Mr. Richardson had somehow managed to fit gracefully into its space— was nearly finished, and we paused to look at it.

"What a heavy-looking building for so ethereal a sect," I said.

He glanced at me, not comprehending. "Cost a pretty penny," he said. "They haven't skimped."

No: he did not understand me. Nor I him, for that matter. Nor did he understand Isabel. Did I?

We walked on, down Newbury, across Dartmouth, up Commonwealth. Buildings in all stages of completion lined the streets. Everything was new, and raw, and dusty. One day, I thought, these streets, this broad avenue bisected by a strip of mud, would be lined with full-blossoming trees; there would be no more scaffolding and piles of brick and stone, no more rubble and dust and ugly gaping spaces waiting to be filled. This was all money, I thought—new money displaying itself alongside the old.

As we passed the vast whiteness of the Hotel Vendome, Avery slowed a bit and glanced at me in an anxious way. "Your skirts are dusty," he said. So personal a remark, coming from this man whom I had known for so long and yet never known at all, surprised me into a moment's laughter. Filthy hemlines were a constant worry, but not many men ever seemed aware of it.

And then, before I could think of a tactful reply, he surprised me even more by saying, "D'you think she'll live?"

We were walking up the southerly side of Commonwealth. The western sky ahead of us glowed crimson with the setting sun. Behind, to the east, the avenue lay shrouded in dusk, lights twinkling here and there, carriages rumbling by. I paused: I put my hand on his arm, I stared into his impassive face. For the first time— but not the last—I saw pain there, and a kind of bewilderment.

"I don't know," I said at last. "Dr. Slocomb said he hoped for the best."

He studied my face for a moment and then began to walk again. "She should not have overtired herself," he said. "She begged me to allow her to entertain Lady Rathmore, but I should not have."

"It meant a great deal to her."

"She must stop all this. It is too much for her. I told her, weeks ago, that that was the last. And now you see that I was right. She has made herself ill, she has

275

endangered the child, endangered herself—possibly she has killed herself. She may die tonight, Marian—think of it! If she dies—"

His voice broke. He quickened his pace, as if by so doing he could control his emotions. "She will die, she will die and leave us here without her, her children without their mother, her husband without his wife—I cannot bear to have her die, Marian! I cannot! If I have been strict with her it is only because I love her. I cannot lose her."

I heard the terror in his voice; lamely I tried to comfort him. "Avery, the doctor said—"

"Why is she not like other women, who find happiness in their families, in caring for their husbands and children? Why must she always have half a hundred people about? Why are we—why am *I*—not enough for her?"

I had no answer for him; I did not know, any more than he. I glanced at his anguished face and looked away again, unable to bear such pain. He loved her—yes, he loved her, but her discontent—her restlessness, her striving—was a constant reproach to him.

"I am not sure that that is so," I said. "Many women are devoted to their families, and yet they have a need to—to have some worldly success, just as men do."

"Then let her engage in some less strenuous work. And less expensive, I might add. The Church Aid Society, any kind of charitable work—"

"Can you really see Isabel making visits to the poor?" I said. "And besides, Elinor does enough of that for all of us."

276

"Elinor is a disgrace," he said shortly. "They ought to prevent her. She carries it to an extreme—"

"As if it were her profession?"

"Exactly. And for a woman to have a profession—any profession—is nothing but a shame on the family that produced her. Do you know I almost lost a client the other day because the man found out that Elinor January is my sister-in-law? She'd been visiting tenants of his, stirring them up to petition for repairs. I had a hard time of it to convince him that she acted totally against all our wishes. She is mentally unbalanced, in my opinion, and they ought to put her into treatment. No. I do not want Isabel to become like that, I assure you. But a little charitable work to fill up her time, instead of all this social business—"

Not five minutes ago, I thought, you were worried that she might not survive. Now you want her to live, but only on your terms.

"Why not take her to Nahant for the summer?" I said. "Let her recuperate. Then, in the fall—"

"I warned her that Lady Rathmore was the end," he said. "But if she persists—"

"What is wrong with it, after all? Many men are delighted at the social triumphs of their wives. Isabel has a talent for that, just as some people have a talent for music, or art."

"It is a talent for spending money."

"Yes: that too."

Another silence; then: "I've had a good year. I could let her entertain the world, if she wanted."

"Why not, then?"

He could not find an answer for me, and so I pressed my point. "Let her do as she will," I said. I could have added: There is little enough happiness in this world, do not deprive her of her share. But he would not have understood. He was a practical man, a man of business. Something as intangible as happiness was beyond his power to comprehend.

Isabel survived that night, and toward dawn her daughter—her last child—was born. And when she had sufficiently recovered, by the Fourth of July, she had her summer by the sea to recuperate. But it was not Nahant, and it was hardly restful.

We went to Newport instead—Avery and Isabel, Perseus and I. And Isabel had a glimpse of grander conquests than any she had had in Boston; and I—well, I had Otis Whittemore.

Eight

The sun shines more brightly over Newport than it
shines in other skies, and the color of the sea is a deeper,
richer blue, shifting, myriad shades of silver and purple
and green; the seaweed bleaches on the rocks, giving the
air a sour tang, and odor peculiar to Newport which I
have never encountered elsewhere; and the light is
luminous there, giving the landscape a special clarity not
unlike that of Paris, or certain sections of the South of
France. People play at Newport: they go there to forget
their troubles, they enter that small island of Aquidneck
as if it were a magical kingdom where everyone is young
and rich and beautiful always, devoted only to pleasure.

"Butterflies," said Mrs. Roberts Reed when she
announced her plan to Isabel and me. "They flock there
now, all these society people. Newport used to be as solid
as Nahant: the best brains in Boston and Cambridge used
to be there—the Longfellows, the Agassizes—but the
New Yorkers are taking over now, building cottages—no
matter. You are all welcome to come to me, and we
needn't pay calls all summer if we don't want to."

But of course Isabel wanted to, very much. She was delighted at the prospect of avoiding her parents' establishment at Nahant, which, as she said, had grown stuffy and dull beyond endurance. "Everyone interesting will be at Newport," she said. "And we can see the tennis, and the yachting—the *America* will be there."

To my surprise, Perseus agreed to go. He hated travel, even to so close a place as Newport, although from time to time he had consented to go to Bar Harbor or Nahant. But his Society needed money, and Newport swam in money; he did not say so, but I knew that he hoped to enlist several wealthy supporters to rescue it from bankruptcy.

Nor did Avery protest. He could not be with us all the summer, he said, but he would spend a few weeks, at least, at Mrs. Reed's, and travel down on weekends the rest of the time. After his terror at Isabel's narrow escape from death, he had no heart to protest what was, after all, a convenient invitation from her aunt; and he was prepared, as it happened, to indulge Isabel far more than that.

And so we went. When I told Otis he was delighted. "But of course you must go," he said. "It will be much better than anywhere else. I have friends from New York who have just built a place there. I will present myself at their door and stay as long as you do."

Even then, at the beginning of its heyday, Newport had an aura of scandal about it: men stayed on board their yachts anchored in the harbor and entertained young women of less than impeccable social background, while their wives stayed ashore in their grand summer homes and entertained everyone else.

But we were not scandalous, Otis and I; by Newport standards we were very discreet. We used to drive out in the afternoons to an inn well removed from the fashionable environs of Bellevue Avenue; so hectic was the social whirl that we were hardly missed. Even Perseus, who held his nose, so to speak, at the goings-on all around him, was so busy cultivating his potential supporters that we hardly saw each other from morning till night. He paid no attention to me; it was as if I had ceased to exist for him, and while that gave me my freedom to come and go as I pleased, it caused me some slight unease from time to time, whenever I stopped to consider it.

Where would we end, he and I?

"You must divorce him," said Otis. "As soon as you return to Boston, you must begin proceedings at once."

We sat on the beach under a full moon, watching the rippling silver sea. Behind us, in Mrs. Bigelow's new cottage, a midsummer ball was in progress. Strains of the waltz drifted down across the lawn, and if we looked back we could see through tall windows the figures of the dancers whirling to the insistent tempo of the music.

"Yes," I said; and much as I loved this man beside me, I was amazed to hear myself say it. Divorce was scandalous, it meant instant ostracism for both parties no matter which was at fault. But worse ostracism, of course, for the woman, no matter what her standing in society, no matter that her husband might be entirely the guilty party. My husband, in the eyes of the world, was blameless, and my standing in society was on sufferance only; people had accepted me first as Mrs. January's

281

unofficial ward, and then, more warmly, as Isabel's close friend and Perseus' wife. If I divorced him I would be a pariah; every door would be closed to me. Even Curtis', I thought; even Isabel's.

Isabel suspected my liaison with Otis Whittemore, but in the way of her new circle at Newport she simply smiled at me or raised an eyebrow when she saw me dance with him. I think that she was amused by us; or perhaps she waited to see if I would trip myself up and become part of a delicious scandal. As long as I preserved the appearance of decency, I thought, she would not interfere. A divorce would be another matter. "Yes," I said again. "Yes—as soon as I can. But if he contests—"

"Which he will not—"

"Oh, I think he will. He will be very angry, he will want revenge and that will be it."

"Then leave him," he said quietly. "Simply go."

"With you? Where?"

He laughed then; he was a man who had achieved success by refusing to admit the possibility of failure. "Anywhere! To the ends of the earth if you wish it."

And he embraced me and held me close to his heart for a long moment, and I knew that I existed in that most miraculous of conditions: of being loved completely, unreservedly. It does not happen often. Seize it when it comes: cherish it, hold it fast!

Isabel thrived that summer. Whether it was the change of scene or whether it was Avery's change of heart, I did not know; but her recovery was swift and sure, and by the end of our stay at Mrs. Reed's she was as fresh and blooming as any debutante. She and I (and sometimes even Mrs. Reed) went bathing nearly every day at Bailey's Beach; despite our best efforts to shield ourselves, our faces and hands soon became browned from the sun. Isabel's three older children and their governess came with us: Charlotte, at eleven, was already as tall as her mother and showed signs of being much taller, and big-boned like Avery. Arthur, a year younger and much smaller, was a quiet, reflective child; sometimes when I looked at him I remembered that Ned had been that age when I first met him. The thought made me feel as old as Mrs. Reed. How many years had passed, and still—still!—my life had only just begun. Otis had begun it—had awakened me, made me come alive.

The youngest of the three, Victoria, was not quite six: an impish sprite of a child whose extraordinary beauty came from neither the Kittredges nor the Januarys, but seemed an accident of nature—one of Fortune's favors which happen from time to time.

Often I caught Isabel watching her. "She will be my prize," she would say. "I will marry Charlotte off as best I can, I won't have much choice in the matter, but Victoria will be my triumph." Her eyes squinted in the glare of the sun on the sand, little protected by the shade of her parasol as she watched Victoria running in and out of the water at the edge of the waves, her small feet dancing up and down. The child laughed, challenging the sea. "They will come to court her by the dozen, and I will make the match of the year for her. Of the decade!"

I smiled, indulging her fancies. Small and plump and determined, she looked as the young Queen might have looked, long ago, plopped down improbably on the beach, determining the fate of nations. But I was no Gladstone, no Disraeli: I could not help her.

"She has a mind of her own," I said. "She may not agree to your choice."

Isabel paid no attention. "Do you know the empty stretch of shore frontage beyond that large new white place—that's the Hazeltines', I met them last week."

"Yes," I said.

"Avery has bought it." She gleamed at me triumphantly. "Next Monday we meet with Mr. Van Brunt, who will design the house."

Well, I thought: Avery must indeed have taken my advice to heart, if he indulged her in this way! Or perhaps it was an offering of thanksgiving, an appeasement of God for having spared her.

"So you see," she went on, "I will have the proper setting to display my jewel. And she will outshine them all, when her time comes."

We returned to Boston in early September. Otis went on to New York; like Perseus, he needed financial backing for his work, and he refused even to consider taking any money of mine. "Keep it," he said. "You are young, you will live a long time, and you will need it."

"Not if I have you," I said.

But he was wiser than I. "Keep it," he said. "Let rich men finance me. It makes them feel that they are doing some good in the world. As indeed they are."

By the end of the month I knew that I was carrying Otis' child.

"Are you sure?" he said when I told him. "Have you—

have you seen a doctor?" His voice was low and urgent, his face was alive with joy. He held me gently as if I might shatter in a stronger embrace, and I laughed at him because of it.

"You may hold me more tightly," I said. "I won't break." I had seen Isabel's female physician, but I did not tell him that.

"No. You will not." His love for me was plain on his face, shining in his eyes. For the thousandth time I marveled at the fact that this man who had made a life's work of defying the worst that nature could show, of being strong enough to endure untold hardship, was as tender in love as women are supposed to be.

He held me more closely, and we were silent for a while. Then he said: "I must go once more to New York. William Prentice has promised to make a large donation. If I do not take his money someone else will. He came by it shabbily enough, he was a partner of Gould's. I will be back within the week. And then we will go away."

"Where?"

"Back to New York, for the winter. And in the spring—"

In the spring the child will come, I thought. And you, Otis Whittemore, will go back to that frozen wilderness which calls you with a siren song as irresistible as any woman's.

But I said nothing. I held him close and thought of the child and of what my life would be: and it did not dismay me, it did not discourage me. I wanted it—I wanted the child, I wanted whatever life I might have with him.

He left the next day, and I began to prepare for my

departure. I had decided not to tell anyone before I went. I would write to them from New York, I thought: it would be easier so. For Perseus, I would leave a note. I had no idea how I would phrase it, but telling him that the house was his to do with as he pleased should soften the blow somewhat, I thought. I needed only to inform the officer at the bank about where to forward my quarterly drafts, and this I did, giving to him the address that Otis had given to me.

Only one person knew our plan: Ned. He called on me one afternoon a few days after Otis had gone to New York. I was happy that he did, for I had not seen him since we returned from Newport. Since he left his father's house and the January firm he had lived a bohemian existence. He had been a frequent visitor to Bowditch's studio, and so he knew of my friendship with Otis; what he thought of it, or how much he knew, he never said.

"What have you been doing to yourself, Marian?" he exclaimed when he saw me. "I've never seen you look so—so healthy! Wonderful! Newport agreed with you!"

I could not have said the same of him: his clothes were worn and soiled; his hair was too long, and what little of his face I could see behind his new beard looked pale and unhealthy.

But I was very glad to see him, and I told him so: "Where have you been hiding, Ned, and doing what?"

"Working." He grinned.

"Poems?"

"Yes. I've had a nibble from the *Atlantic* on one of them. Nothing definite yet. But that's not why I'm here."

"You are here to see me, I hope."

"Yes—of course." A slight flush came to his cheeks above the beard. "But also to ask a favor. Not for myself—you know that I would never ask for myself— but for a friend."

"You need money," I said: for what other favor could I grant? I did not mind; money is worthless if we cannot use it to help those we love—or their friends.

"This fellow is truly brilliant, Marian—the most talented man I've ever met."

"A poet also?"

"No. A novelist. He is working as a clerk while he finishes his book. But he and his wife have both been ill all summer, and then a week ago one of their little boys broke his leg. And yesterday the father—my friend—was dismissed from his place because he'd been absent so often. They are desperate. They need something just to tide them over, just until he finishes his book and sells it—"

The eternal dream, I thought: and how many lives had it wrecked?

"I wouldn't ask for myself, Marian—"

"How much? A hundred? Two?"

We settled on a hundred and fifty. "I will take you to meet him when his wife is recovered," said Ned. "He is a wonderful, brilliant man, truly a genius, I think— No?"

Without thinking, I had shaken my head, and so now it was my turn to blush. And then: Why not? I thought. He will understand: he above everyone else, for poets understand the heart's commands, they understand the meaning of love.

I took as deep a breath as my corsets would allow.

"I will not be here to meet him, Ned. Next week I go away. I will not be back, not for a long time."

He stared at me. We sat in the front parlor before a coal fire; between us rested the tea things. The afternoon had darkened, but I had not called the maid to light the gas; if I were going to share secrets, I preferred to do so in dim light.

"So you are leaving Perseus," he said.

"Yes."

"I wonder that you did not do so a long time ago. He has not been a—a good husband to you, has he?"

Even though I sat in shadow I could not meet his eyes.

"No," I said; and feared to say more because I knew my voice would break.

"Marian. Look at me."

But I could not; and so he came to me, he knelt before me and, like a lover, he took my face between his hands and looked deep into my eyes to where my heart was. He was not my lover; he might have been the brother I had lost, long ago, or perhaps even my son. But whatever he was, he understood me and, like a brother or a son, he loved me, and so I saw no outrage in his eyes, no shock or condemnation for what I did, but only understanding and compassion.

"With Whittemore," he said; it was not a question.

"Yes."

"You are sure?"

"Yes."

"Then I can only say Godspeed and wish you happiness."

He embraced me then, the awkward embrace of a young man who has had no experience at it, the artless, heartfelt impulse of an honest soul.

"I will miss you," he said. "Even when I don't see you for weeks, I take comfort in the knowledge that you are here. You have been a better sister to me than either of mine—a better friend than anyone else. But if you can be happy with him, then you must go. And if you ever need me, if ever I can help you in any way, promise that you will send for me."

I bade farewell to him that day with mingled happiness and sorrow, for I would miss him too, and yet his blessing on what I did was a comfort to me; it banished whatever lingering doubts I might have had.

I would not see him again for a long time, I thought. But I was mistaken: he came again two days later, early in the morning while I was still at breakfast. He came in close on the heels of the maid, not waiting to be announced; for a wonder, he did not meet Perseus, who had gone out not five minutes before.

He carried with him an early edition of the *Globe*. In it was the account of a fire at the Hotel Imperial in New York. A dozen people had been badly burned, and seven more had died.

I do not remember his words; I do not remember how he found a way to tell me. But I can see his anguished face now, as I write, and while I cannot remember what he said, I can hear his choked, halting voice, I can feel his tears dropping onto my hands as he clasped them, held them tight as if he were afraid that I, too, would slip into death.

It is one of Nature's kindnesses to shield us from news that is too painful—brutal, unbearable, incomprehensible news—by tricking us, by making us think that we are in a dream, a nightmare from which, momentarily, we will awake. I remember shaking my head hard—two, three, half a dozen times; I remember feeling the terrible pain where my heart was, and wondering at it, wondering how I could bear it until I woke.

And then from the blur of disbelief and agony and shock I remember one thought coming clearly through, and I clung to it as if it were a splintered timber from a shipwreck, and I drowning if I let go.

I have his child, I thought. I have his child: his son. He cannot be truly dead while his child lives.

A letter arrived for me the next day: a letter from Otis. I suppose you could call it a love letter. He wrote it as much for himself as for me, he said, because he missed me: even for so short a time, he was unhappy when he was away from me. But soon we would be together: he would return for me on Monday next.

I have that letter still. Parts of it are illegible because the ink has blurred where my tears have fallen upon it. The lines at the folds are nearly worn through, and the paper is so brittle now after all these years that I fear to touch it. It lies in a small safety box in the armoire in my bedroom, together with my diamond necklace and my ruby and diamond eardrops and my emeralds. The jewels are worth nothing to me: any thief could take them and I would not care. But that letter, and the others that he wrote to me, are all that I have of him, and they are precious beyond price.

I had already written my farewell note to Perseus; with Otis' words fresh in my heart, I took it from where I had hidden it in my desk and I tore it into pieces and dropped them one by one into the fire. I watched them burn until they were black ash drifting up the chimney; they might have been the fragments of my heart, the last poor remnants of my love.

Nine

"Marian! Marian, are you there?"

A bad winter's night, the first blizzard of the new year. I lay comfortably tucked in bed after my solitary dinner, cutting the pages of Ouida's new novel, *Princess Napraxine*. I heard the storm beating against the windows; before I retired I had opened the front door and looked out to see Beacon Street—a white wasteland, a solitary hack fighting its way along, the poor horse's head bowed against the fury of the wind-driven snow.

And so I had turned and climbed the long narrow stairs to my room on the second floor. I went slowly, heavily; the child was growing in me, and somehow, soon, I would have to announce my condition to my husband. Next week, I thought: next week I would tell him. I would ask Curtis and Isabel to help me. I knew that Perseus did not want a scandal; he might even welcome a child, for all I knew, to preserve the illusion of a happy marriage.

"Marian! Thank God you're here—can you come?"

Isabel, her cloak wet with snow still clinging to it, burst into the room.

"What—?"

"It's Elinor. She's—she's very ill, she may be dying for all I know. We have just had the message. Or, rather, Mother had it. She sent for me, and Curtis too. But Elinor has asked for you—begged you to come."

I had not waited for her to finish before I was out of my bed and, heedless of modesty, pulling on my clothes. I had had some loose woolen sacque dresses made for the time, very near now, when I would no longer be able to lace myself; and so now, not troubling with corsets, I put on a warm chemise and two flannel petticoats and then one of the new sacques.

"Where is she?" I said, my voice muffled as I struggled through the layers of clothing. I knew that she was not at home, for she had left the Januarys the previous autumn, shortly after Otis' death. She had gone to live in a house in the South End, not far from where I had lived with my mother years before. How odd, I had thought, that Mother and I—and my brother George too, while he lived—had wanted so much to escape that district, which even then was on the downslide, while Elinor, now, went there willingly, even eagerly. The Januarys had been very angry with her, Isabel had said: "Don't speak of her at all, Marian. Mother's heart is not strong, the doctor said, and she cannot bear to be reminded of what Elinor has done." And I, preoccupied with my own grief which I could tell no one, had been glad to spare Mrs. January any reminder of what must have been, for her, an equal loss.

"There," I said. "I am ready."

As I turned to face her, she stared at me, forgetting the emergency that had brought her. For a moment I thought that she would speak, but she said nothing: this was not the time for questions, for explanations. I took my cloak and some money in a small purse and, in my stocking feet, hurried downstairs to put on my galoshes. "Do not wait up for me," I said to the maid. "When Mr. Motley comes in, tell him that Miss Elinor January is ill and that Mrs. Kittredge and I have gone to her." Where Perseus was, this bad night, I did not know; I never did.

Curtis had come in his carriage, and he and the coachman waited now for us at the curb. The night was a blinding maelstrom; even in the short distance from the stoop to the carriage door we were covered with snow, blinded by icy flakes of it flung into our faces, stumbling through drifts already three feet high and more. The street plow had gone by shortly before, and so we had a narrow path to follow as we made our way.

"You were good to come," said Curtis. "She is very ill, we must try to get her home."

"In this storm? Why not wait?"

"The people she has been living with insist that she go now. I suspect that they fear some retribution; they are afraid that she will die and we will bring charges against them."

"But you could assure them that you will not—"

"We will take her away tonight," said Isabel curtly. "Can you imagine—she has worked for them for years, and now they turn her out. I would die myself before I would leave her there with them. We must get her away, we must take her home where she can have proper medical care."

For what seemed like hours the horses made their way

through the deserted streets, through the storm to
Rutland Street. At last we arrived at number 43: a swell-
front, four-story brick that would not have been out of
place in the Back Bay.

We hurried in, and at once it was obvious that we were
indeed in a different world, for our noses were assaulted
by the stench of stale cooking and unwashed bodies and
all the rank, foul odors of the poor. A cadaverous man of
perhaps fifty met us in the dimly lit hall. He asked no
questions; he knew who we were and he wanted to help us
perform our task as quickly as possible. He led us to a
room on the second floor. As we ascended we heard a
child crying, a woman's voice scolding, an argument
between two men. The people we knew, Isabel and Curtis
and I, lived in decorous silence. The poor are more vocal,
I thought; they give easy voice to all the agony that the
rest of us must stifle.

Our guide opened a door. He did not accompany us
inside but remained waiting as if on guard in the hall.
Elinor lay on a narrow bed in the corner of the room. A
fat, frowsy woman sat beside her; as we came in she
looked at us in alarm and rose to go. Curtis detained her
with a hand on her arm.

"When did she become ill?"

"Two days ago, sir. We dosed her as well as we could,
but then last night she took delirious, and today she's
been as you see her, very bad, and we thought you should
know."

Isabel and I approached the bed. Elinor lay quiet. Her
eyes were wide; she saw us and clearly recognized us, but
she said nothing. Her hair was wet with perspiration; in

the light from the oil lamp on the table she looked as pale as death.

Curtis released the woman's arm, then, and came to Elinor. He bent over her. Her eyes followed him.

"Elinor? Can you speak?"

Her eyes closed for a moment as if to gather strength. Then she looked at him again. She knew why he had come.

"I want to stay," she said. Her voice was faint and weak, but it carried in it the echo of the iron-willed young woman whom I had known.

"No. You cannot stay. You must come home."

She shook her head slowly, weakly.

"Yes, Elinor. You must come now." He straightened and looked around for help.

The guard at the door peered in.

"She must go," he said. "We can't keep her."

"Listen to him," whispered Isabel. "She has given her life to these people, and they turn her out."

"Fetch my coachman," said Curtis.

"No—no, please—let me stay—" Elinor half lifted herself and then fell back. "Marian—Marian, please!"

"I am here." I bent over her; I put my hand on her burning forehead.

"Make them let me stay. I cannot leave—"

"You are very ill, Elinor. If you go home to recover, then perhaps you can return."

"Listen!" She tried to take my hand but she was too weak to hold it. "You understand what I am trying to do. They do not—Mother and Father and Isabel. But you do. Make them listen—please—"

She started to cry. The tears left a trail down her dirty face; Isabel bent over her to wipe them away.

"Dearest, we must take you home," she said, more tenderly than I had ever heard her speak to anyone. I had not thought that she cared about her younger sister, but family feeling is always strongest in times of crisis, and Isabel was behaving in true January fashion.

"Dress her now," said Curtis. We had brought a warm cloak and woolen stockings, and a flannel wrapper and drawers. We worked swiftly, breathing through our mouths, gagging on the foul odor that permeated the room and rose from the soiled bed, from Elinor's unwashed body. I saw a bedbug scurry out of reach and I thought that I would indeed vomit then, but I fought down my heaving stomach and worked on, pulling the stockings onto Elinor's filthy feet. If I catch some illness, I thought, it will harm my child, and in the midst of all our rush I stopped for a moment and prayed to God to keep us both safe.

Elinor sobbed quietly as we worked, but she protested no more. She lay limp, submissive. The woman watched us suspiciously, as if she were afraid that we would change our minds and abandon Elinor to her mercy.

We heard the coachman pounding up the stairs. He was a small man, but wiry and strong. With a look of contempt on his thin, shrewd face, he shouldered aside the woman who had taken the man's place at the door. Like many servants, he was more caste-conscious than his employers; he classed himself with those he served, and he had nothing but scorn for people who, born to poverty like himself, had not had the good sense to attach themselves to people of standing. In one swift motion he stooped and lifted Elinor's limp body and shouldered his way past our spectators. We followed him. As we were halfway down the stairs the man called to Curtis.

"Hey! I bought quinine for her yesterday. Two dollars and forty-five cents."

Curtis halted. I glanced back at his face. He looked so angry that I thought for a moment that he would turn and hit the fellow. But then, saying nothing, he merely continued downstairs and out into that terrible night, helping Thomas to put Elinor into the carriage, helping Elinor and me in beside her, and then climbing in himself.

We took Elinor to her parents' house. I cannot say that they welcomed her, but certainly they took her in with a sense of duty, with a relief that she had survived her sojourn in the wilderness, and that she was safe again where she belonged, with her family.

She did not recover for weeks. And meanwhile, that spring, I had my own difficulties to confront, the greatest of which was telling Perseus of the child that soon, now, would be born.

Isabel, having seen my condition and having suspected my liaison with Otis Whittemore, was not surprised when I told her. But she did show some small alarm when I asked her help in telling Perseus. "And Curtis too," I said. "You must both be with me. You must make Perseus understand that for the child's sake there must be no rupture—no scandal, no hint from him that the child is not his."

Otis' child: but for its sake it needed to be known as

Perseus'. When it is grown, I thought, I will tell it; Otis would have wanted me to do that.

Isabel turned away from me. "Why should I help you?" she said. Her voice took on a hard edge. "You had your little affair, and you enjoyed it well enough while it was going on. I was sorry when he was killed, and I would have told you that if you had spoken to me about his death. But you did not, and so I kept quiet. Now you want me to help you with your husband?"

Curtis, I thought; Curtis will do as I ask.

"Oh, Marian." Isabel took a deep breath; she moved toward me, her eyes glistening with tears. "I am sorry. I should not have spoken so. The truth is, I envy you. Can you understand that? I envy you because—because you have been loved, truly loved by a man whom you loved in reutrn. While I—"

She caught herself; instinctively she put her hand over her mouth to keep from saying more. And all unbidden, rising to the surface of my thoughts from some deep, dark pool of memory, appeared a vision of a man who had spoken to me on Marlborough Street one warm spring evening years ago, an impetuous young man who had begged me to give his message to Isabel, whose photograph I had seen as it lay broken at her feet. . . .

She could not speak. She turned away from me again, and now it was I who went to her and embraced her and held her as if she were the sister I had never had. And two days later she and Curtis together helped me to confront my husband with the news that I was to bear a child that was not his.

He was very angry at first, although he said little. His

eyes, glaring behind the spectacles which he wore always, were fixed on me for the entire time that Curtis spoke— for it was Curtis who pleaded my case, as if we were in court, while I, like a dutiful client, sat quietly by.

At last Curtis finished what he had to say. Perseus did not reply at once; he looked around at us, his head lowered as if he would charge at us; but the effect was that of a goat, not a bull.

Then: "And I am simply to accept this—this *bastard?*" he said.

"*No!*" The cry broke from me; I started up but at a warning glance from Curtis I sank back.

"You will accept your wife's child as if it were your own," said Curtis.

"And if I do not?"

"You are free to leave her, of course. But you will be penniless, as you were when you married her."

"I will have a settlement—"

"You will have nothing."

Perseus sat crouched in his chair, his mouth working, his body twisting this way and that. I found the sight of him too painful, and so I looked at Curtis instead. His face was a mixture of contempt and pity; I could not tell which was the stronger.

"You will go on as though nothing has happened," said Curtis. "People will congratulate you on the birth of your child. You will thank them for their good wishes. You will continue in your work which is so important to you and which you could not do without your wife's support. You will make no scandal."

"Curtis—" Even though I had begged his help, I did

not want to see him rub salt in Perseus' wounds.

"We made a bargain, my wife and I," said Perseus. "A fair exchange. I have kept my part. And never once have I insulted her by demanding that she perform—"

He stopped of his own accord, glancing at Isabel. "I beg your pardon," he said. He spoke with a curious formality, as if they had met at one of her receptions. "I am not myself, as I am sure you understand." He paused, collecting himself. He looked at the three of us: an uneven contest, one against three. No, I thought; you will not act now. You will withdraw, you will hold your revenge and nurture it and someday—when? five years? ten?—you will have back at us. At me.

I was afraid, then; and I thought that perhaps we had been mistaken to appeal to him. I should simply have left him, I thought.

But no: I wanted my child to have a name, a proper home, a place in the world. I would stay with Perseus, I would make a life for the child.

He was born at the end of April, when the spring came. When I held him for the first time I felt a rush of love as I had never known, not even with Otis. My son, I thought, my joy, my life. And because I could not name him for his father I named him Edward, after Ned.

Ten

Some years later, quite by accident, I found Perseus' diaries. Like the meticulous, obsessive man that he was, he had recorded in them every detail of his involvement with his Society, of all the arduous work that he did for it, day after day, night after night.

And, too, he added from time to time his thoughts and comments on his personal life: on me, on the child:

April 29, '84

The bastard child has been born. Pray I may never touch it!

I could not return to that house—not then, not to her and her shame. Women are punished for what they do; they cannot hide their sin. I would brand the scarlet A upon her if I could. She parades as a virtuous woman, but she is no better than a streetwalker. She used her filthy woman's body just as they do; but she is worse than they, for they at least have cause, they sell themselves to live. She had no need to do that.

Why? Why did she submit to him, why did she allow herself to be so fouled?

I do not understand her. How can women permit such things to happen to them?

And I—I had to listen to Kittredge's congratulations. Does he know the truth? Was he laughing at me?

I will never recover from this shame. I have done nothing to deserve it, and yet I must suffer it.

A man came into the office today to complain of a bookseller in Washington Street who sold a filthy book to the man's wife, a novel, a story of seduction and betrayal. The man found it under his wife's mattress and demanded to know where she got it. Finally she told him, and he went to the place and saw that the proprietor had many others like it for sale. He refused to remove them from the shelves. So the man came to me. I will visit the bookseller tomorrow, and I will have his shop closed if he does not agree to stop selling filth.

This man complained of the shame that his wife brought on him. What does he know of shame? Let me tell you about my wife instead, I thought, so that you can know what some men suffer.

I left the Society's offices at six and took a bite to eat at Sheffield's. By seven, when I had finished, it was full dark. I began to walk. I went to the familiar district; I saw many faces that I have seen before, men's as well as women's. Many of the men regularly go there, they are slaves to their filthy habit as an opium eater is.

A woman approached me: pale, heavyset. She offered herself and as usual I rebuffed her. She turned away, and as she did so I heard my voice—surely it was mine?—call her back.

"Wait!"

She came to me again.

I stood before her, trembling, uncertain, and then I took heart, I found my courage and continued:

"Tell me—tell me why you do this."

She stared at me, uncomprehending. I tried again.

"Can you understand? I want to know why you do this. Why don't you find decent employment?"

She backed away from me and I followed her.

"I won't hurt you. Here—" I fumbled for my purse. "Look—I'll pay you if you will talk to me—"

She turned and fled; I saw the flutter of her cloak as she vanished around a corner.

I will try again. Watching them is not enough. I must discover the secret of what they do. I will go with them if need be. But I must—I *must*—learn more about them.

Eleven

"The stupid little fool," said Isabel. "She has run to London."

"Who?" I asked.

"Elinor."

"Elinor!"

"Yes. Gone, with a young man. With Harry Lathrop, of all people."

It was the day after our return from Newport where once again we had stayed with Mrs. Reed while Isabel's cottage was being built: Isabel and her children (and Avery when he could get away) and my infant son and I. I had hardly expected to see Isabel so soon again, but here she was in my drawing room at five o'clock of a warm September afternoon, her plans for the evening in disarray, her face a picture of outrage and stupefaction, her voice rising in the anger that she could not show to the world.

"When—how did you hear?" I said.

"She was at Nahant with Mother and Father. She told them last week that she was going to Bar Harbor to stay with the Griswolds. Instead they received a telegram from her that she was en route to England."

"And who is—what's his name? Lathrop?"

"He's six years her junior, only twenty-two, just out of college. He's related to the Phelpses—he's good enough family, but his head's as fuzzy as Elinor's, if not more so. Poor Mother! The scandal will be very hard for her. She knows perfectly well what people will say, and of course they *will* say it."

"But are they married—engaged—?"

"Nothing at all, that's the worst of it. She isn't in love with him at all, they haven't eloped, they're simply traveling together. Can you imagine it? She's done it now—burned every bridge. It was hard enough for Mother to hold up her head when Elinor went to live on Rutland Street, but this is the end, absolutely. She'll never be received in Boston again."

"Obviously she doesn't care."

"No. Not a bit. Stupid—stupid! She was always selfish, she never cared for anyone's feelings."

"She has devoted her life to the poor," I said. "Do you call that selfish?"

"She has caused her family great pain. And, yes, I do call that selfish. I question her so-called charity. She has not cared whom she offended, she has given endless worry to Mother and Father, and now this. Well. Good riddance, I say. I shan't miss her. Oh, you needn't look so shocked, Marian. You know how she was always reproaching us for having enough to eat, for having good clothing and decent houses. Why shouldn't we? Father and Avery and Curtis work hard enough. Why shouldn't they profit from it? But no: if Elinor were in charge, she'd have them give all their money away and then we'd all be as poor as the people she says she's trying to help.''

Not even a year ago, I thought, I had written my own message to the husband I would have left behind. Fate had determined that I must stay. Now Elinor—of all people!—had gone instead, impelled not by love but by some need to rebuff her family and all that it stood for; even, I thought, to publicly denounce them, humiliate them, punish them for crimes which they had not known they committed—the crime of being well off, perhaps: the crime of being comfortably fed and clothed and housed while others, those others whom Elinor was driven to protect, had nothing.

Isabel had troubles of her own that day, and soon they came to a head. When she left Newport, Richard Van Brunt had given her a revised estimate of the cost of her house. The new figure was half again as much as the original: Isabel's imagination had taken flight over the summer, and almost every day she had thought of some change in Van Brunt's plan, or some addition to it, which drove up the cost. Never, apparently, did she have an idea that would have meant less expense rather than more. Avery had given her, I suppose, a more or less free rein, and she was determined to have the grandest house on Bellevue Avenue. Ten years later, of course, her efforts were eclipsed by the Mesdames Vanderbilt, but for now, for a season or two, she would be the acknowledged ruler of that little kingdom, and she intended to live up to that role. She had marble mantels quarried from Siena, gold fixtures in the bathrooms, antique tiles on the floor of the courtyard and the loggia, carved wainscoting around the library walls, a coffered ceiling in the ballroom, fountains in the garden and copies of Roman statues—she wanted it all, and more besides.

The house was designed as a villa in the Italian style, with rooms arranged around a glass-roofed atrium, rough, stucco walls, and a red tile roof, a campanile—"The country style, Mrs. Kittredge, a rustic seaside retreat," the architect had said.

Since it was to be cheek by jowl with all the others on the narrow strip of land between Bellevue Avenue and the sea, it was hardly to be a "retreat": each one, whimsically referred to as a "cottage," rose grander than the next, piles of masonry and granite and shingles in a dozen European styles, miniature castles perched above the Cliff Walk, strung out along the bluff like garish ornaments. These were not comfortable summer homes like the Januarys' place at Nahant: they were ostentatious showplaces, built mostly by the invading New York crowd who flocked increasingly to Newport during the season and who were not content to summer in the old way, with spartan comforts, innocently coming to the sea to take the air and the benefits of salt-water bathing. These holidaymakers were of a different breed, and it was their women who commanded them. The men had made their fortunes in the railroads, or in mining, or by some other means fair or foul; and now, to show the world their success, their women spent their money by the millions.

All summer while the foundations for her cottage were being laid, Isabel laid another sort of groundwork. She met everyone—everyone who mattered, that is—and by the time we returned to Boston she had established herself as a person to be reckoned with in the coming season. She worked as hard at what she did as any man in his profession; once, coming upon her as she snatched a moment's rest on Mrs. Reed's veranda, I asked her why she did not simply stay at home for the afternoon, and the evening too, for that matter, since she seemed so tired.

"Stay at home!" she said. "What should I gain by doing that?"

"Nothing, I suppose. But you look done up."

"I am done up. Why shouldn't I be? But Mrs. Warriner is leaving tomorrow, and I must call on her before she goes. She will be a tremendous help to me next year."

"You do all right on your own. And in any case, what does it matter? Why do you do any of it?"

She looked at me as if I had lost my wits. "Why—I do it because it's what I have to do. What else should I do? Sit here and wait for Avery to come down every weekend?"

As the summer passed and Isabel's house rose from its foundations day by day like some fantasy materialized, her face took on a hard, determined expression, her voice rang ever more sharply, she knew no rest as she flitted from one engagement to the next, as she and Van Brunt badgered the workmen at the site. Sometimes it seemed that she survived on will alone: "See me," she seemed to say, "I make my mark, I build my house, I am a person to be reckoned with."

Ambitious? Yes, indeed—as ambitious as any man.

309

And what was she to do with her ambition? How was she to live quiet and complacent when she carried within her soft woman's body the temperament of a captain of industry, a copper king, a robber baron?

But Avery's fortune was not inexhaustible. Nor was his patience, as she learned to her dismay a few days after she brought me the news of Elinor's escape to London.

She had put Van Brunt's bill in her escritoire, knowing as women have known from the beginning of time that she needed to wait for a favorable moment to ask her husband for money. Several days later she thought that it had come. They had dined at home—for a wonder—and after dinner Avery had retired to his study. She had had no hint during their meal that anything troubled him, else she would never have gone afterward to present him with Van Brunt's bad news. She knocked and entered; she seldom went there, and she felt like a stranger in her own house as she did so now.

He did not look up at once. He was reading a book—what, she could not tell—and he finished the page and went on to the next before he acknowledged her. He sat turned away from her, so that she could not see his expression; had she been able to do so, she might have fled to the safety of her room before saying one word to him.

"Avery?"

At last he recognized her. He did not relinquish his book but closed it and looked up. And now suddenly she saw that he was angry, and she cast about for some reason—some other, plausible reason—for interrupting him.

But he gave her no chance. He tapped the leather cover of the book and said, "Have you seen this?"

"What? Oh—that!" she said, relieved. But why was he angry? "Charlotte promised me that she would write in it every day. Did she give it to you to read?"

"She did not." He was only thirty-eight or -nine, but just now he seemed much older; more like her father, she thought, than a man of her own generation. His square, pale face was without expression, but his mouth was drawn down in an unpleasant way, and his eyes, never large, were ominously narrowed, glinting at her. "I found this on the window seat in the third-floor hall," he said. "I thought that it might be yours. I intended to return it to you. I glanced at it to see what it was."

He paused. He seemed to be accusing her of something, she had no idea what.

"*Have you seen this?*" he said. She had never heard such a voice from him.

"I don't— What is it? It is only Charlotte's journal, she doesn't show me—"

Suddenly he lunged up from his chair. She was so startled that she stepped back, narrowly missing a plant stand where rested a big, lush fern. He thrust the volume at her. "Read it!" he said. "Open it at any page and read—read aloud to me!"

She had taken it from him, an automatic gesture to keep it from dropping. Now she looked at it, dismayed, as if it were an artifact from some unknown place, a strange thing from savage people with a curse upon it, perhaps— something that might harm her.

"Read it!" he said again; he was angrier than before,

his voice was strangled with rage—why?

She did so. She opened it at random and began: "'July 15. To the beach this morning with Vicky and Arthur and Miss Dolland. Found a new shell and took it for Mama. After lunch, went to find her. She was on the veranda with Mr. Van Brunt. Aunt Reed said not to bother them, so I did not. Mama always looks so pretty! I do not like Mr. Van Brunt. He laughs at everything I say whether I am trying to be funny or not. Usually I am not. Mama went out with him'—I don't understand, Avery. What is wrong with this? It is simply a recitation of her day."

"Go on," he said.

"But—"

"Go on! Do not argue with me, just do as I say!"

She continued. "'Mama came back while I was bathing again. When I went to find her, she was lying down, not to be disturbed. After supper, went to find her again. She was dressing for a party. She said I could watch her if I stayed quiet. But Vicky came in too and tried to play with Mama's jewelry, so Miss Dolland made us both come away. I practiced my wool-work for an hour and read two chapters of *Little Men* before I went to bed.

"'July 16. I went early to see Mama, but she was still sleeping. After we went bathing, I met Mama's friend Mrs. Tucker. She said that I must stand up straight or I'll get a hump. I am much taller than she is, but not nearly so pretty. She and Mama went to a luncheon party. After afternoon rest, Mama came home but she went out right away again with Mr. Van Brunt. Mama is always busy. I wish I could see her more often. I went to find the shell I had saved for her. I wanted to put it on her dressing table with a note. But I can't find it anywhere. Maybe Vicky took it.'"

She stopped. She raised her eyes to his.

"Did Charlotte ever give you that shell?" he said.

"No."

"Never mentioned it?"

"No."

"I would remind you, Isabel, that your primary responsibility is to your family. You are the mother of five children. Your life should be devoted to them."

She stared at him. We have had this quarrel before, she thought, why does he begin it again now? And Charlotte! To be so stupid as to leave her diary lying about for anyone to find!

Just then a newspaper clipping slipped from between the back pages and fluttered to the floor.

"What is that?" he said.

Her instinct warned her not to retrieve it, and so she did not.

"Let me see it," he said.

"It is nothing. You see—" And in one swift movement, surprisingly agile for so plump a woman, so tightly laced, she picked it up and glanced at it. "Gala at Wysop's" read the heading, followed by many names, her own among them.

He held out his hand and she gave it to him. He read it quickly, the anger on his face overlaid by disgust. "You make a public spectacle of yourself. This is outrageous! Did you know about this? And who is this man who wrote it up? Have you met him? Do you actually speak to such people?" The clipping trembled slightly in his fingers, and she began now to be frightened. What would he do? Surely she could not ask him, now, for more money for Van Brunt. Stupid Charlotte—careless and stupid and irresponsible—

"Well?" he said.

"I—I have seen him. I have never been formally introduced, of course. He stands by the driveway, wherever there is a reception, or a ball, to see who goes."

"And you and all your friends allow your reputations to be ruined by this person?"

"We do not allow it, we cannot prevent him—"

"You can prevent him very easily, by not going in the first place!" He threw the clipping onto a table, where it was almost lost among the piles of books and magazines and papers. "You hold us up to public ridicule! Your name—*my* name—in the gossip sheets! What are you thinking of? Have you no concern for your children? Have you taken leave of your senses entirely? You are a public spectacle—and you make fools of us all!"

She felt a wave of defeat wash over her; she nearly staggered under its blow. Van Brunt would have to wait. And if he pressed her, if he threatened to stop—but he would not. He had invested too much, himself, to stop work now; he had no choice but to proceed, to build this magnificent house which would so greatly enhance his reputation. Damn Charlotte! Twelve years old, a great lumbering goose of a girl, stupid and shy and totally without promise. And Avery wanted her, Isabel, to spend her life with that child, with all the children! She knew women who did that: quiet, dull, domestic women who did nothing, knew nothing except their husbands and children. Never: she could never endure such a life. She would go mad. It was bad enough that she had had to bear the children in the first place; should she bury herself alive into the bargain? She had never wanted them; had never even considered their possibility when Avery came courting. They had simply happened; she had had no way to stop them. Against her will—but what good was women's will against the husband's power? It was all very well for him to complain: he didn't have the burden of them, the agony of pregnancy, the worse agony of giving birth, the helplessness, the fear and the pain and the battering of one's body— Ah, but now it was different, now she had a defense against him, she had her apparatus from Elinor's female physician and she need never suffer so again.

The house was quiet, the children long abed. They faced each other, man and wife, like opponents in a duel. So far, she thought, it is a standoff; and I will never concede defeat, not if he runs me through the heart.

She stared up at him, defiant, undaunted by his height, his bulk. "We will see who is the fool here," she said. "And I will thank you to speak to me with a civil tongue from now on. I am the mother of your children, as you say, and I will be spoken to with proper respect or not at all."

Not waiting to hear his reply, she left him and went upstairs. She had no idea how she would get the money she needed but all the same she felt oddly exhilarated. We do not pretend any longer, she thought: our mutual dislike is acknowledged, and we can deal honestly with each other from now on. She swept up the wide, shallow stairs like a small galleon in full sail; the upstairs maid, coming out into the second-floor hall after having lit the fire in Isabel's room and turned down the coverlet on the bed, took one look at her mistress' face and fled to the safety of the back stairs.

Isabel went to Charlotte's room, however, rather than her own. Charlotte, who was reading in bed, was surprised to see her mother; Isabel did not often pay evening visits to her children.

Isabel sat on the edge of the bed. "Something very unpleasant has happened," she said. "Can you guess what it is?"

Charlotte flushed. "Did Vicky—"

"It has nothing to do with Vicky. It has to do with the diary I gave to you on your birthday."

Charlotte started to cry. "She took it. She says she didn't, but I know she did. I always put it in the bottom of the armoire—"

Isabel sat silent for a moment. "I see," she said. "Your father said that he found it upstairs. I was surprised that you were so careless, but now I understand. And of course she will have to be punished."

"Did he read it?" sobbed Charlotte.

"Yes." And he, too, should be punished for that, thought Isabel; but she did not say it, it would have violated the unwritten rule that adults were free to behave badly as children were not. "Charlotte," she said, "listen to me." She put her hand on the child's heaving, trembling shoulder; she could not remember the last time that she had touched her. "When I gave that diary to you, I hoped for two things: that you would use it to

316

improve your penmanship, and that you would learn to observe and record accurately what you saw. If I had known that you would use it to attack me, to make me look like an unfit, selfish woman who neglects you—"

She saw the child's shocked, frightened face. She knew that she should say no more, that her anger was building in her again and she should leave, now, before it made wounds that would never heal. But all the anger that she had wanted to loose upon her husband, and could not, exploded within her now and erupted upon her child: anger at Van Brunt's bill, anger at Avery's chastisement, anger at bearing children whom she had not wanted, at being told that she must give up the only part of her life that mattered in order to care for them.

And, of course, the deepest, most painful anger of all: the nagging, gnawing rage at that one who, so long ago, had deserted her, had thrown her gift of herself back into her face, had wounded her heart and, worse, her pride— "You stupid, stupid child!" she cried. The pain of her loss was with her still, after all the years; and so now she surrendered to it, she embraced it as she had never embraced that faithless lover. "How dare you write such things? You are a disgrace to me—to all of us! I am building the grandest house in Newport, you will have the most brilliant coming-out of the season when it is your time, you will have your pick of the most eligible young men—and all because of what I do now! And you dare to criticize me? You dare to say those things about me?"

And so on and on, her voice rising until it rang through the house, but she did not know it. The maid, alarmed, had summoned Avery. He took her to her room; he sent the coachman for the doctor. Isabel's maid unlaced her and put her to bed. The doctor came and gave her a sedative. The younger children, sleeping, mercifully had not awakened.

The next day but one, Isabel paid a visit—a special private visit—to her father. She played her part perfectly. She wept a bit as she produced Van Brunt's bill; she called the architect a dozen names, all of them bad; but in the end she admitted that he was, after all, only doing what she had asked him to do.

Asa January, not ordinarily a softhearted man, took pity on her. "I'll make it good," he said, "and anything else he charges—within reason, mind!"

And as she flung herself upon him in a grateful embrace, he reminded himself that he had only one daughter now, and that she was here in his arms. The other had gone away; she would not return. "There," he said, "there! It'll be all right! Drat the fellow—let him do as he will, and don't ask Avery for another cent. Tell him it's taken care of!"

Twelve

"By that time, of course," Curtis told me, "Perseus had begun to lay the groundwork for his own destruction; destroying people at will, he might have expected that they would act in kind."

And he recorded it all, how they hunted him in the night, even as he stalked the streetwalkers.

The woman walked so quickly that Perseus could hardly keep up; she might have been running away from him rather than taking him to her room. He felt his breath come short; the night air was bitter cold, for it was only March and winter still, and as he inhaled he felt the cold go down into his lungs and chill him inside as well as out. His eyes watered, his nose dripped, the skin of his face felt frozen into an icy mask.

The woman stopped at a doorway, waiting for him. When he reached her she turned and led the way upstairs. There was no light; he stumbled once or twice, but he managed to stay close behind her.

She was new; he had not seen her before. He, Perseus Motley, was more familiar with these streets now than many of the women who sold themselves; he often spoke to them, often returned with them to their rooms as he did now. He never performed the act that was their livelihood. He talked to them, he paid them for their time; sometimes he gave them extra for food or coal. He did not know why he acted so: he told himself that he needed to do his work for the Society, but it was not true, no one did such work alone, they always went in pairs.

They came to a door in the upstairs hall. She knocked; after a moment she entered. It was empty. She struck a light and put it to the wick of the kerosene lamp on the table.

"Just lock that door," she said. "You pay for an hour, I want to give you full time."

No, he said, in what had by now become his standard speech; he would pay her, but he did not want her—ah—services, he wanted only to talk to her, he said, to ask her about her life. He had acquired a small notebook in which he made notes on his work, including this; often he felt as daring, as intrepid, as a man who explored, say, unmapped portions of Africa for the Royal Geographic Society.

Warily she stared at him, torn between fear and amused contempt. "A girl told me last month she had a fellow that didn't want her on her back, he wanted her sitting up, talking. Must've been you."

"Perhaps it was. Miss—ah—?"

That made her laugh. *"Miss?* It's been a good long while since anyone called me that."

She pulled a chair from the table and sat down heavily, as if she were very tired. She was perhaps thirty years old; although her face was beginning to show signs of the wear and tear of her profession, it was not unattractive. What gave it its greatest appeal, he thought, was its intelligence: unlike most women of her profession, she was not stupid. He felt a twinge of interest, greater than usual. He hoped that she would talk freely. Without being asked, he sat opposite her; pushing the lamp out of his line of vision, he thought how he must phrase his first question so as to put her at ease. Sometimes women thought that he was from the police, and so they were reluctant to talk to him; other times they were willing enough, but because they were dim-witted or simply inarticulate they were unable to tell him much.

"Now," he said, "if you would tell me your name—" He was conscious of her amused stare; it annoyed him.

"Never," she said, and she laughed. "Never! I've got a new name now and I'll never go back to the old. That way, my man'll not find me, d'y'see?" She spoke with a slight accent which he could not identify.

"Very well, then. Your new name."

"Queenie," she said. "What are you? A newspaper writer?"

"No."

"You just like to talk? What's the matter, is your wife a dummy?"

He did not like to hear her mention his wife; it offended his sense of propriety. She understood, she laughed softly. "How do I know you're not from the police?"

"I assure you—"

"No. If you were from the police you'd have showed

me your hand long since, yes? Well. You're a proper queer one. Put your money on the table, then, and I'll sing whatever song you like."

She gave him the full hour. Her story was the same as all the others that he had heard: different in detail, but still the same sad tale. An unhappy home, a man who betrayed her, abandonment, poverty, starvation. She spoke fluently enough, once she had properly begun, but entirely without emotion; she hardly seemed to be aware that it was her own story that she told, she might have been telling him some other woman's tale. He needed to ask no more questions, after the first; she seemed to know what he wanted, and she gave it to him. He paid close attention, as he always did; even though he could predict what she would say, he wanted to hear it, he never tired of hearing it. Her story, like all the others, spoke to something deep within him, something that he could not have named. When he was safely home again he would write it down in a notebook that he kept locked in his desk in his room. Many pages of that notebook were filled now: soon he would need to buy a second. The Society would benefit greatly from his researches; the Board of Directors would commend him. And not only for his work, which he did after hours and secretly, on his own account; but for all the other work he did—patrolling the city's bookstores, attending theatrical performances, watching for obscene behavior in the streets. His work was never done; he staggered constantly under its burden.

At last she fell silent. Her shawl had slipped from her shoulders; she wore only a blouse underneath. He had watched her face as she spoke. Now his eyes traveled down to her shoulders, her bare arms, the outline of her uncorseted body beneath its thin covering. He could even see the shape of her legs, for her skirt was as flimsy as her blouse and she seemed to wear no petticoats. She let him look at her without comment. She smiled a little, indulging him. He was aware that he trembled; he felt the film of perspiration on his face. Disease, he thought. She carries disease—certain death.

Suddenly she reached out and took his hand and placed it on her breast. He was so startled that he let it stay for a moment, feeling the soft, warm flesh and big, hard nipple. In the next instant he pulled his hand away as if it had touched fire. He heard his breath drawn in in a hiss; he looked at his hand and saw that it was raised as if to strike her. He was very frightened—of her, of himself, he did not know which.

Without a further word he fled. He stumbled down the stairs and burst out into the dark street. Rapidly, he began to walk.

"Of course they had begun to watch him," Curtis told me, years afterward. "Even then—even that night, I am sure, someone trailed him home."

He never knew: not until it was too late.

Thirteen

In May of '85, Isabel's cottage at Newport was complete. She was delighted with it; some of the rest of us did not know what to say. Next to her, at least: to me, Farnsworth Bowditch expressed his feelings quite honestly. "Why didn't she simply go ahead and paper the walls with ten-dollar notes?" he snorted after receiving his grand tour.

The house overlooked a wide lawn which sloped down to the Cliff Walk. This narrow path along the rocks at the edge of the sea was a public way, much to the distress of people whose houses abutted it; they had tried to have the public banned from the Walk, but the courts had ruled that it had always been a free way, and free it would remain. Thus even the wealthiest of the wealthy—an Astor or a Vanderbilt—might expect to see common people walking past the edge of their property, gawking at the great houses going up. The wealthy erected iron fences and stone walls to protect themselves, but still they felt vulnerable. One never knew, strolling on one's own piece of very expensive real estate, when one would

encounter people from the town ogling their betters. But
the presence of the Cliff Walk did not deter those who,
like Isabel, wanted their houses to be in the most
agreeable location—that is, by the water—and so the
houses went up, and ordinary folk took their constitu-
tionals, and the two factions, rich and poor, maintained
an uneasy coexistence.

Isabel's place was a nine-day wonder. Everyone longed
to see it, and of course she planned a great ball to
introduce it to society. To her close friends and family
she gave a private tour in June, before the summer season
had officially begun. She took up residence at the first of
the month and she insisted that I stay with her.

"If there is one thing that I have here, Marian, it is
room—Avery and the children and I will positively rattle
here if I don't have constant company. And you and
Perseus and the baby shall be the first."

He was a year old that summer, my Edward. His hair
was brown, like his father's, although the sun brought
out a reddish tint. His face was plump as babies' faces are,
but already I could see Otis' face in it. He was never still
save in sleep; toward the middle of the summer he began
to walk, and after that his sturdy little legs carried him
everywhere and I followed happily behind, helping him,
watching over him as he explored the world. I had hired a
governess, of course, but she had little enough to do.
"Save yourself, Marian," cautioned Mrs. Reed. "You'll
spoil that woman, she sits all day and reads while you
traipse about." But I wanted to be with him; I did not
want to do as other mothers did, and turn over the
rearing of my child to a stranger. And so we rode in a

pony cart and played on Bailey's Beach and spent our time together, he and I; and once in a while I would attend a luncheon or an evening party, thereby allowing the governess to feel that she was earning her wages.

Perseus, to my surprise, consented to come; but he stayed only a few days before decamping for Boston and a convention to be addressed by the noted reformer Comstock. He seemed to have reconciled himself to our situation; he hardly saw the child and never sought him out, but he was civil enough to me. His work was more important to him than any human tie; and if in order to accomplish it he needed to be polite to me, he was apparently prepared to do so.

And so we went to stay in that wondrous villa by the sea, the Casa del Mare, as it was to be known, with its square bell tower lacking a bell, and its red tile roof, where every room had a different theme and the whole was an uneasy melding of clashing styles. The rooms opened onto corridors surrounding a three-story glass-roofed courtyard with a fountain and a shallow, tile-rimmed pool. On the second floor was a gallery open to the lawn and the sea. Van Brunt had supervised the decoration himself; I do not know how accurate his knowledge of historical periods was. The library was a shrine to the Gothic era, with pikestaffs crossed over the massive stone fireplace and leaded windows and a flagstone floor scattered with the skins of dead animals. The walls were lined with shelves of books—real books: you could, if you wished, take them down and read them. I am sure that Isabel never did, although Charlotte, once or twice, may have done so.

Isabel's bedroom, of course, was French, in the style of Louis Seize. The ceiling and walls were decorated with gold-leaf moldings and plaster rosettes; pale blue silk hangings at the tall windows matched the lace-trimmed coverlet on the wide bed. Fragile gilt tables and chairs were arranged in little groupings here and there; a small pink brocade chaise was the only thing remotely sturdy enough to sit on. But nothing in that house was meant to be used in everyday life, for the house itself had an unreal, dreamlike quality—Isabel's vision materialized. It was meant to be a showplace, a kind of miniature Versailles where Isabel would hold court. Even the bathroom which adjoined her bedroom was Louis Seize, although I doubt that the King of France had sea water piped into his tub as Isabel did. The drawing room was Louis Quinze; the dining room, England of the Renaissance, with two dozen high-backed chairs lining the long trestle table, and heavy candelabra, and tapestries of hunting scenes hung on the walls. The ballroom, which extended as a one-story addition from the main house toward the sea, was walled in mirrors, so that the figures of the dancers would be multiplied again and again into a never ending panorama of delight.

And so we went and we looked at it all, and we told her what she wanted to hear. And in July, when the season had properly begun, she threw open her new and very expensive doors and welcomed in a hundred or so of the best of the summer people, and for a while—for that season, at least—she was the most sought-after hostess in Newport. I heard, later, that women who wanted to make the best match for their daughters schemed and plotted to receive an invitation for one or another of Isabel's events; Isabel was "smart," she was the latest fashion.

On the night of her first ball the moon hung large over the water and the air was warm and fragrant with the smell of roses from her garden overlaying the sour salt smell of the sea, and the house sat like a great lightship at the edge of the lawn, laughter and music pouring out.

Couples swirled around the ballroom to the insistent beat of the waltz. The young women bloomed like flowers—hothouse flowers, blossoming under glass: their waists drawn in, bosoms and hips swelling out, the hems of their gowns billowing about their feet, sometimes entangling their partners' long, slim legs so that for a moment the man and the woman seemed one, whirling and gliding across the floor, one-two-three, one-two-three.

After a time the noise became too much for me and I left the little group of mamas with whom I had been sitting and I slipped through the open french doors to the terrace and then to the lawn below, away from the light and the noise. Grateful for the cool night air on my face and shoulders, I made my way across the grass to the stone wall overlooking Cliff Walk. Beyond it, the dark sea murmured against the rocks, gentler here than at Nahant, inaudible against the music.

"Is that you, Marian?"

The voice startled me, even as I recognized it. I turned to see Curtis standing behind me. The moon was so bright that I could see his face clearly; he was smiling at me as he offered me a glass of champagne.

"Party too noisy for you?" he said. "I trust that Isabel

is enjoying herself. She's worked hard enough to finish the place in time for the season."

"It was the workmen who worked," I laughed. "Isabel—and Mr. Van Brunt—simply directed them."

"Yes," he said. "She's very good at that—at directing."

He leaned against the stone wall, his back to the sea, and sipped his own champagne. Although I had seen him in company from time to time over the winter, I had not had a word alone with him since I didn't know when.

"How is Edward?" he said.

"Very well. He took his first steps last week."

"Ah. A milestone. And you have had no trouble from your husband?"

"No. I hardly ever see him."

He accepted this in silence; he knew what it meant. Then: "Marian, if you want to divorce him—"

"On what grounds?"

"On the grounds of no true marriage."

"You mean unconsummated? But then the presence of my son makes me an adulteress. Perseus would have to bring suit against me, which I doubt he would do now, after claiming paternity. And even if he did, they might try to take my child away from me. Furthermore, even if I were able to get a divorce, my child would suffer far more than I. You know that. I would be ostracized, and he along with me. So I will stay as I am. As long as Perseus is content to live so, as long as he lets us live without interference—"

"As long as you are all right, Marian. And reasonably happy."

"I am that."

"The child makes you happy, doesn't he?"

"Yes. Very."

"Grace would be overjoyed if we had a child. Well. It is too late now." He stood quiet beside me, thinking perhaps of that fortune that he had married, and of how happy—or unhappy—it had made him.

At last he turned to me, smiling, and lifted his empty glass. "Here—are you done with yours? Good. Throw them out—smash them onto the rocks—and wish for good luck for both of us."

He threw his first and I followed. We heard the faint tinkling crash against the rocks beneath us.

"*Christ*, will y'watch what y're doin'!"

The voice was a man's—very prompt, very angry—coming at us out of the darkness below. I was too startled even to scream. In the next moment a face appeared below the stone wall. It was turned up to us, a pale, thin face, angry to match the voice, and now in the light of the moon I could see several people beyond the Cliff Walk, standing on an outcropping of rock. They massed together into one dark shape darker than the moonlit night; none of them moved or said a word.

"Damn!" muttered Curtis. And to his accuser: "Sorry! I didn't know you were there!"

"We've every right to be."

"Yes—yes, I know you do."

"So watch how you throw your glass next time. If you cut me I'll cut you back."

The face disappeared; he turned away from us and stepped across the walk to join his friends. Silently they all stared up at us and we stared down at them; and we all of us heard the music and laughter and the sounds of the celebration of Isabel's dream.

After a moment Curtis took my arm and walked me back across the lawn; it seemed to be a gesture of surrender.

Fourteen

Informants came often to Perseus; he could not have survived without them.

A man came one day that summer to the Society's offices. Perseus, having met with Mr. Comstock, had stayed in Boston alone rather than join us again in Newport. He listened to what the man had to say and then he promised a small sum in payment—"if what you tell me is correct, mind. I pay only for good hard facts. You saw this yourself, you say?"

"At Martin's Farm on the Sudbury Road."

"And the next time—"

"Tomorrow night. Ten o'clock. You're goin' t'go?"

"Of course. I must. The Society cannot act without verifying the facts."

"Then I'd dress down if I were you. They don't like strangers, and particularly anyone well off."

There were thunderstorms the following afternoon, but by dusk the sky had cleared. There was no moon. Perseus did not know whether to hire a horse or hack; in the end, although he was hardly an expert rider, he

332

decided on the horse as being less conspicuous. He went to a stable near the Fens, where he was not known, and he asked for their easiest mount. As he made his way out of the city he took deep breaths of the clean, sweet air; how fresh it smelled after the heat and stench of the city streets! Cities were filthy places altogether: vice and crime of every description flourished there. But he could not leave the city, no matter how disgusting he found it, for his work was there; until yesterday he had never imagined that it was in the country too.

He found the place easily enough, for his informant had given him good directions. But as he approached he saw only a single light in the house, as if the occupants were ready to retire, and he wondered if, after all, the man had said this night. As he came to the gate, which stood open, he dismounted and led the horse through it and along the path to the barn. He heard voices then—men's voices, laughing; he rounded the corner of the barn and saw a flaring torch and more just being lighted. A group of perhaps fifty men were assembled: all kinds of men, young and old, rough country men and a few who would have looked at home in any club in Boston.

Two of them arranged the torches around a square of bare ground. Perseus tied his horse and went to stand with the others who were gathering into an audience around the square. Several of them glanced at him curiously, but no one spoke to him. He wore an old jacket and a collarless shirt and a derby hat pushed to the back of his head. When all the torches were in place on their standards, making the barnyard almost as bright as day, several boys threw buckets of water onto the ground, making mud of what had been dry earth. The men shuffled restlessly in their places; although a good deal of badinage had gone on before, they had fallen silent now. They were waiting, not all of them patiently. "Where are they?" called a voice. "Bring 'em out! We're ready!"

At the edge of the crowd stood a man in vest and shirt-sleeves holding a small sheaf of papers. "Gentlemen!" he called. "Close your bets! Bets closing now! Last call!"

He was met with silence: their business with him had already been transacted.

"All right now!" came a voice from near the barn. "Here they come! Make way!"

A murmur of satisfaction swept around the ring. Every head turned to see. They parted to make way.

Two women walked down the narrow path and into the light. They were naked. They held their heads high; they looked at no one. Both were sturdily built, one slightly taller than the other. One was dark, one fair; one perhaps thirty or thirty-two, the other not more than twenty-five. At their appearance, a hiss began in the crowd; it swelled and then it died until all was silent again save for the crackling torches and the chorus of tree frogs and crickets from beyond the barnyard.

The women faced each other in a combative stance in the center of the muddy ring, hands on their hips, heads held high. From the row of men opposite him, Perseus heard a low laugh. "Couple o' beauties, ain't they?" He did not look to see who had spoken; he could not take his eyes from the figures before him. He had never seen an unclothed woman save in pictures. He had a large collection of those, amassed in the course of his work;

but no picture had prepared him for the fleshly reality. The torchlight played over them, giving them a rosy color which softened somewhat the fierce aggressiveness of their pose. Their uncorseted bodies were as strong and sturdy as men's, their muscles rippling under their skin, only their breasts and the patch of hair at the join of their legs identifying them as female.

"All right, now," cried a voice. "Ready—go!"

Cheers and catcalls filled the night as the two women fell on each other. They seemed to embrace, their hands seeking purchase; they struggled for a moment like frantic lovers, and then they toppled to the ground. A cry of approval went up from the audience. "Go, Rosie, get her good! Come on, girl!" The women writhed in the mud. After a moment they were indistinguishable—two filthy figures performing an obscene ritual. The men hooted and howled, urging on their favorite. Some wrestlers, Perseus knew, were actors rather than athletes: they performed, they were paid, and they went home. That was the end of it: there was no rancor in what they did, they did not dislike the person whom they fought. But these two were different: they seemed to hate each other, to take vindictive pleasure in hurting each other. The goal of their contest—for one to pin her opponent's shoulders to the ground—seemed of less interest to them than the opportunity to inflict pain. Or perhaps that was pretending too: he didn't know.

He glanced around. Every eye was intent on the women. The men were grinning, mostly; some held cigars between their teeth, some chewed and spat into the ring. One fellow, to some applause, landed a stream of tobacco juice on the buttocks of one of the women.

For all his fanatical devotion to his cause, Perseus was no fool. He had been gently bred, gently reared; he knew decent human faces when he saw them. He did not see them now. These men were animals—worse, for no animal brutalizes its own kind as these men did.

The women, all this time, had made no sound. They worked in deadly earnest, total silence. Only their eyes and their open mouths gasping for air were free of mud; every inch of their bodies was covered with it, their hair matted and flapping around their faces. They lay quiet for a moment, entwined in each other's limbs. Were they resting, Perseus wondered, or had they simply agreed to play for time, prolonging their audience's pleasure?

Suddenly one of them moved, and instantly came a high pain-filled scream.

"Stop!" cried a man standing near Perseus. "Foul—stop!"

The women had suddenly gone to work again, more intently now, viciously struggling.

"Stop!" cried the man again. He pushed his way through and ran into the ring, nearly slipping and falling in the mud. He grabbed them both by the hair and held their heads apart and then forced himself between them, trying to prevent one from attacking the other.

"My girl's been hurt," he said. "Look—there."

His hands still encumbered, he gestured with his foot to a place on the woman's body where her breast was. "There's blood," he said. "She's been bit." And, turning on the other: "Did y' bite her, y' bitch?"

She shook her head as best she could under his grip on

her hair.

"All right, Donovan. You can let go. Let me have a look."

The speaker—the referee? the owner of the farm?—examined the injury for a moment and then pronounced his verdict: "Right. This is a foul. Fine of twenty dollars. Where's Billy? Ain't he her owner?"

The man named stepped out; he was an enormous brute of a man, a head taller than anyone else, ugly and menacing in his movement. After looking at the wound he turned on the other; he lifted his arm as if to strike her and was prevented from doing so only by the swift reaction of one of the crowd, who jumped out and held him back.

"Bitch," he cried. "I warned you—"

"No, Bill! She's valuable to you still. Don't hurt her!"

With an angry shrug, the man called Bill threw off his restrainer. "All right then," he said. "Go again. And no more fouling."

The women were released, and they set to work again. A good deal of money apparently rode on the outcome, for the cheering for one or the other grew more intense as the end drew near. At last the larger one slipped and fell and was too slow recovering herself. The smaller pinned her and she could not rise. A great cheer went up. Someone ran into the ring and held up her hand in the manner of champions. The defeated one rose slowly; in the light of the torches they could see tears making streaks down her filthy face.

"That's her last bout, I'll wager," muttered a man next to Perseus. "She fouls too often. She's not made enough profit."

"What will she do then?" said Perseus.

"Dunno. On the streets, I suppose." A sudden grin. "Work there's easier, but the money ain't so good."

It was past midnight when Perseus left the farm. He returned to Boston with a heavy heart; so much wrong in the world, so little time to make it right! Despite his long ride he was not tired, and so, after returning the horse to the liveryman, he walked the distance to Beacon Street and then beyond, toward Scollay Square, toward the narrow streets and twisting slum alleys that he had come to know so well. The exhibition which he had just watched had disgusted him: those were not women he had seen, they were subhuman creatures, poor lost creatures who made the women of the streets seem almost like the decent women he knew.

Except—except that no woman was decent. Every one of them—even those who did not engage in sexual congress—every one was a living reminder of the filth, the degradation that Eve had brought into the world.

He found a girl and went with her. She was perhaps eighteen, prettier than most. He did not notice. His mind was filled with the sight of the women wrestling in the mud. He wanted to erase that image—the image of their filthy bodies. When the girl had closed the door to her room, which was on the top floor of a building near the harbor, she turned to him in a businesslike way. "Well, sir? What's it to be?"

He had no idea how to answer. He wanted to see her body. He wanted it to be clean and white and untouched by any suggestion of dirt.

"Do you have water?" he said at last. "A basin and a cloth?"

"What?"

"I said, do you have water?"

"You want a drink? I'll send for it—"

"No—no. I don't want a drink. I want—I want you to wash yourself."

She stared at him, not understanding. He saw a basin and ewer in the corner. He fetched them and put them on the table in the center of the room. He poured water into the basin.

"There," he said. "Go on—wash yourself."

She took a cloth and wet it and began to wipe her face.

"No," he said. "Do it—do it without clothing. I want to see you wash yourself entirely."

She paused, the dripping cloth in her hand; then quickly she shed her few garments.

He nodded. "Yes," he said. "Like that."

Her body was small, thin, childlike. Curiously innocent-looking, he thought. You could look at her as she was now and never know the foul secret of her life. It was hidden, as it had not been in the women he had seen earlier, the women writhing in the mud.

She glanced at him as she worked. Suddenly he moved, startling her. He meant no harm. He wanted only to take the cloth from her, he wanted to wash her himself. He knelt before her. Slowly, carefully, he wiped her body. The cloth had been white; now it was turning gray but he did not notice. Another man, behaving so, might have been called tender and gentle; but this man worked with an intensity and a kind of fierce purpose in which

339

tenderness had no place. Over and over her body he went, wetting the cloth, smoothing the water down her pale skin, until she stood before him all clean, all white, no trace of dirt or sin upon her; and still he washed her, over and over again, as if she would never be clean enough, as if he could spend his life—as indeed he did— washing and washing to make the world pure, to make it shining clean.

Once, when she was growing tired, she looked through the grimy window and saw that the sky had turned gray, announcing daylight. But he would not stop, he would not let her go. All the night he worked, until sunrise made the sky clear and bright, until the world was fresh and sparkling in the dawn.

Fifteen

And still Perseus' obsession grew on him, and obsessively he recorded it.

He went one day to Maxfield's Book Store in Washington Street. There, from a table marked NEW TITLES, he picked up a volume at random. It was *Nana*, by Emile Zola. After a moment he snapped it shut and carried it to the proprietor, who stood by the big brass cash register at the front.

"How many copies of this have you sold?" said Perseus.

Maxfield, who knew him well, regarded him coolly; he did not answer.

"Well?" snapped Perseus.

"That's no affair of yours. Besides—it's in French. How many people do you think can read it?"

"That makes no difference. It is as obscene in French as any other language."

Maxfield ignored him; he moved to ring up the purchase of the man next in line.

As Perseus spoke, customers had drawn near to see the

offending title. He dropped it onto the counter; someone picked it up and began to leaf through it.

"I've warned you before," said Perseus. "I'll close you down if you continue to sell this filth."

Without waiting for a reply he walked out in the direction of Scollay Square. It was late afternoon. To pass the time until dark he stopped at the Union Oyster House. When he had finished his meal it was past six. He came out onto the street and began to walk. At a corner was a newsboy hawking the late edition of the *Telegraph*. Perseus gave him a penny and scanned the front page. It was an ugly mishmash of advertisements. Some—for new coal stoves, for example—were unoffensive; others were even more objectionable, if that were possible, than the novel he had discovered at Maxfield's. "Certain Cure for the Private Disease"; "Lecture by Professor Whitwall for Men Only"; "Secrets of Masculine Vigor." . . .

He felt a wave of repulsion pass over him. He folded the newspaper and held it in his hand like a club. All around him people jostled by; poor people, workmen and office clerks and sailors on shore leave, here and there a well-dressed man like himself. The only women to be seen were the kind he would shortly seek out: no decent woman frequented Scollay Square. Across the street loomed the garish marquee of the Howard Athenaeum: a place which, through its munificent support of the local authorities, had managed to stay open despite repeated efforts by Perseus and his Society to close it down. A line of men stood waiting to purchase tickets for the evening show. On impulse, he joined them. The evening's entertainment, announced on the billboard, was the Rentz-Santley Novelty and Burlesque Co.—"a fantastic burlesque nightmare." For as little as ten cents one could buy a ticket; a dollar bought the best seat in the house. I need not stay, he thought, if it is obscene.

The theater was packed with a noisy, raucous audience; the air was foul with the stench of alcohol and unwashed bodies. Perseus sat in the first tier. In a moment the show began: a vulgar comedian, a line of dancing girls clad in tights and skimpy tops. A pathetic orchestra played off key. A harlot of a woman (or was it a man dressed in women's clothing?) sang an obscene song. The audience cheered as she began to disrobe; she was a woman after all. Perseus sat silent, trembling, fighting down his nausea. Another comedian; a man who did magic tricks; a short, filthy skit between two men and a girl. One of the men kept whipping up her skirt, thrusting his hand to her private parts. The audience roared its approval. Another comedian, another turn of the dancers . . .

It was just past ten when Perseus emerged again into the street. He stood for a moment breathing the cool, salt-tinged night air; after his experience of the last two hours, he wanted nothing so much as to have a bath. But first he had work to do—urgent work that did not allow self-indulgence.

He began to walk. Soon he was well away from the lights and the bustle of the square; he was deep into the warren of side streets where women waited. He felt an urgency such as he had not known before. He felt that the world was an open sewer, one vast Augean stable, and he alone had been assigned the Herculean task of cleaning it. Why did no one help him? Why did no one care? Why did people—human beings like himself—behave so, like animals? He felt that he would never live long enough to complete his work. Ah, why was he so alone?

A woman stood under a street lamp. Hardly breaking his stride, he nodded and beckoned her to him.

"This way," she said. Her eyes gleamed at him; despite his revulsion he followed her. Around the corner, around another. Her room was on the first floor of a narrow building on a dark alley. She closed the door, shot the bolt, and struck a light to the candle. At once she began to disrobe. All his training, all his upbringing, told him to look away, but he watched her. Her body was like every other woman's, capable of arousing a man's lust. It was his life's mission to keep that lust suppressed. All women aroused all men, all men sought to relieve themselves of their arousal. The problem began with women: men were their victims, their prey.

He had never succumbed; he had never lusted. Thus he had thought of himself as stronger than other men, more in control.

But now, watching this woman, he felt a small grain of doubt beginning to irritate his mind. Should he not know what other men knew in order more effectively to help them?

The woman lay on the bed, legs splayed, arms thrown above her head. Her face was expressionless in the dim light.

He felt his body begin to tremble. How disgusting she was, how like a character risen from the pages of that filthy French novel!

Suddenly she laughed. "What's the matter? Can't you do it? Come here, I'll work you up." She held out a hand to him, flicking her fingers impatiently. For her, as for the captain of industry, time was money; and he was wasting her time.

He approached her as if he were walking in a dream. She grasped his hand and pulled him down beside her. She began to loosen his broad, tightly knotted necktie. He flinched and drew back.

"All right, then," she said. "You do it."

But that was impossible. To undress here, in front of her—!

He sat on the edge of the bed. She stared at him. "Put a dollar on the table," she said, "and then come here again. We've not much time."

Numb, he obeyed her. Numb, walking in a dream, he came back to her and, without removing his jacket, began to unbutton his trousers. He had the sense that he would waken momentarily; he watched himself, horrified at what he saw.

She reached for him; she put her hand on him. He shuddered: a violent tremor that rattled his teeth. Her touch was agony. His flesh lay limp and flaccid in her hand. Innocent that he was, he knew nevertheless that it was not supposed to be so. He felt the beginnings of anger.

She put her mouth on him. He tasted his vomit rising.

"No—no—" And yet he did not pull away. He wanted to see if he was like other men; he had been alone for so long, he wanted suddenly, now, tonight, to know that he was as they were, a member of the same species.

Damned bungling whore—! He heard his voice condemning her, but it sounded only in his mind.

She worked him for a long time but she could do nothing. He remained limp. At last she gave up; she drew back.

"It's no good," she said. "Just lie down here and relax and maybe it'll come up by itself." She reached under the thin mattress and produced a battered flask. "Or have a sip of this. Perk you up in no time." After following her own advice she handed the flask to him. She moved to make room for him; he sat beside her. The liquor stank in the unventilated room; a droplet hung on her lip. He reached out to wipe it away, and now she flinched in turn.

The sight of her fear gave him a curious thrill. She was right to be afraid, he thought. She had failed him. And she had laughed at him—at his embarrassment.

And now she laughed again, not because she thought that he was someone to be ridiculed, but because she was afraid of him. He understood that. In a convulsive movement she heaved herself off the bed, but he reacted quickly and caught her hand and pulled her back. He felt his anger: it blossomed on him like a fever, it overpowered him. He wrestled her down.

"No—"

His blow landed across her startled face, splitting the lip where the drop of liquor had hung. She tried again to rise, to escape him, but again he was too quick for her and again he struck. And again, and again—until her cries were silenced and she lay still on the bed beside him.

Gradually he grew calm. His breath came more slowly, his heart beat at its normal rate. He no longer trembled with the urgency of his need. He stood up; he adjusted his clothing. Carefully, so as to prevent a fire, he blew out the candle as he left.

Sixteen

I do not know precisely how Ned lived during the years
after he left his father's firm and his father's house as
well. With friends, of course—friends gave him a place to
stay, food to eat. He survived as does every aspiring
artist, or writer, or musician who does not have an
independent fortune to sustain him: on hackwork,
placing an article here or a story there, rewriting or
editing for those with something to say but no talent to
say it. He tutored the children of friends; he wrote
advertisements; once in a while he accepted a small loan
from me which he entered carefully in his little pocket
notebook and always promptly repaid. I would have been
happy to give him as much as he needed, of course, but he
would not hear of it. "I'll manage," he would say, smiling
confidently at me under his full mustache. His face was
too thin; he looked drawn and tired, but he would not
admit defeat. He had, I think, some talent; but equally
important, he had what every artist must have in order to
survive: faith in himself and the stubbornness to keep on
going.

And then one day in early March of '88 he came to me triumphant.

"Here," he said. He gave me a small package; I held it for a moment, not daring to think what it might be. "Go on," he said. He could not suppress a grin; his thin face was alive with joy. "Open it! It's not an infernal machine, I promise you." Bombs were all the fashion in those years; anarchists strewed them over the landscape like children dropping daisy petals.

With great care, as if I were handling the crown jewels, I removed the brown paper wrapping. It was a slim volume, not more than eighty pages: *Poems* by Edward January.

"Oh, Ned!" I had no idea what to say to him; no words seemed enough. "When—why didn't you tell me that this was to happen?"

"I wanted to surprise you, of course."

"And you have—indeed you have. I'm overwhelmed." I glanced at the title page, which informed me that the Messrs. Harper and Bros. had published the book. Many would-be poets and writers of fiction were forced to pay for private publication when no commercial firm would take their work; to have one's poems published by a well-known commercial publisher was a triumph indeed. And then I saw the dedication: "For Marian," it said, and, beneath, in his large flowing script, "With love, Ned."

"They sent three advance copies," he said. "And they have promised that books will be in the stores by next week."

"Where, no doubt, they will disappear from the shelves in no time."

He laughed in a self-deprecating way. "These aren't Professor Longfellow's kind of poems," he said. "I wouldn't be surprised if Harper's took a loss on me."

I opened the pages at random. The paper was of good quality, the type rich and black and beautifully sharp-edged. The spare, short, wide-spaced lines lay on the pages like the marks in raked sand in a Japanese garden.

I read aloud:

Lucubrations

We navigate in lamp-dim light
Toward faintly charted, distant shores,
And find yet more and more delight
In cabined darkness of the night.

Where stars break through and oceans sweep
Our love along, my world in yours,
On currents flowing swiftly deep,
'Til we touch earth, and, finally, sleep. . . .

Unnoticed by either of us, Perseus had come in while I was reading. He stood just inside the drawing-room door, silhouetted by the hall lamps. He cleared his throat, now, to announce his presence, and Ned and I looked up as startled as if we had been caught *flagrante delicto*.

He came in. "Afternoon, Ned. I'll have some tea, Marian, if you'll ring for another cup."

I did so, and he settled himself in his morris chair by the fire. He had worn a curious expression when he first came in, but now his face had settled into its customary attitude of anxious watching. He had been somewhat less difficult over the winter—hardly more relaxed, but at least less censorious—possibly because in November his Society had held a testimonial dinner for him to thank him for his faithful service. They had given him a small gold token for his watch chain; he would often rub it between his fingers like an amulet as if it gave him comfort, as indeed I am sure it did.

He held out his hand now to take Ned's book, and I gave it to him.

"Ha," he said, glancing at the front. "Your own? Congratulations. Just out?" And without waiting for a reply he began to turn the uncut pages, skimming as he went. I could not tell if he had seen the dedication. He was a fast reader; often he got through fifteen or twenty books a week for the Society.

After a moment, without comment, he handed the book back to me; and soon, our tête-à-tête ended, Ned went away.

I saw him again the following week. It had been a balmy day, false spring, and I had walked home from the shops across the Common and the Public Garden. The lawns were winter-dead, the flower beds bare, the ice in the lagoon beginning to melt in the middle. But the bright blue sky above the leafless trees promised spring, and the air was deliciously mild. People walked slowly, savoring the day. Children rolled their hoops along the paths, and nursemaids wheeling perambulators stopped to gossip; people sat on the benches, their faces turned up to the sun, warming, blooming.

On such a day Ned's rapid, agitated walk made him

conspicuous even from a distance. Even before I saw who he was, my eye was caught by the tall figure of a man loping down a walkway toward me. He soon reached the point where our paths intersected, and I recognized him.

"Ned!"

Deep in his thought, he was startled by my voice; he stared at me for a moment before he knew me.

"What is it, Ned? Where are you going in such a hurry?"

"Oh—Marian! I was on my way to call on you, in fact."

"I'm delighted to hear it. But you look a bit pressed. Is anything wrong?"

"Yes. Yes, it is. I was just—is Perseus home, d'you know?"

"No. Or at least I don't think so. Why?"

We came to the gate at Arlington Street. He waited until we had crossed before he replied. "I went around today to check the stores to see if my book had come in. And it had. And almost immediately it went out again— shipped back to the publisher."

"Shipped back! Why?"

His face was a study in misery. "They had had a visit from your husband, acting on behalf of his Society. He had warned them not to sell it on the threat of police action. He informed them that it was an obscene book."

"Obscene! But how on earth—"

"So naturally I wanted to talk to him, to make him understand what it is that I am trying to do. If he reads me with an open mind, he must see that what I write is not obscene. He *must* see that, Marian! And he must help me to have the book put back in the stores. They cannot suppress it!"

Ned was so desolate, so near tears, that I took him home and gave him whatever the cook could put together and then sent him home in the carriage with the promise to summon him at once when Perseus returned.

It was nearly nine o'clock when he did. I did not need to send for Ned, for he had come to wait with me. And so once again Perseus came in to find us sitting together by the fire, Ned and I; the expression on his face was slightly different this time, for he had identified this new enemy and had, so he thought, vanquished him.

At once I made as if to leave, for my friendship was no help to Ned in this instance—just the opposite, in fact. But he put his hand on my arm. "Stay," he said. To my surprise Perseus agreed. He knew perfectly well why Ned was there, he knew the difficult half hour awaiting them both as Ned pleaded his case. "Yes, Marian," said Perseus. He shot a malevolent look at me. "Stay, as Ned says. I would send most women away, of course, for we are likely to speak of matters not fit for women to hear. Even married women, who know a good deal about indecency, should not be party to this. But you—" He shrugged, and then he sneered: "To you, no indecency will be too great."

From the edge of my vision I saw Ned half rise as if to leap to my defense and then sink back as if he remembered that he must not antagonize Perseus, that he must endure even insults to me, worse than to himself, in order to persuade Perseus to relent.

Perseus did not sit with us. He stood by the fire

warming his hands, his pale face reddened by the cold. As he grew older he had more than ever taken on the aspect of a long-legged fisher bird—a stork, perhaps, or a heron: his beak—his nose—had grown longer and more pointed from years and years of poking it into other people's business; his small, fierce eyes gleamed with constant hope of discovering some wrong, some human weakness that he could pounce upon.

Of course he knew why Ned was there; but he left it to Ned—or perhaps to me?—to make the opening move.

"Perseus—" I began; but Ned overrode me.

"I want to read something to you," he said to Perseus. "So that you will see that really what I have written is—is perfectly decent." He took a copy of his book out of his pocket, and before Perseus could protest he had begun:

> "Take my hand, that I may lead you
> From the valley—"

"Stop!" Perseus' voice was paler now, warped by its familiar expression of distaste. "I have looked at your work. I do not need to hear it recited word for word."

"Have you looked at this one? It's the last one in the book, it's about patriotism—love for one's country. Listen:

> "Floating on the silver bosom of the sea—"

"Excuse me." Perseus' voice, as irritating as a rasping saw, cut across Ned's. "I am extremely tired. I am going to retire."

He moved toward the door; but Ned, quicker than he, jumped to his feet and barred his way. "No—wait! You must listen! You cannot do this—you cannot ban my book from my own city! You cannot deny me the right to be heard—" His voice broke; he paused to mend it.

Perseus stopped. He looked at Ned in a not unkindly way.

"Ned. Listen to me. You are young, and the young do not always know what they do—"

"I know what *you* do, damn you! I know what *you*— Listen to me, Perseus Motley. You spend your life meddling, meddling, you tell the world what it cannot see, what it cannot read—by what right? Damn you, by what right?"

Perseus' fleeting kindness had vanished. Suddenly, with surprising agility, he sidestepped Ned and moved on; and Ned, overcome by panic and despair, caught his arm and held it.

"No—wait, wait, let me speak to you—"

"*Will* you release me! What are you thinking of? Stop it—stop it at once!"

No maiden defending her virtue was ever more outraged than Perseus Motley at that moment. His fury hissed and spat at us as if he were no longer a heron but a swan—for swans are nasty, vicious creatures, their beauty is a fraud.

But Ned, desperate now, seeing his chances vanish, clung to Perseus and would not release him.

"This book is the most important thing in my life! You cannot order it away! You have no right to destroy me—"

"Ned!"

Somehow I forced myself between them; I pulled Ned's hand away, I held his arms to prevent him from seizing Perseus again. "Stop it! Stop!" And, to Perseus: "Will you listen to him, at least? You can do that much."

Perseus shook his jacket into place and glared at us both—for in his eyes we were equally guilty. For a moment it seemed that he would speak: his thin-lipped mouth worked and trembled but no sound came. Then, without answering my plea, he turned and fled upstairs, leaving Ned and me to comfort each other.

Still I held to him; and now, his hope of persuading Perseus vanished, he went limp in my grasp. I put my arms around him; he trembled in my embrace like a frightened child, he put his arms around me, too, and held me as if I were his refuge, his only hope.

"There," I murmured. "There. You are all right. You are. Ned. Listen to me."

But he would not answer; try as I would, he refused to meet my eyes, he buried his face in my green velvet shoulder and hid there.

We stood so for a long time. I heard the clock strike ten before he lifted his head. His face alarmed me. He looked haunted, and blind, as if he could see only into himself: nothing external.

Finally, dazedly, he spoke. "If I get to New York by tomorrow," he said, "they will give me more copies or I will buy them if necessary and I can take them to the stores myself."

"Ned, please—"

"If I get to New York," he said. "I must go now. I must leave at once. There is a late train. I can catch it if I run."

"Ned, wait until tomorrow. Please. Stay here tonight, and tomorrow, if you still want to go, I will go with you."

"If I get there—" He pulled away from me. "If I get to New York—"

He turned and hurried out.

"Ned—wait!"

He was at the front door; hampered by my stiff, heavy skirts, I could not move quickly enough to catch him. Without a word of good-bye he was gone.

I stood on the front stoop looking after him. I saw him hurrying down Beacon Street, coming into view briefly under the lamps and then disappearing into darkness again. In the morning, I thought, I would go early to his room in the South End. I would carry breakfast to him: hot scones which I would tell Cook to make, a pot of honey, a covered bowl of porridge. Surely he would be there; despite what he said I did not believe that he meant to go to New York.

I stood alone in the quiet night. Ned had disappeared. I could not see the stars, for the sky was overcast. Rain, I thought: rain by morning. The air was damp but not particularly cold for the second week of March; there was a certain thickness to the atmosphere which an older hand than I might have analyzed correctly, but it meant nothing to me.

The storm came after midnight. All that night it raged and into the following day. It swept down on us with a fury that buried everything in its path, it came on us so suddenly that we had no time to prepare to withstand it. The swirling, suffocating snow whipped by the howling winds into drifts ten feet high—every landmark buried, people caught and trapped where they stood, trains stalled, telegraph lines down. And then, when it was done, a still whiteness over the land, country and city alike, an eerie stillness as when a terrible war has been fought and afterward the dead lie cold and silent on the plain of battle. Never in living memory had there been such devastation from a blizzard. Spring had come, we thought—ah, that treacherous, seductive spring for which we yearn, we long to see her, to welcome her, we mistake false signs for real and inevitably we are betrayed.

Ned would have walked, that night, rather than try to find a hack. Overcome by despair, he would have tried to banish it by striding through the nighttime streets; he would have gone on and on, tireless, unaware of the murderous weather blowing up the coast. And when at last he realized that snow was falling, he would have made the fatal mistake that so many others made: it was just a little dusting, people said, a little "sugar snow" to make the sap rise sharp. No one knew: how could they? No storm like this had ever happened before.

Hundreds died that night and day; and Ned was among them. They found him in the Old Granary; perhaps he felt tired at last and simply stretched out for a moment on one of the large flat tombstones to rest his feet and legs. And fell asleep: and so quick came the cold that he froze; and so sudden came the snow that he was buried; and so, alone in that vast, shrieking whiteness, unable to call for help and unheard if he did, he went to sleep forever. He was lying on his back, his hands crossed on his breast. They told me later that his face was at peace: no fear, they said, no pain.

He must have known. How could he not? He could have risen, he could have fled; but he chose to stay. He must have known. He made that choice. It was his right. I could not have borne to think that his was an accidental death. Fate is not kind, but even the most malevolent fate is not that cruel.

They found him in the thaw: a mild, mild blue day, a warm and dazzling day, spring indeed, the snow melting and melting and bodies uncovered everywhere as it went: in the country, in the cities, anywhere a soul might shelter; and sometimes the searchers did not find them right away and they began to rot and stink, and rats came, and maggots, and so sometimes only the clothing allowed identification.

And even today, when people talk of the blizzard of '88, I think not of the general destruction but of Ned and how he died.

And I remember the circumstances leading up to his death; and I charge them, along with so much else, to the man to whom I was married: Perseus Motley.

Seventeen

"My dear Mrs. Kittredge, Lawrence Cushing is the most dangerous man in London," said our visitor, "but I find danger exciting, don't you?" She simpered at us from beneath her flower-trimmed hat and reached greedily for another petit four on the tea tray.

We were on Isabel's second-floor gallery overlooking the lawn and the sea: a summer afternoon the year following Ned's death. It was Isabel's at-home day, early yet, the expected crush of callers still to come. This one, a Mrs. DeBurgh, was a recent arrival at Newport.

Isabel smiled brightly; only someone who knew her as well as I did would have known that the smile was false. "No," she said. "I find danger—well, dangerous." She laughed a little; her hand holding her teacup was perfectly steady. "But why do you call him dangerous? Does he threaten people or commit highway robbery?"

"Ah, Mrs. Kittredge!" Mrs. DeBurgh laughed. "Don't tell me that you don't know what a dangerous man is! Why, he has only to walk into a room and every woman there lights up like a Roman candle! His eyes are positively hypnotic! And of course he is so terribly handsome. A year or so ago we all thought that he was going to marry a great fortune but he did not. Of course he has had affairs without number. I myself—well, I needn't go into detail. You know him, you know what he is. When he heard that I was coming here he asked me to look you up, to give you his—ah—warmest regards." She simpered again. "He may be coming across soon himself, he said. I'm sure you'll see him if he does. Tell me"—and she leaned forward, her face as greedy as if we ourselves were sweet French pastries and she about to devour us—"is it true that he left Boston, years ago, because of a woman?"

"I don't think—" began Isabel; but she was interrupted then by a shout from below, and she and I together moved to the stone railing to overlook the lawn and gardens. My only son and Isabel's younger one were being chauffeured around the paths by the coachman's son, who, at ten, was tall and strong enough to drive the pony cart and command Mr. Micawber, its plump and stubborn locomotion. Mr. Micawber was broad and brown and of a certain age; he moved only upon the command of those he liked, Peter Dill among them. I could not repress a smile; as they rounded the curve and faced me I waved. They saw me and waved in return.

Edward was five that summer, the summer of '89. He was a beautiful child. All children are beautiful to their parents, of course, but he was so to others as well. People stared at him when we went for walks or bathing at Bailey's Beach: they were enchanted, I think, by his grace and charm as much as by his appearance. He had a sweet, forthright manner unlike the awkward shyness of so many children; even so young, he was able to converse, to answer questions in more than single syllables. He had red-brown hair that grew redder in the sun; his eyes were hazel, his skin browned now from the summer but usually pale. He was intelligent, curious, happily comfortable in the life that I gave him. His arm shot up in a salute; he threw me a gleeful grin and then they turned and went down toward the sea and I could not see his face.

As we turned back to Mrs. DeBurgh, her question still unanswered, we were greeted by the butler showing in new callers, and so Isabel was spared having to reply. Soon the gallery was filled with pretty ladies in their white frilly dresses; they chattered like a flock of sparrows, while dainty laughter rippled over the steady stream of talk. Some women, on their afternoons at home, suffered through with only three or four callers, but Isabel always had at least a dozen and often more. It was, I knew, a tribute to her success: undeniably she was making her mark. No general plotting his campaign ever moved with greater care than Isabel plotting her victories at Newport. Had she been a man she would have been a power in the larger world, the world of war or politics or high finance. The likes of Vanderbilt *père* and Jay Gould would have met their match in Isabel; she had a flair for grasping power and using it equal to that of any robber baron. Even as she received her lady callers, as she did this day, she made new alliances and solidified old ones. Every caller was judged not only for what she was but for whom she knew, what entree she could provide. I do not say this as a criticism; it was the way of her world. All women in society did the same.

For instance, she had somehow managed to snare on one occasion or another what seemed like every wealthy and eligible young man in the Boston-Newport-New York circuit. She charmed them, I think, by the very forthrightness of her manner: she let them know unhesitatingly that she could connect them very nicely, not only with similarly eligible young women but with older men, men successful in this field or that, who could give them a leg up, so to speak, in their chosen careers. There were, of course, young men who did not have an occupation: dilettantes, some people called them, although Isabel had a harsher term: "Ne'er-do-wells," she said, her voice dripping scorn. "The new breed. They make me feel positively ancient." (She was at that time thirty-seven or -eight.) "They do nothing! And yet because they are rich they are thought to be a good catch by these foolish women trying to marry off their daughters."

What she said was true enough: money was the order of the day, getting and spending and getting again. Men made money in railroads, and silver, and oil, and natural gas, and manipulations of the stock market; and their wives spent it as fast as it came in—could not spend it fast enough, some of them. And that was the standard by which you were judged: how much money you had, how much you spent and how ingeniously. The old New England standards—a person's family, his character, his reputation for honesty, his moral code—all were vanishing. In their place was the great god Mammon, whose ugly visage, drawn by Th. Nast, leered out at us from the pages of *Harper's Weekly*.

Isabel might have included her brother Leighton in her criticism of the new breed. Years before, he and his wife, Carrie, had decided to try their luck in the West. With a stake from his father, Leighton had invested shrewdly and had made friendships in the right places until he was very nearly rich enough to be called one of the "silver kings." Triumphant, he and Carrie had come back East to show off their wealth and possibly even to enjoy it. Now they were in Newport; it had fallen to Isabel to try to introduce her sister-in-law to the summer colony.

Carrie was a far cry from Newport standards, but despite her weathered, roughened looks, so different from the pampered, porcelain beauty which was favored in the East, she was widely thought to be an attractive woman. Her blue eyes, long-lashed, deep set, were light in contrast to her skin; when she looked at you her gaze was intent, oddly disturbing.

She was at first uneasy in the Newport milieu, and visibly uncomfortable in the fine new clothes that Isabel had helped her to order from that season's fashionable dressmaker. She had worn corsets and silks and velvets as a young woman, of course, but ten years in the West had made her a pioneer woman, with a waist thickened by childbearing and untrammeled by corsets, and a body unused to swaying gracefully across a dance floor.

But Isabel, having determined to launch Carrie as a curiosity if nothing else, was determined to do her best by her. "I've sent her a supply of zinc sulphate and rosewater to make a face wash, but I can't see that she has used it. And I've reserved two entire days of Miss Alcock's time so that Carrie's wardrobe will be acceptable, at least.''

To Isabel's surprise, Carrie was a great success. I saw her one night as we came off a reception line at Mrs. Neilson Battram's and I complimented her on her new dress.

"You are having a regular triumph," I said. "Isabel is very pleased; she told me so."

Carrie laughed in her throaty, forthright way. "I'm a curiosity," she said. "They'll have me for a season and then they'll drop me."

The drawing room reverberated with the chatter of two score and more of early arrivals, and in the pink and gold ballroom the musicians had just launched themselves into a medley of waltzes.

"I don't think—" Carrie stopped, her eye caught by something behind me. She blanched; her mouth dropped open. As discreetly as I could, I glanced around to see what had startled her.

Approaching us—bearing down on us—was the woman who, once upon a time, had been Pussie Mifflin: the girl who had been Isabel's friend, who had, one afternoon, given the garden party which had changed my life and ended my brother's.

For a moment—only for an instant—I went back to that dreadful day; the noise and the lights and the music around me faded, and I saw once again the split in the cliff, the desperate clutching of his hands . . .

". . . as if she'd been very ill—but with what?" Carrie was saying. "I've never seen anything like that, have you?"

I shook my head to clear my clouding brain; Pussie had started through the line, but a delay had occurred, I could not see why, and so she and all the others stood still for our inspection.

How did I know that it was she? I wondered. I had seen her several times in the intervening years—most memorably when she had given Isabel the *Confessions* of Lady X—but then she had looked perfectly well, albeit a little hardened by her troubles. But this! This bloated, scarred, ravaged face bore no resemblance to that of the girl I had known. Something about the eyes, perhaps: something in the set of the lips, the tilt of the head.

Certainly her features were distorted beyond recognition. Her cheeks were puffed so that the jawline was hardly visible, her nose was bulbous and red, her skin was scarred and lacerated, one or two open sores oozing down over what was surely face paint. At last she passed through the receiving line, which had started up again.

"Who is that?" whispered Carrie. "And what in heaven's name caused—"

"She used to be Pussie Mifflin," I said. "She married a man named Brackett. She was quite pretty once. Very sweet."

"Mercy! She's coming here. Marian, I won't know what to say to her—"

She would have fled, I think, if she had had a moment more. As it was, she suffered my introduction with amazing calm. Not by the flicker of an eyelash did she reveal her dismay; I was as proud of her, at that moment, as if she had been my own sister-in-law instead of Isabel's.

"You never change, Marian, not in all these years," said Pussie. "I am so glad to see you." Close up we saw that her lips were swollen and blistered, so stiff that she could hardly speak. I could see that she was attempting a smile, and so I smiled back.

Smiled! At that face!

People turned to stare at us; I felt their eyes. I felt their horror, their sympathy—dear God!

She must have known. How could she not? She must have realized the effect that her appearance had. She must have cringed and quailed before her mirror, searching desperately for the courage to subject herself to the world's scrutiny.

"I have changed very much," I said. "I would not be here otherwise."

"No. I suppose not." She turned to Carrie, whose dismay had softened, I think, into a kind of appalled concern. "And you are Leighton's wife. I was in France when you married. When I returned you had gone West. So now for the first time—"

"How d'y'do," gasped Carrie. "How—yes—no, we didn't—I never—"

We stood, an unhappy trio, in the center of the flow of people from the hallway to the drawing room. They stared: how could they not? They brushed past; some of them might have stopped to chat, but when they saw Pussie they recoiled, they could not bear to look at her, much less to say a word or two.

Pussie accepted champagne from the tray of a passing waiter; Carrie and I declined. She did not sip it but swallowed it all in one gulp; then she looked for a place to put the empty glass. Her hand clutched it so tightly that it seemed in danger of breaking; I did not understand how so fragile a thing could withstand that pressure, I thought that it must shatter in her hand and lacerate it and drip blood all down the front of her dark blue brocade gown.

Would the blood of such a creature be the same color as my own?

People came and went; the orchestra played its repertoire; we three stood alone, shunned, outcasts in the crush of hundreds.

Where was Isabel? Leighton? Anyone at all to rescue us?

People must have known what caused her disfigurement. Otherwise someone—anyone!—would have stopped, would have rescued Carrie and me.

But how could decent, virtuous women ever have known such a thing?

I knew what caused it because I knew something, from Elinor if not from Perseus, about women of the streets and of the diseases to which they were subject. Truly, truly the wages of sin were death, and here was Pussie Mifflin before us to bear witness.

But what sin had she committed?

"She married the wrong man," said Isabel the next afternoon. "He is a perfect cad—a real bounder. Six months after the wedding they found him with an actress. Three months after that he was challenged to a duel by the brother—the brother, mind you!—of a woman who passed herself off as the mistress of a duke. In fifteen years—no, eighteen—of marriage, I don't think Pussie has had so much as an hour of tranquility. She told me once, before things became so very bad, that on their honeymoon he had disappeared for three days— this was in Venice, she was completely alone. She was frantic. She had no idea what to do. Finally he turned up. When she asked where he had been he became angry and threatened to beat her."

So: Pussie's sin—like mine, for that matter: like Isabel's—had been a mistaken marriage.

But she had paid for it far more dearly than we had done: she had paid and paid and paid—God had singled her out for punishment, it seemed, had marked her with this terrible brand.

Why?

She moved among us, that summer, like a phantom from the netherworld of our existence sent to remind us of the ugliness beneath that glitter—beneath the surface beauty of our lives. People shrank at her approach; they drew back and turned their heads as if they understood what she was really: the other side, the dark side of our lives suddenly emerged, suddenly given hideous face.

Nothing deterred her. She went everywhere, she saw everyone. Omnipresent, never acknowledging her dreadful condition, she hovered at the edge of our gaiety that summer and haunted us with the knowledge that any one of us might be stricken as she was.

"She is dying, of course," said Isabel. We were in her landau driving down Bellevue Avenue toward the Ocean Drive. As always on such occasions, we were distracted from any meaningful conversation by the need to decide to bow or not to bow at the ladies approaching us in carriages of their own. "They've given her six months; no more. And she'll be blind well before that."

I glanced at her; under her white straw hat her face was blank and hard. Even though I knew her as well as anyone did—knew her, understood her, forgave her what might have been called her faults—I remember feeling a small shiver of dismay as I looked at that set jaw, the expressionless eyes sweeping up and down the avenue for the next candidate for recognition or rejection.

"Where is her husband?" I said, bowing to Mrs. Barton Trafford and her two daughters.

"In Italy, I believe," said Isabel, bowing also. A rigid smile parted her lips; she spoke through clenched teeth, not looking at me. "And with any luck he will stay here. Horrible man!"

"It was he who—ah—infected her?"

"Of course. Who else? She is a decent woman—pure and virtuous, Marian, as no other woman I know. And he—he was a libertine, a philanderer! Why her parents did not see what he was I will never understand. He infected her. Ruined her! Killed her as surely as if he had taken a knife to her heart."

She was silent for a moment; then, seeing another carriage approach, she seemed to gather herself up for yet another smile, another greeting. The woman approaching was Mrs. DeBurgh, who had brought her news of Lawrence Cushing.

"There," muttered Isabel. "She leaves next week for England, I hear. Good riddance! I hope she tells him—" She broke off; she bowed and smiled again.

Questions bubbled to my lips but I suppressed them. *Him!* Lawrence Cushing! I had never forgotten the young man who had spoken to me on Marlborough Street, who had begged me to give Isabel his letter— Why? Who was he—who was he to Isabel, that is? Had they been lovers? No proper Boston debutante had a lover. Friends, perhaps? More than that, surely. It seemed impossible that two people so long separated would have any memory of each other, and yet first love strikes deep and hard, it leaves its mark for a lifetime.

We bowled down the avenue; we turned in at her gate. She did not speak, and I respected her silence. We climbed down from the carriage; we walked into the house through the cool, dim courtyard filled with the scent of hothouse flowers, the sound of splashing water in the fountain. We went to our separate rooms to unlace. I lay on my chaise and tried to doze, for later we were going to a dinner and a dance at Mrs. Burlingham's Rose Court and I knew that I would be awake far later than usual.

But every time I closed my eyes I saw their faces: Isabel's today, hard and set in its determined smile; and his, long ago, pleading and desperate—so unlike the description we had had of him from Mrs. DeBurgh. I shifted uneasily, unable to find a comfortable position. The room was too warm; I rose and opened the window all the way. No breeze stirred; a sticky film of perspiration covered me. I would have a bath, I thought. But before I did I would ease my mind a bit and look in on Isabel.

371

Dressed only in my wrapper, I went around to her room on the opposite side of the house. Here there was breeze aplenty: her tall french windows, partly open, let in a rush of cool air from the sea.

She too had unlaced and dropped onto her chaise to rest and, like me, she had been unable to. She stared at me as I came in.

"How did you know?" she said.

"Know what?"

"That I wanted to see you."

"Did you? Good. What can I—"

"Look." She fished in the folds of her wrapper and produced a small envelope which she gave to me. "Read it," she said. "It will amuse you."

It was a short note in an unformed hand:

My dear Mrs. Kittredge:

I must speak to you and tell you what is in my heart. You know who I am, for we met on Monday evening at Mrs. Blackwell's. Even long before that, I saw you and knew my feelings for you. Please do not deny me. Please allow me to say what is in my heart. I will be at Rose Court tonight. Knowing that you have read this will make it easier for me to approach you.

Your devoted admirer

"Good heavens," I said. "What is this? Do you know who he is?"

"Yes. A sweet young man—hardly twenty-five, I think."

"But he sounds desperate."

"I imagine that he is."

"What will you do?"

She smiled: that same tight, hard smile that she had worn in the afternoon. "I don't know. Perhaps I should encourage him. It might be amusing to have a—an admirer."

Many women did: the bejeweled matrons who came to Newport in the summer were only human, after all, and while their husbands dallied in the city, or on yachts in the harbor, the women amused themselves with convenient young men.

But that did not seem to be Isabel's style; she had, in fact, spoken contemptuously of friends and acquaintances who behaved so. Why would she suddenly change?

"Isabel—"

"I am tired of watching everyone else have all the fun," she went on. "Why shouldn't I enjoy myself for once?"

"But you do—you enjoy yourself immensely, don't you? Entertaining, being entertained—"

"Stop it, Marian! You insult both of us with such talk. I do what I must. I keep busy. Do you understand me, Marian? It is necessary for me to do that so that I will not think of—of what else my life might have been."

I knew—I knew, even if she could not say his name, I knew: Lawrence Cushing. And she saw my face: she understood. After a moment she relaxed a bit; she nodded, as if she had reached some conclusion. She even managed a small, crooked smile, a jaunty smile that defied me.

"Yes," she said. She tapped the envelope with her index fingernail. "I think so. He appeared at just the right moment. Think of it, Marian. Am I not to be envied? I will have a lover!"

Eighteen

Pussie died at the beginning of November. She withdrew
from the world after the season at Newport: she went to
her parents' home on Beacon Street. She refused all
callers; she sent word that she would see us before she
died but that we were not to come on our own, we were to
await her summons.

It came too late. She lay stinking in her own
excretions, her eyes glazed and sightless, the muscles of
her face and body twitching uncontrollably, her ruined
face a grotesque mask of pain. Her blotched skin, her
clawlike hands, her flaking scalp showing through the
few tufts of hair remaining—wreck that she was, she
knew that we were there and she tried to speak to us but
she could not. We waited until we could bear to watch
her no more and then we went away.

"I'll have nightmares for months, after this," muttered Isabel as we made our way out of the Mifflin house
and across the sidewalk to her carriage. "They ought not
to have allowed us to see her."

"She begged us to come," I said. "Especially

she wanted to talk to you." What, I wondered, would she have said?

Isabel shuddered. "My lunch is still right here," she said, touching her chest. "If I had had to stay there one minute longer, I would have thrown it up."

Pussie died the next day. Her husband did not attend the funeral.

Two weeks later we had news of a birth. We had heard of Elinor from time to time: how she had gone to Paris with Harry Lathrop, how she had been working with poor women in the charity wards, or with homeless children whom she helped to gather off the streets and house and feed in orphanages. Bowditch, who had gone to Paris the year before, had written to us that he had seen Elinor; she was well, he said, and not unhappy. He was painting her portrait.

Now Elinor herself wrote to her parents to tell them of the birth of her child: a girl, she said, whom they named Diana. Almost as an afterthought, she added that she had married Lathrop.

"Surely she will come home now, she will bring our grandchild to us," said Mrs. January. Her eyes brightened at the prospect. For more than a year she had been burdened with the care of her husband, whose failing health was hardly unexpected (he was nearly seventy, after all) but whose care was a trial to her all the same.

During the winter after Pussie's death Isabel threw herself into a frenzy of activity. From morning till night she was busy, organizing charity events for the *crème de la crème* of Boston society, attending dinners and parties and balls without number, enriching an army of support personnel, as it were: grocers and wine merchants and florists and dressmakers. She had been unable to go into society during the previous winter season because we were in mourning for Ned. Now, ensconced in the house of her parents-in-law on Commonwealth Avenue, she made up for lost time.

The move had been the elder Mrs. Kittredge's idea: "Let us exchange houses," she said; it made no sense, she said, for herself and her husband to be rattling around such a big place, while Isabel and Avery tried to squeeze themselves and five children into the house in Exeter Street and manage entertaining into the bargain.

And so the switch had been made, and Isabel had her winter season.

The young man who had importuned her at Newport hung about for a few months that fall until, shortly after the New Year, she sent him packing. "I can't do it, Marian," she laughed—a genuine laugh this time, instead of the mirthless grimace I had seen so often. "He's simply too young. He bores me to death. Always mooning about—I feel like his nursemaid. If I'm going to have a flirtation I should at least enjoy it."

Her eyes darkened momentarily, and I thought for a moment of that other, that one whose name hung unspoken between us. Despite Mrs. DeBurgh's warning he had not appeared. Spring came and went. Isabel prepared for her annual move to Newport. She seemed well, happy with her success. She made no more allusions to Cushing: if any memory of him smoldered in her heart, it was only a low fire, only embers. The summer season at Newport passed pleasantly enough: a few little scandals to enliven the gossip, one elopement, three titles looking for wealthy brides, a rivalry played out between competing hostesses with the loser decamping in mid-season. Isabel enjoyed it all, and I, less intimately involved, enjoyed seeing her pleasure.

Looking back, I wonder now where Isabel found the money to maintain her increasingly lavish way of life. From her father, I suppose. She seemed to have an endless supply of funds; her entertainments were among the most extravagant at Newport, and only a few people from New York outspent her. Favors at a dance given by Mrs. Avery Kittredge might be silver cigar cases for the men and gold and crystal perfume bottles for the women; mountains of food were supplied, pots of plants brought in to decorate the terrace, not one orchestra but two, armies of servants—spend and spend and spend seemed to be her motto.

"I give employment to the native population here," she laughed once. "In my way I am as much a benefactress to the poor as Elinor ever was. They will live all winter on what I pay them now."

Let her have her life, I thought. She is well; she seemed happy. Let her live!

Nineteen

It was inevitable that sooner or later my husband would have an enemy who was angry enough to seek revenge.

He came to me late one night about a year after Pussie's death. I had dined with Edward and had read him a story before he went to sleep—one of the tales from *The Arabian Nights,* as I recall—and then I retired to my room with a fresh pot of coffee and a glass of Madeira and a new novel by Ouida. She was a silly woman, I knew that she was, but silliness is not the worst of sins. She amused me; she took me away from myself into the hothouse world of European nobility.

I was startled when the knock came. I had sent the servants to bed long before, and I knew that only the gravest emergency would cause them to rise, to disturb me. They were too tired, for one thing, and too well trained, for another.

Perseus came in before I could respond. I checked my anger. I had long since decided that I would not argue with him: a peaceful household was more important to me than any temporary victory over him. For the most part I did not need to argue; the house was mine, the money was mine, the child was mine as well. He had nothing to give to me save a kind of facade of propriety, and if worst came to worst I could manage without it.

His face was drawn, paler than usual. He stood just inside the door where the light from the gas jets did not reach; his back was to the wall, and his dark clothing blended into the darkly patterned background so that his face seemed to hang suspended midway between floor and ceiling like some apparition from, say, the tale of the genie that I had earlier read to my son.

"Well?" I said. I was beginning to feel uneasy. On the rare occasions that he had something to tell me he always spoke briefly, efficiently, as if to get an unpleasant task done with as soon as possible; but now he stood motionless, watching me from where he stood in the half-light by the door. "Perseus? What is it? Is anything wrong?"

"Yes," he said; but nothing more.

"What? For heaven's sake, don't stand there across the room where I can't see you. Come here. What is it?"

With surprising docility he obeyed me; he came near and perched on the edge of a straight-backed chair. And now that I could see his face clearly I could see that he stared at me with worried eyes; a line of perspiration wet his upper lip and his hands were clenched. He seemed very carefully to be holding himself together; when he opened and closed his hands I saw them tremble, and when he spoke to me again I heard his voice quake and catch as some men's do when they are making love.

"Well?" I was truly alarmed by then, for this man was

a stranger to me. Even his familiar acerbity would have been preferable, I thought, to this timorousness, this agonizing hesitation.

Suddenly he blurted out his trouble.

"I need money," he said. "I need—well, a large amount. It isn't—I can't tell you—all I can say is that I need it. I need it. I *must*—I need it very badly."

"But what on earth—has happened?"

"I cannot tell you."

"You just want me to hand over—how much?"

He stared at me, breathing heavily.

"Well?" I said. "How much?"

"Five thousand."

"Five thousand! But why?"

"Marian, if you don't— For God's sake! Don't make me beg! Just give me what I ask— You must! These people are ruthless, they will hound me to my grave!"

I did not know what his trouble was; I did not want to know. The money meant nothing to me; I was ready to give him what he asked—partly to keep peace, partly to protect myself. He looked desperate enough, I thought, to attack me if I did not say yes to what he demanded. His eyes glared at me in an oddly threatening way, and I thought that it would not have taken much provocation for him to strike me with one of those tight fists.

A long time afterward, when I told Curtis of that night, he smiled approvingly. "You did the right thing," he said. "He was truly desperate by that time. If you'd refused him, if you'd even hesitated, he might have lost control in some way, or he might even have hurt you. He'd been putting them off for weeks—months. He had no means of laying hands on that amount of money, of course—no means except you, that is; they must have tightened the thumbscrews on him past endurance for him to have come to you at last."

"Why? Who were they?"

"Never proven. But I was told by a source whom I trust that the instigator was a man whom Perseus had ruined. He owned a bookstore. Perseus made repeated calls there. The man had the bad luck, apparently, to stock books that offended Perseus and his Society. Finally he went under and he wanted his revenge."

"Yes."

He threw me a sharp glance. "You know? He told you what he was doing?"

"Ah—no, he didn't tell me, but after he died I—I read his diaries."

He watched me; I saw no condemnation in his eyes but only a kind of compassionate understanding. "Then you knew of his career with the Watch and Ward," he said.

"Yes."

"Did he—ah—record everything that he did for them?"

"Pretty nearly. But not this—he never mentioned the blackmail attempt."

"No. I suppose he wouldn't have."

"How—how did they manage to force him to pay?"

"They set him up. The oldest game in the world."

"How did you learn about him?" I said. "Who told you?"

He watched me. "I can't tell you the name," he said. "But it is a source that I know and trust—a man whose information is invariably correct. I have employed him many times and shall continue to do so."

I did not press him. In his profession he needed dependable, closemouthed informants, and he in turn needed to guard their identity.

"The Society would have dismissed him at once had they known that he went alone to visit whores," continued Curtis. He saw me flinch at the word. "Sorry. In any case, they had a strict rule: whenever light women were to be visited, the visit was to be made by two men—never one alone; and always to a house—excuse me, Marian, do you know about—ah—bawdy houses? Yes? Well then, always in pairs, always to a house—never alone to a room. What Perseus did was wrong—professionally wrong, I mean, although it may have been right for him. He had some terrible need, Marian, some dark urge to explore the foulest kinds of human behavior. Tell me: did he ever—ah—"

And then he stumbled and flushed; experienced trial man that he was, skilled in the arts of direct and cross-examination, he did not know how to phrase an intimate question to a woman.

"No," I said. "Never." And then it was my turn to enlighten him as I told him of Perseus' bargain with me on our wedding night. He nodded slowly, as if he were thinking of something else.

"Does Isabel know of this?" he said.

"Yes."

"Did she admit to you her responsibility in arranging your marriage?"

"Yes."

"She is sometimes a meddlesome fool, that woman."

"She meant well."

"Did she?" He shot an accusing glance at me.

"Curtis, my dear. Listen to me. No—just listen. What is done is done. You cannot remake the past. I have had— Well. I have had my share and more of happiness. Do not forget, if I had not married Perseus Motley I never would have had my son."

"You would have had other sons."

"Perhaps. But not Edward. If I had not married Perseus I never would have gone to hear Otis Whittemore lecture. I never would have met him, or loved him. What has been has been. I am content. Now. Tell me more about Perseus."

He took my hand and held it for a moment and then he finished the sad tale of Perseus' downfall.

The blackmailer—the man whom Perseus had ruined, the man who consequently sought revenge—had waited night after night with a friend, another witness. Repeatedly they had seen Perseus meeting women, going with them to their rooms. One night the blackmailer—I will call him Smith, as Curtis did—visited a woman whom Perseus had just left. She was no better and no worse than any other woman in her place, and certainly she was happy enough to cooperate with Smith once he had explained Perseus' identity to her. "He is from the police," said Smith, "and he is setting you up for arrest."

The woman was terrified. She begged Smith to help her. He agreed. They would set Perseus up instead. "He is acting contrary to police regulations," Smith said. "They are supposed to go in pairs and he comes to you alone. We can silence him for good if you help me."

Smith was so effective in his arguments that he did not even need to pay her. "Go out every night until you see him again," he said. "Go to him and beg him to help you—tell him that you want to be saved and that only he can do it. Say anything but get him to return here with you. Do not lock the door. That is an important point: do not lock the door. Will you remember? Yes. Good. Do what you can to—ah—disrobe, and try to have him at least take off his jacket. I will be watching you. Not more than fifteen minutes after you arrive, I will come in. Be ready: I will come quickly, I will burst through that door and immediately I will start to talk. He will have no chance to collect his wits."

The woman did as she was told—without objection, apparently—and by the time that Smith appeared she was fully unclothed and Perseus wore only his shirt and his underlongs.

"What did he do?" I said. I could not imagine Perseus—who was nothing if not dignified, albeit in a fussy, off-putting way—caught in even the first stages of such a scene.

"He had very little choice," said Curtis. "There he was; there they were. He might have been able to overpower one man, or to silence him, but not two. And of course it is always difficult to be forceful when you are half undressed."

The scene as Curtis described it had a certain humor, but neither of us laughed. For Perseus, trapped and threatened, became a deadly threat himself just as cornered animals are; he could not revenge himself on the men who extorted money from him—my money—but in his twisted way he turned his fear and his anger on us, on Edward and me, and so because I helped him when he asked for help he hated me, he looked for revenge against me. It is a natural human instinct to hate those who help us, just as we sometimes love those whom we assist.

Had I known what bitter fruit my generosity would bear, I would have told him to visit hell for his money, and to strike a bargain with the Devil. At the time, however, I gave him what he asked in order to stop any scandal.

And then Lawrence Cushing came back, and new scandal threatened us all.

Twenty

He came at Christmas: the season of peace and goodwill. And he brought with him turmoil and acrimony, the poisonous seeds of discontent.

He gave no warning; he simply appeared one evening, midweek between Christmas and New Year's, at a crowded, hectic party in Louisburg Square. Both Isabel and I had been invited (with our husbands, of course, although neither one came; Avery was down with *la grippe*, and Perseus never accompanied me anywhere). Isabel arrived some time before I did; I found her standing perilously next to the candles on the enormous Christmas tree, which was laden from top to bottom with gingerbread men and glittering glass balls and tiny tin soldiers and ropes of cranberries.

"Marian. At last." She went up on tiptoe and I leaned down to kiss her. "This is an impossible crush. Come along and I'll introduce you to Mr. Clyde—he's a houseguest at the Tillinghams', I think he'd amuse you—"

"Mrs. Kittredge." His voice was deep and resonant,

like an actor's voice; he was like an apparition at her side,
I had not seen him come up. I did not recognize him at
first: which is to say, I knew that I had seen him
somewhere, probably long ago, but I could not remember
where that had been or who he was.

Isabel glanced up at him, her lovely face impersonally
polite, a small smile on her lips. And then, all in an
instant, her face froze, her smile faded and died, and her
mouth sagged ever so slightly and her eyes glazed over
with shock. Some society women at that time, even in
Boston, had begun to paint their faces, but she did not;
and so now she was deathly pale as if she looked at a
ghost. As, indeed, she did.

"They said that you would be here but I was not sure—
I hardly dared hope to see you." The light from the gas
jets glistened on his golden hair and his eyes glowed
brilliant blue; in the fashion of the day he had grown a
full, showy mustache. He turned to me and nodded. "We
have met," he said, "but perhaps your name is different
now—"

"Motley," I breathed. I felt suddenly weak despite the
strong support of my corsets. Automatically I gave him
my hand. His was strong and very warm; it seemed to
transmit some of his energy to me, and I took as deep a
breath as I could and forced a smile onto my frozen face.

"Lawrence Cushing," he said. He turned to Isabel
again. "Well?" he said. "No word of welcome for the
wanderer home from the sea?"

I could see the effort that she made to collect herself.
Women who were accustomed, as she was, to dealing
with almost any kind of social contretemps have a kind of

automatic patter that they can produce at awkward moments, and that is what she did then. "Of course," she said; and she, too, forced a smile. "Of course I welcome you, Mr. Cushing."

"'Mr. Cushing'!" He gave such a laugh that several people nearby turned to stare. "How very formal we are! My dear Mrs. Kittredge—may I call you Isabel for old times' sake?"

She was never a coquette, and she did not become one then. She smiled at him again but in a grave, almost stern way. "Tell us what brings you back to Boston," she said. She lifted her chin a little, as if to say, "I am equal to any challenge you throw down."

He did not reply at once. All around us people were moving back, clearing a space at the rear of the big double parlors; we heard the orchestra beginning to tune up. An expression of what I can only call sweet yet sorrowful longing—a kind of yearning, if you will—flickered across his face. In such a ruggedly handsome man it surprised me. "I had—let us say—some personal business to attend to."

"I wish you success," she said; and bravely met his eyes.

"Thank you. My success does not depend on me but on—the other party."

The orchestra, just then, struck up a lively waltz and couples made their way to the dance floor. He made a little bow to her. "Will you give me this dance, Mrs. Kittredge—Isabel?"

I thought for a moment that she would refuse him but she did not. She let him lead her out; I watched as he took her into his arms. My thoughts were in turmoil. This man—Cushing! His golden head glowed like a beacon in those rooms crowded with ordinary folk. He had a ruthless look, like a pirate chief come to claim his treasure. He swept Isabel around the floor with a driving, insistent step as if he would sweep her away altogether; and yet he was graceful, too, his tall, muscular frame so elegantly tailored that on a slighter man his clothing would have seemed a dandy's attire.

When the music stopped to allow people to exchange partners, Cushing did not return Isabel to the sidelines but stood waiting with her for the music to begin again. They danced the next waltz, and the next, and then at last she came back to me and he (to my surprise) asked me to dance.

"I don't think—" I began, flustered; I did not want to offend her.

"Go on, Marian," she said. She was panting a little from her exertions; her eyes were sparkling and she was no longer pale but flushed.

Reluctantly, I agreed and he led me out. I was hesitant; I could not give myself to him fully as one must. I felt as though I had been caught up by a whirlwind: my feet could not keep pace, my eyes could not meet his. Finally he took pity on me and slowed his steps. "In London," he smiled, "I am highly prized as a dancing partner."

"This is not London," I said, hearing the nervousness in my voice, "and I am not a very good dancer in any case."

"You are doing splendidly," he said. "Just relax"—as if any corseted woman could relax!—"and let me lead you. There. Much better."

I felt that I should converse with him, but I hardly knew what to say. In an odd way I knew him intimately, and yet I did not know him at all: who was he, this stranger who had so suddenly appeared and yet who had lived in Isabel's heart all the years?

He smiled at me, and his smile was, I thought, honest and friendly. "I asked you for a kindness, once," he said, "and I must apologize now for my—ah—having been so forward."

I felt my face flush. "It wasn't—I didn't—"

"Never mind," he said. "You did what you could, I am sure." He looked at me sharply. "I saw her myself a year or so afterward. Did you know that? I was very stupid that day. I should have asked her then—don't look at me so strangely, Mrs. Motley. I am told that you are her closest friend. I can unburden my heart to you, can I not?"

"It isn't appropriate—"

"Appropriate!" He laughed at me as he engineered a daring turn. "Very good. You have the makings of an excellent dancer. Your husband does not—? Yes. Appropriate! Not proper, perhaps? Desperate men do not consider propriety, Mrs. Motley. I will tell you frankly that I have lived a life that many men would be glad to live, and yet I find that I have no peace, I have no—how shall I say it?—no center to my life. That, I think, is what I came back to find. It lies here—here in this very room. I have been wrong to stay away all these years. I should have insisted—I knew what my life lacked, I knew that *she*—"

"Mr. Cushing." I felt lightheaded, what with the music and the brightly lighted room and the warmth of the crowd, the exertion of our dance; and most of all I felt giddy from his words, the secrets of his heart that I did not want to hear. "I cannot listen to such—such intimacy. It is true that I am her friend, but still you must not—"

"Impose on your goodwill?" He smiled again, the same open, honest smile. "Very well. I will not—at least not until I am desperate again."

And so Lawrence Cushing invaded us, that holiday season, and Isabel, mindful perhaps of the torments she had suffered on his behalf, allowed him entry. She danced that night, and again on New Year's Eve, like a woman possessed. As indeed she was. She was thirty-nine—well past youth—and her figure had thickened with the bearing of five children, and her eldest daughter had recently made her debut, and she had buried brother and friends and suffered through the waning health of her father and waning affections of her husband. No matter. She was a girl again, for these few days at least, and she danced and laughed as I had never seen her do before and have never seen since.

"He is here, Marian!" she said. "Imagine! Here with us—with *me,* exactly as I remember him and even more—"

She broke off. We were in her sitting room on the day after New Year's. We had not had the chance for a good talk since Cushing appeared; but by now she had betrayed herself—if that is the word—by her behavior even more than by her speech, and so she hardly needed to tell me anything.

All during her annual New Year's ball—always one of the events of the year, a red-letter event on Boston's social calendar—she had devoted herself to him to the exclusion of every other guest. She bloomed; she glowed; shamelessly she hung on his arm. Avery saw what she did, of course, but he made no comment—no public comment, that is. What he said in private I did not know; and Isabel, who eventually told me so much, never told me that. Perhaps he played a waiting game, giving her rope to hang herself. From time to time Cushing danced with someone else or allowed himself to be lured into conversation; he was, after all, the topic of enthralled gossip all over Boston, and people wanted to see him close up, to speak to him themselves. But mostly he stayed with Isabel, and he seemed as happy as she.

He came trailing his past like clouds of glory, as the poets say. What had he not done, out in the great world beyond this tight, inbred little city huddled on its land reclaimed from the sea? Cushing had seen great vast prairies of land, oceans of land not only in the West but in the Argentine and in the steppes of Russia; land that had beneath it the riches of Croesus, land that held silver, and copper, and coal, and ancient civilizations. He had gambled down the Mississippi, he had sailed round the Horn—his deeds made him the envy of every man, and woman too.

Isabel was wildly jealous of him. Every time he danced with another woman—even when, at her urging, he danced with me—she suffered torments. "I can't bear it," she said. "To see him again, to know that he returned for me—for *me*, after all this time! And then to have to watch him take another woman in his arms even for a moment—it is too hard, Marian, you do not know how hard it is!''

She looked ten—twenty—years younger. Her perfect creamy skin bloomed as if she were some rare hothouse flower—one of her late cousin's orchids, perhaps. She wore a dressing gown of deep rose and a pair of diamond eardrops that were so large as to be almost vulgar. Her expression was one of what I can only call ecstasy.

''What will you do?'' I said. I was dumbfounded; I hardly knew what to say. For all her radiance, for all her new-found vivacity and the glow that comes only with love, there was in her eyes a hard, sightless look, as if she had suddenly stopped thinking. Or, perhaps, as if her thoughts could not bear telling.

''I don't know.'' She turned that look on me—how it chilled me—frightened me! She was a stranger; I had never met this woman before. ''Did you know,'' she said, ''that once, long ago, he abandoned me?''

''No, I didn't—,''

''It nearly killed me. I did not want to go on living, that summer. Ah, Marian! He bewitches me. I am not myself when he is with me, I take leave of my senses. Many times I have thought that my feelings for him, as strong as they were, were only a young girl's ignorant passion. But I feel the same now—more!''

I watched her with unbelieving eyes. What would she do? What on earth could she do? I no longer dared to ask. It seemed impossible that she would do anything beyond what she had done already, and yet I sensed a terrible restlessness in her, as if, caged so long in the prison of her life, she was now ready to break free. The Isabel whom I knew—cool, levelheaded, even calculating on occasion—had vanished, to be replaced by this passionate figure whose heart overflowed with secrets untold, whose bosom heaved with feelings unconfessed.

I left her soon after, for I could see that if she could not be with Cushing she wanted at least to be alone to think of him; she did not want to be with me. I did not mind. She made me uncomfortable—horribly uneasy.

As I was going out I encountered Charlotte and Victoria just coming in. Charlotte, having recently made her debut, was at that time in her life which is supposed to be every girl's happiest—her "bud" year, when she officially enters the grown-up world. But to Isabel's dismay—and certainly to Charlotte's as well—she was not popular. Invitations came few and far between, and despite Isabel's determination to make a good match for her, despite the legions of young men who gladly came to Isabel's entertainments, none of them seemed prepared to court her daughter. I do not know why this was so, for Charlotte was pleasant and presentable, at least, if not pretty, and as far as anyone knew she had hopes of a reasonably good amount of money. But human beings are a mystery, first and last, and I suppose that one girl, every year, had to suffer the ignominy of being ignored: this year it was Charlotte.

Victoria, even at thirteen, was by contrast strikingly beautiful. She wore a crimson ribbon in her long dark curls, and her deep blue-violet eyes often sparkled with mischief as if she were planning a grand joke. She gave me an impetuous hug and kiss, this day, and demanded to know when I would take her to the theater as I had promised to do when something suitable came along.

"Soon!" I said. "And what are you up to today?"

"Sleighing," she laughed, "if Mama says I may. Will you ask her for me, Charlotte? She's much more likely to say yes to you."

I thought of Isabel as I had just seen her. Perhaps I should warn them, I thought, that she is not to be disturbed. No. I must not intrude, I thought.

"Yes," said Charlotte. "In a minute I will." She walked with me to the front door, where we could see the sun shining through the frosted glass. "Are you on foot?" she said. "It is slippery, you should go carefully." She sounded like a maiden aunt, I thought, rather than a debutante. We both paused, then, and I had the feeling that she wanted to say something more—something important, that is. Surely not about her mother?

But she said nothing; perhaps she thought better of it, or perhaps her courage simply failed her. And so, saying good-bye, I went out into the bright day.

As I picked my way along the narrow path trodden in the snow I shivered despite my heavy cloak, for the sun, for all its brilliance, held little warmth. The sky was winter-blue, and the fresh-fallen snow edged the brownstone roofs and lintels of the houses lining the avenue like icing on milk chocolate cake. But I was nearly oblivious to the day as I pondered what I had heard from Isabel. Would she leave Avery? Would she stay, but carry on a liaison with Cushing? She had confessed her secret to me; surely that meant that she was prepared to take some action. And yet—how could she? I felt confused, and very fearful of what was to happen.

I reminded myself that she had confessed only to me. Certainly she would tell no one else: whom could she trust? She is mad, I thought—mad for him, but mad as well to risk what she has for his sake. She has many years to live. Will she live them with him? Will she give up everything, will she ostracize herself, put herself beyond the pale?

"A dangerous man," said Carrie a week or so later. By that time Isabel and Cushing had gone—fled to Newport in the night like thieves, like the renegades they were. "Isabel said three days," she continued, "but I don't expect they'll be back for a week. That should be time enough for her to get her fill of him." She smiled at me in her vivacious way. She understood perfectly well all of the difficulties and dangers of Isabel's situation, but her natural enjoyment of the *comédie humaine* gave her a certain amused perspective.

I had no reply. Cushing's appearance had turned our little world upside down and I was still trying to find a firm footing.

"Don't look so worried, Marian," said Carrie. She reached out and patted my hand. She wore large sapphire earrings and—even in the daytime—a diamond-studded cuff bracelet over her fawn-colored glove. "Isabel is safe. Do you think I would have let her go if she were not? She is my sister-in-law—my own family. I want no scandal, no more than she does."

"Avery—" I began.

"Avery is not here. He left this morning, did you

know? He has gone West. Something to do with a railroad that he has an interest in. The message came yesterday."

"And the others? What do they think?"

"That she has overtired herself. That she wants to be completely alone—and where better a place than Newport at this season?"

She smiled at me again from beneath her small, tipped hat which matched the silky brown fur piece around her shoulders. She looked comfortable and happy and secure; she was one of those fortunate people who are content with their lot and do not seek to change it. Leighton adored her. Lucky woman!

And so I was left to wait; and not until years later did I learn what happened during those lost, reckless hours, the lovers' hours that they had never had.

Twenty-One

Isabel and Cushing were four days at her cottage at Newport. They traveled in a closed carriage, leaving Boston at dusk, arriving at Newport in the middle of the night. Cushing's coachman drove them while they clung together inside. They had changed horses halfway, but still the animals were near exhaustion. As they drew up by the tall, filigreed, wrought-iron gates, locked and barred for the winter (access for the caretakers and their small wagon being a narrow gate at the side), Cushing jumped out to help the coachman lead the horses in. He pulled the bell hard; it clanged in the silent night as if it would wake the dead. There were only the caretakers to hear it, an old man and his wife. They were there ostensibly to protect the place against thieves, but they were so old, so fragile, that any thief could have overpowered them in a moment. Their true job was to feed the three large mastiffs who roamed the grounds. Once an unwary intruder had scaled the high iron fence that surrounded the property at a time when the dogs were being fed. They were slower to reach him than they might have been; but when they did they nearly chewed his leg off.

Isabel heard their warning bark now, and she leaned from the open door of the carriage to call to them. She was in a frenzy of impatience. He had made love to her as they traveled; now, aroused, she wanted only to shut herself up with him in a warm, dark room forever. Hurry, she thought. Hurry. She twisted her hands so tightly together that her rings cut the flesh of her fingers. Her heart pounded in her ears. She had not known such a feeling before—frantic, desperate, ruthless.

At last the old man came. He hobbled down the path, a lantern in his hand, and peered at them through the opening. They could see his face clearly because of the light.

"John?" called Isabel. "It is I—Mrs. Kittredge. Open the gate."

"Ah—be it really you, missus?" His rheumy eyes blinked against the cold. "I wondered that the dogs went quiet. All right—wait, now, while I unlock."

Isabel had descended from the carriage and she stood now within the faint circle of his lamp, fidgeting, impatiently clasping and unclasping her hands. "Didn't you get my note?" she said. Cushing glanced at her; he saw the face of an irritated mistress of inefficient servants. "Hurry!" she said; "and then go quickly and tell Peg to light the fires and get us something to eat."

And so the gate was finally thrown open, the horses cared for, the coachman given a bed in the dormitory above the stables. The house sat at the edge of the dark winter sea like a deserted palace whose inhabitants have fled to warmer shores. Like a real castle, it had no central heating or even very many stoves. But there was a stove in Isabel's room, a fancy Austrian ceramic thing, and a fireplace as well, and of course the kitchen needed only the big cookstove for warmth.

At last they were alone. The old woman had given them chowder and biscuits and coffee, and Cushing had brought a bottle of brandy, and so they were warm enough that winter's night, what with the fireplace and the lamb's-wool comforters and the ceramic stove. The heat of their bodies alone would have been enough to warm the room.

This was their nuptial night, or so she felt—long delayed, twenty years delayed, not sweeter for that but sweet all the same. He took her as a starving man takes food, he seized her, he devoured her, he sated himself on her and was not sated yet, he would have her again and again all the night. His mouth burned on her body, his hands stroked her sweet warm flesh, maddening her, taking her up to ecstasy such as she had never imagined. And when they had done with ecstasy for the moment, they lay side by side under the comforter, watching the fires glowing at the open door of the stove and in the hearth, listening to the rising wind, the relentless rhythm of the sea below the lawn and the Cliff Walk. Isabel looked around that room—that familiar room where she had plotted her assault every summer. It held the memories of her triumphs. Someone else's triumphs: that woman—the woman who had built this house, who had used it as a battleground to make war on the bastions of Newport society—was a stranger to her now. She looked back on her in wonder: who was she?

Isabel Kittredge, she thought. And now that one has vanished and I am in her place: Isabel January, the girl this man once loved. I am myself again, after twenty years of pretending to be what I am not.

He touched her: he ran the palm of his hand lightly down her body. She lay on her side, her head propped on one hand, gazing at him with adoring eyes. She shuddered at his touch: and when he stopped, just at the curve of her hip, she held her breath: where next would he touch her? He made her ache for him, this man: he made her mad. She felt as though she had lost all sense, all sanity. If he said jump, she would jump; if he said, "Come away with me," she would go.

As she would have done twenty years before.

She watched his face. "Why do you smile?" she said.

"Because you stare at me as if you do not know who I am."

"I stare at you because I do not know who *I* am."

"Do you not?" The hand came away from her hip. He touched her face; he stroked her hair. "I know who you are, Isabel. You are a woman who has haunted me for twenty years. I have never been able to forget you. And believe me when I say that I have tried. I came back to you once before. Remember that."

"And went away again angry."

"I wanted you to come with me."

"I could not. I *could* not—and besides—"

"What?"

"I was angry too."

"After all that time." He did not question it. He

stroked her body, her warm, soft skin; he lowered his head and kissed her, first one breast and then the other. It seemed to her a gesture of inexpressible tenderness: Avery had never done that. She saw the nape of his neck, as vulnerable as a child's; she felt a sudden surge of love for him mingled with desire that swept through her heart and her soul and left her breathless—frightened.

And then, aroused, they took each other one more time. Neither of them thought more about the past, or about the future, or about what might have been or what might yet be.

For three days they hardly moved from her room. From time to time they threw on wrappers and walked to the wall windows; they stood together and looked out to the winter sea, to what in summer were the rose gardens, now brown and clipped and banked against the cold. One afternoon, when the wind had died and the sun seemed warmer than it had been before, they dressed and went outdoors and walked across the lawn to the sea wall. Isabel wore a brown hooded cape like a monk's cape— save that no monk's cape was ever trimmed so richly in sable fur, no monk's cape was made of velvet. Because the lawn was damp, dead and brown and damp, she wore galoshes. Instead of her usual elaborate coiffure, she wore her hair gathered into a loose knot on the top of her head; strands of it floated down around her face, giving her a girlish look, slightly *déshabillée*.

They stood at the wall and looked out beyond the Cliff Walk to the sea shining in the sunlight. The sky was soft blue, the air fresh with the promise of spring. It was only the second week in January; winter would be with them for a long time yet. This mild bright day was a false promise, more treacherous than spring itself. Behind them the house loomed like a fantasy. All up and down the shoreline stood the cottages of Isabel's peers, closed and shuttered for the winter, vast, empty pleasure palaces, their pleasures meaningless to her now.

He took her hand and held it for a moment before pressing it to his lips. He was hatless; he wore a tweed hacking jacket over a gray fisherman's sweater and a pair of flannel trousers. Like Isabel, he looked younger than his years. Perhaps they did that for each other: cheated time, took back their youth. The breeze ruffled his golden hair; his eyes smiled down on her more blue than the sea. She thought that she could drown in those eyes, and she shuddered deep inside herself as she felt herself sink.

"This time I will not go away without you," he said.

"No." She gazed at him in wonder. She felt that she lived in a dream, that at any moment she would awaken and find herself lying beside her husband, ready to face another day of luncheons and teas and evening parties and endless, endless talk. She clung to his hands holding hers; she felt his warmth, his firm, undeniable presence. It is not a dream, she thought; that other is the dream. This is real.

"When we leave here, you will arrange whatever is necessary in Boston," he said. "And then we will go."

"Where?" she said. They stood entirely alone on the promontory and yet she spoke softly, as if someone, somehow, would overhear.

"Wherever you want," he said. "London. Rome. Why not someplace exotic? Constantinople? Damascus?"

"All of those," she said. "We will go to all of those places." Suddenly she laughed. "Do you know what I was thinking just now? I was thinking that I must look in my address book to see whom to invite to dinner next month before the Burgess' Valentine ball." She shook her head slowly, trying to clear it, but unwilling, at last, to awaken. "And I don't need to do that. I will not be having a dinner that evening. They will give the ball and I will not be there."

"And can you live with that knowledge?" he said, watching her closely.

"Yes."

"No doubts? No fears?"

"No."

"You will never be able to come back. Not, at least, as long as *he* is alive."

"I know that."

He embraced her then; he held her close to his heart as if she were infinitely precious to him.

In the evening of the fourth day they came back. They arrived toward midnight. I did not see her until the following afternoon, when, summoned by an urgent note, I hastened to Commonwealth Avenue. It was a raw, dark day, threatening snow; as I descended from the carriage I looked up at the facade of the house and saw that the gas had been lighted everywhere, on all floors— an unusual extravagance. I hurried up the front steps; the maid must have been watching for my arrival—or someone else's?—for I had hardly pulled the bellpull when the door swung open.

"She's in her sitting room, madam," she said. Like all

well-trained servants, she was impassive, but I could see a worried look about her all the same.

As I went upstairs I heard an unfamiliar male voice on the landing. Isabel greeted me with a distracted kiss; Carrie nodded at me in a friendly way, but a frown creased her forehead and her smile was a faint imitation of what it ordinarily was.

"Thank you for coming so quickly, Marian," said Isabel. "I will just speak to Dr. Elliott and then I will be back directly—pour yourself a cup of tea—"

She ran up to the third floor with surprisingly quick steps. I turned to Carrie with a question on my lips which she forestalled with an expressive lift of her eyebrows.

"I don't know," she said. She shut the door behind Isabel and came to me again so that she could speak softly. "I don't know what is going on, Marian. The doctor has been here for an hour, two of the children are sick, but that isn't the worst of it. I think—I *think*—that Isabel intends some drastic thing. I think that she intends to—to *go away with him!*"

I stared at her, too shocked to speak; she was an uncommonly practical, worldly-wise woman of a certain age who refused to acquiesce to the more senseless rules of the social canon. Ordinarily she bore herself with the confidence that money gives, but now, as she stood whispering into my ear, she seemed as fearful and uncertain as a girl before her debut.

Before I could think of a reply we heard the sound of a slammed door, heavy footsteps on the stairs. Avery, I thought; Avery has come early from his office, he will discover us here like two thieves plotting.

I held my breath and waited. The gas jets hissed and sputtered, the room suddenly seemed too warm, and I undid the top buttons—small, jet, difficult—of my jacket. Carrie drew back; she walked to the window, which gave onto the back garden. "I don't think," she said, "that we should—"

The door flew open just then; even though we had been expecting it we were startled nevertheless, frozen into our respective stances.

"I beg your pardon," he said. "I was told that Mrs. Kittredge was here."

The light played on his hair; he looked like a Viking, I thought, tall and strong and golden like a god. He dressed not like a god, however, but like a dandy, fine linen and the best quality wool, and polished leather boots and a greatcoat with a broad, curly gray lamb collar and a large stickpin in his gray silk cravat. But none of that lessened the impression he gave of a pagan prince, some primitive Scandinavian displaced in time.

Carrie recovered more quickly than I. "Yes," she said, "yes, please come in, she's just upstairs. Two of the children are sick, the doctor is here, but she will be down direct—"

He had met us both several times, but he had met many people and it would not have been surprising if he had not remembered our faces, let alone our names. But he turned to each of us, he took first Carrie's hand and then mine. "Mrs. January—Mrs. Leighton January. I was your husband's good friend once, did he tell you? Yes? And Mrs. Motley. How delightful to see you again."

He took my hand; something of his own excitement

passed to me and I felt a faint tremor deep within.

Before we could say anything more we heard Isabel's voice in the hall. I could not make out the words, but there was a shrill anxious note which warned us of trouble. First her voice—sharp, questioning; then a man's—the doctor's, giving answers; then Isabel's reply.

And then in a moment she was with us, bursting in, frantic, half in tears. When she saw Cushing she pulled up short. Her hand flew to her mouth as if to stop her speech; her eyes were wide with astonishment. Or perhaps fear?

"*You*—"

"I had your note," he said. He moved toward her in a protective way. "You alarmed me. What did you mean when you said, 'I must delay'? Why? What is wrong?"

She stared at him—only at him. I do not think she knew that we were in the room. I would have left then, but to do so I would have had to brush past her, to intrude myself upon her total concentration on him. And—I admit—I am only human, I was curious past bearing to know more of them. My life was all on the surface, so to speak: for moments of deep human drama I needed to depend, like so many other people, upon novels and theater and the plots of operas. This glimpse of human emotion normally hidden beneath the proper surfaces of our lives seduced me and I succumbed.

"I cannot go with you," she said. She stood before him perfectly still, her hands twisting, wringing, ceaselessly moving while the rest of her was motionless, her eyes large and staring, fastened on his face, clinging to him while her arms could not.

"What do you mean, you cannot come with me? Why not?"

"Mary and Mason are ill. Very ill. The doctor says— oh, Lawrence, the doctor says that he cannot be sure—it is diphtheria, he says—they are very ill, very ill, I cannot go while they are so bad. I *cannot*—"

He stood impassive before her; and it was his lack of response, I think, that goaded her into further protestation.

"Wait for me! Lawrence, wait for me—do not go away again without me! A week—two at the most—and they will be well, they will not need me for their convalescence, but I cannot go now, I cannot leave them now, but I cannot leave *you*, I cannot do one or the other—oh, Lawrence, please! Please do not go—"

For, to my horror—to hers!—he had taken a step toward the door.

"Lawrence! Please—please—ah, God, *please* do not go, please understand that I *cannot*—please—!"

She threw herself on him then but he pulled away as if she had plague. She came back at him but he held her arms; they struggled like combatants in a deadly battle.

Lovers! Yes—they were lovers then, they had lain together in the night, they had shared that deepest of all intimacies: and yet . . .

And yet they fought. He was very angry, and who could blame him? It was a disloyal thought, for what of Avery, after all? And yet . . .

And yet this man seemed to be her husband. He behaved like a husband—stern and domineering and accusatory—and she was as supplicant as a wife.

409

She had promised to go with him, I thought: and so she would, following her heart's desire.

And instantly was appalled. Had I become so callous that I was deaf and blind to all human decency? This man was an intruder, he had led her into adultery— And what of the children?

"No!" She threw herself on her knees before him. "No! No!"

"Isabel!" At last Carrie seemed to wake herself from our mutual nightmare. She tried to raise Isabel to her feet, to guide her out of Cushing's way—for he was going, he would not stay longer. But Isabel would not be moved, she knelt before him and clung to him and would not let him go. His face was angry; or perhaps it was not anger that I saw, perhaps it was pain as deep as hers, and he was struggling to get away from her to end it, to ease his torment.

At last he bent down and loosened her hands himself. Then he was gone. Isabel knelt on the floor, her head bowed, her face buried in her hands. Sobs racked her body; her breath came in short, harsh gasps through her constricted lungs. After a while she let us help her rise. We took her to her room, we loosened her stays, we put her to bed. We never mentioned Cushing's name.

Her children hovered near death for two weeks. She nursed them day and night, sleeping in snatches, existing on black coffee and frequent doses of Dinmore's Restorative—a concoction with an extremely high alcoholic content.

I looked in on her every day. She grew increasingly pale, increasingly haggard, with dark circles under her eyes, her mouth set in a hard line, her hair undone, straggling down around her face. She slept in her clothes, I believe, when she slept at all—throwing herself down upon a couch for an hour or two, waking again without being called, returning to the sickroom. As the days passed it seemed a question of who would survive, Isabel or her children. Her sickness was of the spirit, of the heart; theirs of the body—but hers was equally dangerous, equally fatal. She seemed to have lost the will to live, I thought: Avery and her mother think that she looks so, behaves so, because of her concern for the children. Carrie and I know differently. Young as they are, Mary and Mason struggled to live, they fought with that inborn, basic human instinct to survive. But Isabel had given up. She does not want to go on without him, I thought. She is beaten: whipped.

In the end the children recovered and so, it seemed, did she. But something had died within her: she was not what she had been. It was a bad winter, everyone said: diphtheria and whooping cough and measles everywhere.

And then my own child took sick, and I had no more time for Isabel.

Twenty-Two

He was ill for nearly a month—very ill indeed, the doctor said before hurrying away to the next house, the next patient in that endless winter of sickness.

I tended him night and day, sleeping on a cot in his room, never leaving the house. On the doctor's advice I hired a nurse also, a woman with an excellent "character," known by reputation to the doctor. He said that I was lucky to have her; nurses were in short supply.

"This child's not so bad as some I've seen," the nurse said. She smiled reassuringly. "How old did you say he was?"

"Six—seven in April."

"Never sick before?"

"No. Not even a head cold."

"Well. You go and rest. I'll just bathe him to keep this fever down, and then we'll see if he'll drink some beef tea. It's all right, missus. I do this all the time. Look in after you've had a bit of sleep, you'll see how well we're managing."

And so I allowed myself to be taken in charge by Mrs.

Rourke, who came, so I reminded myself, with the highest recommendations.

And, indeed, when I had slept for a while and returned to Edward's room in the late afternoon, just as the lamps were being lighted, I saw that he seemed better even in so short a time. His eyes were alert but no longer fever-bright; his skin was cool. He lay looking out at the darkening sky from his bed placed close to the window. The draperies had been removed for cleaning and had not been rehung; during the day, during his lucid moments, he had watched the progress of the clouds, finding animals, castles, fantastic creatures in their shapes. Sometimes at night, as I sat beside him and bathed his fevered face and limbs, I looked out and saw the moon shining on the river—for Edward's room was on the third floor at the rear of the house—sailing high among the stars across the nighttime heavens. Edward had a well-loved storybook, *Mr. Moon and What He Saw;* sometimes, when he was lucid, I read it to him. If the moon shone across your bed while you lay sleeping you went mad, some said; but I welcomed its friendly face smiling down, keeping company with me through the long night.

For of course I was alone in this thing as in every other. Perseus went about his business; he had nothing to do with me or the child. Since the time when he had needed money and had been forced to ask me for it he had withdrawn from me almost completely. Often I did not see him for two or three days running. My friends looked in: Carrie came, and Mrs. Reed, as vigorous in her seventies as she had been two decades previously; and a few others.

Isabel did not come. "She is . . . all right, I think," said Carrie. "The children have recovered, and yesterday I found her at her desk, making up the guest list for the Symphony benefit. She seems—I don't know—a bit distracted. When she looks at me, I'm not sure that she sees me. But certainly she is well enough."

, Good, I thought; for if she were not there was precious little that I could do for her. Even with Mrs. Rourke caring for Edward, I did not like to leave the house. It was as if my presence there, if not actually by my child's side, had a healing effect on him. In his long convalescence he lay patient and obedient under the crazy-quilt and waited for my visits; and when he saw me his small face lighted up and his arms went out to hug me tight, and my heart twisted in my bosom to see such love, such undemanding, unconditional love as my son had for me. I am blessed, I thought; and, having this, I will never ask for more.

One mild day at the beginning of March I went to see him in the morning as usual. Mrs. Rourke sat by his side knitting with blue yarn a sweater for her grandson, a boy, as she told us, nearly Edward's age.

"He's very much improved, missus," she said. Her homely face beamed in a smile.

"Yes?" I said. I sat on the edge of his bed and took his small warm hands in mine and looked at him, as I always did, in wonder and a kind of greedy adoration. How beautiful he was! His long silky hair, browner than mine, redder than Otis', fell over his high round forehead; softly, gently I brushed it back and slid my hand down his

414

pale, thin cheek. "Are you better, indeed, Master Edward?"

"Yes. Much. I think I'll get up today, Mama—"

"Oh no! Never! You'll have a relapse."

"Restless," said Mrs. Rourke. "They're getting better for sure, when they get restless."

"I'll tell you what," I said. "If you stay in bed—if you stay with no complaint, no argument—I will go downtown and buy your birthday present and you may have it today."

He grinned at me. "A castle," he said, "like the one in the *Youth's Companion?*"

He had seen an advertisement for a pasteboard castle to cut out and assemble. Intrigued by the stories of King Arthur that I had read to him, he had asked for it weeks ago, before he became ill.

"Yes!" I said. I smiled, I laughed with the joy of seeing him nearly well again. I hugged him fiercely. "If it can be found in the city of Boston, I will buy it and bring it home to you, I promise!" In the summer, I thought, we will go swimming every day at Bailey's Beach, and perhaps I will buy him a pony.

When I returned, successful, it was not yet dark. Before I even removed my hat and gloves I went upstairs to see him. He lay waiting for me, watching the door expectantly; a great, happy smile flooded his face when he saw me and the package I carried. I rushed to him, embracing him, and then I helped him to open the box.

"There—how many pieces! This will keep you busy for days!"

He had begun to sort it out when suddenly he was seized with a long, painful cough; it was some minutes until he recovered his breath, during which time I held him and felt his shuddering, agonizing attempts to draw breath, I heard the painful rasp in his little chest.

I turned to Mrs. Rourke, aware now as I did so that she was watching us anxiously. More than that: unless I was mistaken, I saw fear in her eyes.

"How long has he been like this?" I said, more sharply than I intended. Something in her attitude alarmed me but I could not have said what it was.

"He hasn't—this is the first time," she said.

"All afternoon he's been quiet? No cough?"

"Missus, this is the first time I heard that today," she said. Something in her eyes—what? I had no time to consider it. He had quieted, finally, and I laid him back on his pillows and put my hand on his chest to feel the slow quieting of his pounding little heart. He watched me with his great dark eyes, and I saw that shadow there, too, that I had seen in the eyes of the nurse. What? Some knowledge, some secret, perhaps, that they kept from me?

What could the two of them possibly know that I did not?

"Has the doctor been by?" I said; for perhaps he had let drop some hint, some warning.

"No, missus."

"Then I will send for him. I do not like the sound of this cough, not when he is supposed to be on the mend."

"Yes, missus." Mrs. Rourke's ordinarily cheerful face was somber, her eyes downcast. What was the matter?

As I went downstairs to give a note to the coachman I was surprised to see Perseus coming out of his study. It was not yet five o'clock; ordinarily he did not return until much later. I said nothing to him, however, concerned as I was for Edward; we passed in silence, he going upstairs, I going to confer with Cook in the kitchen.

The doctor, overburdened, was unable to come that evening, and at eight o'clock he sent word that he would stop by in the morning.

But in the night Edward grew worse, and by morning he was very ill once more. He burned with fever, he shook and trembled with it, he cried out that all his bones ached unbearably, he gasped and gagged and clung to my hand as if he would never let go.

"I can't see any reason for it," said the doctor. "He was progressing very nicely. Usually if there is a relapse like this one can pinpoint the cause." He turned accusingly upon the nurse. "Did he get up at all? You didn't let him walk about, did you?"

And again I watched her, and I saw that indefinable something that I could not capture but that I knew was there all the same, lurking just below her homely, placid surface. But she only shook her head in answer to the doctor's query, and he did not pursue it.

As the day wore on—a dark, raw, dreary day after the previous day's sun—Edward lay insensible, his eyes unseeing behind fluttering lashes. When we spoke to him he did not seem to hear. By evening the doctor refused to offer any hope. "I cannot say," he replied tersely to Mrs. Reed's anxious questions. She had come at once, and had sent an urgent note to Isabel and Carrie and Mrs. January to come as well.

As they sat with me through the night, we understood that the worst was happening after all, the thing dreaded above all others, and we knew that we could do nothing to escape it: Death could take my child as readily as anyone else's. And so we gathered together as people did in times of crisis, we huddled in a corner of the drawing room and drank hot lemon tea and watched the doctor as he came, and went, and came again, and then another man, too, hurrying up the stairs with his bag of tricks.

Even when I sat with them, waiting, waiting, my spirit was with Edward, with the small, precious boy two flights up in his little room at the back of the house where he had lived all his short life since I had brought him into the world. From time to time I was allowed to see him, and then I was sent away again, I did not know why. I knew nothing; I knew only that I was at the mercy of something stronger than I, and that I would lose in the end.

He was a long time dying. His breath came short and hard from his little lungs, and his eyes grew large and dark; his skin was flushed and hot, his soft lips dried and cracked. He lingered that night, and all the next day, and long into the following night. He did not know me, did not know his mother, as I clung to him in frantic, desperate fear, as I held back my sobs through force of will and felt them tear my heart inside me. Even when I was with the others I did not cry.

And even when he died I made no sound, I had no voice for my grief. I do not know why. I had no tears: I sat dry-eyed, numb, while all around me they did what

had to be done, they made the preparations for his
funeral, they supervised the running of the house, they
dealt with people who came to call. I have little memory
of that time. I felt as though I, too, had died. I had no will,
I had no feeling: I did not even have, at first, an
intimation of the depth of my loss. I sat when they told
me to sit; I stood when they told me to stand; once in a
while, on their orders, I ate or drank. I remember that I
was never alone; even when I slept, fitfully, restlessly, I
would come suddenly awake to see someone—Isabel, or
Carrie, or sometimes the nurse—sitting by me, watching.
I understand now that they feared for my life—feared
that I would take it, perhaps. But I would not have done
so, at least not then: I lacked the will.

Then came a time—days, weeks later—when I wept
and lamented and shrieked and they could not quiet me.
They were afraid that I would go mad, then, and so to give
me surcease from my pain the doctor recommended
laudanum. Obediently, I took it, and it did its work: I was
calm again, drugged, hardly alive.

One day, as a kind of test, I deprived myself of the
morning's dose. I wanted to learn whether I could live
conscious and clearheaded through the day. And I did: I
survived it. But as evening fell, and I sat alone in my
room, my self-control slipped away and I was overcome
once again by grief, by a wound that would never heal, an
insupportable pain.

"Edward—"

My room was dark. I stumbled into the hall where I was
blinded by the blazing gas jets. I groped along the
balustrade. I found the stairs going up and I followed

them, hardly conscious of what I did, where I went. I found his room. I opened the door and sank to my knees on the threshold, suddenly weakened by the force of my emotion. Sobbing, I leaned against the doorjamb, my head resting on my arm, my thin body, thinner now than ever before, shuddering with my sobs.

After a while I struggled to my feet. I walked unsteadily to the window. Below me flowed the nighttime river; on the far shore twinkled the lights of Cambridge. The sky was overcast; there was no moon. I pressed my cheek against the glass: it was very cold, it stung my skin. *"Edward—"*

The front door, three floors down, slammed shut with such force that I felt the tremor through the glass against my face. Momentarily distracted, I pulled back. Someone had come in. I was alone, the servants were asleep. Who—?

It seemed to me that the intruder might have a benign purpose. Perhaps it was someone come to tell me about my son. He had gone away, I could not remember why, and I had had no word of him since he left. Perhaps now at last there was news. Perhaps it was Edward himself.

I hurried out into the hall. I hung over the balustrade and looked down into the stairwell—a dizzying tier of ovals, the spokes of the balustrade forming patterns on the walls in the glaring light of the gas jets.

"Edward?"

Instantly I realized my mistake. It was not he; of course it was not he. No little child could slam a door so hard, not even—

Something crashed in the drawing room—from the

sound of it, something made of pottery or china. Clumsy! Why did he not simply come out into the hall and cry up to me?

Perhaps he was looking for me there. Perhaps he—whoever he was—was talking to me even now in the mistaken impression that I sat alone in the dark waiting to hear him.

No, I thought: do not speak yet, wait until I come—

I turned and hurried down the stairs so quickly that I nearly tripped on the hem of my skirt. Down, down—silence below, I heard nothing more. The high heels of my shoes hardly touched the stair treads, my hand skimmed the banister more for balance than support. Down and around the curve at the second floor, on down to the first, through the open door of the drawing room—

Where?

In the light from the hall I saw a figure standing at the table in the center of the room. He had an attitude of dejection: hands flat on the table top, shoulders slightly bent as he rested his weight on his hands, head sunk forward. I smelled strong drink.

With a stab of disapppointment I recognized him. Perhaps I was mistaken. I needed to see more clearly. The long key for turning on the gas hung by the mantel. In one swift step I seized it and thrust it up to the jets. In the instant that the lights blossomed he raised his eyes to mine; his hands stayed planted on the table. Looking down on us was a portrait of a woman dressed in gray, with a haunting, expectant look upon her face.

"*You!*" I gripped the brass rod so tightly that my hand went numb.

This man could bring no news of my son. This man could bring only sorrow. He had refused to give me any children, and he had hated the one I had.

I felt a tremendous sense of injustice. That he stood before me, alive, while my child lay buried— No! It was insupportable—unbearable! I felt my anger rise up in my throat, I felt it swell inside my head and press upon my brain until it seemed that my skull would explode.

In my agitation I did not stop to consider what it meant that he smelled so. Ordinarily he was not a drinking man: he drank nothing stronger than coffee, or an occasional ginger beer in the summer. This night he stank like a still. If I thought of it at all I thought only that he, like everyone else, was only human, and that for once he had behaved so.

"Get out," I said. I did not recognize the sound of my voice.

"Marian—"

"Out. Get out." Please, I thought: go quickly before I start to scream. I did not want to scream, I did not want him to see me lose control. "I will call them to put you out if you do not go peacefully."

He stared up at me; he did not move.

"Out! Damn you! Damn you—this is *my* house, he was *my* child, you have no right to anything—get out! Get *out!*"

Suddenly I flew at him. Before he could move I began to hit him with the rod, I beat him over the head with it. His glasses fell off; blood trickled down his forehead and into his eyes, it spurted from a deep cut on his ear. Again and again I hit him, raising my arm, bringing the rod down upon his head, feeling an immense, inarticulate satisfaction in what I did, a wordless joy as I beat him and beat him—how dared he live while my child was dead?

He withstood me. Drunk as he was, he stood like a dumb animal under my blows, my terrible overpowering rage. In my frenzy I did not pause to wonder why.

At last I stopped. I was dazed and trembling, so weak that I could hardly stand. The rod dropped to the floor at my feet. I turned and walked stiffly from the room. My lacings nearly asphyxiated me. My grief settled down upon me once again, for despite my outburst nothing had changed. My sorrow was with me still, waiting to burden me again.

This man to whom I was bound was alive; and my child—my sweet, beautiful boy—was dead.

When I reached my room I rang for my maid to release me from my corsets. Then, sending the maid away, I unstoppered the small brown bottle which held my drug and, like a lover meeting her beloved and slaking her thirst for his kisses, I raised it to my lips and greedily drank, welcoming the numbed brain, the dulled sensibilities that I knew would come.

It was not death; but it was near enough.

Twenty-Three

In the spring, in the middle of May when the magnolias had bloomed and the trees had fully blossomed and the tulips and daffodils had come and gone, Curtis had a telegram from Paris. It was a message that he had dreaded for months, and now it had come. At once he went to Isabel.

"It's Elinor," he said; and needed to say no more, for Isabel understood. Their younger sister had been ill since the birth of her child; and now at last she had died.

"We were concerned for the child, of course," he told me later—years later, when we spoke freely of our lives. "But we wanted to help you too. Harry Lathrop didn't say so in that first message, but later he wrote two or three letters, all of them to the effect that with Elinor's death he wanted to move on, and he did not feel that he could adequately care for their daughter. We thought of you at once. You were not recovering as quickly as you should, and we thought that it might help you to have Elinor's child. And of course we wanted her here in Boston, not wandering around Europe in the care of some foreign governess."

"Why not you and Grace?" I said.

His face was suddenly somber. "Grace had long since given up hope of a child. She would not have wanted to disrupt her life."

And so they came to me. I hardly remember their visit, but I remember my anger at what I thought of as their intrusion into my private, solitary grief. I turned them away. I did not want sympathy, I did not want another child—I wanted my own boy and, lacking him, I wanted nothing. Not even their pleas for Elinor's sake—Elinor, who once had been my friend—moved me from my selfish desolation.

Isabel went briefly to Newport that summer, her social activities curtailed once again, and when she returned she called on me but I would not see her. I would see no one. I lived alone in my room; from time to time I wandered the streets as if I were searching for my child, only to return exhausted and lie down upon my bed and taste the bitter drug upon my tongue and seek oblivion once again.

Curtis found me one warm, golden day, an Indian summer day, in the Public Garden when the surface of the lagoon was thick with fallen leaves from the surrounding trees and the walkways were clogged with strollers getting the last of the warmth before the onset of winter. The swan boats, normally put away by that date, were still in use; the entire month of September had been unusually fine, and the management kept them running as long as the weather held.

I stood at the end of the miniature suspension bridge where the path continued through the lawns and flower

425

beds to the Arlington Street gate. I felt very weak; the earth tilted under my feet and I steadied myself against the stone parapet. I saw two women approaching. I could not remember their names, but I recognized them, I had met them many times. Although I had chosen solitude, I was suddenly moved to acknowledge them, I did not know why. Cautiously I went toward them, my hand extended in greeting. I remember my unsteady gait; I suppose my face looked strange. It felt stiff; I could feel the tenseness of my muscles as I tried to smile. I spoke to them and my voice slurred, I could not form the words distinctly.

I remember their shocked faces, and how they quickly turned away from me. Curtis was standing near all the while, but I did not see him. I began to walk. My feet, hidden by the heavy folds of my skirts, shuffled like a blind woman's afraid of a misstep. Nurses wheeling perambulators made wide arcs around me; children rolling hoops or running races narrowly missed colliding with me. I came to an unoccupied bench; heavily I collapsed upon it.

"Marian." Curtis stood before me slightly bent, peering into my face. After a moment he saw that I recognized him and he sat down. "Marian, let me take you home."

I looked away from him; I looked out across the late-blooming flower beds, the tiny Bavarian castle on a tall post that served as a birdhouse, the specimen trees and shrubs, to the lagoon and the swan boats plying back and forth, around and around, each propelled by its boy perched at the back, pedaling, overseeing his passengers.

"I don't want to go home," I said, realizing as I spoke that it was true. I did not.

"Well then. Where?"

Still I did not look at him. "There," I said. "On the swan boats."

Accordingly we soon found ourselves being pedaled across the water; we were nearly alone in the boat, for the afternoon was waning, people were going home. Curtis took my hand. The boy at the back will think that we are lovers, I thought, even at our age, and illicit lovers at that. No matter. The water lapped at the sides of the boat; ducks and swans swam alongside us, the sky arched milky blue over us. At last Curtis began to speak. "Marian, we have heard again from Harry Lathrop. He is desperate. He begs us to help him."

I took back my hand; I looked down, I slid away from him, a little farther down the bench.

"If you would take the child just for a while, for a few months—it is a little girl, Marian, and I should think that a little girl would not pain you so much. You understand what I mean, she would not remind you—ah—"

"No."

"But, Marian—listen to me, please. If you—"

"No. No. No." I had begun to tremble so violently that my teeth chattered.

"All right," he said. "You needn't take on so. I simply thought— Well. Never mind. Come—move in toward me before you fall overboard. I will not ask you again, I promise that I will not."

And so he soothed me, and quieted my alarm, and dealt as best he could with my drugged consciousness. And

427

when we had made our stately circuit of the little lake and were safe on dry land once more, he saw me home and said no more about Elinor's child.

His words must have had some effect on me, however, for the next morning when I awoke and reached, as was my habit, for the bottle of laudanum, I did not automatically take it as had been my wont. I hesitated; I was aware that my brain was somewhat cleared and I did not for the moment want to cloud it again. I put the bottle by; I rose. I sent for my maid to help me dress; I ordered breakfast and went downstairs to eat it. All that day, and the next, I withstood my craving for the drug, and on the third day I found the courage to pour it down the sink in my bathroom. It seemed to me that I was waiting for something—preparing myself for something, I did not know what.

One afternoon about a week later I walked downtown—steadily, this time, and neatly groomed as I had not been that afternoon with Curtis in the Public Garden. I spent an hour in the stores and then I retraced my steps across the Common toward Beacon Street. It was a bright, blue and gold October day, real autumn now, the foretaste of winter. The wind blew strong, swirling clouds of leaves from the grass, and I shivered as it cut through the thin black serge of my jacket.

As I came out onto the path above the Frog Pond, now empty for cleaning before being filled again to freeze for skating, I stopped to let pass a dozen or so little boys running down from the gate on Beacon Street. Very little boys: some did not look more than five or six years old. I stood quite still in the middle of the walkway and watched them regroup in the middle of the dry, empty pond. No, I thought. I have not had a drop of laudanum in days. My head is clear, my eyes can see. *No—*

I took one step and then another. I was off the path now, my feet crunching the dry brown leaves covering the grass. No, I thought, no, it cannot be, I am hallucinating—

The children milled about. I saw only one: a boy of six or so, with silky brown hair.

No. No. I had crossed the lawn, I stood now at the granite curbing at the edge of the pond. My arm was raised, my mouth open to call his name. No, I thought, *no*—and yet it was he, it was my own boy come back to life. I devoured him with my eyes: his lithe little form, the way he moved . . .

Please, I thought. I felt my throat tighten as I was about to speak.

The boy turned. For a moment he saw me. He was small, very bright-looking. Our eyes met. He did not know me. I was a stranger to him, he to me. He turned away, he ran with his friends to the playing field by Charles Street. None of the others had noticed me.

I felt my tears well up; my eyes ached and stung, the wind blew cold on my cheeks where the tears trickled down. I could not see. I returned to the path, trembling so that I could hardly walk. I understood what had happened: for one moment I had had my life again, and it had had meaning again, and love, and joy.

My life: my child.

I hurried down the wide walk paralleling Beacon Street. My life: my child. My life . . . Perhaps it is not yet too late, I thought. Perhaps: if I act quickly, if I speak to Curtis at once . . . My brain cleared; I felt the cold wind sweep away the shrouds of grief and self-absorption, I felt strength flow back into my limbs, into my heart.

I arrived at my doorstep breathless, exhilarated. The maid, seeing my face, stared in amazement; she had been employed less than a year, she could hardly remember a time when I had not been half mad with grief or drugged into lethargy. With a word of greeting flung behind me, I ran up the stairs to my room. My heart pounded painfully, my corsets cut my side. Without removing my hat or my jacket, I threw down my gloves and opened the marquetry writing box on the little desk by the window. I took a pen and a sheet of thick ivory paper embossed with my initials; without a moment's hesitation I dipped the pen into the cut-crystal inkwell and scrawled my message:

Curtis:
Send the child to me.

Only then did I pause: need I say more? No, I thought: that is all. He would understand—would understand, as I had done just now, that this was my cry for a new chance at life, that I was done with grieving, and that if I did not soon have some other human being to love I too would die.

Part III

One

At Newport, in the summer of 1896, Mrs. Denton Elliott, for reasons that I cannot now remember, gave what she called her Apple of Discord Ball. Perhaps she had a daughter whom she wanted to show off; or perhaps her husband had come into some money that he wanted to dispose of as quickly as possible; or perhaps she was simply bored. Parties have been given for worse reasons.

Every woman in the summer colony who received an invitation, Isabel not least among them, took it as a personal challenge of the highest order, for this was to be a costume ball for young, unmarried women: their daughters. The girl judged to be the most beautiful would be awarded the prize of a golden apple.

"Surely not real?" said Isabel with some asperity. "Even Mrs. Denton Elliott is not that rich."

We sat with our daughters on the gallery facing the sea: she, Charlotte and Victoria, and Diana—Elinor's child, now mine. Diana was by far the youngest, not quite eight, but already she was acutely aware of everything that went on around her. She watched Victoria now with an unabashed stare. Victoria had made her debut the previous December, several weeks after Consuelo Vanderbilt married the Duke of Marlborough. By now, having attended more parties and balls and receptions and teas than any human being should be asked to endure, she was heartily sick of the whole business. Diana knew that Victoria's life—the life of a debutante—would be her own one day, and so now she paid strict attention as Victoria recited her litany of complaints.

"I must always smile," she said, "even when my feet hurt so that I can hardly stand. And I must always be pleasant to every old horror in Boston—there aren't so many in Newport, thank goodness. They pick us over"— she meant her fellow debutantes—"and gossip about us and criticize us— And the men! The men are even worse! The young ones step all over our feet—when they condescend to dance with us at all—and the old ones bore us to death with their stories—"

"Enough!" Isabel, who had not been paying strict attention, suddenly realized what her young daughter had been saying—and its effect on Charlotte, who, unclaimed at twenty-four, sat listening, stony-faced, to a recitation of troubles which she herself would have been overjoyed to bear.

How different they were: Charlotte, the image of her father, massive and square-faced; Victoria, small and vivacious, having come to look very much like her mother. She had more color than Isabel, who was always pale; her hair was a shade darker, her eyes more sparkling, but now that Victoria was grown, people sometimes mistook them for sisters.

434

Suddenly, unexpectedly, Charlotte spoke. "What about Winifred?"

Isabel stared at her. "Winifred," she said blankly. "I had forgotten all about her. And she's to arrive—when? Next week?" The costume ball was to take place the week after.

"I suppose we could write and put her off," said Charlotte, not without malice. She is glad to see her mother so pressed, I thought; not for the first time I reflected on the fact that a lifetime of being plain and dull in a world that valued beauty and vivacity served only to make one bitter and angry and filled with the desire to hurt others. Even—or perhaps especially—one's own mother.

"No," said Isabel, "we cannot do that. I promised to have her. I've already put her off twice, and this time I promised that nothing would interfere. Well: let her come. We'll deal with her somehow."

The young woman in question was a distant connection from Portland, Maine. For some months her mother had been pressing for an invitation for her to stay with Isabel, either in Boston or Newport. "To find a husband, of course," said Isabel with some bitterness. "It is not enough that I must marry off my own daughters, I must find husbands for other people's as well. No doubt she expects me to supply a title or two from which to choose. Well, I am not Mrs. Vanderbilt and I cannot work miracles."

The marriage of Consuelo Vanderbilt to the Duke of Marlborough the previous November was still a topic of animated conversation in Newport and everywhere else, for that matter. People said that Consuelo was forced into it; people said that Alva Vanderbilt engineered the affair to distract attention from her own divorce, or to feed her own overweening ambition. In any case, marrying a daughter into the aristocracy had been the goal of many an ambitious mama—including, no doubt, the woman in Portland.

Now, tapping her fingertips nervously against her teacup, her eyes staring out to the sea shining violet and metallic blue in the late afternoon light, Isabel focused on her immediate problems: costumes for her two daughters and in particular a costume for Victoria that would ensure her triumph.

On the other hand: "Success will depend not only upon the costume but upon who will judge it," she said. Her face was still turned toward the ocean, but her eyes flickered around toward me.

"Of course you have no idea who that will be," I said.

"No." She looked away from me, she looked out across the water. Her expression did not change. "But I mean to find out."

Two

Some people, that summer, said that extravagant entertainments such as Mrs. Elliott's Apple of Discord Ball were unwise in view of the general depression: times were hard, many people were unemployed. We had heard repeated warnings from the pulpit and from some of the more nagging editorials about the plutocracy, about the great and growing gulf between rich and poor. But the Panic of '93, followed by the specter of "Coxey's Army" marching on Washington the following year in a desperate demand for jobs, did not disturb Newport nearly so much as affairs of the heart like the Deacon killing: Edward Deacon had discovered his wife with her lover in her hotel room in Cannes, and he shot and killed the man. The ambassador to France, Thomas Jefferson Coolidge, was a member of one of the first Boston families; Deacon was not, I believe, so well connected, but he was sufficiently so that Coolidge acted at once to protect him and preserve him from French justice, such as it was.

The Deacon affair was emblematic of the decade: a

cuckolded husband murdering his wife's lover. At Newport, where the Deacons had been well known, the details of the case were traded like Vanderbilt railroad shares. Everyone knew that only fate had kept Newport from enduring—or enjoying—a similar scandal, for Newport had become a place in which the Sun King or one of the Borgias would have felt entirely at home. It was a place of artifice and display and bought pleasures and skulduggery: where women spent obscene amounts of money on their "entertainments," each scheming and plotting to outdo the other, while their menfolk sought pleasure elsewhere. Marriage had become a path to licentiousness, so it seemed: single women needed to adhere to a strict code of behavior, they needed to be eternally vigilant lest through a moment's carelessness their reputations be soiled, thus condemning them to a lifetime of spinsterhood. Once married, however, they were allowed every kind of freedom—not so much as the men, but far more than anyone would have imagined a generation previously.

Styles differed. While Newport tolerated nearly every kind of behavior, Boston remained straitlaced. One Boston woman, it was said, had hired an Irish prizefighter to pose in a one-man *tableau vivant* for a few of her closest friends—an exception to the rule that "No Irish need apply." He wore tights—a small and probably necessary concession to modesty—but they were like a second skin and of course his chest was bare. Such episodes were innocent compared to what went on in Newport town or on the yachts at anchor in the harbor.

The same year as the Deacon affair, what came to be

called the crime of the century took place not fifteen miles away from us in a city that could not have been more different from Newport had it been on the moon. In Fall River—a dreary, ugly mill town—a woman named Borden was accused of murdering her father and stepmother. She butchered them with an ax, the authorities said. But the Commonwealth did not prove its case to the satisfaction of the jury, and Miss Borden was acquitted. Some said that no jury could have found a gentlewoman guilty of such a crime: common women, servants perhaps, could have done it, but not a lady like Miss Borden.

In any case, in the summer of '96, Mrs. Elliott had thrown down the gauntlet, so to speak, and Isabel rushed to pick it up.

"Victoria will win," she said. "She will—she must. We cannot afford to fail."

I wondered if she could afford to win, either. Like so many other men, Avery had suffered in the Panic of '93, and I had no idea whether he had yet recovered. Certainly Isabel behaved as though their money would never run out; she had ordered a gown for Victoria in the style of Marie Antoinette, heavily encrusted with paste jewels and gold and silver embroidery, and a white powdered wig that was a foot high, at least. Charlotte had chosen—so Isabel said—a less elaborate costume, though still French.

As the day of the ball approached, Isabel became more and more irritable and edgy. One morning, stopping by on my way into town to inquire whether she needed anything from the shops, I came upon her berating the dressmaker.

"I told you that I wanted the wig today! And those emeralds were to cover the shoulders, I told you that explicitly! Now you have ruined the effect! You will have to move them!"

The dressmaker, a sullen, heavy-eyed creature who had a reputation for being quick and neat but not for being imaginative, stood silent before her and made no attempt to defend herself. Had I been in her place, I thought, I would at least have said a word or two.

But she had revenge, after all, when she submitted her bill.

"Two thousand five hundred dollars!" said Isabel. She sat at her spindly little desk holding the sheet of paper with a few lines and figures scratched on it in black ink. "Two thousand—but that is insane, there must be some mistake!"

"No," the woman said when Isabel confronted her, "the figure is correct. The material was expensive, and the price of trimmings has gone sky high. If anything I charged you too little. Paste jewels and gold and silver thread are very dear and becoming more so."

"You may bring the costumes for a final fitting tomorrow afternoon at two," said Isabel.

The woman stared at her, not with insolence exactly but with a kind of impermeable hostility. "When you pay three quarters of the bill, ma'am, I'll come for the fitting. And full payment when I deliver the finished outfits."

Isabel was as shocked as if the woman had slapped her; then, as if she did not trust herself to speak further, she dismissed the seamstress and rang for afternoon tea. She was badly unnerved, her voice tight and sharp, her eyes strained. When the maid had finished bringing in the tea things, Isabel shut the door firmly behind her and locked it.

"What," I said, "do you fear robbers so much that you lock our bedroom door?"

"It is not because of robbers," she said grimly. "For one thing, I don't want Avery to come in uninvited— which he is perfectly capable of doing. For another"— she opened the doors of the tall armoire next to her bed and took something from behind the dresses—"I don't care to be caught indulging my vices."

She had brought forth a bottle of liquor, I could not tell what, and a package of cigarettes which she offered to me. I declined. She poured a good tot of liquor into her cup, filled the cup with tea, and began to sip at it greedily, holding it with both hands as a child holds a cup of milk. Then, having slaked her thirst, she took a long, thin brown cigarette from the packet and lit it. She inhaled deeply two or three times before she spoke.

"Can you imagine such insolence?" she said. "Three quarters of the bill in advance!" Her voice was angry, and the hand that held the cigarette trembled slightly. From what I knew of alcohol and drugs—including my own unhappy experience—they were intended to soothe, but they were not doing so now.

"I have no money," she went on. "I have nothing. Avery has cut me off until next month." A cloud of smoke hung above her head; she handled the cigarette expertly, with the ease of an experienced smoker. Sitting in the sunlight, surrounded by the golden cloud, elegant and slightly *déshabillée*, she resembled one of Alphonse Mucha's advertising posters. Charles Dana Gibson was all the rage just then, but Gibson's girls were too wholesome; Mucha captured something else of the spirit of the times—a hint of decadence, a deliciously sinister look.

I realized that I had fallen into a little reverie; Isabel was speaking again. "If I dare to ask Avery for money, he will simply insist that we leave Newport now. I cannot do that. Victoria must be here. She must be seen by the right people. She *must* marry money. Why should she not? She has beauty, she has charm and wit—but this ball is crucial, she cannot afford to miss it. And not only must she attend, she must win! It will be unbearable if someone else wins. There is no one more beautiful than my Victoria. Avery doesn't care, he doesn't have the worry of it, the work of bringing them up and then seeing them well married. I never imagined until I had daughters of my own what Mother went through with Elinor. Poor Mother! Charlotte, I don't mind telling you, is equally a problem but not for the same reasons. Charlotte is willing enough to go along with all the necessary foolishness. The problem is simply that no one wants her. Don't look at me that way, Marian. What I say is true. With any luck she'll find someone when she tours the West in the fall, but I'm not counting on it. But Victoria—ah, Victoria is different. She was unquestionably the belle of the season. The tray in the front hall was not large enough to hold all the calling cards and invitations she received. All winter long people clamored to have her. Luncheon, tea, dinner, evening parties—and she behaved simply beautifully. I know that many times she was exhausted but she never stopped smiling, never stopped charming everyone in sight. At least a dozen young men asked Avery for permission to marry her. None of them was suitable, of course, and thank heaven she didn't fancy any of them. She is headstrong enough to make some terrible mistake—"

She caught herself then; she stubbed out her cigarette—with unnecessary violence, I thought, pounding it into the crystal bowl which served as an ashtray until the end of it was shredded.

"Never mind," she said. "It will be all right. Somehow—I don't know how—this will be a triumph for her. I will make it so."

She had some help, it turned out, in her plotting. That very evening, during a dinner at Mrs. Fisher Wainwright's, she was approached by a man named Freddy Melville. The easiest way to describe him is to say that he aspired to be Mrs. Elliott's Ward McAllister. Which is to say, he was a servant and a master both, following Mrs. Elliott's wishes for social success and dictating to her how they were to be achieved. I hoped for his sake that he met a kinder fate than McAllister, who had died friendless and alone the previous year, sadly fallen from the high place to which he had aspired.

Melville came to Isabel when the men joined the ladies after brandy and cigars. He had met her before, so it was acceptable for him to approach her in that way; he nodded at her and smiled and took her hand with alacrity as she offered it. He was a small man, hardly taller than she, with pale brown hair slicked back and a narrow, haughty face. Only his eyes were eager: they were pale blue, not unintelligent; he had the knack of focusing them steadily on you as you spoke and giving you his full attention. You felt important when you spoke to Freddy Melville; you knew that you were being flattered but you didn't mind.

"Gettin' ready for the big night, Mrs. K.?" He grinned.

They chatted amicably for a moment or two. Isabel thought that the time had come for him to move on, but he lingered. She wondered why. She glanced around the room. It was a scene she had looked upon countless times before: richly dressed, bejeweled women; men in impeccably cut evening clothes; a backdrop of interior decoration that would have suited a Renaissance prince; the sense that, no matter what happened in the world outside, this world, this little hothouse, protected world, would survive. How could it not? For here was money, here was power—including the power to make alliances. This brought her back to Victoria. How would she get the money to pay the seamstress? What would she do if she could not? Demand the costumes nevertheless? Steal them? She turned and smiled brilliantly at Melville.

"We can't wait to see all the costumes, Mr. Melville. What a party it will be! You and Mrs. Elliott must be busy morning, noon, and night. Newport has never seen anything like it. Whatever gave her the idea for it?"

He threw her a private, unobtrusive wink. There was nothing forward about it, for Freddy Melville was not interested in the usual relations between the sexes, and even if he had been, he would hardly have settled on Isabel as the object of his attentions. No: this was, you might say, the opening move in a treaty of friendship.

"Lord Hyslop," he whispered—unnecessarily, she thought, since they stood quite alone near the french doors leading out to the terrace. The moon shone on the manicured gardens and made a liquid silver cobweb of the fountain, whose gentle splash was obscured by the noise of the guests within. Melville did not need to fear being overheard; the whisper was simply another move toward their as yet unacknowledged alliance.

Isabel stood quite still while she digested what he said. Then: "He is coming?"

Melville nodded.

"Anonymous?"

Melville grinned. "Until the great moment. But you'll be able to spot him easily enough."

She waited, her eyebrows arched at just the right level of polite curiosity. Such control takes a lifetime of training; young people can seldom achieve it.

Across the room, Mrs. Denton Elliott was preparing to take her leave. Melville saw her, and so he left Isabel to join her. As he went, he flung his secret over his shoulder for her to catch as if it were a bouquet: "He's the judge, Mrs. K.! Advise your daughter accordingly!"

And then he was gone, weaving his way gracefully through the crush to take his place at his patroness' side and usher her to the door.

Three

The day of Mrs. Elliott's extravaganza drew near; and
Winifred Blunt arrived from Portland, Maine.

"Yes," said Isabel with some irritation when I
inquired; "and she will attend the ball with us in the
usual way of house guests. She is responsible for
providing her own costume, however. From what I
understand, she can well afford to pay for it. At least we
don't have to worry about her winning."

The young woman was, in truth, a homely person
whose too eager manner and nervous, artificial smile put
you off immediately. She was dark-haired, thin, with a
prominent nose and a prognathous jaw. Undoubtedly she
would make some young man an exemplary wife, but first
she would have to catch him: for her, a difficult job.

She was enthralled by Newport. On the second day of
her visit she ran to us as we sat on the terrace and gushed
out her delight, her amazement at how beautiful, how
perfect were the town, the cottages, the alacrity with
which she was welcomed by Victoria's set, the style with
which the young women dressed—"I *am* so happy that I

came to visit you, Aunt Kittredge," she bubbled, showing
all her teeth. "The tennis and the sailing and all the
parties—when I think of what I had in Portland! Or,
rather, what I didn't have!" And off she ran, her parasol
trailing behind her, to accompany Victoria to a garden
party at a cottage farther down Bellevue Avenue. By
rights they should have been driven there in the chaise,
but Victoria, never a stickler for etiquette, had chosen to
walk. She would arrive cool and refreshed, I thought,
while Winifred would be panting and perspiring, her hair
coming undone, perhaps, dust covering her skirts.

Isabel watched her go. Her face seldom revealed her
thoughts, but just then it was a study in contempt. "That
little fool," she said, more to herself than to me. "Does
she think that we do all this for pleasure? For the fun of
it? Ridiculous! We do it to survive!"

That day passed, and then another. The night of Mrs.
Elliott's ball inexorably approached. And Isabel still did
not have the costumes.

There was in the town of Newport a shop near Thames
Street—the rough area near the waterfront—that was
well known to the ladies who summered on Bellevue
Avenue. The owner was a dark, taciturn little man who
seemed to have a jeweler's glass permanently affixed to
his right eye. His hands were delicate and gentle;
sometimes he seemed almost to caress the diamonds and
sapphires and pearls that were brought to him for
appraisal. He gave fair value, so it was said; and he asked
no questions.

Isabel went to him carrying her wedding pearls in her
pouched pocketbook. It was her first visit, but he was no

more and no less friendly to her than to women who had visited him a dozen times. He smiled at her and ducked his head; grimacing, he adjusted the jeweler's glass in the socket of his eye and set to work to examine what she had brought. In no more than ten seconds he looked up at her. "Three hundred," he said.

"Three—" She was taken off guard; she had not expected so prompt an answer. But surely there was some mistake, she thought, surely he was making a bad joke—a most unsuitable joke—when he named so low a figure.

He watched her with a kind of curious compassion. After a moment she collected herself and put out her hand. Desperate as she was for money, she would not take so little. He poured the strand of pearls into her cupped palm. The interior of the little shop was dim against the blazing August sun outside. It was as if she held some of that brightness in her hand—the shimmering opalescence of the sea, whitened, perhaps, at dawn. The pearls were heavy: cool and round and smooth, and of good weight. They were worth ten times what he offered. She put them into her pouch and went out. I will get the money somewhere, she thought, but I will not give these up for nothing.

At home later that day she waged a desperate battle with her better judgment and lost. She told the upstairs maid to let her know when Victoria and Winifred returned from their afternoon's visit to the Casino; then she retired to her room to wait. She sat on her chaise longue by the tall window overlooking the sea and drank a little whiskey and smoked several cigarettes. She put out of her mind the image of the small dark man bending over her pearls. She listened to the wind moaning faintly through the gallery, which was next to her room; above that sound she heard a faint ringing in her ears—caused, the doctor had said, by too tight lacing. Damn the doctor, she thought, he could make his way in this world without showing off his small waist. Women were judged by the way they looked. The new fashions were even more extreme, bustles having given way entirely to a flowing, hourglass shape and leg-o'-mutton sleeves so puffed that two women could hardly sit side by side in a carriage. They would have to have all their last winter's outfits altered—a huge expense, even if they ordered nothing new. And of course they would have to have a few new things: one could not dine out four nights a week and visit balls and receptions and ladies' luncheons and all the other occasions on their calendars and not have some new clothing to wear. At least they would not have to deal with this woman in Newport; their dressmaker in Boston was much more understanding about unpaid bills. She would do the alterations at once without any deposit; and somehow the money would be found for new things.

Meanwhile, she must have money now.

At last, just before five o'clock, the maid came to tell her that the girls had returned. "Send Miss Winifred to me," said Isabel. It was unfair, she knew, to intrude on the visitor's short time to rest before Winifred went with Victoria to dinner and a dance at the Ocean House, but she did not care; the time for good manners, for kindness, had passed.

Winifred came in beaming—why was she always so irritatingly, maddeningly happy? wondered Isabel—and accepted the cup of tea offered to her with a giggle that grated on Isabel's taut nerves. Winifred, after her initial gaiety, looked suddenly tired. Perhaps we are too much for her, thought Isabel; perhaps she will leave us soon. The thought cheered her momentarily.

She had not the faintest idea of how to begin—how to approach the topic which loomed so large in her mind that it nearly obliterated everything else. Like the mythical grail, the finished costume for Victoria hovered tantalizingly beyond her reach, and she did not have the means to get it. She had no money. No money, no way to get money. Her husband was implacable. Her pearls were worthless. Somehow, in the next few days, she must raise the necessary cash to retrieve the dress from the seamstress.

Winifred smiled hesitantly at her; and then: "Victoria's very kind to get me an invite to Mrs. Elliott's ball. Mama telegraphed this morning that our woman will finish my costume by tomorrow and Mama is sending it down with one of our hired girls."

Each word stabbed Isabel's heart. To be able simply to order a dress and pay for it without thinking! "What will you be?" she said, hoping that the girl did not hear the tremor in her voice.

"A Spanish dancer—like Carmen. I wanted something more elaborate, but Mama said we—well, she said we couldn't."

Isabel stared at her.

"As a matter of fact—" Winifred began. A flush spread over her already rosy face. She reached into the fold of her wide sash and pulled out a small envelope. "I had a letter from Mama today," she said. "It came an hour after the telegram. She asked me to give this to you."

With a sense of dread at what she would find, Isabel took it and opened it:

Dear Cousin Isabel:

You have been very kind to take my Winifred and introduce her to all your friends.

She is thrilled to be invited to this grand ball. I had her costume made here because she said your women in Newport were so busy.

But now, dear Cousin, I am in a bad way and I must ask your help. Mr. B. has had reverses in his business, and I find now that I cannot pay the seamstress.

Could you, dear Isabel, lend me the money? I don't have to tell you how important something like this is for a girl like Winifred, and it would only be until October when the quarterly dividends come in and I could repay you—with interest if you like. Thanking you in advance,

                    Ever your devoted cousin,
                                Mary Blunt

Isabel looked up sharply at the girl, who sat before her, dejected, hands clenched in her lap. Although she had little sense of humor, she felt now an almost irresistible impulse to laugh. She controlled it; she pressed her lips together and then opened them to speak.

"My dear—you have read your mother's letter."

"Yes." The girl kept her eyes down.

"But this is impossible. I will be perfectly honest with you. I haven't the money to pay for Victoria's costume, let alone Charlotte's—let alone yours! You must tell your mother that. I cannot. I haven't even the strength to write a short letter to her. Tell her that I am very sorry but I cannot help. I was going to ask her to help me, as a matter of fact. Tell her—no, not that."

She stood; Winifred followed her example, understanding that she was being dismissed.

"Do not tell Victoria what we have said."

"No, ma'am." Winifred was a study in dejection, but Isabel was beyond sympathy.

"And I wish you luck in breaking the news to your mother." Isabel heard the bitterness in her voice; she felt her face go slack as she watched Winifred take her leave. Now what? she thought. Now, in heaven's name, what?

Four

Isabel dined, that night, with Diana and me and all her children save Victoria. I do not know where Avery was: in Boston, I suppose, and coming down late for the weekend as so many of the men did. He would have been preoccupied, of course, by his rearguard action, trying to hold off disaster for his firm. The crash of '93 had not affected him at first, but now, three years later and the country still feeling its effects, he was being hurt. How badly no one of us knew or even suspected: he was closemouthed as all good investment men must be, and in any case he would never have told a woman of his worries. Not even his wife. Most especially not his wife, for his wife, when it came to money, was his enemy: she spent what he brought in—spent and spent and spent, a hemorrhage of spending what he acquired. All women in her set did this: it was their calling, their life's work. Sometimes I think that it was their revenge as well.

We sat in silence, progressing through the several courses—the soup, the fish, the meat, the fruit and cheese—and making a little desultory conversation for the servants' sake.

Heavy rain streamed down the windows; the room was chilly and damp and drafty. For once, I imagine that Charlotte did not envy her younger sister who, attending a dinner with Winifred, had had to sacrifice a pair of shoes to the storm.

After the meal Isabel excused us all and went to sit by herself in the drawing room—a place that she did not usually frequent when she was alone. Charlotte offered to keep her company but she refused. She sat in a tapestry chair beside a round marquetry table in the center of the room. An oil lamp with a delicate, leaded Handel shade provided the only illumination. She had a piece of embroidery with her, but it lay in her lap; she was too distracted to concentrate on embroidery. She listened to the storm; she rehearsed the speech that she must make; she waited for her husband to arrive. Nine o'clock passed, and then nine-thirty. Her heart lay heavy in her breast; she felt a sense of dread. Only the urgency of her need kept her there, waiting for him. As the clock struck ten she stood and began to walk around the room. Her feet tingled, stabbed with pain. She held onto a high-backed chair for support and shook first one foot and then the other. She wore thin satin high-heeled slippers, blue to match her gown; she did not ordinarily dress so elaborately for a meal with the children, but this night, reduced to begging, she wanted to look her best. She shivered and drew her embroidered shawl higher around her shoulders. This room was colder than the dining room. The enormous fireplace, eight feet across, held a few sputtering logs that threw off no heat at all. She had begun to pace the room again—it was a big room, and to walk its length was more than a matter of a few seconds—and as she reached the easternmost wall she heard a new sound. She paused, lifting her head to listen.

Plink! Plink!

Drops of water striking metal. Where?

She followed the sound to its source: the ceiling above the tall windows overlooking the gardens. From it, drops fell with that steady relentless noise onto a piece of decoration: a fifteenth-century knight's helmet which rested on a narrow fluted marble column to one side of the french doors.

Plink! Plink!

In the silent house the sound echoed like a struck gong. It irritated her: she felt that she could not possibly make her case to Avery with that noise to distract her. She tried to lift the helmet, to move it out of the way of the leak, but it was fastened somehow to the column. The water was coming faster now: the drips became a steady little stream. *Plink plink plink plink*—Some drops splashed onto the front of her dress, staining it. Silently she cursed the architect, the builder, the slovenly carpenters and plasterers whose services had cost so dear. This room extended, a single story, from the main house, like the ballroom on the other side; there were no rooms above it. Its flat roof, imperfectly graded perhaps, was unable to withstand so heavy a rainfall.

Knotting her shawl over her bosom to free her hands, she seized the marble column and slightly tilted it and rolled it on its bottom edge away from the offending leak. Even at so slight an angle it was intimidatingly heavy:

how had they moved it in the first place? She braced herself against it—it was almost as tall as she—and, mindful that the helmet stayed firmly on top, she maneuvered it a few inches across the floor.

"Isabel?"

The sound of her husband's voice startled her so that for an instant her grasp loosened. The column crashed to the floor, narrowly missing her foot. The helmet, dislodged, rolled rapidly away to come to rest against the leg of a narrow refectory table. Its polished metal gleamed against the surrounding shadows like an impossibly large nugget of something more precious than silver. Some people kept such helmets, and even entire suits of armor, with authentic claims that the wearer had been an ancestor, but Isabel had no idea whose helmet this had been. For her, it had been only a decoration. And now that it had been guillotined, so to speak—struck off from its support—it looked oddly ghoulish, as if it still held someone's head within.

Avery came in, shutting the big double doors behind him. She caught the pungent odor of his cigar. The smell of tobacco caused her a momentary spasm of desire: how she would have liked a cigarette!

"They said you wanted to see me." He came into the center of the room. The marble column, crashing down, had gouged a deep dent in the parquet floor but he did not look at it. He watched her, impassive, waiting to see why she had summoned him—a thing that she did not ordinarily do.

She came toward him. Her knees were suddenly weak but she showed no fear. She had had long years of discipline, of hiding what she felt: this was her cruelest test and she must not fail. She tilted back her head to an uncomfortable angle and looked up at him.

"Yes," she said. "I did. Have you had supper? No? I will ring, they can have a tray for you in no time—"

But he shook his head. He looked tired, she thought: she realized that she had not seen him—had not looked at him—in weeks. His broad, pale face sagged with fatigue; his eyes were sunk deep under his brows and his hair had gone from brown to gray seemingly overnight; she had not noticed it before.

They stood facing each other for a moment, gathering strength. In the way that married people have of each knowing what the other is thinking, he knew at once that she had some serious problem; given her way of life, it could only involve money.

She felt tongue-tied, as shy and awkward as a schoolgirl—worse than that, for a schoolgirl would not have been left alone, unchaperoned, with a strange man.

Yes: a strange man. She did not know him. Certainly she did not love him—did not now, perhaps had never. She loved—who? That other, who had left her not once but many times? Like a curse, his face flashed across her memory and she shook her head and blinked her eyes to be rid of it. Her husband watched her, waiting. But his patience was not endless: he was tired, he was wet, he wanted to go to bed.

Uneasily he shifted his weight from one foot to the other. She saw the look of irritation on his face. I must begin, she thought. She had only three days more in which to get Victoria's costume. Blast that woman's soul, to put her, Isabel Kittredge, through such torment—

"I need money," she said abruptly. As soon as the words were out of her mouth she stopped, appalled at her stupidity. That was not the way to succeed! Begin again, she thought, and be more careful. She forced a smile. "I mean—no. No. I mean—wait until you see Victoria's costume." Her voice sounded high and bright and brittle. "It is exquisite. She will win—unquestionably she will. This is a very important occasion for her. You do understand that, I know that you do. And the dressmaker refuses to give me it until I pay her in full, can you imagine?"

She paused. She saw not a flicker in his face. The storm, having lessened for a time, now came again with new force: the tall windows shivered with the beating of the wind, rain streamed down the panes and had begun to seep in around the edges. The leak which had first annoyed her had spread: a wide patch of ceiling was wet and dripping, looking as if it might crash down at any minute.

Abruptly she turned and walked away from him. She stood with her back to him, looking out at the black night, seeing her watery double in the glass. She loosened the heavy crimson velvet drape from its cord and let it fall across the window, eradicating her image. She turned to face him and saw that he had followed her; he stood not five feet away. Good, she thought, he is not hostile; at least he will listen to what I have to say.

"I wouldn't trouble you with any of this, except that it is so very important for Victoria," she said. "This house badly needs repairs"—and here she glanced at the ceiling again—"but it can wait if you say that it must. But Victoria cannot wait. This affair is only three days away. She *must* be ready for it—she must go to it and win!"

He said nothing. He watched her, expressionless. It occurred to her at last to wonder at his silence. Even so stolid a man must give voice either to approval or disapproval, agreement or disagreement.

"Avery? Do you hear what I say? I *must*—"

He reached out, startling her. He came a step or two closer; he touched her arm. She glanced down at his fingertips against her flesh and then up at his impassive face. Relief flooded her heart. He will help me, she thought: I have won, I can do for Victoria what must be done.

"Oh, Avery. You do understand. I was afraid you wouldn't. You see, the judge will be Lord Hyslop, and if he says that Victoria is the most beautiful, as she will be in this costume, then she will be his partner for the evening, and perhaps—"

"No."

She did not understand him at first; that single syllable, spoken so soft, needed a moment to penetrate her sluggish brain. He saw this; and so he shook his head and said again, "No."

That time the word hit her with the force of a blow across her face. *No!*

"Avery, I beg you—I know that I have spent too much in the past, but now I apologize for that, it is just that it is my life, I have nothing else to do—Avery! Please! Listen to me, listen—"

Panic seized her, for he had turned away. Now he

paused and came around to her again.

"It is out of the question," he said. "Until the end of the month—no."

"Avery, listen to me—can you borrow it? Can you? This is more important than anything else, this is her future—"

He shrugged. "I am sorry," he said. His voice was light and dry, lacking feeling. He turned away and walked toward the double doors. She stood quite still, frozen in place. *No?*

"Avery!"

He had reached the center of the room. Now he stopped and turned to her once again, one last time—a slow, heavy movement of his big, heavy body as if he were bracing himself against the onslaught which he knew must come.

But she was nowhere near him. She stayed behind, at the far end of the room, seemingly unable to move. Her head held high, her eyes wide, a curious, wild expression on her face—she might have been the model for the figurehead of a clipper ship from whence had come his ancestors' wealth, and hers.

But not his own: those days were done, money came differently now, and harder.

"Avery—" All at once she crumpled, so quickly that he had no time to react. She fell to the floor on her hands and knees. He stared at her, fascinated as if she were a freak and he had paid to see her and must now watch, unable to turn away before he had his money's worth.

She began to crawl to him. As she did she half moaned,

half sang her litany of desperate need. She kept her head up as she moved. The heavy folds of her dress caught at her knees; her corset nearly suffocated her. She cried as she came, she sobbed and choked and moaned, awkward and blindly moving forward, abasing herself.

"Isabel—"

On she came, inexorable, awkward, impeded by her dress, driven by her need. At every other move she needed to use one hand to pull forward the cloth under her knees. Like a horrid, misshapen animal she came, moving in spasmodic jerks, crawling blindly toward shelter.

"Please—Avery, please—I will never again ask you, but this time I must—please—I beg you, I beg you— don't think of me, think of Victoria. This could mean everything to her—Avery! Don't—don't go—" She clung to his knees. He shook his leg convulsively to throw her off, and when still she held fast he reached down to pry loose her clutching fingers.

"Avery! Avery—"

Her voice had risen to a shriek which, inevitably, was heard beyond that room. In a moment the door burst open. Victoria and her visitor, only that moment returned, stood thunderstruck on the threshold. It was as if they had stumbled out of the storm and into a nightmare whose characters they knew but whose action, as is the pattern of nightmares, was strange and frightening beyond belief.

Victoria, surprisingly, kept her wits and immediately withdrew, taking Winifred with her. And some time later, I do not know exactly when, Avery maneuvered

461

Isabel upstairs and into her bed and poured a sedative down her throat.

The next day she came to see me. And when she told me her story I gave her as much as she needed with no thought of repayment: I am a realist, after all. And so Victoria got her costume dress for Mrs. Elliott's ball, and Charlotte did too.

Five

Mrs. Elliott's Apple of Discord Ball, said *Town Topics*, was the most thrilling extravaganza since Mrs. Astor's ball celebrating the completion of her Fifth Avenue château more than a decade previously.

It was hardly that, but it was colorful enough; and since Lord Hyslop was to pick the most beautiful girl, we were spared any eccentricity or misplaced humor in what people chose to wear.

I was there with several other unattached middle-aged ladies who had been invited to act as chaperones-*cum*-aides-de-camp. We helped the girls to form their presentation line, in which they paraded at a stately pace in front of Lord Hyslop for his consideration; we prevented as best we could the inevitable catfights that accompany such an event; we monitored the anterooms and the terraces and gardens to make sure that no young woman's reputation was compromised. No mother of a participant could be trusted with such work, for sabotage was not unknown in Newport: during the previous season, so the rumor went, a certain Mrs. Billingsley

463

caused the daughter of a rival to be lured onto Bailey's Beach after midnight on a false pretext, and the girl was ruined—shut out, never again invited anywhere.

Mrs. Elliott had spared no cost. She was not a vain woman, or a proud one, but, coming from the provinces west of the Hudson, she had been snubbed for many years by the reigning Newport matrons and now she wanted to have back at them.

And she did: I cannot remember a more elaborate evening.

Under Freddy Melville's direction she had spent money like—well, like water. Her house—her "cottage" —was festooned with garlands of golden flowers. A champagne fountain bubbled in the ballroom. Small tents had been set up around the grounds to accommodate those wishing to take supper away from the crowd, and a thousand golden lights illuminated the gardens until they looked like fairyland. Gold plate held the food: the favors were golden baskets of tiny golden apples. Even the evening's program, which told the names of the costumed participants (but not their judge), was printed in gold and embossed with a gold seal. Mrs. Elliott, while not herself in costume, glittered like a fantasy goddess in a gown of some thin golden stuff that caught the light as she moved and made it impossible to overlook her even in the midst of all the costumed beauty that she had summoned up.

All of this, of course, was secondary to the fact of Lord Hyslop: he was Mrs. Elliott's drawing card, her bluest chip, her *éclat des grandeurs*.

We chaperones met him before the costumed guests

arrived. Freddy Melville greeted us as the butler showed us in, and when he had accounted for all of us, six altogether, he took us upstairs to meet the guest of honor. "I will give you only ten minutes, ladies, because his lordship has a grueling night ahead of him. But he requested especially to meet you. He said it would be pleasant to meet ladies whom he did not have to judge, or mamas whom he did not have to fear, ha-ha!"

Lord Hyslop was hardly the popular idea of a lord, English or otherwise. In novels, the lord is always lordly—tall and strong and rugged, if not actually handsome. This specimen before us was potbellied and bandy-legged, with a weak, watery-eyed face and thinning, sandy hair (a fact easily ascertained since he was so short that most of us could see the top of his oddly shaped head). He grinned at us affably enough, buck teeth sprouting under an attempt at a mustache, but we came away unimpressed all the same.

"No wonder they kept him under wraps until tonight," muttered one of my companions. "No one would have bothered to come if they'd seen him first."

I thought of Isabel and her frantic attempts to salvage Victoria's costume from the dressmaker. For this! I shrugged and smiled to myself and went downstairs to take up my battle station, as it were. It might, I thought, be a more interesting evening than any of us had expected. I positioned myself carefully near the dais where his lordship was to stand: I wanted to see the expressions on the faces of the girls as they came up to present themselves to him.

At nine o'clock they began to arrive (the invitations

having read "eight"). Melville was in his element: he bustled back and forth like an impresario—which he was—alighting from time to time at Mrs. Elliott's side like a homing pigeon and then flying off again on some new task. For an hour or so, he had decreed, there would be dancing; then the judging; then dancing again; then supper. Lord Hyslop did not dance at first; he stayed on his dais and watched the whirling crowd below and wondered, no doubt, why he had come.

"He's supposed to be very rich," murmured my neighbor, a stout, pleasant woman whom I had met once or twice before.

"Does anyone know for sure?" I said.

"I don't think so. But I've heard it from several people."

Rich he might be, I thought; but still he was no prize. Poor Isabel, whose hopes for Victoria must surely be dashed!

But I was wrong: she was not discouraged, not put off at all. She came to me before long. Her eyes were shining, her face a little moist and flushed. She looked wonderful—better than she had done all summer.

"Have you seen her?" she said, beaming (meaning Victoria, of course). And, despite the crowd, I had. She wore her costume with a grace and élan that would have become royalty itself: her perfect heart-shaped face framed in the thick white wig, sausage curls draped over her shoulder, her slender body encased in the flat-front décolletage of the French court of a century ago. Her gown was magnificent, all jewel-studded brocade, and her costume was complete to a large black beauty patch near

466

her right cheekbone.

"Bless her," said Isabel. "She's magnificent, if I do say so!"

Victoria flung me a wink as she whirled by in the arms of a young man whom I did not recognize. The music was a waltz—the most popular dance, and deservedly so, since dancing the waltz made both men and women seem as graceful—and as grand—as any member of the Hapsburg court. *One* two three, *one* two three—around and around they went, two by two, dipping and swooping like great birds—swans, perhaps, or eagles. The orchestra, a popular local group, played with fervor and a good deal of volume. Their leader stabbed the air with his baton as if he were skewering enemies; the fiddlers sawed for their lives, not daring to glance at those for whom they played.

Suddenly, in the middle of a measure, the music stopped. The dancers stood stranded on the floor; all eyes turned to the dais, where now Freddy Melville stood clapping his lavender-gloved hands for attention. He had it at once, of course: everyone was on tenterhooks for the judging to begin. Lord Hyslop sat on a high-backed carved Gothic chair looking like a bank clerk. No—that was wrong: he did not seem to have the intelligence to be a bank clerk. Someone's half-witted cousin was more like it, I thought.

"Ladeez and gentlemen!" cried Melville in a self-conscious imitation of a P. T. Barnum ringmaster. "We are honored to have with us this evening a distinguished visitor, Lord Hyslop! He has kindly consented to judge our little contest and to award the prize of the golden apple to the most beautiful young lady here tonight!"

A smattering of applause and an approving murmur rose from the audience, while on his improvised throne Lord Hyslop nodded and clucked and made little bobbing bows in several directions.

"And so now, if you *please,* ladies, form your line to your right—*your* right—according to the numbered card which you received when you came in. Yes—yes, that's it, number 1—and number 2—"

Isabel stood across the room from me. Her expression was both proud and apprehensive; a proper mother's face, I thought. I reminded myself that I had paid for the costume that Victoria wore this evening, and I looked to find her. She was number 6. She stood with perfect posture, her chin raised, her shoulders squared, so that she looked taller than she was.

One by one they passed Lord Hyslop. Each girl stopped directly in front of him, dipped a little curtsy, and then stood for his inspection until Melville gave the signal for her to move on and the next to approach. There were twenty-five girls in all, and after the first ten or twelve Lord Hyslop's eyes began to glaze over; his smile remained unvarying, fixed wide upon his face. Victoria had safely passed by that time. I looked for some sign that she had particularly pleased him, but I saw none: it was impossible to tell whom he liked best. Charlotte looked better than I had thought she would in her more modest gown; Winifred made an awkward Spanish dancer; I saw a Renaissance lady, and a Tyrolean peasant, and the Queen of Hearts, and a lady of the Middle Ages with a high, pointed hat and a flowing veil. Not one, I thought, had a chance against Victoria.

At last they were done, the last girl gone by. The two men conferred briefly, heads together, eyes downcast so as to avoid giving any hint of preference. Then Melville approached the lip of the dais and, not needing to ask for all our attention, made his announcement.

"Will the young ladies holding the following numbers please step forward and form a line to your right—*your* right, thank you. Numbers 1, 4, 6, 7, 12, and 22. Thank you—thank you!"

A buzz of indignation and excitement greeted those words. Those who had been eliminated—and their mamas—looked angrily at those still in the running. I caught Isabel's eye and she threw me a quick, triumphant smile as if to say: "You see how good an investment she is!"

The select half dozen paraded past his lordship and then, at Melville's direction, they paraded past again.

"Thank you, ladies! Thank you! If you will just step aside now, join the others—thank you!"

Victoria waited until the rest had obeyed; and then, solo, she walked gracefully across the room to stand at Isabel's side. She looked oddly triumphant; even in that ornate mirrored and gilt-encrusted room she stood out like a swan among ducks.

Melville stooped over the seated figure of his lordship. They whispered together for a moment and then Melville took a card from his pocket, wrote something on it, and handed it to the Englishman. His lordship stood. At a signal from Melville the orchestra played a short ruffles and flourishes. From a small table at the rear of the platform Melville took the prize—the golden apple, probably gilt, as Isabel had surmised. With a small, neat bow, he handed it to Lord Hyslop. His lordship took it, held it up on the flattened palm of his hand for us to see.

"And the winner is—" cried Melville.

Lord Hyslop read from the card, "Miss Victoria Kittredge!"

At once there were cries of admiration and envy and applause, and a cluster of congratulators to escort her to the lip of the dais. Lord Hyslop leaned down to present the prize to her; and before he gave it to her he took her hand and kissed it and held it for a moment as he stared at her. She was, indeed, the most beautiful young woman at the ball; it was a pity, I thought, that his lordship's appearance did not match hers.

I glanced at Isabel. She watched the little performance with an avid, hungry expression; she paid no attention when the woman beside her leaned in to speak to her but kept her eyes riveted on her daughter and Lord Hyslop.

Something inside me rebelled. I wanted to take Isabel away from this room and give her a proper shaking up. Would she really sacrifice Victoria to this poor, weak specimen, simply because he had a title and a rumored fortune? How could she chain her child, her youngest daughter, to a man like this? Consuelo Vanderbilt was known to be bitterly unhappy. Would Isabel consign Victoria to the same fate?

The orchestra struck up a waltz, and Lord Hyslop let Victoria out onto the floor. She was a skilled, graceful dancer who had been, all her girlhood, the pride of Miss Willett's dancing classes, but even she could not disguise her partner's ineptitude. He hopped and dipped sideways across the floor with a curious crablike movement, waving his elbows, grinning, nodding, apparently completely unaware of his grotesque appearance.

In that shining ballroom overlooking the sea—a glowing jewel clinging to the darkened shore—the revelers danced together two by two into the night. Mrs. Elliott's Apple of Discord Ball was a resounding success, I thought, for Victoria at least. Or perhaps, more accurately, for her mother; for the next day Freddy Melville left Mrs. Elliott and came to Isabel.

Six

All Newport shivered with delighted horror at the news. Mrs. Elliott, of course, was furious. Some people said that her anger was a sham, that she was tiring of Melville and would have dismissed him—without a "character," as it were—had he not acted first. And then there was the business of Victoria's winning the golden apple: had Isabel bribed him with the promise of her patronage in return for a guaranteed win, a sure shot at Lord Hyslop?

No matter: the alliance was forged the following afternoon at Bailey's Beach. Isabel wore the newest bathing fashion, a cumbersome heavy-skirted affair of black linsey-woolsey, with black stockings and a mobcap to protect her hair. Diana and I, similarly attired, had been there since midmorning: we often spent the entire day at the beach together, picnicking under our large umbrella, dabbling in the shallow water and venturing occasionally deeper when we became too warm.

On that day we had had our lunch and a short rest and we sat now on damp sand near the water, heedless of the sun on our necks and hands and faces, building a drip castle with a scallop-shell moat. Diana was a serious child; she concentrated intently on whatever she did, and so it was I who noticed Isabel's arrival. She came with an umbrella of her own, carried by one of her footmen. Isabel could make a short walk across a stretch of gravelly sand seem like an entrance of the Queen; even uncorseted, even in her bathing dress, she moved with the upright majesty of a fully laced, regally costumed figure.

I waved; she waved; expertly the footman plunged the umbrella shaft into the sand near to ours and then retreated. Diana, having seen her at last, waved also, but it was obvious that she wanted to continue her task. "I'll go," I said, rising with creaking knees. She tilted back her head and smiled up at me: a sweet, closemouthed smile that was so like her mother's—Elinor's—that I stopped and stared down at her, at this small girlchild not quite eight years old; for a moment I was oblivious to the bright day, the sun sparkling on the water, the crowded shore, the familiar tangy air that was Newport's exclusively, and I was taken back through the years to a time when I had been her mother's confidante and all our lives were yet before us.

And then the moment passed and I went to Isabel.

"Have you seen Mr. Melville?" were her first words to me: a peremptory demand. "He said he'd be here by one unless there was some terrible emergency. Oh well. I might as well begin. Will you have some lunch?"

I declined. I sat next to her on a large striped blanket under a large striped umbrella and watched her take the food from the big wicker basket: cold fried chicken and potato salad and leftover petits fours, complete with china plates and freshly starched linen napkins. She held a drumstick in her delicately crooked fingers and gave me a steely glance before she attacked it. "What did you think of Victoria last night?"

No parent who asks such a question wants an honest answer.

"I thought she was magnificent," I said; and in fact it was true.

"Worth every penny that you spent on her." Her voice took on a bitter edge. "It is too bad that her father did not see her. But then, he was not interested in her— he did not care whether she won or lost. Sometimes I think that he does not care whether she ever marries at all."

She gazed unseeing out to the glittering water, the gentle waves curling up on the sand—even the waves were genteel at this little enclave of the rich. I kept silent. It would have been tactless to remind her that Lord Hyslop danced with at least a dozen other women, young and not young alike.

"In any case— Ah, there he is." She dropped the half-eaten chicken leg onto her plate, wiped her fingers on her napkin, and instantly became someone new: someone smiling and gracious without a care in the world. Freddy Melville approached, nattily dressed in a knee-length red and blue striped bathing costume and a wide-brimmed straw hat. His skinny shanks were bare. From under the shade of the umbrella Isabel smiled up at him and held out her hand, palm down, fingers gracefully drooping. He took it, kissed it briskly, and gave it back to her—an appropriately businesslike transaction.

"My dear Mrs. Kittredge." He beamed at her; only after a lengthy, mutually admiring moment did he consent to recognize me. "Mrs. Motley."

I nodded at him, suppressing a smile as I did so. We must look ridiculous, I thought, playing at manners in such costumes. My companions seemed unaware of it, however, and certainly this was not the time to comment on our appearance. At Isabel's invitation—or command—Melville seated himself beside us. I made as if to withdraw but Isabel motioned me to stay. I understood: she wanted a chaperone. She reached into the basket and produced a bottle of champagne, which she handed to Melville to uncork. Expertly he did so; she held out glasses and he poured.

"To our success," she said. Her face was grave: a silent smile hovered around her lips but she looked as solemn as a bride about to exchange her vows.

We drank to it, and then Melville, assured of my discretion, began to discuss with her some of his plans for their triumph. They were as thick as thieves: plotting and counterplotting, laying the groundwork for what Melville described as Isabel's "renaissance." I had not known that she required one.

I listened to what I could not avoid hearing; I sipped one glass of champagne and then another; I watched Diana where she labored at the water's edge. The castle had grown from a single tower to a many-spired vision from *The Arabian Nights*. I had heard that Melville had bragged about his power: "I can make a woman or break her," he was reported to have said—not only those

475

women like Isabel or Mrs. Elliott whom he actively
assisted, but also other women whom he excluded or
included on guest lists, women whose daughters were not
named to lead the cotillion, not asked to stand in a
reception line. He was like a petty princeling, I thought—
a little despot.

And why had he come to Isabel? There were many
possibilities, I thought. I sifted the hot sand through my
fingers and squinted against the sun's glare. Perhaps
Mrs. Elliott was tiring of him. Perhaps he was tiring of
her. Perhaps he saw in Isabel (by way of Victoria) a
greater opportunity—greater scope for his talents, a
bigger stage on which to perform. Perhaps he wanted to
arrange for Victoria—poor child!—a marriage even
grander than Consuelo Vanderbilt's. If so, I thought,
repressing a smile, Lord Hyslop was out of the picture.

Even in the shade of Isabel's umbrella it was hot on the
beach that day. The sun blazed down from a whitish sky;
there was no breeze. And so after a while I left them to go
wading with Diana. They nodded to me in an abstracted
way as I went; Melville scrambled to his feet and almost
immediately sat down again. "And in November," I
heard him say, "you must have a ball—a night to end all
nights."

The success of all their schemes, of course, depended
on a steady supply of money.

And unbeknownst to any of us, Avery was about to go
bankrupt.

Seven

September had more rain than usual that year—the result, we were told, of an aberrant hurricane pattern—and so by the middle of the month Newport was deserted, the great houses empty and echoing, as we gave up the season and returned to our winter homes. Freddy Melville had rooms at the Botolph Club on Newbury Street. With the arrogance peculiar to a certain kind of upstart, he moved in the same circles frequented by Mrs. Elliott and all the people he had met and manipulated while he was in her employ. He carried it off well: after a few months even Mrs. Elliott was on speaking terms with him again.

He spent long hours with Isabel; they might have been planning the overthrow of the Republic rather than a series of social triumphs.

"Why do you need him?" I said to her. "You've always done well enough on your own."

"He gives me—well, I suppose you could call it credibility," she said. "People take me more seriously if they know that he is my—my partner, if you will. He has such hopes for Victoria! And he is very clever, you cannot deny that he is."

Clever he might have been, but even his agility could not get around the fact that Avery's fortune, such as it was, was nearly depleted. Melville discovered this unpleasantness one day in October when he trotted around to Isabel's to put the finishing touches on the charity ball that they were planning for an evening in December. He found her at her little desk confronting a stack of bills that already had begun to descend on her like an unwelcome blizzard.

"Well?" he said with some impatience. "You'd better pay them—in part, at least—just to keep your credit going. Mrs. Elliott was always very sloppy about her bills. That's one of the reasons I left her."

Ordinarily Isabel was quick to obey his command, but now he simply stared at him in a helpless way and made no response.

"Well?" he said impatiently.

"I—I don't think that I can."

He had been riffling through the stack of invitations that would be sent in early November. "Don't forget to add Mrs. Tarbox to this," he said as if he had not heard her. "She is not the best family, I know, but she has interesting connections and she may be useful. Her daughter made a great success in London last summer, I am told."

Isabel did not reply, and so, after a moment, he put down the neatly addressed envelopes and turned to her.

"What did you say just now? I must have misheard."

"I said, I don't think I can pay these. My husband

says—well, he told me this morning that we are in a very bad way. We may even—I can't believe it, but he says that we may even have to sell this house."

Melville's expression, which had been his usual one of polite and easy familiarity—a partner's expression—changed to one of caution: "As if," she told me, "I had suddenly betrayed him somehow, as if he no longer trusted me."

"Sell—but that's impossible!" He spoke with contempt; in Freddy Melville's world no one was forced to sell his house because of financial difficulties. Melville moved in the very best circles (as he would have been the first to inform you) where such calamities were unheard of.

"Yes," she said. "Nevertheless—there it is."

"But—" He struggled for a straw to grasp. "What of your daughter? What of Victoria? She will make a brilliant match if you keep on. You cannot simply stop! You can never make a good match for her if her father is ruined!"

Isabel simply shook her head and put her hands over her eyes. She knew very well the consequences of Avery's financial ruin; she did not need Melville to tell her. Had she not struggled for months to stave off this very disaster?

Like a schoolmaster lecturing a recalcitrant pupil, Melville drew himself up and presented to her the facts of her situation as he saw them: she must not allow Avery's difficulties to stand in the way of her most brilliant season yet, for if she did not somehow find the money to continue she would not only destroy Victoria's chances but she would lose him, Melville, as well. Clearly, he felt that the latter was the worse fate.

Isabel might have come to me, then, as she had done for the money for Victoria's costume, but she did not: her pride prevented her, I suppose. She went instead to Mrs. Roberts Reed who, well past eighty, was confined to her bed and could no longer attend any of Isabel's entertainments. Not even Mrs. Reed's fortune was enough to save Avery; but she did advance enough for Isabel to pursue her vision for Victoria—that is, to see the winter through, entertaining as she and Melville saw fit, until, as Mrs. Reed put it, Victoria was "settled."

"It's all foolishness, Marian, all this spending and showing off. But Isabel is my first husband's niece, and it's his money I'm giving her, after all. I'd leave it to her when I die, and she might as well have it now. Just tell her to keep a sharp eye out for a likely prospect. Even my money will run out at the rate they're going."

I thought—but I did not say—that long after Victoria was safely married to whatever mythical nobleman Isabel had envisioned Isabel would still continue her life of extravagance—for she lived in that way as much for herself as for any of her children; they were only her excuse. But I simply patted Mrs. Reed's shriveled, mottled hand and kissed her withered cheek and promised to do as she had instructed—a promise that I never kept, for to have spoken so to Isabel would have been like crying into the wind, one's words vanished, whipped away as soon as they were uttered.

And so Isabel and Freddy Melville gave their extravaganza, and all of Boston's best came to it, and everyone agreed that it was a triumph. It did not, however, produce a husband for Victoria. I watched her dance, that evening, with a dozen different eligibles, but none of them was destined to be her husband.

Isabel made no bones about her dilemma: "Not suitable," she said flatly. "Any one of them would have her, of course, but none of them is the right one. I hate to say it, Marian, but Freddy thinks we may need to go to London next summer for the season. The pickings are much better there, he says, and heaven knows we've seen everything that Boston and Newport have to offer. And New York, too—half the people at Newport are New Yorkers. Well. If we must go abroad, then we must. I *will* not rest until she's properly settled."

Or until your husband is properly ruined, I thought.

Diana turned eight in October; and because, like most only children, she was lonely, and because I had had good reports about the place, I enrolled her in Miss Gregory's School for Little People on Marlborough Street. Every morning after breakfast one of the maids would walk there with her; if it was raining, Henry would drive her in the carriage. She enjoyed Miss Gregory's; she made friends there, she learned to write a pretty hand, she learned a little independence. She grew; she was happy. I could not have asked for more.

One afternoon shortly before Christmas I was delayed at a reception and did not arrive home until after dark. On the silver tray in the hall was an envelope addressed simply to "Mrs. Motley." It was not the sort of envelope that I usually received; the paper was flimsy, of poor quality, and the handwriting was that of an uneducated person, uneven, badly formed. It had been hand-delivered: no street address, no stamp.

I knew that Perseus was not at home because his hat and his walking stick were not on the hall-tree; even had he been there, however, I would have seen him only accidentally.

I went upstairs to my room, carrying the letter, giving instructions that Diana come to me when she had had her supper and bath. I felt a sense of dread, all the worse because there was no reason for it. Get on with it, I thought. Rather than call the maid I lighted the fire myself and turned up the gas and then I sat in a straight-backed chair at the little Winthrop desk in the corner. My hands were trembling; for a moment, as I stared at the scrawled sheets of paper which I had taken from the envelope, my eyes would not focus.

Mrs. Motley:

I bin sick for 2 wks now and I know about it, I know I won't get better this time.

So Ill write this wile I still have strength, and when I go they will take it to you.

Ill be honest with you, Mrs, I don't want to die without telling what happened. I bin looking for Heaven ever since I was a little girl, and I don't want my chances spoiled now.

He said I had to let him take the boy out for an airing. I tried to stop him, as God is my witness I did, Mrs, but he said I had to, he said Id never work anywhere again if I didnt, and he said I wasnt to tell anyone.

The boy's name was Edward, I remember. He was a sweet child, Mrs. I never knew a sweeter one. He used to talk about you. He used to tell me how much he loved you. Little boys is dear, aint they? I had a girl but shes gone away, I can't find her.

Mr M said I had to let the boy go out with him. No, I said, hes too sick. Yes, he said, he needs the fresh air. Hes been cooped up too much.

And then he said a strange thing. He said, Im his father and I know whats best for him.

Youll pardon me, Mrs, but I never believed that. I shouldnt say so, but I wont be here to suffer if you get angry. I dont want to hurt your feelings. But that man was never a father in his life.

He said hed hurt me, Mrs. I didnt want to let him take the boy, but what could I do?

And I wanted to tell you. You was out, remember, and when you came back I wanted to tell you. But I was afraid. I couldnt do it. You brought him a little paper castel, remember. But he never made it, he was too sick.

And Ive troubled about it every day since, Mrs. I should have stopped Mr M, even if I had to fight him. Even if I lost my place with you, if I didnt work again.

It was my fault, Mrs, and I had to tell you.

Remember, he loved you right to the last. A beautiful boy.

There was no signature. In a different hand—a well-formed, educated hand—someone had written at the bottom of the last page: 8 December, 1896.

Today's date.

Remember . . .

He had been a long time dying. His little lungs had stretched and strained for breath; he had lain, panting and suffering, for two days and nights before he died. What had he done to deserve such a death? What God would allow it? Once again I saw his small, tormented face; he had been very frightened, he had known that he would not live—

And Perseus. Drunk. Coming home late at night, and never retaliating when I hit him. Until this moment I had not thought to wonder why.

Remember . . .

He had taken Edward outdoors. He might as well have murdered him.

Why? He had never shown any overt dislike. After his first, venomous opposition to my bearing Otis Whittemore's child, he had seemed to accept our situation readily enough. He did not care about me, he had married me for my money and he had always had enough of that to do as he pleased. I had even paid his blackmailer for him. Why, suddenly, had he needed to revenge himself? To punish me: to punish me, at last, when he saw his chance. He might not have had another for years.

Remember . . .

Ah, God! I cannot write it, it is too painful. Even now, so long afterward, I cannot. But I must: I have determined to do it.

I did not shed a single tear that night. My mind was numb—suspended in limbo between the years.

So small he had been, so precious—the living
testament to the love that I had had.

My heart pounded in me, hurting me. I stared at the
scrawled sheets of paper, but I did not see them. I saw
through them far back in time, to a day when a great tall
man took my hand in his and smiled down at me and took
me into his life. And later: hot in the room, and the blinds
drawn against the sun, and his body in mine—

I was aware that someone stood at my elbow. It was
Diana. I had not heard her knock. She stepped back when
she saw my face, but I reached out and pulled her to me.
She did not resist. Once before she had saved me, and
now she did so again. Her small firm body clung to mine;
her arms, surprisingly strong, went around my neck. She
kissed my cheek once, twice, and then pulled back and
looked at me. Her face was grave.

"What is it, Mama?"

"Nothing, pet. I am tired, that is all."

She waited for a moment. "Good night, then."

"Good night, sweet. Did you have a good time at school
today?"

"Yes. I had every word right in spelling."

"Good. That's my clever girl. Now. Off to bed."

Taking her hand, I led her out into the hall. Together
we climbed the stairs to her room. She kissed me again
before I left her; she lay quietly on her fluffy white
pillows and solemnly watched me as I drew back the
curtains and opened the window an inch and extinguished the lamp. The pain of knowing how—why—my
son had died bore me down with its terrible weight, but I
was comforted to look at her. And when the room was

dark and I had opened the door to go out I whispered a last good night to her and I heard her say, "I love you, Mama," and my heart eased a bit under its burden.

As I went downstairs I saw Perseus. I had not heard him come in. His back was toward me: he was locking the door of his room as he always did when he went out. The sight of him just at that moment sent a shock through my body as if I had been struck by lightning. I stopped, frozen, on the stairs; he was fussing with the lock, he could not get it right, and I heard him muttering to himself as he fiddled with it. He did not know that I saw him.

And I saw myself just then, too: and I knew that that woman on the stairs, that tall thin redheaded woman whose hand gripped the polished banister and who held her breath lest she be heard—that same woman, had she had the weapon, could have murdered this man on the spot, without remorse, without hesitation.

At last he got the lock to work. He straightened; he turned to go downstairs. It was a Wednesday night: his weekly Symphony night during the winter season.

He caught sight of me. He acknowledged me with only a glance; without breaking stride he went on. I stayed where I was; I felt as if I were under a spell. After a moment I heard the front door slam, and the spell was broken. I went into my room and closed and locked the door behind me. Once again I picked up the letter, but I did not read it. I sat in a low chair before the fire; I held the letter lightly in my fingers as if mere contact with it would poison me. As indeed it had.

For a long time I sat watching the flames flicker and lick at the coals and finally devour them to ashes. I heard the clock strike the hours, nine and ten and eleven. I heard muffled sounds which I assumed were made by Perseus coming in. I sat in a kind of trace, not moving, hardly even conscious of the breath going in and out of my lungs. I heard the sound of his feet as he climbed the stairs; I heard the click of the lock on his door as he opened it and closed and locked it again.

I could get up now, I thought, and confront him. I could demand explanation, confession—penance, I supposed; I could even demand a kind of reparation.

But I wanted none of it: not then, at least. All night I sat; the fire burned low and went out. The room grew cold. The clock chimed one and two and three. I sat, the letter in my hand, memories flooding in: Otis' face above the crowd in Bowditch's studio; Otis' face as we loved; and the last time I had seen him; and Edward's birth.

I sat in a trance, suspended between past and present—even as I sit here now, fleeing back through the long years to the time when my son was born and I first held him in my arms and cherished him.

Dawn came. When the sun was well above the horizon I stood, flexing my stiffened muscles, and went to the window to look out on the new day. The river was not yet frozen; it flowed dark and fast to the sea, whitecaps flecking its surface. I put my hands flat against the glass and felt the cold penetrate my skin. It seemed to flow all down through my body; for a moment it steadied me, for I was lightheaded from my long night's vigil. Down my arms, down through my torso to my lower limbs, up into my brain I felt that astringent, bracing cold, awakening me, giving me strength.

And finally it found its way into my heart, which had never been truly cold before. And I knew then what I must do.

Eight

As it happened, Perseus had not gone to Symphony that evening after all. He went instead to the theater, to a new play, *The Widow's Mite*. A member of his Society had sent him a note earlier in the day, alerting him to certain questionable lines of dialogue.

Victoria saw him in the audience assiduously taking notes. She had gone to the performance with a party of friends, chaperoned by the two elder, married sisters of one of them. As she assured me later, there was nothing in the play that could have been called more than mildly risqué. "But he looked as fierce as anything, writing in his notebook, and every now and then lifting his head to stare around at the audience—to *glare* at them, very angry, as if he were warning them to go home."

I saw him in my mind's eye: a fierce, solitary figure, peering at the offending actors from behind his spectacles, his nostrils quivering, chin trembling a bit perhaps with the effort of holding back his rage, God's anointed stamping out sin.

"And when I looked around after the final curtain,"

she went on, "he was gone."

To the manager (who knew him well), to demand that the play close.

The manager would have eyed him warily, recognizing danger when he saw it, but unwilling to relinquish a profitable run. They would have sparred for a moment or two, Perseus unyielding, the manager alternately defensive and placating—for Perseus was a well-known figure now, and his reputation went before him. His run-in with the blackmailer some years previously had apparently done nothing to temper his zeal.

For reasons of her own, Victoria had told me less about that evening and its aftermath than she would have done ordinarily; but still I heard more than Isabel, who should properly have known it all.

And yet: who could blame Victoria for what she did? Not Isabel; and certainly not I. Victoria simply fell in love—instantly, passionately in love, swept off her feet, as they say, by a consuming infatuation.

It happens to us all.

The leading man in *The Widow's Mite* was a handsome, dashing fellow named Montrose Fletcher. From the moment he bounded onto the stage, resplendent in brown velvet doublet and tights and a frilled shirt (the play being set in the seventeenth century), Victoria and her friends had been enchanted by him. So handsome! So courtly, so debonair! So unlike the boys she knew, the eligibles from among whom, one day, she might be expected to choose a husband, and even more unlike her mother's candidate, Lord Hyslop.

On the day after the performance they had gathered at

lunch to gossip and do their bit of charity sewing. One silliness led to the next, and before anyone could remember how it had come about Victoria had accepted a dare: to go to Fletcher's hotel and steal into his room and leave a rose and an anonymous note. It was an appallingly risky thing to do, of course: but at nineteen our fears are very different from what they are at fifty.

She wore a sealskin capelet with a collar of shirred beaver and a toque and muff to match. The soft, dark, shiny fur matched her hair, her brilliant eyes. Her coloring was naturally vivid, and she did not need to enhance it as some girls did: her red lips, pink cheeks, milk-white skin provided a perfect backdrop for any color she chose to wear.

She wrote the note at home and then she set off for the hotel. On the way she stopped at a florist's on Tremont Street; she bought one red rose for Fletcher and a nosegay of violets for herself which she pinned onto her high fur collar. Their color matched the delicate veining on her eyelids, and their scent made her feel like a woman of the world.

The Parker House late on a winter's afternoon would have been a bustling, busy place; a solitary young woman could have made her way to the elevators without attracting undue attention. She gave a quarter to a bellboy to tell her which was Fletcher's room; then she made the ascent in the ornate brass cage. When she stepped out into the corridor she was relieved to see that she was alone. She had begun to have second thoughts about her little adventure: what had seemed to be a deliciously enticing dare had begun to be a foolish, frightening episode.

She reached the door; taking a deep breath to steady herself, and reminding herself that her honor was at stake, she silently turned the knob. To her surprise the door opened. She went in and closed it behind her. The room was dim, the draperies drawn against the late afternoon light. She took one step and then another. She saw a large round table in the center of the room—a sitting room, for this was a suite as befitted a man of Fletcher's celebrity. On a hat tree in the corner were a top hat and a black satin-lined cape; along the mantel were several photographs of women and children—his? A decanter of some golden-brown stuff stood on a sideboard, an oversized volume beside it. A pair of black evening shoes was by the fire. She could see no other evidence of the inhabitant. The door to the adjoining room—the bedroom—was closed.

Quick, she thought: drop the flower onto the table, drop the note beside it, and get away safe.

But then she remembered that she needed to bring proof to her friends that she had indeed been here: she needed to carry back some small personal thing of his, or at least of the hotel's. What? Gingerly she approached the table. She put down the note and laid the rose on top of it. For a moment she contemplated them, imagining him as he came in and found them. Would he be pleased? Indifferent? Curious to know who had left them, and how?

"Don't move. Your profile is perfect. Perfect!"

She froze. She could not have moved had her life depended on it.

"There—yes indeed, I didn't expect so lovely a flower, who has herself brought me a rose! Braithwaite promised to send me a pretty little morsel, but I must say, my dear, that you look—ah, now, what is it, what is wrong?"

He had approached her and put out his hand to caress her cheek in a way that no gentleman would. His movement shocked her into action and she pulled back, angry color flooding her face, her gloved hand raised to fend him off.

"Come now," he laughed. "You're being paid well enough, you needn't try to hold out for more. I know what Braithwaite gives to girls like you, and you've no reason to complain, believe me." He reached to embrace her, but she pulled away and put the table between them.

He was too good an actor himself not to know when someone else's behavior was genuine; and so he did not pursue her but stood with an embarrassed half smile on his handsome face and a shrug of his broad shoulders as if to say, "I think I have made a mistake. Please tell me how."

She held her head high and prayed that the tears that filled her eyes would not spill down her cheeks. To be taken for *that*—!

"I beg your pardon," he said simply. "I thought you were—well, never mind. Obviously I have made an unpardonable error. Nevertheless I ask you to forgive me, Miss—ah—"

She did not yet trust herself to speak. She wished that he would stop staring at her and give her a moment to collect herself. She took a handkerchief from her muff and dabbed her eyes and nose; she did this with great dignity, almost comical in one so slight and young and pretty. But he did not smile; his smile had vanished, to be replaced by a look of baffled pleasure.

"Tell me your name," he said softly, "so that I may call you it and begin to be your friend."

Hesitantly she obeyed him. She had a sense that she was dreamwalking, that at any moment she would awaken in her own familiar bed and know nothing of this hotel, this strange man, save a fragment of dream memory.

"Well, Miss Kittredge. This is an unexpected pleasure. Sit down, sit down—here, right here at the table—and I will send for tea and we can have a very pleasant half hour."

It was madness for her to stay: they both knew it, but still she was sorely tempted to do so. Such an escapade could ruin a girl's reputation. No decent man would court a girl who had spent an unchaperoned hour in the company of any man, let alone an actor—and in that man's hotel suite.

And, it turned out, an actor whose play was too strong for the stomach of the Watch and Ward. Before she could reply, he had gone to the sideboard and poured himself a healthy drink from the decanter. "If you'll pardon me, Miss Kittredge, I'll just fortify myself against the night. We don't know yet whether we'll be on or off, and there may be a tremendous fight brewing. Mr. Braithwaite, the manager, has got to deal with a man named Motley. Wants to shut us down. Heads up an organization called the New England Society for the Suppression of Vice. More commonly known as the

Watch and Ward. You've heard of 'em? Yes. Very vigilant. Mind everybody's business for 'em. This man Motley has been to see Braithwaite, threatens to close us unless we close ourselves. How about that, huh? A very chilly reception in Boston, I'd say."

He drank the whiskey in three or four quick gulps and poured himself another. She could not take her eyes from him. She had never seen his like: his ruddy, large-featured face with its lock of hair strategically fallen over the left eyebrow, his deep-set eyes, the full lips from whence came, now, a steady stream of talk, his famous, sonorous voice—the voice that had helped to make his fortune—wetted by the golden liquid, the voice becoming as warm, as golden and glowing, as the liquid itself.

And as dangerous. I must leave, she thought: I have made enough of a fool of myself already. I should have given him a false name. I should have left the note and the flower at the door. I should never have come at all—

". . . to be alone," he was saying. She was aware that he watched her with an intensity unknown to the self-conscious, self-centered adolescent males whom she saw at parties. "Can you imagine the effrontery of this man? Even Comstock himself, in New York, does not dare to openly threaten a theatrical manager the way this man threatens Braithwaite. I missed a rehearsal this afternoon because I was so angry. I needed to be by myself, to calm myself before the performance tonight. Otherwise you would not have found me here, and I—well, I would have missed the very great pleasure of meeting you." He gave her a little bow, mock gallant. He did not take his eyes from her. He devours me, she thought; she felt her heart flutter in delighted dread.

"So. I may leave your fair city ere the sun peeks roguishly o'er the topmost trees—isn't that dreadful? A playwright wrote that line for me once and I refused to say it in public."

He put his glass, now empty for the second time, beside the decanter on the table. With a swift, smooth movement he was instantly at her side. So quickly that she had no time to protest, he took her hand. Peeling off the glove, which he thrust into his pocket, he put his lips to her fingers. "Speak," he murmured, "so that I may know you."

She gazed at him in wonder as he bent over her hand. Boston boys did not behave so. She did not know whether she was flattered or frightened. Both, she thought. I must test him, she thought, and quickly, while she retained her courage, she said: "If you would know me, you should know that Mr. Motley is the husband of my mother's closest friend."

Without taking his lips from her skin, he raised his eyes to look at her. Then, slowly, he straightened.

"Why did you not say so before?"

"I—"

"Never mind. I know: I hardly gave you a chance. Tell me, do you think that he would listen to you, or your mother, perhaps—"

They heard a loud peremptory knock, followed immediately by the entrance of a small round man in a brown tweed suit, cigar clenched between his teeth, lips drawn back to reveal those teeth in a triumphant smile.

"We've won, Mr. Fletcher! The show goes on! Ah"—
for the first time noticing Victoria—"afternoon, miss.
Excuse me, Mr. Fletcher, I didn't know you were—ah—
busy. I thought you'd want the news."

"The police?" said Fletcher.

"The top man himself. Bought and paid for. He won't
touch us if we run into the Fourth of July, or the Fourth
of July after that."

Fletcher, grinning, clapped him on the shoulder.
"Well done, thou good and faithful et cetera! A
celebration is in order, yes? Yes! A celebration—supper!
You see this young lady, Braithwaite! Miss Kittredge,
this is, as you may have guessed, the man who manages
the Majestic Theater, and who manages me whilst I play
there. Mr. Braithwaite, Miss Kittredge—who is not what
you presume her to be, but who is a proper young lady
paying me her respects. Am I not a fortunate man,
Braithwaite? Fortune smiles upon me, I am Fortune's
plaything, her willing toy." He beamed at them, relieved
of his worry, assured of the play's run and of his own
salary therefrom. "Supper, Braithwaite! Supper is what
we must have! A bounteous feast to celebrate the
venality, the greed of this good man who takes your
bribe. I will drink to him, I will toast his health in
champagne. Yes!"

As Victoria dined with them that night she tasted the
victuals of Paradise, for she returned home (sent safely
in a hack) transformed, as she told it, from a silly girl on a
prank to a grown woman deeply in love. He courted her,

497

after that, with the devotion of a Romeo—a role which, no doubt, he had often played both on the stage and in life. And for once Isabel and Avery agreed: they both cordially disliked him. But if they could agree on that they could come to terms on little else. They were so estranged, hardly speaking, going their separate ways, that they were unable to agree how to keep him from her; and so, inevitably, he continued to appear.

Every day some new offering came: flowers, boxes covered with pastel watered silk and filled with French chocolates, love letters, many pages long, more pages than might have been needed because his handwriting was outsized even as the man himself. Some pages contained only four or five lines: extravagant flourishes, large loops and long dashes, many exclamation points. Once he sent a nosegay of violets in memory of the flowers she wore on their first meeting: but these flowers were amethysts, nestled in a bed of enameled leaves.

Victoria received his tributes happily enough—she was more than happy, she was glowing, elated, filled with a secret joy—but hardly with surprise. Like all women, she knew from the first moment when she had made a conquest. Such knowledge encases a woman in an impenetrable armor: nothing in the world can hurt her, nothing can intrude upon the satisfaction of her triumph.

Isabel, busy with Freddy Melville's program for her success and preoccupied even more with the problem of money, was at a loss to deal with her daughter's highly unsuitable suitor. "He will ruin her," she said, "just by paying calls, by sending presents to her. No decent young man will interest himself in her after this. Even if she does not encourage him, it is common knowledge that he pursues her. That alone will compromise her."

"Does she encourage him?" I said. We sat in a tea shop on West Street, just off the Common. It was a lowering afternoon in February, not particularly cold but with that penetrating coastal dampness that defies all attempts to warm the bones. Particularly middle-aged bones, I thought. I did not mind growing older, but I was sure that Isabel felt differently: how could she not, living in a world which valued beauty almost as much as money and ancestry?

"She is infatuated, as any girl might be. I cannot reason with her. I forbade her to accept anything from him, but at best it is only a temporary victory. I cannot keep her a prisoner in the house, and if they are intent on communicating they will find a way to do so. They say that Mrs. Vanderbilt kept her daughter prisoner until the marriage took place, but that was different. And besides, I am not such a barbarian. I could send her away, but where? And for how long? Why should I be forced to give up my daughter simply because the wrong man has chosen to pay suit to her? She is a fool to encourage him, but she is *my* fool. I do not want to lose her."

The waitress had replenished the hot water, and to warm my frozen hands I curled my fingers around the earthenware pot. We sat by the steamy window. The shop was busy, a steady stream of late afternoon customers, but we did not feel pressed to leave. And, indeed, I wondered at Isabel, for ordinarily at this hour, nearly five o'clock, she was preparing for the evening's activities. There were very few evenings when she had nothing scheduled, for Freddy Melville was a hard taskmaster. But now she sat quite still, oblivious to the bustling restaurant, the flaring gas jets, the noisy talk, the stench of damp wool, of horse dung tracked in onto the sawdusted floor.

"She *is* a little fool," she said, so abruptly that she startled me. "Avery says we must stop her somehow, and he is right. For once he is right. But how? How can we, Marian?"

I had no answer.

The Widow's Mite, after a highly profitable run undisturbed by the police, had its last performance on March 20. It was a bright, blustering day, the sun in and out, a brisk wind ruffling the blue surface of the Charles.

It was also, although we did not know it, Victoria's last day in Boston, her last day as one of the most eligible debutantes in the city: for that night, after the performance, when Montrose Fletcher left Boston, Victoria left with him.

They were very clever, the two of them: for some days he had not sent flowers or any other token to her, and she had seemed to take interest once again in her accustomed round of social engagements. That night she attended a party in Chestnut Street. Somehow she managed to slip away unnoticed at about eleven o'clock: Fletcher had a cab waiting for her, and she went directly to him at the theater. When he had taken his last curtain call and acknowledged his last congratulation, the two of them boarded the late train to New York and were gone before anyone knew. The note that she left for Isabel had as its paperweight her golden trophy from Mrs. Denton Elliott's Apple of Discord Ball.

But I did not learn all that right away; I had my own concerns that night, and they did not involve Victoria.

Nine

I had spent that day shopping with Diana; she was growing at an amazing rate, and nothing from the past year fitted her. The warm weather would be upon us before we knew; she needed an entirely new wardrobe, and I had the dressmaker do only her best things. We came home in the late afternoon, and after resting for a while we took an early supper. I had had an invitation to a recital that evening, but at the last moment, prompted by some instinct that I obeyed without understanding, I sent a note to the hostess, a woman I hardly knew, to say that I could not attend. Feeling released from an unpleasant duty, I read to Diana from *The Tales of King Arthur* for half an hour before she went to sleep: a much more worthwhile way to spend my time than going out, I thought. When I saw that she was drifting off I closed the book and bent to kiss her. She opened her eyes drowsily and smiled up at me. Although she has turned out so well, she was not then a particularly beautiful child: she was thin, with eyes too big for her face, her hair straight and limp, her complexion pale, the parts of her face—nose, forehead, jawline—too large for the whole, not yet in harmony. She was a genuine ugly duckling: how I loved her!

"Good night, sweet," I whispered, pressing my cheek to hers.

"Night, Mama." She smiled a sleepy smile; I pulled the coverlet more closely around her shoulders and kissed her one last time. And then, for no reason, the thought of my son came into my mind. I stopped as if I had been struck. Once upon a time it had been he whose face I saw on the pillow; once I had had to whisper "Good night" when really I meant "Good-bye." Yes, I loved her; yes, she had brought me back from the brink of death; but still that pain remained and nothing—not even Diana—could assuage it.

And I had received that letter, some weeks ago, telling me why he had died.

Suddenly close to tears, I left Diana and went down to my small sitting room on the second floor. I rang for the upstairs girl; when she came I asked her to bring me a pot of coffee and a slice of the cherry pie that we had had for dessert. She hesitated before turning away to obey me.

"What is it, Ella?" Perhaps the servants have eaten all the rest of the pie, I thought, and she does not have the courage to confess.

"I don't know if I'm supposed to tell you, ma'am, but the master isn't well."

I hesitated for a moment before I replied.

"What do you mean, isn't well?"

"Just—not well, ma'am. No one told me to tell you, but I thought you'd want to know."

"I see." I sat still in my chair, looking up at her with my bland, mistress' expression. I knew what she was thinking: why did I not get up at once and go to him as a dutiful wife should? "And how did you come by this information, Ella? Did he tell you?"

"No, ma'am. Mrs. Beasley said so at supper."

"Mrs. Beasley is generally right, so I suppose we must believe her. Very well, Ella. I will go to him. And you may bring my coffee and then go to bed and tell the others to do so too. If I need any help I will send for someone."

"Yes, ma'am." She departed looking somewhat relieved, as if I had reassured her by showing a proper wifely concern for him. I knew that I must not act in haste. For weeks now—ever since I had received the letter—I had been waiting for the chance to take some action.

No. That is not right.

I had been waiting to discover what action to take. I had felt that whatever I should do would be revealed to me and that I needed only to wait to learn what it was.

Now I knew.

When Ella came with the tray I permitted myself a small falsehood—a little transgression indeed, I thought, compared with what would come.

"I have looked in on Mr. Motley, Ella. I will see to him tonight, and if any emergency arises, or if I need help, I will send for you."

"Yes, ma'am." She ducked her curtsy and went away when I dismissed her.

I poured the coffee into the eggshell-thin cup. The coffee was very dark, the way they know I like it, and

steaming hot and smelling rich and slightly bitter the way
good coffee should smell. The cherry pie was properly
tart, made from sour cherries that Cook had put up the
previous summer. I finished it and poured more coffee
and I sipped it and I waited. The porcelain clock on the
mantel said nine o'clock; I heard the grandfather clock
downstairs begin to chime, and then the bells in the
Church of the Advent on Brimmer Street. Then they
stopped and I heard nothing save the wind rattling the
glass. I sat rigid in my chair, waiting.

He was ill, the girl had said.

Nine-thirty came, and then ten. Wait: wait: the
servants might be wakeful still, and who knew what they
might hear?

I sat immobile. Memories overtook me.

Ten-thirty, and then eleven. When the bells fell silent
again I got up from my chair. I stumbled a little as I went
to the door, stiff from the cold, but I was very steady,
very calm. I noted particularly that I did not tremble.

I opened the door and stood for a moment in the
darkened hall, listening. The house was silent. A line of
light showed under the door of Perseus' room. I
hesitated: should I wait longer or should I go to him and
force the issue? But before I could decide his door
opened.

He stood silhouetted against the light; I could not see
his face but, from the way in which he clung to the
doorknob and the -jamb, it was obvious that he was in a
bad way. He sagged a bit and then swayed forward. I
checked my instinctive move to help him. I simply
watched him. He took one step and then another, moving

into the hall; he lurched to the banister and clung to it.

I said nothing.

After a moment, breathing hard, he turned his head toward where I was. "Dr. Weybridge," he said. He was panting; the words came hard and he could say no more.

I watched him.

After a moment, leaning heavily on the banister, he took a step toward me. He paused; then, lurching, he took another. He came close to toppling over the rail into the front hall one flight below.

The telephone was there: the lifeline.

Another step. "Weybridge," he whispered.

The staircase lay between us. I went to it; at the top step I paused.

"If you can get downstairs," I said, "you can call Dr. Weybridge yourself and ask him to come."

I caught sight of his face as I started down. He clung to the banister looking at me, his face not three feet from mine. A little light reflected from my room glittered on his spectacles: small twin opaque discs. They made his face blind. It was a stranger's face. Worse: an inhuman, alien face. The face of a man who had—

"Please."

So faint: almost a sigh. He had never said "please" to me before; I was hardly sure that I heard him correctly now.

I went down one step and then another. Despite the blankness of the spectacles, his face now seemed to take on some expression. Fear, I thought; he is very frightened. The mouth fell open. To moan? To gasp, to try to get air?

I went on; I went all the way down. I turned at the bottom and looked back. He had managed to get to the newel post; he stood staring down at me, swaying slightly, ready to topple.

"Here is the telephone," I said. It was attached to the wall near the bottom stair. "If you can reach it you can get help."

He made a noise that I could not understand. He slid down until he was on his knees, hovering above the steeply descending stairs. If he let go the post he would fall, he would tumble all the way down and land broken at my feet.

"Please—" The voice was hoarse, the single syllable wrenched out.

"Come down," I said. "Call him yourself." I stood quite still; I made no further move.

He seemed at last to understand that I would not help him. I had thought that perhaps he would give up, but he did not: he began to descend. Because he was so weak he needed to come half sliding, half crawling—but he came on, he came down, breathing hard, hand over hand down the balustrade.

I went to fetch the key to turn up the gas. I wanted to see him clearly, to watch every move he made. He was in pain, he was probably frightened—ah, I loved to see him so! Had not my child been in pain, had he not been frightened when he knew that death was near?

The gas hissed and gave light. I could see him very well now. His face was shiny wet; veins stood out on his temples and forehead. Oh yes: he was very frightened. He knew that he had only me to help him; and he knew that, of all places in the world to find pity, I was the last.

I saw his shadow on the stairway wall, thrown there by the harsh bright light of the gas. It was larger than he: oddly menacing. His sharp, wolflike profile was thrown in vivid outline upon the pale flowered wallpaper. The shadow moved with him like a doppelgänger: his dark self.

Perhaps he knew that he was dying, and knew my pleasure in it.

I prayed so.

He was one third of the way now.

Suddenly he made a misstep. He slid, grasping the rail, falling against it. His head knocked it; his spectacles flew off. They fell down into the first-floor hall. They did not break; they lay on the carpet throwing off small glints of light from the gas jets, sidepieces upright, lenses flat against the floor.

Now Perseus could not see. He stared down at me, blind, groping, his face having that defenseless look that myopic people have without their glasses.

"Perseus," I hissed.

He squinted down at me, peering at me. He knew perfectly well who spoke, but it is disconcerting to have to listen to a voice from a face you cannot see.

"Perseus—I know! I know! I had a letter from the nurse!"

He clung to his support. He stared down, but I knew that I was no more than a blur to him. He was breathing hard, trying to hear, trying to understand.

"Perseus! Listen to me! She wrote to me before she

died. She told me what you did! Yes! You remember—
Edward!"

I longed to see some sign that he understood me. I felt
no shame at what I did. What I did was nothing compared
to what he had done. But revenge is meaningless if its
recipient does not know that it is being taken.

And then, quite suddenly, his grip loosened and he
fell; disjointed as an unstrung marionette, he careened
down the rest of the stairs, his body and his booted feet
making loud thumping noises as they struck carpet and
bare wood.

He landed in a heap at my feet. I stepped back to avoid
having any part of him touch even the hem of my skirt.

He lay still. He might have been merely unconscious,
but I knew that he was dead. I could not bring myself to
feel his pulse but I did not need to. He was beyond help.

I felt a surge of triumph.

Dead!

I wanted to kick him—to stomp him, grind my heel
into his mean, pinched face. But I did not dare. I wanted
no trouble with the law. Even as it was, I might have
committed some offense by not getting help for him. I
could not risk more.

But one thing I could do. I stepped back into the hall to
where his spectacles lay, and those I smashed, I stomped
them to pieces, I pounded them again and again with my
heel until they were ground into the carpet. I felt my
breath come fast, I felt my skin flush with—what?
Excitement? Pleasure?

At last I stopped. My paroxysm of hate was spent. I felt

as though I were awakening from a bad dream, but whether the dream was only this evening's events or my life entire I did not know.

And then the telephone rang. The noise of its bell, harsh and urgent, frightened me so that I nearly cried out. Pain stabbed my heart; I felt my throat constrict. The noise was so loud that I thought that it must awaken all the household—that is, Diana and the servants—but no one seemed to hear. *Ring-ring! Ring-ring!* For one dreadful moment I thought that Perseus would arise and answer, but he lay still. I told myself that he would never hear anything again. The thought comforted me. My knees were weak, and as I lifted the earphone I balanced myself against the wall.

"Hello?"

"Marian? Is that you?" The voice sounded far away, scratchy and fading in and out. Even so, I recognized it.

"Yes, Isabel. What on earth—"

For it was late, past eleven-thirty. In my daze I thought that perhaps she was calling to console me on Perseus' death. When I realized my mistake I had to clap my hand over my mouth to keep from laughing—or sobbing, I hardly knew which. Whatever noise had been about to issue from me I strangled. I held my hand to my mouth and bit the flesh of my fingers and palm until blood came. It had a bitter taste: like metal.

"Marian, listen to me. Are you there?"

"Yes. Yes, I am here."

"Something terrible has happened. I know that it is late—very late—but something terrible—"

Perhaps she knew after all. I felt my stomach begin to

heave and churn, and I clenched my teeth to keep from gagging.

"Marian, you must help me. Avery is raging. I don't know what to do with him, and in any case I can't deal with anything else, I am frantic myself—"

"Isabel. Isabel, please—"

"Marian. Listen to me. Victoria has run away."

"Run away?"

"With that actor. Marian—Marian, can you hear me? With that dreadful man. She is gone—"

I heard crackling sounds and faint, wheezing whistles —the by-products of Professor Bell's invention rather than Isabel's distress. I leaned against the wall and listened to the noises coming down the line and fought to stay on my feet, fought to keep from vomiting, to keep from crying out in terror at what lay on the floor behind me. I must tell her, I thought; I must say it, I cannot keep silent—

"Marian, what am I to do? What will become of her? And of us—of us! She has ruined us all! Even the boys' chances are spoiled now!"

And then my laughter came, unbidden, uncontrollable, and I clung to the earphone and slid slowly down until I, too, was a heap upon the floor, and I laughed and laughed and laughed until I wept and then I wept because I could not stop my tears.

I heard the noises down the line: Isabel's exclamations, the static of the machinery.

"Marian? Marian, can you hear me? What is it—what is wrong? Marian? Are you crying, is that what I hear? Marian—speak to me!"

511

Ten

Isabel had not intended to tell her mother about Victoria. Mrs. January, widowed for some years, was nearly eighty; her sight was failing, her heart had weakened, and her movements were severely restricted owing to both obesity and arthritis. She was tended to by a hired companion who read aloud to her from the latest newspapers and periodicals; novels, she said, were frivolous—immoral. "I can't do it," said Isabel. "Mother always set great store by Victoria. I can't upset her now by telling her what the foolish child has done."

But Mrs. January had the news anyway: Winifred Blunt from Portland, whose visit the previous summer had been so unsuccessful (that is, unproductive of a husband), had come to Boston for another try. One afternoon, while calling on Mrs. January, Winifred let slip the information that Victoria and Fletcher had run away.

"I almost hit her," said Isabel later. "Mother looked so stricken—as if someone had kicked her in the stomach, poor dear. But then do you know what she did? Really, she is amazing. She simply thought about it for a moment and then she smiled up at us and said, 'Well, my dears, we must do something to distract attention from poor Vicky. Isabel, why don't you have a big crush—invite everyone we know and put me right at the head of the receiving line. I'll have to sit but that doesn't matter. People will say how plucky I am.' Can you believe it? And you know how sensitive she has always been to any hint of scandal."

I was glad that I had no new scandal of my own to sorrow her. Perseus' death was accepted for what I said it was: an accident. He must have gone downstairs in the night, I said, trying to reach the telephone. People were very kind. He had no friends to speak of, but a respectable delegation from his Society turned up at the funeral and so appearances were preserved.

I went into mourning as though I truly grieved over him. It meant nothing to me whether I wore black or any other color, and certainly I did not mind not going into society. I was perfectly happy staying home with Diana, who mourned him as little as I. I wept at Mount Auburn on the day that they buried him: I wept bitter tears such as any bereaved woman might, but I wept for my boy whose stone was there before me in the Motley ground, for the child who never reached even Diana's age, who never sailed or skated on the Charles, or rode a pony. Curtis stood by me and kept his hand under my elbow as if he were afraid that I would collapse; but I had collapsed for the first and only time on the night that Perseus died; I would not do so again.

One night, when Victoria had been gone for perhaps

two months—that is, toward the end of May—Isabel went to a reception at Mrs. Silliman's. There she saw Freddy Melville. She had not heard from him in weeks—not since Victoria's defection, in fact, for Freddy had hitched his wagon to Victoria's beauty. Now that she was gone—off the market, so to speak—his interest in Isabel and her career had markedly waned.

As it happened, Lord Hyslop was there as well. After his introduction at the Apple of Discord Ball the previous summer he had had an extremely successful winter season—a season, that is, in which he dined out every evening and was invited to all the best dances. He stood in the center of an admiring crowd of anxious mamas, receiving them with the air of a feudal landowner receiving homage from his serfs. Isabel could not have been happy to see him. Inevitably he would remind her of what might have been: a daughter married into the British aristocracy, rather than abducted—for so she saw it—by an actor.

One of the other ladies present that evening was English also: a lady of some station, it was said, although not a member of the aristocracy. After lingering briefly in the group surrounding his lordship, she came away with a perplexed expression on her face. She approached Isabel, to whom she had been introduced half an hour before. "Where was that man presented to American society?" she said.

"At Mrs. Denton Elliott's in Newport," said Isabel. "Last summer," she added, somewhat more hesitantly. With her long experience in reading people's behavior, she had sensed just then something in the Englishwoman's tone, her expression, that boded ill for someone.

The Englishwoman—a tall, big-goned woman who spoke with an air of studied rudeness—fixed Isabel in her cold blue stare and said: "Mrs. Kittredge, is it not?"

Isabel allowed that it was. This woman's name, she thought, was Mrs. Manion. Or Manfred, perhaps. Or Manting? Minion?

"Am I to understand that ever since last season in Newport he has been parading himself as Lord Hyslop?"

Despite the warmth of the room, Isabel felt a sudden chill.

"Why, yes," she said. "Mrs. Elliott presented him so."

Mrs. Manion snorted. "I've heard of brazen impostors," she said, "but this beats all. I know Lord Hyslop, I've known him for years. He's almost ninety. He lives down in Hertfordshire. I saw him only last winter."

Isabel had begun to feel ill. Her mouth had gone dry, and it had an unpleasant aftertaste of sour champagne punch.

"Perhaps this is his son," she said.

"If it is, he was born on the wrong side of the blanket. Lord Hyslop has never married."

"But Freddy Melville *said*—"

She broke off and abruptly turned away. Long years of discipline as rigid as that of any army would not allow her to show her anger in public. Anger was undignified, it was unladylike. There was not one word that she could say in rebuttal. Mrs. Manion was so obviously in the right, so surely in possession of the facts, that to disagree, to question her, would only make the questioner look more foolish than before.

The guests crowding through the room became blurred as tears filled her eyes. An impostor! How near she had come to foisting off Victoria on him! Poor Victoria! How dreadful it would have been. Truly, truly dreadful, a scandal beyond imagining. They would have been the laughingstock of every city in the East. She could never again have appeared in society. Victoria, in her foolish impulse, had acted on the prompting of her heart; but her crime, if indeed it was a crime, was committed out of honest emotion—not from a cool calculation like Isabel's decision to try to marry her into the nobility.

The nobility! Mrs. Manion was saying something but Isabel did not care that she missed it. Nobility! And Freddy Melville had dared to pass him off—!

She peered around the room, looking for Melville. There: in an alcove by the window he was talking to a woman whom she did not recognize. Some new prospect, she thought bitterly, whom he could exploit until she, too, was impoverished—for Mrs. Reed's bounty had run out, and although Avery had not, in fact, had to sell their house, he had had a close call with disaster. But she could do nothing here, she could say nothing to Melville in front of all these people, for she might lose her temper and disgrace herself forever.

The next day she sent for him. Like lovers who realize that their love has died and who must come to terms with that bitter knowledge, they faced each other over cups of tea in Isabel's sitting room. Melville was not apologetic. He shrugged his slight shoulders and fingered his pale blue neckpiece. He remarked that from time to time everyone makes a mistake.

"A mistake!" cried Isabel. "It was much more than a mistake! To pass him off for what he is not—how could you be so careless? What if Vic—what if someone had married him?"

Melville's face took on a look of scorn. "Pretending to be what you are not should be sufficient grounds for annulment, I should think."

"Annulment! What good is an annulment when a girl has been ruined?"

But he refused to do penance for her, and so in the end she dismissed him—banished him. As she put it, "If you hire an appraiser you expect him to be able to spot a fake."

After he went away that afternoon she sat for a long time without moving, until her hands and feet grew cold from lack of circulation. A woman of Isabel's age—and mine—did not lace herself so tightly as a debutante, but still she needed to move around or the blood could not flow. The late afternoon sun shone full through the window; then it sank behind the rooftops to the west and the room grew dim. Still she did not move.

She had invited eight people to dinner that evening, and for once Avery was home early: many times, when company was expected, he came in later than some of his guests. As he told me afterward, he arrived to find the maid laying the silver—ordinarily a task accomplished much earlier in the day—and the cook carrying on as best she could without her mistress' direction.

"She was always so meticulous about her entertaining," he said. "That was my first warning: where was she? I'd never known her not to be on hand at the last minute when people were coming. So I went looking for her because the servants said she hadn't gone out. And I found her sitting in that little room of hers. She didn't answer when I spoke to her. And then when she did— when I finally managed to get through—I could see at once that she was—well, upset. She spoke in a controlled way, as if she was afraid that she would break down." His face betrayed pain and puzzlement: he had no idea what was wrong with her.

Poor Avery! He had hardly been the most sympathetic of men, but at times I felt sorry for him.

Eventually he persuaded her to rise and change her dress and go downstairs to tell the servants what to do and to greet her guests when they came.

But afterward, when the guests had gone, she took to her bed and would not—could not—get up. After three days Avery sent for me.

"What does the doctor say?" I asked, even before I went upstairs to see her.

"Nothing. He says—that she should rest, that is all." His heavy face was worried, and I thought I saw a faint tremor in his hands.

I had played this scene before, I thought: years ago Avery and I walked the streets of the Back Bay one twilit evening. He had confessed then that he loved her: did he still? After all their disagreements, all their difficulties, did he still?

I knocked softly at the door of her room and entered without waiting for a summons. She was alone. She lay wide-eyed in her bed, the draperies drawn against the bright warm day—a true spring day, a taste of summer. The room was stuffy. I pulled one drape and opened the window. A warm breeze blew in, sour with the smell of the streets. Then I turned to her and sat beside her on the bed. I had done that before also: when her life was in danger in childbed, I had been with her and then with Avery, comforting him, reassuring him. A strong sense of *déjà vu* settled over me. How inextricably my life had been entangled with theirs!

"Isabel," I said, but she would not look at me. Her hair had not been properly taken down and brushed since the night she took to her bed, and it lay now in a tangled, ugly mass on the pillow. In this uncompromising light more than a few silver hairs showed, and I could see lines in her face—around her mouth, under her eyes—that I had not seen before. Her eyes, which always sparkled with wit and often with malice, were open wide but blank and dull.

Her hands and arms were underneath the covers. I patted the place where I thought her arm would be and she pulled sharply away as if I had attacked her. One hand came out, and I saw that she held a photograph. She looked at me now, readily enough: her face was tense with recognition, and I saw pain in her eyes, and a shadow of defeat that I had never seen there before, not in her worst days.

"What is that?" I said, meaning the photograph. "May I see?"

She did not give it to me, but neither did she offer resistance when, after a moment, I reached to take it from her.

It was a scene from the past: a dozen girls in pale

dresses arranged on a lawn, a few young men in white flannels in the periphery. I knew perfectly well where it had been taken, but the name of the place escaped me. There had been peach ice cream and small chicken sandwiches, and a strong breeze from the sea that whipped the trailing roses around the piazza: and beyond the cliff a murderous, drowning sea. . . .

I realized two things then: that I was holding the photograph so tightly that my fingers ached; and that Isabel was watching me intently.

I met her eyes and glanced away. I could not look at her. Years ago I had buried my sorrow, my anger at her for what she did; it was an accident, my brother's death, I said. I believed it then; I believed it still. She did not deliberately send him down.

"I am sorry, Marian," she whispered. "I—I have never said so before but I am sorry."

I could not speak for the pain in my throat, the sudden choking. And I did not know, now, whom to pity most: my poor brother, so long dead, hardly having lived; or Isabel, who had carried all these years the guilt of his death; or myself, whose life had been so changed by my association with Isabel and her family—an association that never should have happened had George not died.

I leaned down and touched my cheek to hers. "I know," I said softly. "I understand."

"No. No. You do not. I was—I was not myself that summer. Victoria—Victoria has done what I would have done, if he had not—"

She choked a little then. I waited for her to continue. Cushing, I thought. Always Cushing. I remembered the terrible scene when he left her, when her children had been ill and she could not go with him. "I think that Isabel intends some drastic thing," Carrie had said. "I think that she intends to go away with him!"

I pulled back from her a little. Our eyes met. "Yes," she said. Her voice was very faint, hardly more than a sigh. She closed her eyes; it was, I understood, my dismissal. I put the photograph on the table beside her bed. I could not bear my silent thoughts; I needed to talk to someone—anyone, I thought. My heavy mourning chafed my skin, and I was perspiring so freely that my bodice was damp all down the arms and around the neck and shoulders.

I left her then; and before I went home to Diana I stopped again to speak to Avery.

"How is she?" he asked.

"I don't know."

"You mean she didn't speak?"

"She spoke, but nothing—nothing much."

"The doctor recommends letting her come out of it on her own. A delayed reaction to Victoria's—ah—"

"Yes. A shock to the nerves." More than that, I thought: a lifetime of mourning that other one. Did he know? Did he have the imagination even to suspect?

"Exactly." He put out his large, fleshy hand and held mine longer than necessary. "You are a good friend, Marian."

He peered down at me. His small eyes were worried, baffled— How do we read expressions? Are they shown in the eyes only? Or in the arrangement of the features, the slackening or tightening of the muscles of the face?

I did not know what to reply: I agreed with him, but it was hardly fitting to say so. And so, after murmuring some noncommittal reply, I went away again and with the warm May sun at my back and a cool wind from the river to dry my dampened skin and clothing I walked home.

That was at the end of May. By the middle of June, when ordinarily she would have been in the midst of preparations to leave for Newport, she had sunk into a melancholy so profound that it seemed as if she could never come back. Much of the time she lay quiet in her bed, not moving, not responding or only very rarely. But every now and then, for no apparent reason, she went mad—a different kind of madness. She would cry, and rave, and call down invectives on the heads of all her enemies real and imagined; she would gnash her teeth and roll her eyes like the heroine of some Elizabethan tragedy; she would weep with a sorrow beyond our ken. She was, indeed, like a person bewitched—and she could not tell us who had enchanted her.

Poor Charlotte! It was she, I think, who suffered more than any of us—save Isabel, of course, whose ravings were signs of torment in the extreme, but who perhaps through Nature's mercy was spared the realization of what she did. Or perhaps she realized and then forgot: I did not know.

Charlotte came to me one day when I had left Isabel and was on my way upstairs to the children's quarters to look in on Mary and Mason. They were fourteen and fifteen, respectively—old enough to rightfully expect to be told something of their mother's condition, and yet too young to be burdened with the truth of it. Charlotte held a letter which seemed to have had bad news, for her face was taut with unhappiness and her manner agitated.

I smiled at her, for I was fond of her almost despite myself. She was not an easy person to like: she was too earnest, too matter-of-fact, lacking both wit and humor. I prefer a lighter touch—a smarter, slightly more cynical view of the world. Nevertheless I had to admit that in this, as in other crises, Charlotte was a brick.

"Do you have a moment?" she said. "This has just come and I don't know whether to show it to Mother or not."

"What is it?" I said.

"A letter from Victoria."

"Victoria!" I remember the physical shock I felt at hearing the name. It was as if she had died and Charlotte had announced her resurrection. They had not had one word from her since the night she ran away. "What does she say? Where is she?"

"She says that she is well and happy. They are in San Francisco. He has just finished the tour." She did not give the letter to me, and I could hardly reach out and take it. "She says—she asks us to forgive her." Charlotte's voice was flat, controlled, purposely without expression. I wondered at her: Victoria had had all that Charlotte would never have—or feared that she would not—and so what did Charlotte feel? Curiosity? Envy? Contempt?

"Ah—no," I said. "No, I wouldn't show it to her, Charlotte. I wouldn't even tell her that it came."

She was silent for a moment and then all of a sudden she burst out: "Because it would remind her of what

Victoria did. I know that I am not supposed to say so, but it was Victoria who caused her to collapse. You know it, I know it, Father knows it—but we are none of us supposed to say so for fear of being impolite. Or disloyal, perhaps—although Victoria wasn't very loyal to us, was she? It is no wonder that Mother broke down, it is no wonder that all her worry finally caught up with her. The disgrace is enough to cause anyone to collapse. But do you know, I'll wager that if Victoria were to come home today—if she were to appear on the doorstep this very moment—the family would welcome her and forgive her and no one would ever say a word of blame. And yet if I—"

Her voice broke and she paused to calm herself. I could not argue with what she said, for I thought that it was true; but I would not have argued in any case, for I saw now that she was indeed upset and I did not want to exacerbate her hurt.

"Do you know," she went on, "one afternoon last summer in Newport Sam Brigham came by in his two-wheeler and asked me to go for a drive. And I did. Mother was out making calls, so I couldn't ask her permission. But when she returned I told her, of course. She was simply furious. Furious! She said I'd compromised myself. I went for a drive, that was all, we were in an open buggy, everyone could see what we did, everyone could see that we were behaving in a perfectly proper manner, we weren't even holding hands, but Mother acted as though I had ruined my reputation. As if it mattered."

Isabel had not mentioned the incident. I could see her in my mind's eye, angry, protecting as best she could her daughter's only marketable quality. This summer, I thought, she might not be so harsh—if, indeed, she were in any condition to know what was happening.

I said nothing, however, for it was obvious that Charlotte wanted only an audience, not a commentator. If only I could explain to her, I thought: Victoria had been only the occasion of her mother's breakdown, not its cause.

But of that I could not speak—not to Charlotte, at any rate. As far as I knew, Charlotte had never been in love; she had never known that blissful agony. Only someone who had experienced love could comprehend the heart's demands and sympathize with their victim.

Victoria would have understood perfectly.

Eleven

Isabel's villa at Newport was vacant that July; in August, Avery found tenants—a socially ambitious family from, I think, Chicago—who took the place through the end of the season. They were millionaires, of course, but that meant nothing in Newport, where millionaires were as common as earwigs. They would learn the same hard lesson that others had learned before them: a family often needed to stay two or three seasons at Newport before it was accepted, and even then there was no guarantee of success. Many ambitious mamas had to return, defeated, to Cleveland or Pittsburgh or Prairie Flats, Kansas; for Newport was Newport, after all. As it happened, this family was luckier than most, for they at least received a few cards, if not invitations: many people would have been ecstatic to have so much.

Isabel summered in Brookline: a green and pleasant suburb, the next town out from Boston, the home of so many of Boston's physicians that one of its districts was called "Pill Hill." Among them was Dr. Endicott Gardner, who specialized in female neurasthenia—those nervous afflictions to which women, supposedly, were especially susceptible. He had an estate not far from where Cousin Sam Swift's had been: a large brick house set in spacious grounds. The casual visitor, or someone driving by, might have noticed the beauty of the setting, the well-kept formal gardens, the attractive furnishings and decorations of the house. But there was a wing that casual visitors never saw: a place where the rooms had barred windows and the doors had double thickness and triple locks. And the grounds, too, had locks and bars: a high iron fence ran completely around the property, and dogs and groundskeepers patrolled it.

Dr. Gardner was the most frightening man I ever met. He was a small, thin person with pale gray hair and skin that almost matched it. His hair was sparse, barely covering his narrow head; his face was pinched, his cheekbones high, his eyes pale and cold, his mouth surprisingly—revoltingly—full-lipped. His lips were liverish, and constantly wet: you could see little bubbles and trickles of saliva at the corners, and occasionally he sprayed you as he spoke. The skin of his hands was dead white and waxy, the fingers small and slim and without character.

But it was his attitude that frightened me far more than his appearance. He had a way of speaking to you that made you feel like a bug under a microscope. He was arrogant, of course—all doctors were arrogant—but it was more than that.

"He won't talk to women," said Charlotte. "He told Papa all about Mama's condition. But he doesn't like to talk to women. He doesn't think they can understand him."

And I realized that what she said was true, and it was

that that I found so frightening. He made me feel that I did not exist—had no right to exist.

Dr. Gardner's private asylum—for that is what it was—was run on strict rules of cleanliness, order, healthful diet, and obedience. This last was most important: obedience not from the staff only but from the patients as well. If a patient behaved badly—if she were unruly, say, or even if she only protested some small thing—Dr. Gardner's discipline was swift and sure, for, like his patients, he needed the security of an ordered world; he could not tolerate deviance or any questioning of his rules.

Avery took Isabel there in June. For two weeks we were not allowed to see her: she was, in effect, in solitary confinement. I wondered whether this was the best way to treat her illness—if indeed it was an illness—but Avery and Dr. Gardner between them had charge of her and so I could do nothing.

At last we were allowed to visit her. Charlotte and I went together one afternoon. It was one of those glorious New England summer days: brilliant sun, cool breeze, sky as blue as Italy's. We drove in the Kittredge barouche. We did not speak much, but we were comfortable with each other: we shared a concern for Isabel that overcame our differences. Charlotte seemed to have taken special pains with her appearance that day: she wore a summer walking suit of royal blue, its skirt flared at the hem, and a large hat set at an angle on her bouffant pompadour.

An attendant opened the high iron gate. As we passed through and proceeded down the drive I turned to look behind us and I saw him pull it shut. Despite the beauty of the day I felt a sudden apprehension, as if I myself were coming to be incarcerated here.

We drove the quarter mile or so to the house, where we were greeted by another servant, who held the reins while we descended. The house was quiet, shuttered against the sun; a dark-coated manservant met us at the door and led us away from the living quarters through a heavy door, unlocking it for us to pass through and locking it again behind us. We proceeded down a long, bare corridor: white walls, scuffed parquet floor. At its end was another door identical to the first; like its twin, it had a heavy lock whose very sound, a loud grating sound followed by a *thud*, felt like a blow to my heart.

We were in a corridor which ran at right angles to the first, but this one gave access to the rooms. Walls and ceilings were painted white; the floor was worn linoleum. Electric bulbs gave a harsh light, but they were needed since there were no windows. There was a strong smell of lye. Perhaps half a dozen doors led off this corridor, each with a six-inch-square pane of thick glass at eye level through which the attendants could look in at the inhabitants. The glass was covered with wire mesh; it looked impregnable. I heard our footsteps and the soft sound of my skirts: there was no other sound in this place, closed off as it was from all the world. As we progressed I saw that on one of the doors the glass was cracked—smashed, splintered into a spiderweb held in place by the mesh, as if, say, a brick had been thrown at it.

I paused to look at this evidence of—what? Rage, I supposed: anger beyond anything I had ever known.

Why? Who lived inside that room and what tormented her?

That the occupant was female I had no doubt: Dr. Gardner treated only women. Men, perhaps, were not so susceptible to nervous disorders: or perhaps not so amenable to his treatment?

I turned to move on; Charlotte and the attendant had paused to wait for me. Suddenly—suddenly! no warning, no chance to brace myself—I heard a scream, a shriek of agony from the room behind that door. It lasted for perhaps ten seconds: an eternity. I stood transfixed, frozen there in that passageway; I could not have moved to save my life.

The shriek died. I could not take my eyes from the door, although what I expected to burst through it I could not have said. A moment's silence, and then a new sound: a muffled thump. Over and over it came, its rhythm unvarying: thump. Thump. Thump. Thump—

The attendant shouldered me aside. Taking a key from a ring at his waist, he unlocked the door and opened it. I had a moment's glimpse only before he slammed it shut in my face, but what I saw there will be forever imprinted on my brain, for it was what any woman might become, given bad enough luck.

A human female crouched in the corner. From the waist down she was naked. Around her arms and upper torso was wrapped and tied a white thing like a mummy's wrap. Her dark hair hung about her face so that you could not see who she was, but then she gave a quick, impatient shake and revealed herself to me. Our eyes met. Her face was dark and thin; I could not take it in all in one glance, but the eyes—ah, the eyes! Dark and gleaming and filled with pain, like twin coals glowing in the night. She stared at me and I stared back. I could not have looked away, not for anything: how she held me with those eyes! Help me, she seemed to say; and: Stay away, for I am beyond help. And then, even as I watched her, she leaned over and struck her head against the wall: once, twice, three times.

The attendant slammed shut the door, glancing at me angrily. I waited, listening, straining my ears, hearing the echo of that but nothing more, no new sound.

Nothing. What was he doing to her? Why, suddenly, could she not at least cry out? What was her affliction, that she was kept in that way, wrapped and tied? No sound—nothing. I heard only the echo of my heart hammering in my ears. The silence frightened me more than noise: it allowed my imagination more play. I remember thinking that if they had tied Isabel in that way I would set her free no matter what.

I had been staring at the door. Now from the corner of my eye I saw a movement at the end of the corridor. I turned my head slightly to look and with a little shock of surprise I saw Charlotte. I had forgotten her. Now I lifted my hand as if to caution her to wait, not to come near me. I stepped up to the small meshed square of glass but, shattered as it was, I could see nothing. I turned away then and walked on to join Charlotte.

"What was that?" she whispered when I had caught up with her.

But I shook my head; I would tell her in good time, but not now. "Where is your mother?" I said—not loudly, but not whispering either.

"The attendant said the last door."

We stood before it. I looked in. Isabel lay on the bed, her eyes closed; I could not tell if she were asleep. She wore something long and white—some sort of smock, I supposed. I knocked softly so as not to startle her. Her eyes flew open and she turned her head to look. There was mesh over this little window, too, and so I suppose it was difficult for her to see who knocked. In any case she showed no recognition, nor did she get up to open the door. I tried to open it myself but, like the others, it was locked.

"Isabel! Can you hear me?"

Charlotte shushed me: "They will force us to leave without seeing her."

The door was heavy, faced with a sheet of metal. I assumed that Isabel could not hear me. And yet, in an unnerving way, she kept her head turned toward me and her eyes open, staring wide.

"Isabel! It is I—Marian!"

Charlotte grimaced in an agony of embarrassment, but I did not care. Avery was paying a fine high fee to Dr. Gardner, I thought; at least someone could be on hand to unlock. What if there were a fire? What if she suddenly went into a convulsion or started to choke?

And then it seemed that Isabel heard me after all, or at least knew who I was, for she leaped up as if she would run to the door to let me in.

But before she had taken three steps she was pulled up sharp and short like a dog at the end of its leash. She rebounded and fell half on the bed, half on the floor.

"What is it?" whispered Charlotte, who saw my expression.

"A tether," I replied, speaking softly also, but because of my shock at Isabel's condition, not from fear of the authorities. "They have put a strap around her waist and harnessed her to the bed. And she cannot get as far as the door to let us in. No—no, I will not let you look. No one should see her mother in such condition. Oh, that terrible man! Wait until I tell your father. Isabel! I am coming, I will get help!"

We heard a door open down the hall. The attendant stepped out and closed and locked it behind him. For a moment the image of that occupant flashed across my mind and I wanted to run to that door and look in and, perhaps, unlock it and go to her. And unlock *her*—

The attendant was at my side. He looked very cross.

"Talking in the halls against the rules," he said peevishly. He selected a key from the ring and slid it into the lock and stood back to let us go in, and so poor Charlotte saw her mother tied like an animal after all.

We did not say much, for there was nothing to say beyond the usual sort of greeting. We embraced; we wept; we sat together on the bed, for there was no other furniture, and in any case Isabel could not move more than three or four feet away from it. We tried to free her but there was a lock on the buckle and we could not get it undone.

"We wanted to come before," I said, "but Dr. Gardner would not allow it. Isabel, listen to me. Do you want to come home? Because if you do I will speak to Avery and he can speak to Dr. Gardner. No one should be kept in a place like this against her will."

She sat quietly on the edge of the bed, her eyes downcast, her hair undone, looking like a little girl instead of a woman of forty-five or -six.

"We are all here against our will," she said. "There is a woman who screams—"

"Yes. I heard her. I saw her, in fact."

For a moment her face lighted up. "You did? Who is she? What did she look like? Night after night she screams—oh, it is horrible! It frightens me so! She might be screaming for all of us—doing for us what we are afraid to do for ourselves. Is she young? Beautiful? Did she speak to you? How I would love to meet her!"

I had no heart to tell her the truth about the poor wretch I had seen, and so, avoiding Charlotte's glance, I made up a lie. "She is quite beautiful," I said, "and exquisitely dressed. Except for the screaming, she might be a guest at a house party."

Isabel gave me the ghost of her smile. I think she knew that I lied. I did—I did! I told one lie after another. She listened quietly. Then, after I stopped, and after Charlotte had given her some small domestic news, she leaned over and put her head on my shoulder. I felt her body shake with muted sobs. The room was warm; sun streamed in through the barred, uncurtained window, which was raised only a couple of inches to let in air. Avery should have taken her to Newport, I thought. This is doing her no good, and probably a great deal of harm. What was the purpose of it, after all? How could a nervous disease be treated by allowing her to stifle in this hot little room, tied to the bedframe, forced to listen to the shrieks of a woman truly mad?

"Marian."

"Yes, dear."

"Marian, you must help me."

"Yes. I know." I patted her back, I comforted her as best I could. I heard the panic barely concealed in her voice.

"I cannot stay here."

"No. No. Of course you cannot."

"But they won't let me out. They make me lie here all alone, all day long. Sometimes they put me into a bath—a cold bath, so cold, I think I will die of it. I protested and they threatened to make me stay longer. I see Dr. Gardner for five minutes in the morning and five at night. I see the attendants who bring my meals. I see Avery when he comes. They haven't let anyone else until today. I am all alone, all the time. I am not allowed to read, to do needlework, even. They say I have been overstimulated, that I must learn to be quiet and obedient lest I unsex myself. I am not normal, they say—not properly domestic. But if one came here as sane as—as Dr. Gardner himself" (a simile which I found unconvincing) "one would be mad within a week, surely." Her voice broke then and she sat silent, leaning against me. Her hands were clenched in her lap, and I could feel her breath coming hard and fast through her uncorseted body. "Marian—please. Please. Make them let me out. You must! I will die here!"

And of course I promised to do what I could, I promised to speak to Avery, to Dr. Gardner if necessary, to do anything in my power to secure her release.

But both Avery and Dr. Gardner were unyielding: Isabel had had a nervous collapse, Dr. Gardner was a specialist in such problems, and therefore she must stay at Dr. Gardner's asylum until she was recovered or at the very least improved.

They let her out in September; and it seemed to me at least, and possibly to Charlotte too, that she was worse off than when she went in. She wept constantly; she raged, she railed at us when we were near, she cried out to herself in solitude. For three days in succession after she had returned home I went to see her. On the fourth, when I presented myself as usual at the door, the maid did not admit me.

"They've gone to Philadelphia, ma'am," she said.

"Philadephia!" I could not have been more surprised had she said "the moon." "Why?" I said. "And no message for me?"

"No, ma'am. They've gone to see another doctor."

"Another—but who? Do you know his name?"

"Dr. Parkin, ma'am. They went on the train. This morning, it was. Mr. Kittredge, and Mrs., and Miss Charlotte, and the nurse."

"For how long? A week? A month?"

"I don't know, ma'am." And then, no doubt because she knew me well, she allowed herself a confidence; "I heard Mr. Kittredge say to Miss Charlotte that the missus probably won't be home before Thanksgiving."

Twelve

It was the first week in December before I saw Isabel again. She had come home three days previously but, as Charlotte said, she needed time to recuperate from the journey as much as from the treatment she had received at the hands of Dr. Parkin.

I was anxious to see her, of course, but apprehensive too. We often do not know how to speak to friends who have been ill, for to be ill is to be away—to be someplace else—and we are somewhat strangers therefore, shy and awkward until new bonds are forged.

She waited in her sitting room on that bright, mild day; I was her only visitor. She wore a mauve velvet receiving dress; her hair was freshly done and—so it seemed—freshly hennaed, too, for I saw not a strand of gray. The room smelled strongly of smoke, although she did not have a cigarette in her hand. Her face was slightly puffy and her eyes were dull; nevertheless she smiled at me and gave me a welcoming kiss which I fervently returned.

"Welcome home, dearest! I've missed you so—but you look wonderful, you look as if you'd been at a health resort."

She smiled rather vaguely. "Dr. Parkin's isn't a health resort, I assure you. Rather more strict."

Her voice was slurred, like that of a patient emerging from chloroform. She turned round and round the ring on the little finger of her right hand: it was a large baroque pearl in a setting of thin twisted gold rope.

"How?" I said. I settled myself across from her and poured myself a cup of tea—that innocuous lubricant of so many tongues.

Slowly, fumblingly, she opened the chased silver box on the table beside her and took out a short brown cigarette. I lit a match for her and gave it to her so that she could light the cigarette for herself. She inhaled deeply, closing her eyes and then slowly opening them again to stare at me through the little cloud of smoke that she had made.

"They operated on me," she said. "They—I don't know, they wouldn't tell me, but it was something to do with my—with down here." She patted her gown over the place where her abdomen was. "They said—*he* said, Dr. Parkin—that it would calm me. He said that hysteria is a female disease and that to eliminate it we must eliminate its cause."

She shuddered then, and I moved to put a shawl around her. But she waved me off. "No—no. I was thinking of some of the poor creatures I saw there, at Dr. Parkin's clinic. They were far worse off than I. And the worst of it is that they must stay there, they cannot go home after a few months. And he has operated on some of them two or three times—"

She broke off then and stubbed out her cigarette. "Never mind," she said with an attempt at cheerfulness. "I am home again, that is all that counts. And look—people have been very kind, see all the notes that I have had, and invitations—Mrs. Stuart Gibney is having a monstrous crush on New Year's Eve, and she wants us all to come—Avery and the boys as well as Charlotte and me."

"You will be well enough to go?" I said, alarmed. I had received an invitation to the same affair, but I had not yet decided whether to attend.

"Of course," she said. She smiled in an unwontedly gentle way. "I must get back into the swim, mustn't I? I am not yet well enough to entertain here, but certainly I can go to other people's affairs. And I must do it for Charlotte. It still may not be too late for her."

And in fact Isabel's instinct guided her correctly, for at Mrs. Gibney's crush Charlotte found a suitor.

"He has left his card every day since he met her," said Isabel with a bemused smile. We were two weeks into the New Year—1898—and she and I were lunching at the Hotel Bellevue. Ladies did not lunch at restaurants in those days as frequently as they do now; Diana thinks nothing of meeting one friend or another any day of the week. But then it was less usual; we both took it as a sign of Isabel's recovery.

"And New Year's Day as well?" I said.

"Yes. Not twelve hours after he said good night to her at Mrs. Gibney's he was on our doorstep."

He was someone's cousin several times removed: tall, open-faced, somewhat shy but bright enough when you had won his trust and persuaded him to speak openly to you. His name was Ellsworth Barnes. He was from Butte, Montana. He had money; he was decent and honorable and kind; he had come East for purposes of business and also to find a wife if he could; and he wanted to marry Charlotte.

He proposed to her the following week, having dutifully spoken to Avery. "I simply can't believe it," said Isabel. "After all this time. I'd nearly given up hope. They want a summer wedding, they say."

"You have no objections to him?" I said.

"How can I? She could do far worse, as you know perfectly well. And she is obviously not going to marry a duke! Have you seen Freddy Melville, by the way?"

I took that last as an indication of her complete recovery. She could not have mentioned Melville's name, I thought, had she been anything less than well.

"I think he went to New York," I said. "Someone told me she'd seen him there."

"Good," snorted Isabel. "The farther south the better."

The family's happiness over Charlotte's engagement was shadowed the following month by the attack on the battleship *Maine* in Havana Harbor. In April, when President McKinley issued a call for volunteers, their eldest son, Arthur, announced that he was going to enlist.

I have said little about Isabel's boys because I did not know them as well as I knew the girls. Arthur would turn twenty-five that summer. He had of course graduated

from Harvard; then he took a six months' Grand Tour—
at his Uncle Curtis' expense, since his father could not
have afforded it. For the last two years he had been
working in his father's offices. He was a quiet, decent
young man, rather dull, with nothing to recommend him
other than an inoffensive temperament and a certain
understanding of the insurance and banking businesses.
But now, all of a sudden, he took on some importance.
The country was in a frenzy after the *Maine* was blown
up; William Randolph Hearst fanned the flames of war
and the future President, Theodore Roosevelt, proved
his manhood by rounding up a pugnacious little troop
and preparing to invade Cuba.

"Why must he enlist?" said Isabel. "It is so pointless.
Haven't they anything better to do than play at war?
They are like children shouting at each other. They have
no more control than that. Why must my son offer his
life for them? For what?"

She threw down that morning's *Globe*—a publication
not ordinarily seen in her house, but since the
President's declaration, followed closely by Arthur's, she
had had a morning paper delivered every day. "If they are
going to take my son," she said, "the least that I can do is
keep up with the news."

Arthur went in late April. For a month, while he was in
training, he wrote faithfully once a week; but then his
company moved out and she did not hear from him.
During that time she prepared to go to Newport. "I
missed it last season," she said in an offhand way, as if
she had been in France, say, or Germany, rather than at

Dr. Gardner's. "And Charlotte says that they want to have the ceremony there. It will be easier that way, rather than asking everyone to come up to Boston in the middle of the season."

And so the transfer was made, the entourage making its way to that improbable red-roofed villa perched at the edge of the sea. I went with her, and Diana, too, of course, and we helped her to prepare for the season.

Isabel was very lovely still: have I said that? It is important to remember it. She was forty-six and still she was beautiful. I saw men turn to look at her in the street, and at every party she attended she had her little circle of admirers. Her ordeal of the previous year had not dimmed her physical appeal; but it had somehow dulled her brain and slowed her vivacious temperament, so that those who had responded to her lively charm found her less interesting now, while those who clung to her for her beauty's sake had reason still to stay by.

At Newport she often wore white. One of her favorite dresses, I remember, had an organdy bodice and a high choke collar and cuffs trimmed in point lace. The skirt was narrow at the waist, heavily gored, swirling and full at the bottom like an upturned lily.

She wore it to dinner one warm evening not long after we arrived. Because the days of June are the longest, we dined while it was still light. Afterward Isabel announced that she would walk in the garden awhile and take the evening air before she went upstairs to dress for that night's entertainment.

I had gone to Diana's room as I always did to spend a

little time with her before she went to sleep. We sat at the
window, opened wide to catch the breeze, and looked out
over the lawns to the sea. After a moment we saw Isabel
emerge, oddly foreshortened, and walk down across the
terrace steps. In the eerie, dusky light, with the thunder
muttering in the west and heat lightning playing around
the horizon, she seemed in her white dress to be a
character in a Gothic tale—one of Mrs. Amelia Braden's
heroines, perhaps.

She walked slowly down to the low stone wall at the
edge of the lawn. A movement to her right caught my eye.
On the adjoining property, separated from hers by a high
yew hedge, a man was walking across his own lawn,
walking parallel to her but unseen. He was the new
tenant, I supposed. We had heard that the owners of the
place, a small stone château, had let it for the season.
Isabel had not been eager to meet the newcomers, for
ever since the panic five years previously Newport had
been invaded by upstart unsuitables trying to take the
places of those of the old guard who had been ruined. The
two figures reached the sea wall, which continued from
one property to the next, at almost the same instant. He
looked toward her. The hedge ended just there, so that
you could see your neighbor's portion of the wall. And if
someone stood watching you, you would be aware of it.

She turned only her head. Probably she meant to give
him a dismissive glance intended to discourage any
attempt at neighborliness. But instead of one swift look
she stayed fixed in that attitude: her body straight-
forward to the sea, her head turned to her right—like a

figure in an Egyptian wall painting, I thought.

His attitude was more relaxed. He faced her, not the water; his hand in one pocket, he might have been lounging against the wall. In that strange light his hair glowed like golden fire. His head was inclined to her. It is true that you can read a person by his stance—men far more than women, of course, since men are not constricted by corsets.

How long? A moment—two—three. Diana spoke to me but I shushed her; then, aware of my preoccupation, she looked out and saw them and said no more but watched as I did.

The two of them stood in that enchanted twilight as if they were under a magical spell and it seemed as if some grand thing must happen: the threatening thunder must erupt, perhaps, or the pulsing lightning suddenly flare into long jagged streaks. There was so much emotion—so much pent-up, charged emotion—in their stance that I could not believe that one of them would not go running into the other's arms.

But they were no longer young, and that impetuousness of youth had left them. And Isabel (so I reminded myself) was not what she once had been: Dr. Parkin had changed her.

For what seemed an eternity they stood so. And then, slowly, he put out his hand and she gave him hers; and slowly, gently, with infinite care, he lifted it to his lips. She allowed him to do so. She did not rush into his arms, but neither did she run away; she simply stood before him like a figure in a dream and let him kiss her hand, let him hold it. They did not move; they hardly seemed to speak. They might never have been apart all the years; they stood that way as darkness fell, two new statues in that Italian garden, and so close they seemed, so inextricably joined, that I thought that they never must part again.

Thirteen

A bright moonlit night, near midnight; the moon, full and white high over Newport town, glimpsed from time to time through the trees as we went.

A late night: and Lawrence Cushing had me in his runabout. We were taking a midnight spin down Bellevue Avenue and out to the Ocean Drive. A young woman might have refused him for fear of scandal, but my reputation was secure enough. Only women hunting for a husband needed to fear being compromised.

We had met at a reception at Mrs. Plunkett's—a crowded, hectic affair, running late, which I had been only too glad to escape when Cushing asked me to drive. He seemed edgy, distracted; I saw him speak abruptly to several women—very pretty women—whom ordinarily he would have taken the trouble to charm. Now, as we bowled down the avenue, he sat silent, expertly handling the reins, never glancing at me but keeping his eyes straight ahead. The trees made patches of black and white on the road, and on either side, set well back, were the big houses which in this month of June were just opened for the summer. Some of them were dark and silent, their owners elsewhere for the evening, but from some came lights and the sound of laughter, voices raised in revelry. We traveled through the landscape, Cushing and I, like strangers. I might never have been to any of those houses, I thought (although of course I had); I might never have made the acquaintance of any of those people.

We came out onto the Ocean Drive and now the houses were behind us: to our left stretched the shining sea, a long swath of silver moonlight across her bosom. The night wind blew stronger here, and I clutched my thin silk mesh shawl more closely around my shoulders.

Cushing glanced at me then. "Too cold?" he said. "We can turn back."

"No. I am all right, for now at least. Go on."

He slowed the horses and we rocked along at a gentle pace, savoring the night, the star-strewn sky, the sense of being alone in the universe. A night for lovers, I thought.

"Would you speak to her?" he said abruptly. His voice was tight, a bit hoarse. "Would you—would you explain to her that I am sincere, I am not trifling with her, I am not amusing myself?"

"What does she say?" I was stalling for time, I hardly knew how to answer him.

"She says no."

"Just that—no?"

"Everything else she says comes to the same thing. I have begged and pleaded with her but she will not listen."

I did not need to ask him what his plea had been, for she had told me. "He wants me to go away with him," she had said. It had been only a week since their meeting in the garden. He had seen her every day since, including this day. I had taken tea with her at five o'clock and she had told me of his latest proposal. "He wants to go abroad again," she said. "He has lived most of his life in Europe, and now he wants me to go there with him." And not for the first time, I thought, remembering Cushing's abrupt appearance some years past. She had been willing to go then—would have done but for her children's illness, and would have thrown over her husband, her children, her entire life. But Mason's and Mary's illness had prevented her, and now, it seemed, she could not make the break.

But of course she had changed: had had the operation which was to have calmed her willfulness, her driving ambition. Avery had wanted her quieted, not so headstrong. Did Cushing know of that? I wondered. I felt that it was not my place to tell him.

"Perhaps it has to do with Charlotte," I said. "Perhaps if you gave her some time—she has the wedding to plan for, she will need to be here for Charlotte's sake."

"I understand about the wedding. I told her that I would wait. We could leave in September, October even—I do not insist that she go at once. But she will not listen."

I heard the anger in his voice, a desperate kind of anger, I thought, for he was a man accustomed to having his own way and he did not take rejection lightly. It was amazing, I thought, that he was here at all. After all the years he still loved her—or wanted her, at any rate, which was perhaps not the same thing. He could have had his pick of women, either here or abroad; but he had come one last time for Isabel, and now she would not have him. The mysteries of the human heart are surely that, I thought: beyond our comprehension.

Suddenly he pulled the horses to a stop and, putting a hand on my arm, turned to face me. In the bright light of the moon I could see his face plain: I saw suffering there, and anger, and utter bafflement.

"Help me," he said. "You are her closest friend—and more than that, you are a good woman, you have a kind heart. You helped me once before. Now do so again. Speak to her and try to make her understand!" His brilliant eyes seemed to shine even more brightly with what I thought must be tears.

Despite my misgivings my heart was touched; and so I agreed, with some trepidation, to do as he asked.

I had little chance in the next few days, however, because Isabel was embroiled in last-minute preparations for Charlotte's engagement party and had no time for anyone save Charlotte and the servants. Charlotte herself was calm: quietly happy, I thought, but certainly not worked up into that ecstatic state of dreamy bliss which so many girls assumed as their wedding day approached. But then, at twenty-six, Charlotte was hardly a girl.

She had invited several of her old schoolmates to stay for a few days before the party and, on the day before, Isabel gave a luncheon for them. They were a pleasant enough group and got on very well with the rest of us, the older generation, Isabel's friends whom she had invited to fill out the table. We had cold turtle soup, I remember, and chicken in aspic.

Charlotte was very happy. She laughed and joked in a way that I had never heard her do, and more than once I saw Isabel watching her. This makes up for Victoria's betrayal, I thought—for that is what it was. But now Isabel must feel that she has not failed completely, one daughter at least will be properly married. She gave no hint of the strain of the past two weeks, Cushing's pleas to her, her own anguish, which surely, I thought, she must have felt.

After lunch we wandered out onto the terrace, but the weather had turned, the morning's sun had vanished behind a thick cover of clouds and the wind blew cold and raw off the sea. Shortly a few drops of rain began to fall, and so the ladies took their leave and Charlotte gathered up her friends to gossip and sing in the music room. Isabel turned to me. "Come upstairs," she said. "I must get my stays off before I break in two."

And so I went with her to her boudoir, wondering as I did so whether she knew that I had a message for her and wanted to give me an opportunity to present it. Her room overlooked the sea. When we went in we found the french doors, which gave onto a little balcony, standing wide open and the damp air and the rain blowing in. She hurried to shut them and stood for a moment looking out, shivering; then, without turning, she said, "Would you mind unhooking my bodice, Marian? I don't want to bother ringing for Elsie."

I struggled with the tiny hooks that ran up the back of her pale blue organza bodice, and then I helped her out of the dress and began to loosen the long ties of the whalebone corset. She stepped free; wearing only her chemise and her underpetticoat, she went to the closet and took out a turquoise silk kimono. Over this she threw a mohair shawl and, sighing in relief, threw herself onto a brocade chaise longue. "Come and sit beside me," she said. "Tell me how you liked the luncheon. This new cook came very highly recommended."

"I have never had a bad meal from any of your cooks," I said, "and this one is as good as the rest."

She smiled at me. "And Charlotte seems very happy, does she not?"

"Very happy. Why shouldn't she? He is a fine young man by all accounts."

Her smile faded. "Yes. By all accounts. And very rich, too."

"Well then. What more could she—what more could anyone want?"

She did not answer me at once. She put her hand over her eyes as if to shield them from some vision; then, after a moment, her eyes still covered, she said, "Life."

"Life? But she will have everything. What more—"

"Life!" Suddenly she took her hand away. She stared at me with the eyes that I remembered so well, the eyes of her youth, before her illness, before whatever it was that they had done to her at Dr. Parkin's. She had thrown off that terrible dullness, the apathy, the sense of being somehow drugged that I had seen in recent months, and now she was my Isabel again.

"I want her to have that, Marian—to have life, to *be* alive, to *feel!* I want her to feel what I have felt, to know real love, true love, not just this tame affection that I see. I want her to know what it means really to love a man, to feel passion—yes!"

She spoke in a low voice, rapidly, leaning up from the chaise and stretching out her hand to mine. We clung to each other for a moment; I looked deep into her eyes as if they could tell me how much I might say in reply.

"To suffer?" I said at last. "Would you have her suffer, too, as you have done?"

She understood my meaning. She held my gaze for a moment longer and then she looked away. I heard the spatter of rain against the glass and, down the bay, the foghorn and its melancholy song.

"He took you driving last week," she said. "No—do not try to explain. It does not matter. I have no claim on either of you; certainly not on him."

"He wants to give you a claim. He asked me to tell you—"

She shook her head as if to clear it. Her skin, still perfect, still flawless, took on a faint flush; her eyes darted around the rich appointments of the room as if somewhere there she would find the words she needed. I waited. Suddenly she burst out:

"What do they know of love?" she said. "Charlotte and her friends—do they know what love is? Do they? Do *you?* Ah, yes—" For she saw that she had touched a nerve in me still raw after all the years. "You know. As I do. You know love, you know our need for it, the truth of it, the terrible pressing pain of loving someone always whom you cannot have, the agony of living life without him, forever repressing and denying that desire. You know how it drives everything else away, how it maddens you, how you think you cannot live, you *cannot* live without him—and yet you do, *you* do, *I* do, we live from day to day with that awful need, we know that we will never, *never*—"

Tears streamed down her face. Her eyes were wide and staring, not at me—at him, perhaps, at Cushing. I longed to take her in my arms and comfort her, to soothe her as one soothes a mourning child, to hold her close and protect her, if I could, from any further pain. How did she live—how do any of us live with that desire always unfulfilled?

She will break again, I thought, she will go mad once more—if indeed she was ever mad—and this time, perhaps, she will not recover.

Damn Cushing! Why could he not leave her alone, why did he need to come back to torment her once again?

"I know what he asked you to tell me," she said. Her voice was quiet again, she was in control. "He had no right, of course—no right to put such a burden on you. But that is the way he is. He makes his demands, he does not care."

"He wants you—"

"Ah, yes. He wants me." I heard the sardonic undertone; her good, quick mind, I thought, was reasserting itself, it would save her after all from the treachery of her emotions. "And I have wanted him all these years. I have wanted him, I have never stopped wanting him, I have lived my life here and yet I have not lived it at all, for I have been with him always, wherever he was. And there has not been a day, not one day, when I have not wished myself away from this life of mine, when I have not wished myself with him."

"And I am to tell him that?"

"You are to tell him—no."

"Just that? Just one word?"

She nodded but she could not look at me for fear that I would guess that she was lying.

"Just that," she whispered. "Just—no."

Fourteen

Cushing did not take my news well, but I hardly expected that he would. Our first chance to meet was at Charlotte's engagement party the following night. He saw me at once across the crowd and he made his way to my side directly, hardly bothering to respond to those who spoke to him on his way. I had seen him bending over Isabel's hand as she and Charlotte greeted their guests by the door, but he had done no more than say a word to her.

He took two glasses of champagne from a tray carried by a passing waiter and, handing one to me, steered me out onto the terrace. It was a raw, chilly night; the bad weather which had come in the previous day had stayed, and Isabel's plans for fireworks on the lawn had had to be abandoned at the last minute.

"Well?" he said, not bothering with the usual amenities. I gathered up my courage; I am not a timid woman, but this man had a ruthless, intimidating way that threatened to overpower even someone who was not taken, as I was not, by his particular kind of attractiveness.

Japanese lanterns had been strung outdoors despite the weather, and so he could see the expression on my face before I spoke. His own expression, accordingly, began to harden into anger before I said a word.

"She is so very busy and distracted—" I began; but then I stopped, casting about for a better way. There was none, of course: he wanted to hear only one thing, and if he could not hear that, nothing else would suffice.

"She cannot," I said.

"You mean she will not."

"She wants—"

"*She* wants!" He drank his champagne down in a gulp and threw the glass into the shrubbery—a theatrically violent gesture, I thought, which he did not need to perform for my sake. Perhaps for his own? "She has always had what she wants! Always! A respectable marriage, a respectable husband, respectable children—"

Victoria, I thought; but I did not interrupt, I lacked the will.

He went on. "She has had money—"

"Not so much as one might think," I said, unable to resist interrupting him then.

"Enough, at any rate, to have this—" He cast a glance at the house. "Enough to maintain her position, her precious position in this precious, stuffy little world. She has climbed to the top of this festering heap, and do not tell me she did not want that!"

For a moment I thought to tell him of Isabel's agony that I had witnessed the day before, but I kept silent. He would not believe me, I thought; it would do no good, it would only make him angrier.

We stood silent for a moment, looking out to the dark sea, the noise and gaiety of the party going on behind us, without us. At last he turned to me and smiled. His face was still angry, but he seemed to have calmed somewhat.

"Very well," he said. "You have done what I asked of you, and I can ask no more. I am in your debt."

Abruptly he left me. I did not mind his rudeness. I understood that he feared that if he stayed he might betray some further feeling; and that, for him, would have been unbearable. I watched him through the tall glass doors. He made his way slowly through the crowd this time, stopping to speak to gentlemen, bowing over ladies' hands.

The dancing had begun. Couples stepped out onto the floor and surrendered themselves to the seductive strains of the waltz. Standing alone on the terrace, I looked in on them as if I had only just arrived from some distant place where dancing was unknown: the crowded ballroom filled with light and music and laughter, the young women in their flowing gowns, their hair piled in pompadours, their heads balanced on their long slim necks, their lovely faces glowing with life and the beginnings—the anticipations—of love. Guided by their partners, they whirled around the floor to the rhythm of the dance which mimed that deeper, more urgent rhythm of bodies caught in passion's ebb and flow—an ancient, primeval call which none of us can ignore.

The night air was cold, and so at last I went in. I saw Charlotte dancing with a young man whose name I did not know. Because this party was in her honor and because the gentlemen at Newport were thoroughly schooled in etiquette, this would be perhaps the only night in Charlotte's social career that she had a full dance card, I thought; now that she was safely spoken for, they would not mind dancing with her. I took my station with the other matrons who sat in gilt chairs along the wall and looked for Isabel. She was making her way around the room, speaking to each guest, smiling, chatting easily. She had had a letter from Arthur that day assuring her that he was well—a much-needed bit of good news in the midst of all the past weeks' strain. Avery had not yet appeared, but that was nothing so unusual at Newport, where husbands often deserted their wives for weeks at a time. Newport was a woman's town, the place where women wielded their power and made their careers as the men did in the boardrooms of Boston and New York.

Exchanging pleasantries with my neighbor, I caught sight of Lawrence Cushing and for a moment I forgot what I had intended to say. He stood talking to a young woman whom I had never seen before. She wore a pale pink gown which revealed half her bosom and she wore camellias in her pale blond hair; her manner was slow and languid, unlike the lively air of New England girls, and even from a distance I could see that she was not one of us, she was an outlander. Southern girls occasionally made a foray to the watering places of the North, to Saratoga Springs and Newport and Bar Harbor; they came, said Northern mamas, in search of the rich husbands who could no longer be found in the South. The Confederacy had never recovered from its defeat thirty years ago; the money was in the North and West, and so the Southern belles followed it as hounds follow the scent. This girl, I was sure, was one of them. And even though I could not hear a word they said, it seemed that she and Cushing had found something very interesting indeed to talk about.

Someone else came up to speak to me then, and so I lost sight of them; but from time to time during the evening my eyes sought them out again. The young woman danced occasionally with someone else, but for the most part she was in Cushing's arms, and even her dancing set her apart. She seemed almost to swoon, so that her partner needed to hold her more securely, more protectively, than New England girls were held. When she danced with Cushing—which was most of the evening—the prescribed six inches of distance between partners vanished to nothing; they went as one around the floor, as oblivious to their surroundings as if they were alone. So much for his devotion to Isabel, I thought; even if this is only a performance for her benefit he is playing his part superbly. I could not tell if Isabel noticed his behavior, although most certainly she saw him take the newcomer in to supper.

By the end of the following week, however, all Newport was abuzz with rumor and gossip about Lawrence Cushing and Julia Jeffries, and there was no longer any question of whether Isabel knew about the affair.

"It is disgusting!" she said, her eyes bright with indignation. We had snatched a quiet half hour alone on her gallery late one afternoon. She had not yet changed from the white organdy dress that she had worn to go to

559

the Casino to watch the tennis, and she looked nearly as young and fresh as one of that season's debutantes. "They were there together today. They hardly spoke to anyone else. When Charlie Musgrove went over to say hello Lawrence practically ordered him away. And the way that girl dresses! Daytime décolletage may be the fashion in Richmond, but it certainly is not in Newport!"

Julia Jeffries was, indeed, a Southerner, a houseguest of the Randall Jepsons, Southerners themselves originally but for the past twenty years residents of the North. She had come to Charlotte's ball as a courtesy, since houseguests were always welcome to the events their hostess attended.

Charlotte joined us just then and, overhearing Isabel's last words, she said: "Miss Jeffries has made a conquest, so it seems."

I should have interrupted then; I should have forced the conversation into a different path. But I was too slow; I missed my chance.

"What do you mean, a conquest?" said Isabel.

"Just that." Charlotte dropped a kiss on her mother's cheek and deposited herself on a wicker and bamboo chair opposite us. Her plain face was placid and smiling; she had no idea, I was sure, of the damage she was about to inflict. "A conquest," she repeated. She plucked a grape from a bowl of fruit on a low table and, to tease her mother, took her time chewing and swallowing it before she continued. "It seems," she said at last, "that Mr. Cushing, as unlikely as it may be, is courting Miss Jeffries and that, despite the difference in their ages, they are rumored already to be secretly engaged."

Isabel sat very still; she did not move a muscle, her face was a pleasant, slightly smiling mask. After a moment she managed a short laugh. "If Miss Jeffries is hunting a fortune," she said, "she will not find it with him."

"Perhaps she is simply infatuated," said Charlotte. "He seems a very charming man."

"And nearly thirty years her senior," retorted Isabel.

"Really? He looks much younger." Charlotte took another grape. She does not know, I thought. She has no way of knowing. Silently I begged her to be quiet, or at least to talk of something else. I tried to catch her eye but she did not look at me. "In any case," she said, "it is no affair of ours."

"Of course not," said Isabel. Her pleasant mask remained. She was, I thought, a miracle of self-control— for I could not believe that she would accept Charlotte's news with such equanimity. Surely, I thought, she must be raging inside.

Before many more days had passed I saw that I was right. The Cushing-Jeffries liaison was one of the warmest topics of gossip in Newport that summer; people said that he had swept her off her feet, they said that they had never seen an affair proceed so swiftly, so single-mindedly.

And then, before long, they said that the thing had soured and that she had not ensnared him after all. He had suddenly cooled. Word had gone round—from where, no one knew—that Miss Jeffries had a "rep," a clouded past which had ensured that no young man in Richmond would have her. In desperation her mama had sent her North, but bad news travels fast, and suddenly Miss Jeffries was not the prize that she had seemed a few weeks earlier. Shortly Cushing dropped her cold.

Isabel burst into my room one night upon her return from an evening at Sea Crest, the newest (and, some said, the most extravagant) of the summer "cottages": fifty rooms, at least, and marble everywhere, and gilt, and crystal and mirrors and priceless paintings, a ceiling from a Florentine palace, a mural by Singer Sargent himself.

"Have you heard the news?" she said. "I'm sorry—were you asleep?"

I was in fact in bed, having nodded off over my book, one of the silly romances which I devoured like bonbons.

"I saw your light," she went on, taking the chair beside my bed, "and so I thought I'd chance it. I couldn't wait to tell you. She's gone—decamped! Vanquished!"

I had come fully awake by then, and I did not need to ask of whom she spoke. However, I did need some reply to her excitement. "Why?" I said.

"Why—because I caught her out, that's why! There are advantages, after all, to living to a certain age, and one of them is that you get to know a great variety of people. I have acquaintances everywhere. Even in California, or in England, or—"

"Richmond," I said.

"Yes. Even in Richmond."

"Who?"

"It doesn't matter. The daughter of an old friend of Mother's who married South. Much to her family's distress. I've never even laid eyes on her, but she knew who I was right away when I wrote."

"You wrote—and asked—"

"Yes!" she said triumphantly. "Ask and ye shall receive, Marian! I have her letter locked in my desk. I'll show it to you if you like. She told me everything—everything! More than enough to discourage anyone from courting that minx. Oh! It is disgusting how some women try to pull the wool over men's eyes!"

I smothered a smile at the thought of anyone pulling anything whatsoever over Lawrence Cushing's eyes, but I said nothing. For the moment, at least, he was for Isabel the injured party, the party who needed protection.

She sat silent for a moment, just beyond the circle of light thrown by my little reading lamp, and so I could not see her face distinctly; I saw that she had her hands clasped in her lavender silk lap but I could not see her expression, I could not see the moment when her face changed from elation to despair. I was startled when her voice came suddenly harsh.

"Why should he be happy when I have not been?" she said. She did not want an answer; she hurried on before I could reply. "I have struggled—you know how I have struggled! I have worked myself half to death to make a place for my children while he has been free to come and go as he pleases, living his easy life—"

I did not even try to argue with her. In a way I agreed with her. She had indeed had a difficult life compared to many women in her circle: her own ambition had made her difficulty.

Because Newport was awash in gossip it was not long before Cushing had discovered the source of the rumor that had dethroned Miss Jeffries. He appeared one day as

Charlotte and I were lunching at the Casino; he was resplendent in his white flannels, his hair glowing, his eyes taking us in in his rapacious way.

I was slightly embarrassed, remembering the unhappy man who had left me on the terrace at Charlotte's party, but he behaved as if no unhappiness had ever visited him; he seemed not to have a care in the world. He promptly accepted my invitation to join us for coffee, and afterward he strolled with us to watch the players thwacking about on the velvety grass courts.

It is one of life's ironies that a girl like Charlotte, who had never been particularly popular all during the years between her debut and her engagement, should now, just when she had been taken off the market, as it were, suddenly become one of the most sought-after young women of the season. Proving, I suppose, that women hardly exist in their own right: they need a man's identity, and a fiancé will do as well as a husband. Charlotte, this summer, safely secure as Ellsworth Barnes's intended, was enjoying a season of popularity such as she had never had. A trio of young women beckoned to her now, and with a smiling "Adieu" she went to join them. Of course I did not mind; I was happy to see her enjoy herself for this little time. Marriage was a gamble, even when the prospective husband was a "brick" like Ellsworth Barnes; if worst came to worst, she might never be happy again.

Cushing followed her with his eyes. "She does not resemble her mother," he said.

"No. More's the pity."

"I don't know." I heard the suppressed laughter in his

voice. "Avery Kittredge has a certain monumental, imposing quality which Miss Charlotte seems to have inherited. Perhaps that is better than mere ordinary feminine beauty." A half smile played at his mouth. It occurred to me that he privately laughed at us all. Perhaps in that way he mastered the very real pain which, briefly, he had allowed me to see.

He took my arm and walked me away from the courts. I was conscious of people's glances—not at me, certainly, but at him. He would have been stared at anywhere, I thought: at the court of the Czar, at Versailles had he lived in the time of the Sun King. We walked out to Bellevue Avenue and began to stroll. Soon we passed the Gothic Kingscote, a quaint little gingerbread affair, and then we had the broad sidewalk to ourselves. I said nothing, waiting for him to speak. Soon enough he did.

"Will you tell me now that she does not care?" he said. His smile, his hidden laughter, had vanished; his voice was hard, peremptory.

"I can tell you nothing." I did not look at him. I watched the tips of my green morocco shoes as they peeped from beneath my full ecru skirts, right and left, right and left.

"You know what she did to Miss Jeffries," he said.

I kept silent, refusing to be enticed into criticizing Isabel.

"I might have been very happy with that young woman," he went on. "Isabel had no right to interfere."

Still I said nothing. I did not look at him. After a moment I was startled to hear his short, harsh laugh. "I cannot get free of her," he said. "Even when I resolve to

565

give her up forever I cannot. She will not have me, but she will not let me go. Tell me—" He stopped suddenly. "Where did she get her information?"

At last I relented. "From Richmond."

"I thought so."

We began to walk again. We were alone; a parade of carriages passed up and down the avenue, filled with ladies and the occasional gentleman, some of them staring at us, the eccentrics who walked.

"She was right, you know. About Miss Jeffries, I mean. I would have found out sooner or later, but I suppose you would say that I should be grateful to Isabel for saving my time."

But again I made no reply; I was an unwilling confidante, I could not understand why he insisted on telling me things that I did not want to hear. Suddenly I heard my name and I looked up: an open chaise was clattering by, carrying Charlotte and three of her acquaintances. They laughed and waved to us, and then they were gone, all heads turned, staring at Cushing and me. They vanished in the sea of traffic.

Cushing stared after them but he said nothing. His expression was curious, cunning almost, but he did not comment again, as I was afraid he might, on Charlotte's plainness. How unfair men were to damn women for their lack of looks, when the homeliest man in the world, had he sufficient fortune or family name, could have his pick of women!

But he said nothing. Looking back, I am struck all over again by the cruel whimsy of fate, or luck, or chance— whatever name you choose to call it. Had Charlotte been ten minutes later we would not have seen her; and had we not seen her . . .

Well. My story would have been different indeed.

He left me at Isabel's gate. I did not mind; I hardly wanted him to accompany me to the door, where perhaps he might encounter her. I watched him as he walked rapidly down the long stretch to the next entrance which, for the summer, was his. The two cottages were neighbors, but because of the extensive grounds, the small patch of woods between them, the high shrubbery, they might have been a mile apart for all the occupants saw of each other.

He had, I thought, a markedly purposeful stride for a man who had just been once again set adrift.

Fifteen

"My dear Marian," said Mrs. Sprague. "You are exactly the person I wanted to see." She lowered her lorgnette, peered at me from her small, avaricious eyes, and then raised it again to look around the room. We were at a ball at Eaglesmere, given in honor of some visiting nobility, but as was the custom for ladies of a certain age, we clustered on the sidelines except for an occasional whirl. "There," she said. "Look there. At Charlotte Kittredge."

I glanced out onto the dance floor. I knew perfectly well why Mrs. Sprague had told me to look. Charlotte was dancing—again—with Lawrence Cushing. I smiled at Mrs. Sprague in a deprecatory way.

"Where is Isabel?" demanded Mrs. Sprague. "I cannot believe that she would allow her own daughter to be so compromised. Three people have spoken to me in the last hour, wondering what on earth is going on."

"Isabel could not come tonight," I said. "She felt unwell—"

"I don't blame her," snorted Mrs. Sprague. "If my daughter carried on like that I'd take to my bed for a month. Whatever can Charlotte be thinking of? I know that her fiancé is from the West, unaccustomed to our ways perhaps, but a man would have to be blind not to see what is happening here."

"Mrs. Sprague, I don't think—"

"Of course you will defend them, but if you don't believe me, have a look at this," she said. She dropped her lorgnette so that it dangled from its silken cord onto her broad, spangled bosom and opened her small black and gold beaded bag. From it she extracted a newspaper clipping which she held gingerly between two fingers as if it were red hot—as, indeed, it was.

"From *Town Topics* yesterday," she said triumphantly.

I seldom looked at *Town Topics*, Colonel Mann's scandal sheet, a compendium of innuendo, half-truths, and outright lies that made William Randolph Hearst's publications look like Sunday school tracts. But under the challenge of Mrs. Sprague's glare I took the clipping, a column of chitchat labeled, "Of Note," and read the portion underlined.

We hear that a prospector from the West who made a *large* strike in Boston last winter may lose it to the attentions of a more experienced hand. This unpleasant experience will stand as a warning to all Western men that our Eastern belles, large and small alike, have notoriously cold, capricious hearts.

I handed it back to Mrs. Sprague. "Typical," I said evenly. I willed my expression to be calm and pleasant.

"Probably not true—almost certainly not true—but typical." I stood up; I took my leave of her and made my way around the crowded periphery of the room. I could feel her eyes watching me, and so I refused to give her the satisfaction of looking at Charlotte again.

Charlotte—and Cushing: they were that week's item, and what Mrs. Sprague had said could not be denied. He had taken her up, despite the fact that she was to be married in less than a month's time to Ellsworth Barnes. Had taken her up—had been allowed to take her up. I could not understand it. Why did she not refuse him? Why did Isabel not see what was happening? Why did Ellsworth Barnes not fight for the woman he loved—if, indeed, he still did love her after the gossip of the past days?

Safely out of Mrs. Sprague's sight, I looked again to find Charlotte. I did not see her at once, although I found Ellsworth Barnes readily enough. He was the tallest man on the dance floor, and he danced the most atrociously, rough and awkward, lumbering, putting great effort into it, getting very little result. But the girl in his arms was not Charlotte. I looked again: there was a large crowd, I might have missed her. No: she was not there. Nor was Cushing. I felt suddenly unwell, anxious and just at the edge of fear. The music throbbed through my head; the room was hot and bright.

Why did I need to concern myself? I thought. Charlotte is not my daughter, I do not need to care what happens to her. But even as the thought came to my mind I pushed it away. I needed to concern myself because the lives—the fate—of these people, Isabel and her family, had been intertwined with mine for nearly thirty years. I could no more have abandoned them than I could have abandoned Diana. It was not a matter of choice: I was with them until death, their trouble was my trouble, their happiness (and little enough of that there had been) was mine as well.

I found myself standing near the entrance of the ballroom, and on impulse I stepped out into the vaulted reception hall off which branched the family's living quarters. I had been in this house several times before, and so I was more or less familiar with its arrangements. I knew, for instance, that beyond the deserted drawing room lay the conservatory, whose harvest, this night, filled the house with heavy fragrance. I stood, hesitant; then I heard the imp of fate whisper in my ear: "Go there!" I waited for a moment more and then I obeyed. I walked the length of the empty room; I came to the open doorway of the conservatory. No light shone there; the air was heavy with the odors of plants and moist soil and the few flowers that were left. I heard nothing; only the sounds of music and voices drifting from the ballroom.

But that dark, damp place was not deserted, and, indeed, I had somehow known that it would not be. Someone was there—two people, in fact, although as my eyes adjusted to the gloom they seemed at first only one. They stood in a close embrace and they stayed so after I appeared, for they did not see me.

Then they did, and I heard a startled "Oh!" from Charlotte as she sprang apart from him. They both peered out at me from the gloom of their hideaway; to them, I was silhouetted against the light and so perhaps at first they did not know me. I could not muster up even a single syllable; I felt as though I looked upon the ruin of Isabel's hopes and nothing that I could say could make them right again. Perhaps five seconds passed. I had no idea what to do—nor, apparently, did they.

The imp of fate came to rescue me, then, from the trouble he had made, and at his command, without a word, I turned and fled through the drawing room, back to the noise and light of the evening's festivities.

And not a moment too soon: as I turned to reenter the ballroom I saw Mrs. Sprague just coming out. If she had seen that little *tableau vivant*, I thought, Charlotte would have the same value in Newport as Julia Jeffries—less, for Julia Jeffries was an outlander, and people were often not surprised when outlanders stumbled and fell; New Englanders were supposed to have surer footing.

I had feared lying awake that night until dawn and passing the next day groggy and out of sorts, but I fell asleep with surprising speed. In the dawn I arose and walked out into the garden. The dew was still heavy on the grass and the birds still sang their chorus to the sun. This was a peaceful time in Newport, where dawn was often the end of an evening rather than the beginning of a new day; I knew that I would have the seaside garden to myself.

The roses were just past their best bloom, but there was still a profusion of them, pink and yellow and the purest white. Covered with droplets, they sparkled in the first sun: the delphiniums stood like sentinels to one side, fronted by a patch of yellow lilies and purple Japanese iris. Small grassy paths led between the beds down to a low box hedge which was flanked by curved stone benches. A gazebo lay beyond, and then the stone wall above the Cliff Walk. The sea lay pale and flat beneath a sky that grew deeper blue with every moment. A hot day, I thought; a hot fine day for whatever entertainment Newport has in mind. I looked back to the house, Isabel's Italian palazzo clinging to the rocky New England shore. The red tile roof glowed in the early sun; the house stood silhouetted against the sky as if it were indeed in Italy, along the Amalfi shore, perhaps.

Alone in that garden by the sea, alone in that bright warm dawn, I wrestled with my conscience and my conscience lost. Should I tell Isabel what I had seen? Should I rob her of her chance to see her daughter safely married? Should I disturb her possibly fragile mental state to inform her of a momentary slip of Charlotte's— for I was sure that it was that, it could not have been anything more.

Round and round went my thoughts on their treadmill of worry, and higher and higher climbed the sun. I felt like a fly trapped in a spider's web. No matter which way I turned I only bound myself more tightly: anger and guilt played equal roles in my silent dialogue. As I struggled with it, first one way and then the other, full day came and I felt the sun beating hot on my exposed hair and neck and arms. Time to go in: to awaken Diana, have breakfast with her, plan our day.

I heard a shout just then, and the clatter of a carriage. Bellevue Avenue was not too far distant, it did not come from there; it came from the direction of the Cliff Walk and the narrow strip of beach below, exposed now at low tide. Swiftly I went to the stone wall and looked down. I could hardly believe what I saw: a two-seater pulled by a fine chestnut mare careening along the shore. Seated on its high bench were two people, a man and a woman: Charlotte and Cushing. No, I thought, I am mistaken, it cannot be. I stared and stared. He had his arm tightly around her to prevent her falling, while with his free hand he held the reins and gave the horse its head. They were laughing—she shrieked with laughter, or perhaps it was fear. She clung to him as if she would never let go, as if her life depended on him—as, indeed, at that moment it did.

They whirled past me. In a moment they were gone, vanished around a great curving outcropping of rock. I leaned against the rough stone wall, staring at the point at which they had disappeared. I had seen them for a few seconds only: perhaps I had dreamed it, I thought. I took a fold of my pink linen skirt between my fingers and felt its good firm texture, I smelled the winy air, I looked back along the narrow beach and saw the line of wheel tracks, the heavy indentation of the horse's hooves.

No. I had not dreamed it. What I had seen had been real enough: unbelievable, impossible—but real.

With a heavy heart and a sense that events were running beyond my capacity to absorb them, I turned and walked back to the house.

Diana and I took a picnic to Old Tower Farm that day, for I needed to be away from everyone in Isabel's ménage for a while. I wanted some time alone to wrestle with my increasingly difficult dilemma: should I tell Isabel what I had seen, thereby risking all the dislike—and disbelief—

574

which bearers of bad news traditionally received, or should I keep silent for a while longer, perhaps, just speaking privately to Charlotte to warn he of the danger of her behavior? But what could I tell her that she did not already know? She must understand what she does, I thought, and yet she goes on with it as if she were under a spell, she is bewitched by him—even as her mother once was!—and she cannot help herself.

Caution won: I said nothing to either of them.

We were then in mid-July; Charlotte's wedding was scheduled for the second Wednesday in August. Somehow, I thought, we will get through the days until she is safely married, somehow it will all come right. But I went my accustomed rounds—luncheons, teas, balls, musicales—in a state of apprehension. I was terrified lest Isabel discover what Charlotte was up to, and I was even more terrified that she would discover that I had known of it and had not told her. The item in *Town Topics* had somehow, miraculously, escaped her notice; perhaps, I thought, I was not the only woman in Newport who feared to tell Isabel news that she did not want to hear.

The days passed quickly in a flurry of last-minute preparations. Charlotte's wedding gown was brought for a final fitting, and Isabel, for a wonder, pronounced herself satisfied. "Of course she should wear mine," she said, "but it would be impossible—she is twice my size, at least, and no amount of alteration would make it right. It will simply have to wait for Mary." She did not mention Victoria; Victoria's name never crossed her lips. The kitchen staff was rehearsed on the menu; the groundsmen received their final instructions on the way in which they were to transform the lawns and terraces into a bower of potted orange trees and camellia shrubs. A thousand other details were dealt with; half a dozen crises nipped before they blossomed to disaster. All Newport was to attend, it seemed—"all" being the *crème de la crème,* of course.

Undoubtedly Isabel needed a great deal of money for such a show. I remembered the time, two years ago, when she had come to me for money for Victoria's costume for the Apple of Discord Ball. Where was she getting it now? From Avery? Or had Ellsworth Barnes agreed to share the cost? Naturally I did not ask; one did not ask such things even of so close a friend as Isabel. I seldom saw Avery. He kept clear of his wife's affairs, appearing only rarely, unexpectedly, at lunch or dinner and then disappearing again. He looked peaked, I thought; his fleshy face was unhealthily pale, and his movements, always deliberate, had slowed to the pace of an old man. Once, when he was walking across the foyer, I saw him stumble and catch himself. He seemed remote; he almost never spoke, and when he did his voice was dull, devoid of life.

Nor, to my relief, did I see much of Charlotte during this time. I was hardly able to speak to her when I did. Once, sitting on the gallery, I felt her stare and I looked up to meet it, but her face was a blank. Several other people were with us and so, of course, it was not possible to speak to her other than about the most trivial thing, and in any case I had no idea of what I would have said. What would she have said to me?

The wedding day drew near, and I began to feel some

sense of relief. On the few occasions that I saw Charlotte and Ellsworth Barnes together they seemed happy enough, and Cushing, it was said, had gone for a week's cruise with the Arthur Lambs. Perhaps it would be all right after all, I thought; perhaps we would escape the disaster which hovered over our heads, threatening to descend on us at any moment.

But I was wrong.

Cushing returned to Newport, to his rented cottage next to Isabel's, just five days before Charlotte's wedding. That night Mrs. Hetherington gave a champagne *fête*. Isabel had been invited, and Charlotte and Ellsworth; I had not. Diana and I took supper with Mary and Mason, therefore, and Diana went to bed around eight. Isabel left shortly thereafter with Charlotte. Before I retired I took a brief walk about the garden, watching the moon rise over the water. Later, nodding over a new novel, I heard a carriage in the drive. My room was at the front of the house, and so I slipped out of bed and went to the tall windows and peered through a crack in the draperies.

I could see nothing, for the carriage had stopped under the porte cochere; nor did I hear any voices. After a moment the carriage pulled away and disappeared down the drive and through the massive gates onto Bellevue Avenue. It was Isabel's, I thought; why had she returned early? Had something happened—the disaster, perhaps, that I had feared so long? She will come directly to me, I thought, and I must strengthen myself to hear her. I did not return to bed but sat in a high-backed chair before the fire, which, as an extravagance, I was allowed to have as often as I liked. I waited. She did not come. Perhaps, I thought, she is ill; perhaps I should go to her. Pulling my soft woolen dressing gown more tightly around me, I opened the door to my room and waited for a moment, listening. The house was dark and silent, the children asleep upstairs, a few servants waiting in the kitchen, perhaps, to lock up for the night, the others in their tiny rooms on the top floor. Light shone from below and let me see as I went quickly around the gallery to Isabel's room. I knocked; having no answer, I knocked again more loudly.

"Isabel? Isabel, are you there?"

Silence. The door was thick and heavy like all the doors in the house, carved in imitation of Renaissance style, but even so she would have heard me had she been there, for my knocking in that quiet house sounded like a thunderclap of doom. There was no answer.

So it had not been Isabel who returned but Charlotte. And Charlotte was the last person on earth I wanted to see. I returned to my room and rang the kitchen bell. After a time a parlormaid appeared.

"Yes, ma'am?"

"Who came in just now?"

"Miss Charlotte, ma'am."

"Why? What is wrong?"

"I don't know, ma'am. She didn't say."

"Did she send for Reena?" Reena was Charlotte's maid.

"No, ma'am. She told her when she went out earlier she wouldn't need her again tonight."

"But she didn't ask you, either, to help her with

her dress?"

"No, ma'am."

The girl was young, new that summer, I thought, and she was growing uneasy under my cross-examination. I heard the sharp edge to my voice; it was caused by fear, but she could not know that.

"Very well," I said at last, and sent her away.

I looked at the little clock on the mantel; it was just past eleven. Ordinarily Isabel would not be home for hours, but this was not an ordinary night. If Charlotte had left the party because she was ill, why had Isabel not come with her? And if she was not ill, why had she left early? Had there been some incident—an encounter with Cushing, perhaps? Had Charlotte committed some further folly and been banished in disgrace? Would the scandal which I had so dreaded come upon us now at last?

I was too restless to sit, much less to read. I walked back and forth across the flowered carpet, going to the windows to look out, returning to my pacing, going to the windows again. The fire burned low but I did not replenish it; the little clock ticked inexorably, rapidly, and yet the minutes dragged, the hands seemed hardly to move.

At last, near midnight, I heard the carriage once again. As before, I could not see who came, but this time I heard Isabel's voice bidding the coachman good night.

I waited. She will go to Charlotte first, I thought, and then she will come to me.

Five minutes passed; ten. I heard her knock; swiftly I went to admit her.

She said not a word but brushed past me and into the

room. In an instant she knew that she had been mistaken.

"Where is she?" she demanded.

"I thought—she is not in her room?"

"No. I came home as quickly as I could, it was a dreadful party, I could not get away before, they kept on introducing me to people—ah, I *knew* that Ellsworth should have come with her. I told him so, but she would not have it, it would not be proper, she said. People would talk. People would— Oh, *Marian.*" Her face was suddenly stupid with fear. She stood in her evening finery—a gauzy gray-blue gown picked out in seed pearls, an egret's feather and diamond headdress, diamond and pearl necklace and earrings, a fine gray mohair shawl. "Where is she? Did you hear her come in?"

"Yes. About an hour ago."

She looked desolate—devastated. "Then where—?"

"Would she have gone upstairs to the children's rooms for any reason? Or perhaps—perhaps she is in the library. Come—I will go with you to see. She is bound to be here somewhere." Isabel stared at me. I heard my voice: bright, determinedly cheerful, speaking words that we both knew to be lies. But I kept on; I did not know what else to do. "Come," I said. I held out my hand to her as if she were a child. "Come, we will find her."

She did not take my hand, but she did consent to follow me. We went downstairs. The lighted chandelier in the reception hall did not give enough light to see into the rooms, and so as we went we turned up the gas, illuminating the dining room, the ballroom, the library, the billiard room, the drawing room . . . Nothing. She was not there. As we ascended the stairs, back to the second floor, we saw in the foyer below the startled faces of two maids (including the girl whom I had questioned) and a footman. They had emerged from the kitchen and stood now looking up to their mistress as if she had taken leave of her senses. Not yet, I thought, but soon, soon—

We paused halfway up. The footman cleared his throat. "Yes, Robert?" said Isabel.

"Is there anything—can I help, madam?"

"No, Robert. You cannot."

"Can I put out the lights, or does Madam wish them to stay up?"

"Yes, you—no. No. Let them stay. I do not want the house to be dark. Let the lights stay."

"Yes, madam. Is there anything else?"

"No. Nothing. You may all go to bed. Is anyone else up?"

"No, madam."

"Very well. Good night."

"Good night, madam." The three of them chorused in unison, the maids bobbing a little curtsy. They turned and vanished toward the back stairs while their mistress and I continued up the front. My hand trailed the marble balustrade: how cold it was, how cold this house.

At the top of the stairs Isabel turned toward Charlotte's room. She paused; then she knocked and went in. She turned up the light; she stood in the center of the room, looking, peering—I thought for a moment that she would drop to her knees and look under the bed. Then without a glance at me she withdrew, leaving those lights up as well. On she went, to all the guest bedrooms ranged around the corridor. In each she did the same:

lights up, quick inspection; retreat. Soon the house was ablaze with light. She never once called to Charlotte or even uttered her name; her search was conducted silently, with an air of frightening determination all the more frightening for being without sound. When we had done with the second floor, her room and mine included, we went on to the third. At the last moment, however, she checked herself. "I will not disturb the children with the light," she whispered, "but let us just look in." We did so: Mary, Mason, and Diana each had separate rooms and we did no more than glance at them. We knew— Isabel knew—that the search was hopeless, that Charlotte was not in the house.

Then where was she?

She had come in and slipped out again. There was only one possible reason why: to meet him. And Isabel knows, I thought; she cannot help but know.

We descended, Isabel in the lead. When we reached the foyer again she touched my arm. "Come," she said. She led me through the empty, echoing ballroom, glittering with light, to the tall glass doors leading to the terrace. As she reached for the door to unlock it she uttered a sharp little cry and pulled back; then she leaned forward to examine the lock.

"Look!" she said.

The bolt was off, the doors unlocked.

Our eyes met for an instant; there was no question of the meaning of what we saw. Still, like a fool, I tried to reassure her.

"Perhaps Robert overlooked this when he was locking up," I said lamely. "There are so many doors and windows to check—"

"He never overlooks anything. I do not permit it." She visibly pulled herself together, gathering her strength. She twisted her shawl more closely around her shoulders; she seized the handle, turned it, and pulled open the door. I followed her outside. She strode out onto the terrace, to the edge of the flagstone where the lawn began, and turned to look back at the house. Every window in the first two floors was alight. There might have been a glorious entertainment going on. The dark silent night surrounded us, the great silent lighted house confronted us. It seemed an eerie thing, as if perhaps a fancy ball or a costume party were taking place there and all the guests were invisible; ghosts, perhaps, of years gone by. I shivered; I turned my back on the house and gazed out across the dark lawn to the garden which I could not see and to the sea beyond, shining pale, murmuring, filling the night air with its acrid smell.

A movement caught my eye: it was near the wall of shrubbery, ten feet high at least, which divided Isabel's property from the next—the house that Cushing had taken for the summer. It was a shimmer of white which detached itself from the dark bulk of the hedge and moved across the lawn toward us. I saw that it was a woman's figure. It came quickly, but halfway across the lawn it stopped. Isabel saw the direction of my gaze and she followed it.

"Marian—what is that?"

"Someone coming."

She peered, squinting. "My God," she said. "Oh, *Marian*—"

I put my hand under her elbow to steady her, for I thought that she might sink to the ground. We stood together, silhouetted against the house, and waited for Charlotte—for of course it was she—to come to us. She had seen us and stopped, but now she came on again. She was limping. In a moment she was beside us on the terrace and I saw that in her left hand she carried one white shoe.

Isabel stared up at her as if she were one of the ghosts I had imagined. None of us spoke. Charlotte was disheveled, her hair loosely caught up in a knot, the ribbons and bands of lace across the bodice of her dress in disarray. She wore no gloves or shawl. Silence: what, after all, could any of us say? Charlotte's appearance said everything.

At last Isabel turned and with one short word— "Come!"—she led the way back into the house. We followed her. She bolted the french doors behind us and swept through the ballroom with us in tow. When we reached the foyer she stopped. "Will the two of you please wait for me in my room," she said. "I will just ring for Robert to take care of the lights and then I will come up."

Poor Robert! He had, no doubt, only just gone to sleep.

We climbed the broad marble staircase, Charlotte and I, still in silence. She looked troubled, I thought—as well she might—but she said nothing, not a word, and I had no idea what to say to her. When we reached Isabel's room we sat in opposite chairs by the fireplace—empty, unlit, decorated with a large embroidered fan—and stared at our laps, waiting. We knew each other well enough to be silent. I felt like her guard, which indeed I was: Isabel did not want her left alone, I knew, for fear she would escape again. And so we sat and waited, never looking at each other, never speaking, until Isabel appeared.

It seemed an eternity until she came; I suppose it was ten minutes. She shut the door firmly behind her and came to stand between us. Now, I thought, I will go: I did not want to be a party to what I knew must come. I half rose from my chair, but she motioned me back.

"I want you to stay, Marian. I want you to hear what we have to say to each other, Charlotte and I."

"Isabel, I really think—"

"Aunt Marian, please stay." It was the word "please" that won me over, I think, for I did not dislike Charlotte, and I wanted to help her if I could. Had I helped her, in fact, by keeping silent, by not telling Isabel of the gossip that had begun to filter through the summer colony like a dirty fog?

I sat back, feeling very awkward in my woolen wrapper, and waited to hear what Isabel would say. Of course she demanded an explanation at once.

"Surely you know?" said Charlotte.

"I want you to tell me."

"I had—an assignation."

"With—?"

"Mr. Cushing."

Not by the slightest move did Isabel betray her thoughts.

"You left Mrs. Hetherington's for that purpose?"

"Yes."

"You deceived me—you deceived Ellsworth, all of us, by saying that you were not well—?"

"Yes."

"You risked ruining your marriage, you risked ruining all of us, simply to see that—that man?" Her control was beginning to slip; she stood straight and steady, but her hands clenched and unclenched as if she were wringing the life out of something.

"Yes." And now Charlotte, too, had begun to break, I heard the panic in just that one word.

"Have you taken leave of your senses?"

"Yes! Yes! I have taken leave, I have—I have succumbed—"

The word hung in the air: *succumbed . . .*

Isabel was very pale. She stared at Charlotte, her mouth slightly open, unable to form any further question or accusation. Succumbed!

"No."

Charlotte nodded; she closed her eyes. I saw no trace of remorse in her face but rather a kind of weary patience, as if she wanted to say, "Here is the truth, take it and leave me be."

But of course Isabel could not do that: too much was at stake.

"Charlotte. Look at me."

Charlotte obeyed.

"Let me understand you. What do you mean, 'succumbed'?"

"Just that, Mother. Just that."

"You mean he—he seduced you?"

"Yes." It was almost a whisper.

Isabel swayed slightly. I sprang up from my chair and took her arm. "Sit down," I said. "You must sit down. You will faint." She should get her laces off, I thought, she has worn them since early evening and in any case they are far too tight. To my surprise she obeyed me. She sat heavily in the chair, staring at Charlotte, staring as if she were confronted by a stranger who claimed to be her daughter, a stranger who needed to be got rid of quickly lest her activities ruin the entire family. I felt fear rising in my throat, and to quench it I spoke to her.

"Isabel, let me ring for Elsie, she will bring you some tea, or a glass of hot milk—"

She shrugged me off: she waved a hand in the direction of a small cabinet near her canopied bed. "In there," she said. "Brandy."

I fetched it and gave it to her. She sipped it steadily in small quick gulps. Charlotte refused, but after a moment's hesitation I took some for myself. I had no idea how long this night would last and I was beginning to feel weak.

After a moment Isabel seemed to revive and she resumed her interrogation. Her first question surprised me; in its hard, shrewd practicality it reminded me of Mrs. January's response to the news of Victoria's escapade.

"Who knows about this?" she said.

"Who—why, no one."

"As far as you know."

My face must have betrayed me then, for Isabel pounced next on me.

"What, Marian?"

587

"There was an item—in *Town Topics*."

"When?"

"A week or so ago."

"And you did not tell me?"

"I thought—I was afraid—"

"Never mind. Never mind. I would have done the same in your place, I suppose. None of us likes to be the bearer of bad news."

She returned her attention to Charlotte. "So Colonel Mann has had wind of your adventures and he has put them in his paper for all the world to see. Tell me now that no one knows."

But Charlotte did not—could not—speak. She sat with her eyes downcast, her hands clenched together in her lap.

"In five days," Isabel went on, "you will become the wife of Ellsworth Barnes. Oh yes, you will"—for Charlotte had looked up, then, as if to protest—"indeed you will. This is a match far beyond anything that I had dared to hope for, and you will not throw it all away now."

Charlotte shook her head. "No," she whispered.

"Yes. Yes! What do you mean, 'No'? Do you think that simply because that—that man seduced you he is ready now to marry you? And even if he were, do you think that I would permit it? Never. Never! Have you taken leave of your senses?"

Charlotte did not utter a sound. She simply sat and shook her head, over and over again, no, no, *no* . . .

"Stop it!" Isabel heaved herself up from her chair, she crouched before her daughter and took her by the shoulders and began to shake her; and Charlotte, so much bigger, so much stronger, was limp, she was a rag doll, she allowed herself to be whipped back and forth with never a cry of protest, her head lolling on her shoulders, her hair falling down around her face.

"Listen to me!" said Isabel. She held tightly to her daughter, she peered into the sorrowing face not six inches from her own. She spoke in a low, measured voice as if she were speaking to a very young child, perhaps, or an adult who had no sense to be reasoned with. "Listen. You will marry Ellsworth Barnes. You will not see Lawrence Cushing again. First because I forbid it, and second because he will not want to see you. No—believe me! I know him. I knew him before you were born. At the first hint of trouble he disappears. He does not love you. He was only amusing himself. Believe me. *Believe me.*"

Charlotte, eyes still downcast, had begun to cry. Tears streamed down her face, her body shook with sobs. "No," she moaned. "No—"

"Yes! Yes! This is over and done with! Now we are going to put you to bed, and in the morning you will behave as though this night had never been. Come. Get up now."

Still weeping, Charlotte obeyed. We helped her to her room, we helped her out of her dress and her corsets and undershift and put on her nightdress and got her into bed. She never stopped weeping. As we left her in her darkened room the sound of her sorrow was in our ears.

Over my protests Isabel walked me to my room.

"Let me help you with your dress at least," I said. "How will you manage?"

She gave me an oddly defiant look. "I am not ready to retire," she said.

"But then just let me loosen your stays—"

"No. I have an errand to do." Her eyes gleamed in the half-light; I thought I heard a note of bitter mirth in her voice.

"An errand? What do you mean?"

"Just that. A small bit of business that needs tending to."

Suddenly I understood. "You don't mean that you are going to see him?"

"Yes. I must."

"Isabel—not now, not in the middle of the night. Let me come with you in the morning—"

"In the morning he may be gone."

"Why? He has no reason to suspect—"

"He has had his way with her. Now he has no reason to stay longer in Newport. He can go away, he can find someone else to ruin."

"Then let me come with you now. Wait until I dress. I won't lace, I won't be a minute—"

"No. No. This must be a private call, Marian. Mr. Cushing and I have an account to settle. I know very well why he has done this, and I want to confront him once and for all."

"You mean because of Miss Jeffries?"

"That—and other things. You know them as well as I."

I did not, but I let it pass.

She reached up and kissed my cheek. "Good night, dear heart. I will be with you in the morning. And I will give you a full report, never fear.''

She left me then and I went to bed. As I lay there in the dark, sinking down into the luxury of the big feather mattress, soft sheets and coverlets pulled close around me, I thought of her going out into the night to confront the man who had so nearly destroyed her daughter. And, I reminded myself, Isabel too: she had come near enough to throwing over everything for him, for his love. Now she went to him in anger. In my thoughts I followed her: down the drive, through the small side door beside the carriage gates, along the avenue to Cushing's. She had no fear: she was fighting now for her child, nothing could deter her.

As she told me the next morning, he was still awake, dressed in a lounge robe, taking brandy and a cigar in the library. He was hardly surprised at her visit; it was almost as if he had been waiting for her. He ushered her in with a kind of mock gallantry that did nothing to soften her fury.

"What a pleasant surprise," he drawled. "I have never received a visit from such a lady—such a socially prominent lady—at such an hour. From other—ah—ladies, yes, but not Mrs. Avery Kittredge of the Casa del Mare."

But she would not be deflected from her purpose.

"I have spoken to Charlotte," she said.

"Sit down. You look quite tired. The social calendar can sometimes be too full, I think."

Isabel ignored his banter. "She told me what has happened."

"Indeed?" His grin flashed out at her. "Not in too

much detail, I trust."

"I ought to have you horsewhipped."

"That would be very unwise. Think of the scandal."

"If Avery knew—"

"Avery! That poor sod. Every time I see him— infrequently, I admit—I feel more sorry for him. He is working himself to death for you and he hasn't even the pleasure of a wife who stays home at night to comfort him. No—don't tell me. I understand. You have nothing else to do with your life but to make your way in society. I sometimes think that if we let you society women run the country we'd be a damned sight better off. You put more energy and intelligence into one of your social triumphs than Congress gives to the entire year's agenda. Are you sure you won't have some brandy? I won't offer you a cigar. I know that you are a perfect lady—most of the time—"

She hit him then—struck him across the face with all her strength, catching him off guard so that he staggered back, raising his hand to his cheek where she had left her mark.

"Horsewhipped!" she cried. "At the very least. How dare you—how *dare* you ruin my daughter, try to destroy her marriage—"

"I have not destroyed her marriage. On the contrary, Ellsworth Barnes may come to thank me one day for giving his wife an elementary education in—ah—the nuptial bed."

"I *will* have you whipped," she said. "You are beyond belief. You deliberately took her and ruined her. For what? To amuse yourself? To revenge yourself on me?

592

You did not need to do that."

"I do not need to do anything, dear lady. Least of all stay here and listen to your abuse and threats and take your assaults. If you cannot be more polite I will have to ask you to leave."

He turned away from her, then, to fetch his brandy. He lifted the glass to her in a mocking salute before he drank.

"Now," he said, "what can I do for you at this unlikely hour?"

"Apologize."

"For what?"

"For—for what you did."

"But I have already explained to you, I did her no harm and indeed I may have done her a great service. She will be a better wife because of her—ah—acquaintance with me. As a matter of fact—"

"I came here to hear you apologize. I will not leave until you do."

And now he dropped his mocking, smiling mask and he too showed his anger.

"You will leave when I tell you to. Not before, and certainly not more than a minute after. Now listen to me, Isabel, and perhaps we will both win this little game."

"What do you—"

"Listen. I need—ah—a certain sum of money. I believe that you can get it for me. If you do I will go away quietly. Neither you nor Charlotte will ever see me again, I promise. And—more important—no one will know of Charlotte's little adventure. But I must have what I ask."

Always it came down to that: money. She heard him as if she heard a figure in a dream—or, rather, a nightmare, for where was she to get money? And what if she did not get it? He would tell his filthy story, he would ruin them . . .

"It is not so very much," he went on. "About the cost of Charlotte's wedding, I should imagine."

She did not want to hear the amount, but he would not stop now, he had gone too far.

"Ten thousand dollars," he said.

She stared at him; she could not believe what she heard. Ten thousand—!

"As soon as I have it I will go, I promise," he said.

"But—that is impossible. I cannot—"

And now suddenly his mood changed again, and he softened, his voice grew gentle as once she had known it. He came to her; he took her hand and lifted it to his lips. She felt nothing, she did not even try to pull away.

"You will," he murmured; "I have great faith in you. You are resourceful, you have managed triumph after triumph all your life. Somehow you will get what I ask— for Charlotte's sake if not for mine."

For Charlotte's sake . . .

She felt suddenly clearheaded, as if the fog shrouding her mind had lifted and now she could think clearly, she could see what she must do.

"You must give me a little time," she said. "I cannot get such an amount on a moment's notice—"

"How long?"

"I don't know. A few weeks, a month perhaps."

"After the wedding, in other words."

"Yes. You must wait."

"Until Charlotte is safely married and will not lose her

prize catch because of any tales that I might tell."

"I cannot do anything before then. It is impossible. But when they return from England I will speak to Ellsworth."

He held her for a moment longer, giving her a long, deep look such as lovers give; but these were lovers no more, they were deadly adversaries now, and she was fighting for her daughter's life.

At last he let her go. He uttered a short, sharp laugh. "Ellsworth!"

"I cannot go to Avery. He would never—he would rather die. And besides, I do not think he would have such an amount. He has been very pressed, he has cut my allowance. He tells me nothing directly, of course, but he does not need to. He canceled my standing order with the florist, and he refused to hire a new downstairs maid when the last one left."

"Ellsworth! Very well. I must trust you. I have no choice, it seems. Since your son-in-law is to provide the money it would hardly do to alienate him now. Wait until he is safely in the family and then—"

As she repeated this exchange to me the next morning I watched her closely. She was, I was sure, telling me all that had passed between herself and Cushing, and yet something was missing.

How did she feel about him—about this man whom she had so passionately loved, who had so cruelly betrayed her? I searched her face for a clue to her emotions but I saw none. She sat by my fire, sipping her coffee, her feet on the fender, looking for all the world as if she had just come in for a cozy chat instead of the ugly revelations which she had given me.

My fire burned bright to warm her; it was not a luxury today, for the good weather had vanished and a heavy fog had come down. Beyond my windows lay whiteness; looking out, I could see only a little portion of the drive before it vanished in the thick shroud—as thick as a blizzard, I thought. For no reason I remembered Ned— dear Ned! He had died in such whiteness, colder then, deadlier. . . . The muffled dirge of the foghorn lent a mournful counterpoint to our conversation.

When Isabel finished I hardly knew what to say to her. What could one say to such a tale? She sat quietly before me, her pale blue skirts neatly arranged, her hair perfectly dressed, her face as pleasant and impersonal as if she were paying a social call to someone she did not know very well.

"Come," she said then, getting to her feet. "I looked in on Charlotte earlier, but she was still sleeping. We will go to her now together, and she will be far happier to see you than me."

We found Charlotte sitting up in bed taking her morning tea. She looked dreadful. Her eyes were red, with dark hollows underneath, and her face was swollen with weeping. She refused to speak to us. I thought that Isabel would become angry then, but she did not; she simply left, promising to come back soon, and we returned to her room where she summoned the housekeeper.

"I want Miss Charlotte watched," she said. "Not by you—but choose someone reliable, someone discreet, one of the maids, I should think. Miss Charlotte is not to leave the house without my knowledge. You will know where I am at all times and you will be able to send for me."

"Yes, ma'am." The housekeeper was a stolid, supremely competent woman whose face revealed nothing. Before coming to Isabel she had served two other mistresses at Newport; what a tale she might tell if she chose, I thought.

After the housekeeper had gone Isabel gave me a defensive look. "I am not Mrs. Vanderbilt," she said, "but I cannot take chances now."

I left her then, for she had much to do; the wedding was less than a week away and last-minute details crowded in on her. She would call on me, I knew, if she needed help; meanwhile she wanted to be left alone. I went downstairs. The household staff was busy with the daily routine of dusting, sweeping, polishing—Isabel was a demanding mistress, and often she would make inspection tours, armed with a clean handkerchief, poking into the farthest corners of the house.

I wandered into the ballroom where, the night before, we had searched in vain for Charlotte. Through the glass doors I saw the beginnings of the terrace, only a few feet of it before the white wall of fog pressed in close upon the house as if it would smother us. I crossed the polished floor and unlocked the doors and went out. There was a strong odor of rank seaweed, the stench of ocean life flung up on the rocks to die and rot, and today there was no strong sea breeze to blow it away—only the dense, choking blanket. Heedless of my shoes, I walked out toward the garden and the wall above the Cliff Walk. I could not see ten feet in front of me; I might have been alone in the world. There was no sound save for the foghorn. I labored under a heavy sense of dread. I longed to go away, to go back to Boston, to Bar Harbor—anywhere but this place where we were all trapped, waiting. For what? For Charlotte's wedding? Less than a week away, it was: it might have been a lifetime. I could not imagine how we would survive until then.

Once upon a time a wise man said that our worst fate is to have our wishes granted. I remembered Isabel's wish for Charlotte: "Life!" she had said. "I want her to be alive, to know true love, to feel passion—"

And now it had happened, with what disastrous results I could not imagine. What if Cushing grew impatient? What if he could not—would not—wait? He held our lives in his hands; one word from him and Isabel's hopes would be ruined, he would destroy her once for all.

He *must* wait, I thought. I stood alone in the fog at the edge of the lawn and breathed in the raw, wet air. It burned my throat, and surely, too, I thought, it must have been that same fog that caused the tears to come hot and stinging to my eyes, slipping cold down my face, blinding me so that I could not see what must happen to us all.

Sixteen

To my surprise, Charlotte's wedding took place after all. It was not a large affair: two hundred people or so.

Charlotte looked—well, not lovely, perhaps, but certainly as attractive as might be. She seemed subdued, but many brides are that and no one thinks it odd. A woman's wedding day is the most important day of her life; it is proper that she approach it with a certain solemnity.

She had passed the days before the ceremony in a kind of inner fog as thick and blinding as that which had shrouded us on the morning after her misadventure with Cushing. She spent that day in bed; the next in her room. Ellsworth was told that she had an attack of prenuptial nerves. He believed it. He sent flowers to her and a box of chocolates. On the third day she arose, dressed, and came downstairs to breakfast. She spoke little, but she seemed composed. Her eyes were dry, her face no longer swollen with weeping.

"Thank God," said Isabel. "She has come to her senses."

Isabel herself looked tense, as all mamas do before a daughter's wedding, but she would, I thought, survive very well if Cushing kept his distance, if he did not press his demands.

But to my amazement he attended the ceremony. He sat near the middle of the church; I saw him as the usher led Diana and me to our seats just behind the family at the front. His bright hair gleamed even in the subdued light which streamed through the stained-glass windows. Why had she invited him? Had she been afraid not to? What if he created a scene—made a declaration of some kind? But he would not do that: he was a Boston gentleman born and bred, and no matter what despicable thing he did in private, he would always practice good manners in company.

His presence disturbed me all the same; he should not have been there. I was so unnerved that I hardly paid attention to the ceremony. Charlotte and Ellsworth stood before us, bathed in that special glow that new couples always have. Avery gave her away with a proud, satisfied smile and they made their vows and pledged their lives to each other and kissed chastely at the end and it was done. She—and Isabel—had got him. I dared not turn my head to look at Cushing. What was he thinking? Was he smiling as we all were, but for his own special, unmentionable reasons? Or was he stern, worrying over whether his blackmail would succeed after all?

Afterward we lunched under green and white striped tents on Isabel's lawn. The heat was intense; I could eat no more than a bite or two, and even Diana, whose appetite was normally unaffected by anything, only picked at her food. The guests were in a happy mood, as wedding guests always are, and they laughed and chattered ceaselessly, unaware that in our midst, like a viper hidden under cover of growth in the jungle, sat one who could destroy the bride, and her mother as well, with only a word.

Beautiful man! For he *was* beautiful, physically beautiful; he sat among a group of admirers at his table and enchanted them with a running monologue, smiling, self-deprecatory, deferential to the men, charming the women. They hung on him, they surrendered to him (even as Isabel had done, and Charlotte!).

I could not bear to look at him, so loathsome he was. How I longed to reveal him to his stupid circle of admirers! How I wanted to disabuse them, to open their eyes to the truth of the man! Beautiful he might be in his outward self; but inside lived a vile creature not fit even to know ordinary decent human beings. We were none of us without fault; some of us had committed grave wrongs in our time; but no one of us was what he was.

At last it was time for Charlotte and Ellsworth to depart. Their wedding journey was to England; they would be gone six weeks. Although it was customary for the bride to say good-bye to each of her guests, Charlotte did not. She does not want to speak to Cushing, I thought; and who could blame her? She had been perfectly composed all day, but to have to say even a word to him would be beyond her.

Afterward the guests took their leave in rather a hurry; the men to the Reading Room, which served as the gentlemen's club of Newport, and the women to their

601

homes, where they could be unlaced and seek relief from the heat in peignoirs, with cold cloths on their heads and glasses of iced lemonade to drink, or perhaps something stronger. Avery, looking very pale, retired to his room; the younger Kittredge children, Mary and Mason, went off to find their friends and Diana trailed after them.

Cushing, to my disgust, made a great show of his departure. He kissed Isabel's hand, he bowed to me, he had a pleasant word for all. I felt a knot of vomit rise in my throat as I watched him. Then he was gone, everyone was gone, and Isabel and I were alone as the servants came to clean up the debris.

It was late afternoon, still very hot. The sun cast long shadows across the lawn and garden; the sea shimmered silvery blue beyond. The air was heavy with the premonition of thunder. Isabel turned to me; to my surprise she asked me to walk down to the sea wall.

"Don't you want to go and change?" I said. As far as I knew, she had no engagements for the evening; she could relax in her room, restoring herself from the ravages of the day.

"Not now," she said. She held out her hand to me as if we were children. "Come—be with me for just a little while."

And so we walked toward the water, the two of us in our finery alone after all the guests had done. She did not speak at first; then, as we reached the wall, she turned and looked up the coastline to the next house, the house that Cushing had taken for the season.

"He is gone," she said abruptly.

"Gone—from Newport?"

"Yes. He only stayed for the wedding." A sour, bitter smile crossed her face. "It was kind of him to come, was it not?"

"But—" The implication of what she said began to dawn on me. "If he is gone, then he does not mean to trouble you. He will not insist—"

"He will trouble me for as long as he lives. He has never done anything else."

"But if he understands that you cannot get for him what he asks—"

"He knows that I will. I must. He has given me no choice. But even if I get the money and give it to him, what is to prevent him from coming back again to ask for more? At any moment he chooses he can ruin Charlotte—ruin me. As good a man as Ellsworth Barnes is—and there is no better—he cannot be expected to keep a wife who deceived him less than a week before he married her."

"But he promised—"

"Promised!" Her voice cracked on the first syllable. "What does a promise mean to a man like that? He can bleed me for the rest of his life if he chooses, and I can do nothing to prevent him."

I felt suddenly very tired; and if I felt so, I could only imagine the depth of her exhaustion. The heat pressed down upon us; not a leaf stirred, the sea was flat, the sun burned low in the western sky.

"What will you do?" I said.

She closed her eyes; but even so we cannot shut out

the most terrible visions. She did not respond, and suddenly I was overcome with the need to know the answer to my question. "Isabel? What will you do?"

She looked at me then—such a look of desolation, of desperation, as I had never seen.

"What will I do?" she said. She paused. "Why—whatever I must."

Seventeen

The next morning she too was gone—back to Boston, the housekeeper said.

"But why? In all this heat—what exactly did she say? Did she give a reason?"

"No, ma'am. Nothing. Master Mason and Miss Mary too." And Avery, as far as I knew, had left the night before.

The news left me profoundly uneasy, for the season still had three weeks and more and no one whom we knew was in Boston save those men who, like Avery, kept their offices open during the summer months. My disquiet increased that afternoon when I was lunching at the Casino. My companion was a Mrs. Tuttle, a shrewd little person of some wealth whose chief attraction was her encyclopedic mind; she had retained, it seemed, every shred of information that she had ever heard about anyone, and she had catalogued it, so that she could give you a neat little dissertation on almost everyone at a moment's notice. Her topic of conversation was exclusively other people; no idea ever crossed her brain, and if it had it would not have been recognized. We spoke, of course, of Charlotte's wedding, which Mrs. Tuttle had attended; and then, in passing, she dropped Lawrence Cushing's name into the conversation. She might as well have slapped me across the face; I felt my color rise, my heart beat fast. *What does she know?*

"He has returned to Newhall Gardens," she was saying. "He has had a flat there since the spring, it seems, although he did not announce himself to his Boston friends. I do not know why he chose not to go out into society until he arrived here in June; he came to Boston in March from London and lived the life of a perfect hermit. Isn't he handsome? Do you have any idea why he never married? He has money, of course—he must have, to live at Newhall Gardens." This was a new set of French flats on Clarendon Street at Commonwealth. They had been built by a speculator from Worcester, Strafford Newhall, who unaccountably had got hold of that prime parcel of Back Bay land. His wife had had visions of entering Boston society but Isabel and my present companion, among others, had put a stop to that scheme even before it began, and so Mrs. Strafford Newhall, pretty and stupid and vain, had sat alone in her fine new house in the Bay State Road and wondered what she had done to offend the circles she wanted to join. Her offense, of course, had been the same as mine: she had been born into the wrong family, she had chosen the wrong ancestors. I had been luckier than she, that was all.

But I had no time to think of her. I needed to digest the news of Cushing. Back to Boston—and Isabel gone too. What was I to make of it? Nothing, perhaps—of course it meant nothing. It could only mean nothing. My mind worried on the fact of it while I tried to keep up with the endless flow of Mrs. Tuttle's conversation. Cushing gone; Isabel gone— No. No. It meant nothing. Nothing at all. Cushing gone—

At last we were done; we said our good-byes, we summoned our respective carriages. All during the drive down Bellevue Avenue I heard Mrs. Tuttle's dry, drawling voice, I saw her narrow, avid face as she spewed her gossip. *What did she know?*

I spent a restless afternoon at Bailey's Beach with Diana; we paddled in the sea and built our castle at the water's edge, but I did not enjoy myself as I usually did. I was hardly there; I was in Boston with Isabel, with Cushing . . .

She must have gone to see him. Why else return so abruptly? She must have gone to beg him off, to tell him that Ellsworth would never pay. It would be a worthless trip, I thought: he will never let go. She told me so herself. She must have been desperate indeed to have gone to him. Foolish woman!

I turned with a start at Diana's touch on my arm. "Can we go home now, Mama?"

"Why, pet—the afternoon isn't half over. Why go?"

"Because you're not having a good time. You're not even listening to me."

Ah, Diana! The world is not always kind to clever, blunt-spoken women—and yet I would not have her otherwise, she is exactly what I want her to be.

And so we left the sand and the sea and we returned to Isabel's house, empty now and echoing where twenty-

four hours before it had been filled with celebration. I
was uneasy; I was worried; I was, at last, beginning to be
frightened. We had our tea; we rested; we had an early
dinner. Round and round went the images in my brain;
Isabel and Cushing. Isabel and Cushing. *Why?* The house
oppressed me; I too wanted to flee. At dinner my hands
trembled so that the wine slopped over onto the linen,
causing Diana to stare at me in astonishment. The heat
continued unabated. Toward midnight, as I sat reading in
my room, a thunderstorm came and went, leaving us as
uncomfortable as before. No, I thought, I cannot stay
here, I must go to her.

And so the next day Diana and I too left Newport and
returned to Beacon Street.

The heat, that August, was the worst in memory.
Boston lay prostrate, the red brick and brownstone
buildings radiating the sun, the dusty streets reeking
with the stench of horses' droppings, the greenery in the
Public Garden parched and drooping. Here and there I
saw a solitary figure—a maidservant, perhaps, or a
roughly dressed man—but for the most part the streets
were empty. The long straight expanse of the Commonwealth Avenue mall stretched into the distance without
one human figure to relieve the landscape. Beacon Street
too was deserted, the blinds of the houses pulled against
the sun, the houses locked and barred until their
inhabitants' return. As we pulled up to our doorstep I
paused for a moment before accepting Henry's hand to
help me down; I felt like a stranger, like an unexpected,
uninvited guest who would be turned away. The servant
who came to the door would say that the mistress was

gone, no one knew when she would return. . . .

"Mama?" Diana was staring at me again. I had frightened her with my woolgathering.

I gave her what I hoped was a reassuring smile and climbed down and ascended the shallow brownstone steps and saw my shiny black front door open to me as if by magic; I would not be turned away, after all. Bessie, looking rather wilted in her black uniform, greeted me as if she were glad to see me—"Yes, ma'am, very warm, a little breeze comes off the river at night"—good discipline not allowing any surprise to show.

And so we settled in. I telephoned Isabel at once, but the voice on the other end of the line—a voice that I did not recognize—said that she was not at home.

Where, at four o'clock on this broiling afternoon, could she be? Round and round went the worry in my brain. I could think of nothing but the bleakness, the hopelessness, of her last words to me: she would do what she must, she had said. But what was that? For one moment I thought of telephoning Cushing but I could not. I must not meddle, I thought: it is enough that I am here.

With Bessie's help I unpacked, and then Diana and I had cold supper—sliced ham, tomatoes, peach compote. We sat in the dining room at the back of the house; the french doors were open and we looked out onto the river as twilight came, the lights on the Cambridge shore beginning to shine through the dusk, a little breeze springing up.

After Diana went to bed I telephoned Isabel again, and again that strange voice, a man's voice—had she taken on

a new butler?—announced that she was not at home. I
was half inclined to disbelieve him, to order up the
carriage—or go on foot, if necessary—and go to see for
myself. I returned to the dining room and sat in near
darkness and drank my coffee. I could only wait, I
thought. But my worry would not leave me: it weighted
me down so that my limbs were heavy, my brain groggy, I
felt drugged, lethargic, burdened by my fears, my dread
of I knew not what. I waited. The room was dark and
warm, the house quiet. I felt alone in the great heat-
ridden city. Where was Isabel? Where had she been
today? Yesterday?

The bell in the Church of the Advent tolled eight. I
stirred; I felt my brain begin to clear. There was someone
else, after all, whom I could see: Curtis. He was, like
Avery, one of the city men in the summer while his wife
went to Nahant with her uncles and aunts and cousins—
an unfashionable place, now, but that was no matter to
her. Curtis would undoubtedly be at home, and alone,
and he might very well have seen Isabel. In fact—and I
felt relief wash over me as I realized—it had undoubtedly
been to see Curtis that Isabel had returned. Why had I
not thought of it before? He would be able to advise her—
to prepare her to deal with Cushing's demands. Of
course!

I felt my worry drop from me as I went again to the
telephone. The girl put the number through and I waited
impatiently as I heard the tinny ring at the other end.

Please, I thought: please. On and on it rang, not even a
servant to answer it. There is this about the telephone,
wonderful invention though it may be: that even though

it is an instrument designed to give instant contact with one's fellow human beings, there is no feeling in the world more desolate than to ring someone and have no answer. And so this instrument, intended to bring us closer, has the power to isolate us too. At last I gave up; I replaced the small black earphone onto its cradle and stood for a moment trying to think what to do.

And at that instant the doorbell rang. Before any of the servants could respond I was there to open it. For a fraction of a second I hesitated, my hand on the knob. In this vast, unpeopled city, who could it be? A stranger? A thief? A ghost from our past given flesh?

I shook myself free; I opened the door. Isabel stood before me—of course, who else could it have been? Her face was in shadow, for no light came from the house. Even so I could see her wide eyes, her drawn, frantic face—for she wore no veil, she did not even wear a hat. Her carriage stood in the street; at least, I thought, she did not come on foot, possibly to collapse along the way.

She came in; I closed the door behind her and sent away Bessie, who had finally appeared. I led Isabel back to the dining room and turned up the gas. Her face was white—dead white, and her hair was undone, simply thrown up onto her head. Her eyes stared and stared, and yet I hardly thought she saw me. She seemed stunned, unable to speak and yet her eyes spoke a frantic need to tell me . . .

She carried a folded newspaper in her ungloved hand, and now she thrust it at me.

"Marian," she whispered. "Marian—look—"

In the instant before she collapsed the headline

registered: "Murder in Newhall Gardens." And then she lay at my feet and I tossed the paper aside in a frantic attempt to revive her, and with all the commotion of summoning the servants and loosening her dress and applying smelling salts the newspaper lay on the floor; and it was not until some time later, when Isabel had revived and lay on the sofa in the drawing room, that I could read the story itself.

But I already knew what it would say, for there was my dread, the heavy foreboding that had dogged me—there it was on the page, in that story, that account of murder, that description of the victim whose description I knew so well, the attempt to estimate the hour when the deed had been done, the telling of the bloody scene—he had been murdered in his bath, stabbed until his blood ran red and he lay in a sea of crimsoned water, his golden head sinking, his life run out.

What the reporter did not know—what no one knew— was the name of the person who had killed him.

Eighteen

The news of Lawrence Cushing's murder shook Boston like an earthquake. There had been no news so sensational since the Borden murder six years previously—and that had been not Boston's news, after all, but Fall River's.

The police were highly embarrassed. Confronted every day by deaths both natural and unnatural in the city's poor districts, they remained unperturbed—for the poor died everywhere and often violently, and the world took little notice. The violent death of a person of quality, however, was another matter. Such people had friends in high places, they controlled the city's money and power and therefore they controlled the police—and if the police could not prevent the occasional murder of such a one, they were expected at least to solve it quickly and bring the murderer to justice so that all the other people of that class might go on living unthreatened.

But Cushing's case was a bafflement, and therefore embarrassing. The police had few facts to go on: Cushing had been seen entering Newhall Gardens on the evening before his death—that is, on the evening of Charlotte's wedding. He had gone out the following morning and returned in the early afternoon—this according to the doorman. He kept no servant, nor had he kept any since taking up residence there several months previously. He had, during the spring (that strange time when he lived in Boston yet did not move among his lifelong acquaintances—many of whom, admittedly, had more or less forgotten him during his long absences), occasionally had a caller or two: two or three different gentlemen, a lady (heavily veiled, unidentifiable). His neighbors did not know him. No one, on the day of his death, had heard sounds of a struggle. He had no known enemies. (At this I gagged; how little we know of each other's lives! Cushing had undoubtedly left a string of outraged, cuckolded husbands across the European continent—or wherever he had lived all the years that he had not lived in Boston.) Lastly, and of some importance, the police had been unable to find the murder weapon— the knife that had stabbed him while he lay in his bath. The man who wielded it must have had terrific strength, the theory went, for the wounds were very deep and some of them were surrounded by bruises; further, Cushing's face was bruised as if he had been repeatedly struck.

One day about a week after the death I was visited by one of the investigating officers, Detective Sergeant Mullaney. He was a stocky, blondish man with pale skin and pale gray eyes whose demeanor was what the Irish call "cute." Had he been an attractive woman his manner would have been termed coy. Despite his politeness, even his deference, I did not like him; he alarmed me because he was so unlike what I thought a policeman should be. He spoke perfect English without a trace of a brogue.

"You understand, ma'am, that we are talking to everyone who ever knew the gentleman."

"Yes."

"So if you could just speak as freely as you can, any little detail, even something that you think might not apply—just go on as you please."

"Yes." I was, in fact, very frightened of him—his manner, so unpolicelike, instantly put me on my guard.

"Now. You first met Mr. Cushing—ah—some years ago?"

"Yes."

"And how many times have you seen him since?"

"Only once or twice."

"And most recently?"

"At Miss Kittredge's wedding. Last week—ten days ago."

"Ah. Yes. We will need to talk to everyone who attended that affair. Yes—it is the last time, you see, that he had contact with any of his friends and acquaintances, and we hope that someone can tell us—yes."

If the police intended to talk to every guest at Charlotte's wedding, I thought, the investigation would take months. Sergeant Mullaney did not spend much time with me; he left with a small bow and an even smaller smile and asked me to contact him at once if I should remember something, no matter how small or seemingly insignificant.

Fortunately he did not ask me how I came to hear of Cushing's murder; nor did he speak to any of my servants.

Isabel, that night, had lain on the sofa for two hours and more, speaking to me in a faint, strained voice, commanding me with a movement of her head not to call the doctor, or Avery, or Curtis. And so I had sat with her, and she gradually got back her strength, and at last she sat up and announced that she would return home.

The odd thing was that during the entire time, that evening, she spoke not one word about Cushing, and I, fearing to bring on another faint, dared not mention him. And so we spent the evening, consumed by him, unable even to speak his name.

It occurs to me now that it was—and is—the same in the physical relations between the sexes: everyone thinks of them, many people are obsessed by them, but no one dares speak of them; the topic is simply unmentionable.

Of course the police went to her too, and they spent more time with her than they had with me, possibly because he was her guest so shortly before he died. Sooner or later, I thought, someone will tell them of Cushing's involvement with Charlotte; and once that connection is made, they will hound Isabel without mercy. And they will ask her about her flight to Boston, they will want to know what she did with every moment of her time. . . .

The newspapers had their field day with the case, but as time passed and the investigation foundered the story was to be found buried deeper, given less space, until finally, in mid-September, it vanished altogether.

Gossip was another matter, however; matrons spoke of

the case in hushed tones as they took luncheon and tea together; girls in the Sewing Circles exchanged their tidbits; schoolchildren, who had chanted cruelly of Lizzie Borden and her ax, now sang:

> "Cushing, Cushing in his bath,
> Someone, Someone crossed his path,
> Someone, Someone raised the knife,
> Someone, Someone took his life!"

Worst of all were the servants. They whispered among themselves and watched us with sly eyes and never, never said a word of what they thought—but we knew. They are laughing at us, I thought: they see how we suffer, and now they take their revenge. Even my Bessie, even faithful Henry were the enemy now: they watched as we suffered, and they could not find it in their hearts to pity us.

On a golden afternoon in late September, when I was just preparing to walk out into the Public Garden to pass the time until Diana should return from school, the maid came to announce that a man was asking to see me. She did not say "gentleman," and this judgment of his status, which was reinforced by the fact that she had not admitted him but had kept him waiting at the door, caused me to hesitate.

"Did he say what he wanted, Bessie?"

"No, ma'am."

"And no card?"

"No, ma'am. I started to turn him away but he said it was important."

All my instincts told me to refuse to see him, but curiosity got the better of me and so, dressed in my hat and walking suit, I told her to admit him and I went down.

He was a small man, very pale, with a badly cut dark jacket and a dusty bowler which he held under his arm. His dark hair was plastered back from the center part with a sticky, odoriferous pomade; his eyes were ravenous, taking in, I thought, possibly more than there was to see.

"Mrs. Motley? Linwood Hooper. Very kind of you to see me."

His voice was soft and pitched so low that I had to strain to hear it. His expression was solemn—as if, I thought, he had come to bring bad news—and yet the softness of his voice, the melancholy expression in his eyes, gave him an attitude of regret, as if he were sorrowing for both of us because he had to cause me grief.

"I will be short. And to the point. I am in the employ of a certain gentleman whose name you may know."

It was his melancholy air, I think, that caught me off guard; had he swaggered in I could have met his bluster with my own and ordered him out of the house. But his attitude was disarming; I did not know how to protect myself from what he would say.

"Colonel Mann," he said; his voice was no more than a whisper, his shoulders shrugged in apology.

Colonel Mann!

Linwood Hooper lifted a limp hand to forestall the objection that he read on my face.

"Before you send me away, hear me out. Colonel Mann is—ah—not without mercy."

It was a lie: Colonel Mann was the most merciless, the most ruthless man in all America. His filthy yellow sheet purveyed the most salacious gossip imaginable. He destroyed reputations left and right as carelessly as if he were crushing insects under his heel. Sometimes, for a price, he offered not to print his information; that blackmail, and not his newspaper, was the source of his wealth.

"I have here"—he tapped his breast pocket—"a piece of information which may be of interest to you."

"Nothing that you have is of interest to me. You may print what you please; it cannot hurt me."

"Oh, it is not about you, Mrs. Motley. No, indeed. It concerns a friend of yours."

"Who?"

He smiled sweetly, apologetically. "Let us not be so crude as to name names. You know the person—the lady, I should say—very well. Very well indeed. And I am sure that you would want to help her."

"Why do you not go to her? Why come to me?"

"I did. I tried to see her, not an hour ago. She would not admit me. She lives not so very far away; it took me only five minutes to walk here. I wanted to give her another chance, you see, by coming to you. I am sure that she cannot realize the importance of this little paragraph that we have. If she did she would have seen me. But we all make mistakes. I know that you are her good friend— her best friend, indeed—and so I came to you. I am giving you a chance to help her, since she will not help herself."

All during this recitation I felt my anger rising, and now it burst.

619

"It is you who have made the mistake, Mr. Hooper. I know how you operate, you and your employer. You blackmail people, pure and simple. You are trying to blackmail me."

"I am only—"

"No! I will not listen! You may leave—get out before I have you thrown out!"

But even as I spoke I heard a warning voice inside: should I not at least try to discover what information he had? And when Isabel refused to see him, why had he not gone to Avery? For the damning tidbit, whatever it was, could only be about Isabel, I had no other friend so close, so much in peril.

His manner had changed. He was no longer fawning and apologetic; he spoke arrogantly now, not bothering to hide his contempt for me. "You must be frightened to speak so foolishly," he said. "I understand. But I must warn you, there is little time. I am offering you a chance to suppress information which could be extremely harmful to this lady. She is a woman of high position, and when she falls she will fall very far."

"Her husband—"

"Her husband has nothing—not a penny to spare. You, on the other hand, are well able to afford what we ask."

I felt naked—completely vulnerable. Was there nothing that these men did not know? And how did they get their information? Servants, of course, were easily bribed; but even servants did not know everything as Linwood Hooper seemed to.

"Get out." Wait, said the warning voice; find out

what he has. I ignored it. Already I had rung for Bessie. "Get out. You are mistaken. You will get nothing from me—nothing!"

He shrugged; he raked me with his eyes; then he turned and followed Bessie to the door.

My knees were shaking badly. I sank down onto the little sofa by the fireplace and tried to collect my thoughts. My hat weighed heavily on my head but when I tried to lift my hands to remove it I was so weak that I gave up the attempt. Had I dreamed him? No: I could still smell the rancid odor of his pomade, I could hear the soft, menacing tones of his voice.

What in God's name had Isabel done to set Colonel Mann on her heels? Of course it had to do with Cushing, it could be nothing else. Was it her aborted interval with him early in the summer? Or—more likely—was it his seduction of Charlotte? Or was it something else, something more serious even than that?

Cushing: I saw him in my mind's eye, I saw him lying dead in his blood-red bath, his eyes open perhaps—had they seen his murderer?

And Isabel: she had returned to Boston unexpectedly, she had left the comfort of Newport and had come up in that hellish heat, the broiling August sun, when she might have remained ensconced at Newport for a few weeks more. . . . Why?

I imagined her: I saw her walking those hot, dusty, deserted streets as clearly as if I had been watching her then. I saw her small, solitary figure, walking, walking . . . to him? To one last assignation?

She would not have called the carriage. She would

have walked, heavily veiled despite the heat, straight and steady she would have gone, down Commonwealth, past Dartmouth, around the corner onto Clarendon, unrecognizable in her veil, past the doorman guarding the ornate entrance doors lettered with the words "Newhall Gardens" . . .

I shook myself free of my thoughts. Nonsense! Worse than nonsense—Isabel was no fool, she would never commit murder.

And yet: they had made no arrests. And this odious little man was on the prowl.

I should not have sent him away. I should have stalled for time, I should have asked him to come back the next day when I would have had time to consider his offer—or at least to consider what to do. Now it was too late. He and Colonel Mann would print their damning information and Isabel, perhaps, would suffer for it.

The afternoon was slipping away. I needed to act quickly if I were to act at all.

I went to the telephone and gave the operator Curtis' number at his office. The polite young man who answered informed me that Curtis was in court and I left instructions for him to call me immediately upon his return.

That done, I could only wait for Diana to come home; when she did, bubbling as usual with tales of the day's events, I drank a cup of tea with her and sent her in care of one of the maids to Brimmer Street to play with a friend. And finally, in the late afternoon, Curtis telephoned and promised to stop on his way home.

I had not seen him since the wedding; now, face to face, I decided to tell him everything: not only what happened at Newport, including Charlotte's misadventure, but also my suspicions about the real purpose of Linwood Hooper's visit. Curtis' fine dark eyes filled with disbelief as he heard me out.

"You can't mean that you think that Isabel is somehow involved in Cushing's death. *Do* you mean that, Marian?"

"I don't know. I simply don't know. She did come back, she left Newport in a great hurry—"

He sighed: a long, exasperated sound. His fingers danced a nervous tattoo on the green brocade arm of his chair.

"Have you seen her?" he said.

"No. I thought I'd call around after dinner. Would you come with me?"

He made a wry face. "We have an engagement. Besides, I think that she would suspect something if we both appeared. You will see the lay of the land, of course, but I shouldn't think that you'd want to say anything about this. Not just yet, in any case. It would only upset her."

I understood; it was less than a year since she had been in Philadelphia, since the operation which had been intended to quiet her.

He stood up to take his leave: a tall, elegant man, a good man—how good he was! I felt enormously relieved: he had shifted my worries onto his own shoulders, he would make things right. "I will find your Mr. Hooper and press him a bit." He took my hand; he smiled his warm, sweet smile and then he was gone.

Accordingly, after saying good night to Diana, I called the carriage and went around to Isabel's. I had no idea what I would say to her. As Curtis had advised, I would simply see how she did without mentioning the mysterious Mr. Hooper.

The night was warm: a balmy September darkness, the street lamps shining on trees still heavily in leaf, on the evening traffic carrying people to their dinners or their parties or downtown to the theaters.

We arrived at Isabel's about half past eight, and I sent Henry to inquire whether she was at home.

"Yes, ma'am," he reported, opening the door of the carriage and extending his hand to help me step down. "She's here. And somethin' up, too."

I paused before I alighted. "What do you mean, 'something's up'?" Servants had a network of communication between themselves—a wink, a shrug, a muttered word—which functioned as efficiently as the telegraph.

"Don't know. But somethin', for sure. Minna looks about to burst." Minna was Isabel's longtime downstairs maid; ordinarily, however, she was not on duty to admit evening visitors, that being the task of the butler.

Curious now, and not a little alarmed, I stepped down and ascended the broad marble steps. Minna held the massive door open; she ducked her head in greeting but I could tell nothing from her brief, smiling glance.

Isabel had told them to show me up straightaway, and

so I climbed the polished oaken stairs behind Minna's starched black skirts. I sensed an air of excitement in the house. The lights were turned on in every room and passageway, although I saw no one coming or going, and that alone was evidence of something unusual, for Avery was pinchpenny, he refused to allow the gas to be used unless it was absolutely necessary. I remembered Linwood Hooper's contempt: "He has nothing."

The broad upper hall, too, was deserted, but as Minna led me to Isabel's door I heard muffled laughter and a little shriek of joy. What—?

"Come in—come in!" cried Isabel at the maid's discreet tap.

The door opened, and I stepped in to be met by Isabel's embrace. She flung her arms around me, she kissed me, she was radiant with joy. "Oh, Marian, how wonderful that you are here!" She pulled me into the room; Minna discreetly disappeared. I saw a woman standing before the fireplace. I did not at first recognize her. She wore a plain dark dress, and her hair was not fashionably done but pulled back severely. And although she too smiled to greet me, her expression was cautious, her eyes wary, as if she were not sure of the greeting that she would receive in return. But she put out her hands to me, and stepped forward, and said shyly, "Hello, Aunt Marian."

And then, of course, I knew her; and I abandoned all caution and rushed to embrace her: long lost, long given up for dead, home to her family once again! I was overcome; I could not speak, I simply held to her as if she were a ghost who would vanish as unexpectedly as she had appeared. I too began to laugh and then I wept, I wept for Isabel, her daughter now restored to her; I wept for that daughter, for my own girl, for all of us; and then I laughed again and put her away from me to gaze at her, to reassure myself that she had really come home. Victoria!

Nineteen

Within twenty-four hours all Boston knew that Victoria had returned, and in twenty-four hours more all Boston knew why. In the manner of such escapades, hers had turned out badly. She told me, that night, the essential outline of her story, and I knew only too well how to fill in the details: how Fletcher had adored her for three months; how they had traveled from city to city as he completed his tour of *The Widow's Mite;* how the question of when they would marry was never answered; how they had at last turned up in San Francisco where his attention seemed to wane; how ultimately he had abandoned her for a cabaret dancer; how she had struggled to survive, alone and penniless; how she had found employment with the elderly widow of a man who, half a century before, had made his fortune in the goldfields; how she had met, in those frantic months, more types of the human species than most of us meet in a lifetime—"I have seen the world, Aunt Marian, and what a world it is!"

Her reappearance gave rise to a good many agonized

discussions over the teacups in Boston's best families.
Should she be received? Should anyone call on Isabel
while her renegade daughter was in residence? Should
Victoria—but the thought was really outrageous—
should Victoria be included in invitations sent to her
mother?

The problem was complicated by the fact that Victoria
was absolutely unrepentant. She admitted her mistake—
"Infatuation and sheer pigheadedness," as she put it—
but she refused to play the sinner's role. "If I was to be
punished for my wrongdoing," she said, "that punishment has been dealt to me already. How do you think I
survived out there, completely on my own, without any
resource whatever?"

Isabel would shudder when Victoria spoke in that way;
she did not want to hear. "You have come home to me,"
she would say, "and that is enough. Do not punish *me* by
telling me too much."

Our Boston circle soon grew accustomed to the fact of
Victoria's return; the problem of whether to receive her
was decided by each woman individually, and while some
refused her, most did not. Gradually Victoria made her
way back.

But the tepid waters of Boston society were not enough
for her now, and within a month she was casting about
for something to do. She refused to take part in any
charity work whatever, not even the North Bennett
Street School for Boys. "If I were poor," she said, "as I
have been, I would resent terribly the well-meaning
efforts of the rich to keep me poor—and to make me
humble as well."

We walked out together one brisk October afternoon. Heavy wind and rain the night before had stripped the trees, but now the sun shone brightly, if with little warmth, and a blustering wind swept puffy clouds across the bright blue sky. The red brick and brownstone buildings rising up Beacon Hill glowed as if they had been freshly scrubbed, and above the long slope of the Common the golden dome of the State House gleamed like the original beacon. It was an invigorating day, a day to set the blood running fast to charge the brain, and Victoria seemed appropriately lively. Her air of caution, so noticeable the first few days after her return, had vanished to be replaced by her former insouciance; she laughed easily again, and bubbled over with energy, and skipped a step or two every now and then as if she were ten instead of almost twenty-one. She wore a puce-colored walking suit and a gray hat trimmed with ostrich plumes; we had lately been accosted, those of us who wore plumes, by women in the streets who handed small printed cards to us: "God's creatures sacrificed to women's vanity!" Fortunately we met none of them this day.

"I have decided how to spend the winter," Victoria announced. "I know that Mother, and you too, have been worried that I have nothing to occupy my time—as indeed I do not."

I was delighted that she had at last found some charity work that suited her; she could not, after all, fill her days with social engagements as if she were a debutante.

"I intend to make good use of my experiences," she went on. "I am going to write a romance about them—a penny dreadful, more likely."

I stopped short in the middle of the walkway and stared at her. She saw that I was horrified and with an impatient little laugh she took my arm and led me on. A strong gust of wind hit us just then, so that we were both obliged to hold our hats, which were large and heavy, wide-brimmed, far too much for any hatpin to secure. The wind was fierce, stronger than either of us; it propelled us both, heavy skirts blowing, and nearly unbalanced us. We could not fight it; we staggered to a bench and fell onto it. The ridiculousness of our appearance struck us both, then, and we began to laugh; several passersby stared at us, for decent women did not laugh uproariously on the walkways of the Boston Common.

"A romance! But, Victoria, you cannot do that! You will be disgraced—"

But the obvious inadequacy of this objection struck us both, and off we went again, dissolving into peals of laughter.

"Yes," she gasped, "I will be disgraced, no one will receive me."

Gradually I recovered myself. "But, Victoria, listen to me, do you think that it would be wise?" Poor Isabel, I thought; this surely will be too much.

But I misjudged her. Like her mother before her, Isabel wanted no scandal; on the other hand, she had a shrewd Yankee practicality which always sought to turn every situation, no matter how compromising, to her advantage.

"Let her do it?" she said to me the next day, when Victoria had broken her news. "Of course I'll let her do it. How can I stop her? And besides, it will keep her busy, and it may even earn her some money. God knows she has nowhere else to get any. And she has promised to use a pseudonym, although of course everyone will know the truth."

And so Victoria, having returned to face the scrutiny of Boston, retired from it again and began to work on her opus.

The autumn drew on. Curtis, after an intensive search, had failed to find Linwood Hooper, and when, in desperation, he sent an emissary to Colonel Mann, that gentleman denied any knowledge of such a person.

"We can only wait," said Curtis, "and hope that nothing is printed."

I felt as though the sword of Damocles hung over my head, but as the days passed and we heard no more of the matter I began to hope that it had all been some kind of insane mistake.

Curtis told me, too, that the police investigation of Cushing's murder had come to a halt. They would be able to make an arrest now only if someone came forward to offer information—an unlikely possibility at this late date.

That bit of news seemed too good to be true; as indeed it was.

Twenty

"Vile swine!" hissed Victoria. "How can men stoop so low? This is nothing but filthy lies and innuendo—"

She paced the room, too agitated to sit. As was her custom when she was working at her manuscript, she wore a loose woolen smock; her hair hung down her back so that she looked like a schoolgirl, hardly older than Diana, but her language, her blazing eyes, her ferocity, were those of an Amazon. In her trembling hand she held a copy of Colonel Mann's *Town Topics*.

"Has Uncle Curtis seen this?" she said. "I think Mama should sue. They can't be allowed to print this—this *swill*."

At last it had come, the item that we had dreaded for weeks:

In their investigation of the Cushing tragedy, we suggest that the police need look no further than the *calendar*. There is a certain lady of *wintry* cast who was observed *frostily* castigating the victim shortly before his death. Has her *icy* heart *frozen* in

632

this matter? Let the authorities *thaw* her and they may solve the mystery which perplexes them.

Why Colonel Mann had chosen this time—mid-November—to print it was a mystery. Perhaps he had given up hope of getting his hush money and had decided to have his revenge.

Even more mysterious—and more unpleasant—was the way in which the copy of the newspaper had come to Isabel. Someone—some anonymous someone—had mailed it to her. The label, addressed to Mrs. Avery Kittredge, had been typewritten—"In *Town Topics'* office, no doubt," said Victoria. Her lovely face was flushed with anger; even in the midst of all my fears crowding around me again I could not help but notice her beauty and think what a shame it was that her family feeling, so strong now on behalf of her mother, should have deserted her in that one crucial moment of meeting Fletcher. Now she will suffer all her life for that one lapse, I thought, and never make a proper marriage.

Her outrage, however, prevented me from any meditation on her fate; the immediate crisis was too demanding. Willy-nilly, I thought, she will find out one way or another my part in this affair, and so I decided to confess.

"A man came to see me," I said, "a man from *Town Topics*. He offered to sell me that information."

For a moment she let me see her contempt. "And you refused?"

"Yes. Curtis tried to find him later, but he could not. Even Colonel Mann denied knowing him."

NANCY ZAROULIS

"You did what you thought was right."

"Yes. Once give in to a blackmailer—"

I thought of Isabel's words about Cushing, and I
faltered. If the police discovered that Cushing had tried
to get money from her it would look very bad for her. I
had already resolved that they would not learn it from
me, but who else knew? Did Charlotte? I was sure that
Isabel had not mentioned the matter to Ellsworth!

I had gone that day to call on Isabel, but she was not at
home and so I visited with Victoria instead. I admired
Victoria's industry: she worked every day save Sunday,
and already she had a thick pile of manuscript. She did
not offer to show it to me, and of course I did not ask.

"How—what did she say about it?" I said. "Was she
upset?"

"No. She seemed quite calm."

And, indeed, when she came to me the next day she
was positively bubbling, for word had come that Arthur
was coming home from his military adventure, and all the
family were thrown into preparation for a welcome
home. "He is well—only a touch of fever," said Isabel.
"We will have him back by Thanksgiving."

She did not mention *Town Topics*, and I did not want to
spoil her happiness by asking her about it, so the matter
lay unresolved between us. It meant nothing, I told
myself. It is just the usual gossip and scandal. No one—
least of all the police—will pay any attention.

Curtis was not so sanguine. Having had no luck in his
initial inquiries, immediately after Linwood Hooper's
visit to me, he now began again to try to discover *Town
Topics'* informant. I saw him a week later and his worried

look, his pessimistic tone, threw me back again into the doubts and suspicions that I thought I had left behind.

"I have been to Newport," he said.

"Newport! Why—to see Colonel Mann?"

"No. He is a lost cause now, and in any case he is in New York. But I found the man who worked as butler in the house that Cushing rented. I am sure that he was Mann's informant."

"But—did he tell you so? Surely not."

"No. Not even for the substantial sum of money that I offered. The fellow was positively impudent. Said his conversations were no business of mine, said I had no right to question him. Met me at his door—a house down near the docks—in his shirt-sleeves, a cigarette in his mouth, insolent as you please. I told him he'd never work in Newport again if I had my say. He was Cockney, I think. I told him I'd have a look at deporting him if he wasn't careful but it didn't faze him a bit. In my day," he added grimly, as if he were a regular graybeard, "no servant would have dared to speak so."

Poor Curtis! A gentleman himself, he had no idea of the resentment—the very real hostility—of many in the servant class. Men in general did not understand it, for women, by and large, were the overseers of servants, while men simply enjoyed the benefit of their labor.

I watched him; he was lost in thought for a moment and I did not interrupt. I had never seen him so; he always seemed cheerful, competent—the wisest man I knew. We sat before the fire in my drawing room. It was a dreary, rainy day, darkness closing in now, the storm beating against the glass; if the temperature dropped during the night we would have ice and snow, an early winter. I fingered the soft green wool of my skirt; I sank back onto the deep cushions of my chair; I sipped my hot, strong tea and felt once again as I did every day of my life the comfort—the luxury—of my existence, the security that Uncle James's money had given me.

And yet: the dragons lurked, the demons hovered near, waiting to snatch us. Every day since the news of Cushing's murder I had felt the other thing, the great yawning pit which had opened at our feet and from which I, at least, had scrambled back, seeking firm ground, the earth under my feet always threatening to give way. We were not safe yet: the police were stalled but they had not given up.

"Curtis," I said, unable to contain my worry any longer, "what will it mean? This thing in *Town Topics*—it doesn't say anything really, does it? Just innuendo—"

"It stirs things up again, if nothing else," he said. "It sets the police on a new trail. Someone, seeing this, may go to them with new information."

"And if Avery gets wind of it?"

He shrugged. "Avery is embroiled in trying to save his skin. I doubt he has time to notice anything unless someone shoves it under his nose."

"What can we do?"

"Nothing. There is nothing we can do at all. Except wait."

And so we waited. A few days later Arthur came home, weak and yellow from fever but otherwise well. Isabel gave a great party for him on the Saturday after Thanksgiving. All the family came, the most distant relatives, and many of her closest friends. She was very happy—happier than I had seen her since the Apple of Discord Ball when Victoria's promise had seemed so bright.

I am glad she had that happiness; for that, at least, they were unable to take away from her. Truly, as some wise person has said, we are fortunate that we cannot see the future, that we live day by day without the curse of foresight; for if we knew what would happen on the morrow we often would not want to wake to greet it.

On the following Monday the police came to Isabel again; and this time they arrested her and charged her with the murder of Lawrence Cushing.

Twenty-One

I write now of nightmare: of that strange netherworld that haunts our waking hours, public shame and private agony, long nights without sleep and longer days of waking torment.

I cannot see it whole; even now, ten years later, I see only darkness illuminated by flashes of light, as a storm sweeping over a vast plain will show in streaks of lightning the turmoil beneath for a moment only, and then vanish, leaving darkness again.

I see Isabel's face as she stood in the dock: pale, immobile, unmarked by tears, her eyes dry, her lips firm—no trembling, no swooning, but only a terrifying stillness there, concealing her soul's anguish.

I see the faces of her children, gathered together in this, their most terrible hour—her family, that good solid support which would sustain her through her time of trial.

Her trial: I see her trial, the worst nightmare of all, it comes back to me still, the crowds fighting to get in, the stern faces of the men on the jury, the old judge—far too old, surely for such an ordeal?—the prosecutor, a lean, hatchet-faced man whose dry voice scraped my nerves raw, and the defense, Isabel's lawyers, a trio of dark-garbed, respectable men called upon to deal with this scandal.

Dark days—dark February days, and at the end of each day we went out into the frozen streets to be greeted by ragged newsboys hawking the headlines, and curious passersby snapping up the papers, and the desolate journey home from the courthouse, home to supper with Diana, who, as the niece of the accused, had been hounded from school by the taunts of her classmates so that now she spent her days with a tutor, growing even lonelier and more withdrawn, and yet I was unable to be with her, for I needed to be at the court, I was called as a witness and even aside from my testimony I needed to be there for Isabel.

"They have no case," said Curtis, "none at all. If ever a grand jury was influenced, this one was—pressured unmercifully. The police have been embarrassed, public pressure has been brought to bear to make an arrest. They are always accused of favoring the rich, of not prosecuting people of standing; now they will make an example of her whether they have a case or not, simply to silence the public outcry."

"I think it's a disgrace," said Carrie. "To put Isabel on trial for murder. Isabel! It's ridiculous! Why doesn't Avery simply buy them off? In New York you can buy district attorneys very cheaply. Judges come a bit higher."

Curtis looked at her as if she had uttered an obscenity.

She stared back defiantly. "I meant it!" she said. "I wasn't joking."

"I know you meant it. We operate differently here, and pray we always will. Although when the Irish finally take over—as they will—there's no telling what will happen."

Knowing what I did of Avery's and Isabel's marriage, I wondered if he would have done what Carrie suggested even if he had had the chance, even if he had had the money. It was an unpleasant question. Did he some-how—awful thought!—feel that this was retribution for the life she had led, the life of which he had always disapproved?

I had known Avery for nearly as long as I had known Isabel, and yet I could not have called him a friend. Save for that one time, years ago, when Isabel was near death in childbed, he had never reached out to me nor I to him. I had no idea what he was thinking now. But times of trouble prompt us to unaccustomed action, and so, more from a sense of duty to the family—to Isabel—than from any particular feeling for him, I went to him.

"I am sorry," I said. "I don't know what else to say to you. I don't know what I can do to help. You can call on me for anything, you know that."

He stared at me for a moment before he replied. He seemed to be thinking of something else; I was not sure that he understood what I had said. "Thank you," he said at last.

"I mean—this is all so impossible. As if it cannot be."

"Nevertheless," he said, "it is."

"Avery—Avery, listen to me. She is innocent. She

could never have done such a thing. You know that. It is inconceivable."

He made no reply.

"Avery—don't you know that? Don't you know your own wife?"

He stared at me. I could see nothing in his eyes but—what? Hostility? Resignation to his fate—and hers? Or simply exhaustion?

I could not bear his silence. "Tell me," I begged. "Please tell me that you believe that she is wrongly accused. She is! You know that she is!"

He closed his eyes and opened them and licked his lips before he spoke. Then: "If she is innocent they will find her so."

"Avery!"

But he would say nothing more to me; and I had no heart to say another word to him.

The trial was set for early February, but the lawyers got a delay so that it was nearly March before they began. The judge, it was said, had a long-standing feud with the prosecutor, arising not out of any personal encounter but from a dispute between the families going back a generation and more; in the manner of Boston families the antagonism had lingered down the years. The defense attorneys, whom Curtis recruited, were the best in the city—in all New England; they seized upon every point, they kept the jury selection going for three weeks, they argued over the admissibility of every shred of evidence.

The courthouse was a huge forbidding pile of masonry and stone in Pemberton Square, not far from the red-light district. Every day the way there was clogged with

curiosity seekers. In the cold dark hours before dawn the
spectators lined up for seats, and occasional fights broke
out between early arrivals and latecomers trying to force
their way in. Often people nearly froze, waiting there, but
the crowds increased day by day as the trial went on,
people could not get enough of this sensation.

The Commonwealth's case rested on three points:
Isabel's opportunity to commit the crime, her means of
committing it, and, most of all, her motive.

"They have no case," said Curtis; and yet they had—
at least enough to bring her to trial.

The police were the first witnesses. A bluff little
sergeant testified that they had been called to Cushing's
apartment at Newhall Gardens on the morning of August
12. That they had been admitted by the doorman. That
they found Cushing lying dead in his bath.

Bloodstains?

Smears on the edge of the tub; on the floor of the
bathroom; on the bedroom carpet.

Evidence of burglary? Drawers ransacked, doors or
windows jimmied?

None.

What found?

A bracelet.

This? (Holding it up: a woven pearl cuff, emerald
clasp.)

Yes.

Defense: At the inquest you testified that there were
bloodstains on the doorjamb between bathroom and
bedroom, and on the bedclothing. Do you say so now?

Sergeant confused; contradicts himself; cannot remember now.

The testimony of the medical examiner: Death had resulted from a stab wound in the heart made by a blade not more than one inch wide. There were many other wounds upon the upper portion of the body, and bruises on the face. How many? Ten stab wounds in all, some with bruises. Deceased had been dead for not less than twelve hours or more than twenty-four.

Defense: In your opinion, Doctor, these wounds were very severe?

Yes.

Have you ever before seen wounds as severe as these?

Once or twice.

No more?

No.

Can you tell us about one of those other cases where the wounds were very severe—savage, would you say?

Yes. Savage. Ah—five years ago or so there was a case of a seaman murdered on Long Wharf. He was pretty badly cut up.

As bad as this?

Pretty nearly.

And was the murderer apprehended?

Oh yes, they got him right away.

And can you describe him?

The fellow who did it? He was a Russian fellow, hardly spoke English, about six feet three, I'd say, about two hundred and fifty pounds, a big Russian bear, he was.

The testimony of Isabel's coachman: He had driven her, Mason, and Mary to Boston from Newport on the morning of August 11. He had been given notice only the night before. Usually he had at least several days to prepare for a long trip.

Defense: Had Mrs. Kittredge ever gone anywhere on short notice?

Yes; several times. Last year to Nahant; the year before to Franconia Notch.

The testimony of Isabel's servants: On the day of her arrival from Newport she had gone in and out at least twice; once with Mason, at least once alone. They could not remember the exact times: like the coachman, they had been put on short notice, the house needed to be opened three weeks ahead of schedule, food brought in and prepared. They had had only Mr. Kittredge to care for during the summer, and the house had been as good as closed. Mrs. Kittredge had seemed somewhat agitated.

Defense: Had she ever seemed agitated before?

Yes.

So this agitation was not unprecedented?

No.

Can you give us an instance—when something upset her?

I remember one time when the florist sent the wrong bouquet.

The florist sent the wrong bouquet. And she was upset?

Yes. Very much so.

To the coachman: Any other?

Ah—one time she was to go driving in the afternoon and the carriage wheel was loose and had to be fixed and I was late coming around.

And that upset her?

Yes. She cried very much.

At missing her afternoon drive?

Yes.

So in your experience Mrs. Kittredge could become upset over very little things—things that might not bother someone else?

Yes.

So it might on this occasion have been some little thing also?

Yes.

So little that she did not mention it to you?

Yes.

The testimony of Isabel's maid, Elsie: Mrs. Kittredge had come in after her visit to the tailor. Not upset. Had gone out again shortly afterward.

Did you see her go out?

No.

How did you know that she had gone?

They told me.

Did you see her return?

No.

When did you see her again?

Before dinner.

How much time had elapsed?

Three hours or so.

And what was her demeanor?

Quiet.

Not upset at all?

No. She was calm.

Holding the bracelet: Is this Mrs. Kittredge's?

Silence. Isabel had been a good mistress. Maid reluctant—

Is it?

It—it looks to be.

Yes or no?

Yes. (Very soft.)

A murmur through the room.

You have seen her wear it?

Yes.

Are there any articles of clothing missing from Mrs. Kittredge's wardrobe?

The maid is confused: she does not know what is meant by "missing." Her mistress' wardrobe changes with the seasons, clothing comes and goes. Many items go to charity; many more are made over by the dressmaker . . .

Defense: Did you at any time last August or since that time see any of Mrs. Kittredge's clothing that was stained with blood?

No.

Or any stain at all?

No.

Nothing needed to be cleaned in any special way?

No. Nothing.

The testimony of the tailor: Mrs. Kittredge came to see him on the afternoon of August 11.

Was she alone?

No. Her son was with her.

Do you remember how long they stayed?

Not more than an hour.

Do you remember the time?

After lunch. About two o'clock, I'd say.

The testimony of the doorman at Newhall Gardens: Mr. Cushing had come in March, just about a year ago now. A quiet tenant, no loud parties, no trouble. He had occasional visitors, mostly gentlemen. A lady came once in a while—that lady there in the dock.

The courtroom hushed: this was what they had come to hear. How I despised them!

The lady's appearance? Short, he would say; heavily veiled always. Often she wore a black coat or a brown cape. He had never seen her face; her voice, when she spoke to him through her veil, had been muffled. How many times had she come? Perhaps two dozen in all. And on the day of Cushing's death? He had not seen her come in; he had been around at the back overseeing the delivery of another tenant's trunks. He saw her go out but they did not speak.

Defense: A short woman, heavily veiled?

Yes.

You positively stated before that the woman was Mrs. Kittredge. You are sure it was she?

Yes.

Why?

The way she walked.

A door opens. Two women come in got up in cape and veil. They walk to the witness box and back.

Defense: Can you tell us which of these women is Mrs. Kittredge?

Witness silent, struggling.

Well?

That one—on the left.

Thank you. Would you (to the women) remove your veils, please?

Veils removed to reveal Isabel on the right; woman on the left identified as Elizabeth Brown; occupation music teacher, no connection to the present case.

A heavier murmur from the crowd; the judge frowns and coughs, picking up his gavel but not rapping it.

Defense: Do you say now that you can positively identify the defendant as the woman you saw leaving Newhall Gardens on the afternoon of August 11?

No.

A soft sighing sound sweeps the courtroom: tension broken, breath expelled. *He cannot. . . .*

The testimony of Dr. Parkin, the alienist who had treated Isabel at Philadelphia: Do you have an opinion, Doctor, about the defendant's mental stability while she was under your care?

I do.

And can you tell us what it is?

She was hysterical.

Can you describe that condition for the court?

She was subject to extremes of behavior—very passive, very—ah—distraught.

And you treated her for this condition?

Yes.

How?

I placed her in a darkened room. No visitors. No reading material or sewing. Once a day she was brought out for a cold bath lasting for half an hour. I regulated her diet—no stimulants, no red meat, no sweets.

And did she improve under your care?

Not at first.

And then?

I operated on her. I—ah—removed her female organs.

I see. And this operation cured her?

It always does except in the most severe cases.

But it cured Mrs. Kittredge specifically?

Yes.

Can you describe her condition afterward?

She was calm. Rational.

And in your opinion could there be a recurrence of her hysteria?

Of course anything is possible.

But probable?

It is possible.

The defense: Dr. Parkin, do you have any memory of any patient reverting to her former hysterical state after you performed your operation on her?

No.

So when you say that it is "possible" that Mrs. Kittredge would become hysterical again, it is a very small possibility indeed, is it not?

Yes.

So small as to be almost impossible?

Yes.

And you have examined her recently, have you not?

Yes.

And what is her condition now?

She is calm. Even, I should say, passive.

Not violent at all?

No.

Nor capable of violence?

Of course anything is possible. But I should think not.

But now more damaging material: a letter unsigned but written in Isabel's hand, testified to by an expert in handwriting. A letter undated—when was it written?

Found in Cushing's desk. Not recent: impossible to tell when it was sent. Contents never meant to be exposed—a painful letter of good-bye, a heart-wrenching confession. The first meat of the trial. The groundlings devour it, eyes avid, courtroom as silent as the tomb while the prosecutor reads it and offers it in evidence:

> . . . and so I must say farewell, I cannot and yet I must, I cannot live without you, I cannot bear your loving someone else. . . .

Isabel like a graven image—like the statues of the pharaohs, distant, enigmatic, unlike the vigorous, lifelike statues that we put up now, striding generals, grave philosophers visibly thinking. She is not here, I thought: by the mercy of God she has removed herself.

The defense: Did the witness recall the trial of Jeremy Stout held in November of 1897?

Witness, looking uneasy, admitted that he did.

In that trial witness identified a letter as having been written by the deceased's mother, did he not?

Yes.

When in fact it had been written by his sister. Was that not correct?

It was the only time in twenty years—

Yes or no—the witness had incorrectly identified the author of that letter, had he not?

Yes.

Hour after hour, day after day the drone of voices went on in that hot, crowded courtroom. The judge sat like an old turtle, hunching his head down into his robes, his old eyes flicking back and forth, back and forth, from attorneys to witness to the jury and, occasionally, to the prisoner in the dock. The jury sat impassive, twelve men called to judge one woman: what were they thinking? In the first rows of the spectators sat Isabel's husband, her older children, Leighton and his wife and Grace. Curtis sat with the defense lawyers and lent his skill to theirs.

After each day's session, coming out into the city's cold damp night air, I often felt as though I had been away for weeks instead of just a day—the hustle and jumble of the city after the stern decorum of the court, the freedom to come and go after the iron rule of the judge's gavel.

For Isabel, of course, there was no freedom, since she was their prisoner. They made a special cell for her in the Charles Street jail, and there she was taken each evening. I went to see her on Saturdays. She was always frighteningly calm; once, when I was near tears, she soothed me with her smile, her shining eyes.

We were not allowed to touch.

"They have no case!" said Curtis; and yet . . .

They had Charlotte. Poor child! They brought her back from Montana and forced her to take the stand and admit her shame for all the world to hear; and why Ellsworth did not leave her then, and file for the divorce which undoubtedly would have been given him, I cannot say except that he is—and always was—a faithful and trusting man who, quite simply, loved his wife. Even the revelations that they pulled from her in that terrible trial did not lessen that love.

"They are trying to establish motive," said Curtis.

"But it won't hold, it won't hold. It is too flimsy."

I searched the faces of the jurors as Charlotte, near tears, testified to her brief infatuation with Lawrence Cushing. Would they not have sympathy for a woman whose daughter behaved so foolishly?

But then I reminded myself that they needed no sympathy for her, for she was not guilty.

But—again—they needed to find her so.

On it went, on and on, a nightmare never ending. Charlotte's testimony, damaging as it was, was only the prelude to something far worse. I was sitting with Carrie in the front row of spectators. As I glanced at Curtis I saw him stare at a witness just being ushered in and onto the stand. He was a big man, dark and glowering, neatly but not expensively dressed in a dark suit. He took the oath easily enough and gazed out over the courtroom as if to say, "You all fancy yourselves my betters, but we will see who comes out better in this contest."

The witness, whose Cockney accent grated on our ears, gave his name as Chester Barlow. He was a resident of Newport. He had been in service for the last ten years to a variety of employers, some of whose names he gave. During the previous summer he had worked for the gentleman who had leased Green Harbor—Mr. Lawrence Cushing.

The prosecutor: I would ask you to look at the witness whom we have just heard—Mrs. Ellsworth Barnes. Have you ever seen this person before?

Yes, sir.

Where did you see her?

At Newport.

And can you recall any specific occasion when you saw her?

Yes, sir.

And when was that?

She came to Green Harbor one night with Mr. Cushing.

Could you say about what time?

It was just past eleven.

And how do you know that?

I was sitting in the kitchen. When the front bell rang I looked at the clock because it seemed early for him to come back.

You had not expected him until later?

No, sir.

What did you do then?

I went upstairs to admit him.

Was he alone?

No, sir.

Who was with him?

A lady.

Could you identify her?

Yes, sir.

Do you see her now?

Yes, sir.

Can you point her out for the court?

Over there, sir. In the brown hat and coat.

Silence. The judge held us all in his power; no one dared move or make a sound.

That is the witness we have just heard—Mrs. Ellsworth Barnes, who was at that time Miss Charlotte Kittredge?

Yes, sir.

You are absolutely sure?

Yes, sir.

Very well. Can you tell us what happened next?

Nothing, sir. That is to say—I went back to the kitchen, not knowing if I would be needed again.

And what did they do?

They went into the library.

And did you see Mrs. Barnes again?

No, sir.

And what did you do?

I waited for Mr. Cushing to tell me that it was all right to retire.

And did he?

Yes, sir.

When?

It was just on one-thirty.

Can you tell us how he appeared? Was he calm, or upset—how did he seem to you?

He seemed—content.

Content. Ah—how was he dressed?

He had taken off his jacket, and his collar and his white tie. He had on a silk robe.

And he was alone?

Yes, sir.

You did not see Mrs. Barnes again?

No, sir.

And what happened then?

I retired.

And was your night's rest undisturbed?

No, sir.

What happened to disturb it?

The bell rang about a half hour later.

The bell—to the front entrance?

Yes, sir. It is connected to my room.

I see. And did you go to answer it?

Yes, sir.

Even though you were presumably in your—ah—nightclothes?

Yes, sir. I pulled on my coat and trousers and went down.

And who was at the door?

Mr. Cushing had admitted her, sir. They were in the library.

Did you see who it was?

Yes, sir.

Is she here today?

Yes, sir.

Would you be so kind as to point her out?

Yes, sir. The lady in the dock—Mrs. Kittredge.

This time the judge found it more difficult to silence the spectators. How I hated them! Buzzing and nodding and winking their knowing eyes—but they knew nothing! Nothing of all the years that had brought us to this—nothing of her pain, her anguish!

Silence. The relentless questioning began again, spinning a web of half-truth and innuendo that would catch her and never let her free.

Now, Mr. Barlow. You are positive that it was the defendant whom you saw with Mr. Cushing?

Yes, sir.

And could you hear what was being said between them?

Yes, sir.

The door was open?

Yes, sir.

And you listened?

Yes, sir.

The prosecutor had turned halfway round so that I could see his face. Even though Barlow was his witness, even though Barlow was helping him to build his case against Isabel, he wore a look of contempt now for this man, a member of the servant class, who admitted to eavesdropping. How we depend on our servants, and how we despise them!

And what did you hear?

Mrs. Kittredge accused him of ruining her daughter.

A low murmur, prelude to something more, dying away at the impatient tap of the gavel.

Ruining, Mr. Barlow? Is that the word she used?

Yes, sir.

And what was Mr. Cushing's reply?

He threatened to tell Mr. Barnes unless Mrs. Kittredge got ten thousand dollars for him.

Pandemonium—quickly and fiercely silenced. But they smelled blood now, they would not be silenced for long, they hovered on the edges of their seats, they licked their lips, they blinked their eyes, hungry to see her brought down, torn limb from limb or stoned, at least, as women were stoned in the old days.

The defense went at him with a vengeance as if he

himself were on trial. They attacked him—savaged him until (so they hoped) no word of his on any subject at all would be believed.

He had been in service for ten years? Longer than that, surely? In 1882, for instance, had he not been in service in the home of Mr. John Farley in New York City? And was dismissed for forging Farley's name upon a bank draft? Yes?

Yes.

They attacked his character, his veracity, his honesty. They called one former employer to testify that Barlow had been dismissed for stealing and had in fact been convicted and imprisoned for it; they called another to testify that he had been dismissed for impregnating a maid and procuring an abortion for her. They called Barlow's former wife, whom they located in western New York State, to testify that he had lied when he married her, that he had a wife still living in England. When finally he left the box, I thought that he could have sworn that the earth was round and no one would have believed him.

And now it was my turn. I climbed slowly into the box; my knees were trembling but I heard my voice strong and steady as I took the oath. I dared not look at Isabel. I looked only at the prosecutor, a tall, balding man who looked unhappy—profoundly sorry at having to perform the distasteful task of questioning me.

"Mrs. Motley, how long have you known the defendant?"

"For nearly thirty years."

"You would describe yourself as a lifelong friend,

would you not?"

"Yes."

"Perhaps her dearest friend?"

"Yes."

"And did you know the deceased?"

"Slightly."

"Can you describe what you mean by 'slightly'?"

"I knew him—only to speak to."

"You would not describe him as a close friend?"

"No."

"Not someone you would have—for instance—invited to dinner at your home?"

"Probably not."

"Not someone who would have—ah—called upon you?"

"I would not have expected him to."

I saw his trap—*what did he know?*—but I could not see how to avoid it.

"Would you have—ah—allowed him to put his name upon your dance card at a ball?"

"Probably."

"You did in fact dance with Mr. Cushing last summer, did you not?"

An objection from the defense: what did Mrs. Motley's dancing partners have to do with the business at hand?

Sustained. The prosecution continued unruffled.

"Mrs. Motley, did you ever have any extended conversation with the deceased?"

The trap sprang open.

"Yes."

"Can you tell us about it? Where did it take place?"

"At Newport."

"When?"

"Last summer."

"Can you be more specific? June? July?"

"Late June, I believe."

"Late June. Go on."

"It was—at a party."

"Whose party, Mrs. Motley?"

"Mrs. Peter Plunkett's."

"And only there? Nowhere else did you speak to him?"

What does he know?

"We went driving."

"Then? The next day? The next day after?"

"No. That night."

"You went driving? You left Mrs. Plunkett's?"

"Yes."

Pause; pace a bit. Return to the attack.

"With a man you say you hardly knew?"

"Yes."

"Is it your habit, Mrs. Motley, to go driving at night with men you say you know only slightly?"

"No."

"But with Lawrence Cushing you did. Why?"

"He asked me."

"Ah. He asked you."

Pause again. Smirk. Return to the attack.

"It is not our purpose here, Mrs. Motley, to—ah—sully your reputation." A snicker from the audience, a warning glance from the judge. "Can you tell us why Mr. Cushing asked you to go driving with him at that unlikely hour?"

"He—he was bored, I think."

"Bored. So he asked you—forgive me, madam, I do not wish to seem discourteous—but you are a lady of some years, you are not—ah—you are not one of the debutantes who so frequently adorn festivities at Newport and in our own fair city as well. If Mr. Cushing was bored and wished to amuse himself—I must be blunt—why should he have asked you to accompany him? Why not some—ah—younger lady?"

Objection: the witness cannot be expected to have known the motive for the deceased's having asked her to go driving.

"Your Honor, bear with me for one moment. I am trying to establish the motive for this crime—for this man's brutal murder."

Objection sustained.

"Now, Mrs. Motley: what did he say to you that night as you went driving?"

Pause. The trap yawned in front of me, its steel teeth gleaming, waiting to snap shut.

"I don't remember."

Pause. Pace. Turn. "You don't remember? When a man you say you hardly knew asks you to go driving at midnight—it was midnight, was it not?—to leave a grand party, to walk away in the face of all your friends—and you say you don't remember?"

"It was—he spoke of Newport, of the people there, mutual acquaintances—"

"Mutual acquaintances. For instance—"

"Our hostess, Mrs. Plunkett."

"And?"

"Several of the other ladies who were there."

"Yes? Their names?"

"Mrs. Southard, Mrs. Lamb."

"Did he mention the defendant's name?"

"I believe he did."

"You believe he did. Can you remember what he said of her?"

"Not particularly."

"Nothing?"

"Only—that I was staying with her—which I always did, it was known that I did—"

"Because you were her close friend."

"Yes."

"And that is all? Nothing else?"

"About her? No."

"About anything, Mrs. Motley."

"He said—that he would go away soon again."

"Ah. That he would go away soon again. Can you remember how he phrased that?"

"Not exactly. Only that he would stay the season and then go."

"Did he say where?"

"To London, as I recall."

"Nothing else?"

"No."

Pause. The courtroom was silent. I heard the echo of my voice in my ears. A moment's respite, and then the attack again.

"Mrs. Motley, were you aware of any trouble between the defendant and the deceased?"

Objection.

Sustained.

"Mrs. Motley, did Mr. Cushing pay particular attention to any lady in Newport last summer?"

Careful now: very careful.

"I believe he did, yes."

"And who was that?"

"Her name was Jeffries, I believe—Julia Jeffries."

"And do you know what their relationship was?"

"Not exactly."

"Did you hear that they were to be married?"

"I heard it, yes."

"And did you believe it?"

"I don't know."

"Do you know why, Mrs. Motley, that relationship between Miss Jeffries and Mr. Cushing was broken off?"

"No."

"No idea?"

"She returned home, I believe."

"She returned—why?"

"I don't know."

"Could it have been because her reputation was called into question?"

Objection, Your Honor. This line of questioning is not relevant.

Your Honor, I am once again trying to establish motive. I assure you that this matter is most relevant.

Objection overruled. But proceed carefully.

Thank you, Your Honor.

"Mrs. Motley, what was said in Newport about Miss Jeffries?"

"I don't remember. I never heard anything."

A baleful look. He disliked me, I was not a helpful witness.

"Which, Mrs. Motley? You don't remember, or you never heard anything?"

"I don't remember hearing anything."

"The defendant never mentioned Miss Jeffries?"

"No." *On my sworn oath . . .*

"Now, Mrs. Motley. Let us come to the day that the defendant returned to Boston. You were staying at her home in Newport, were you not?"

"Yes."

"As you had done for many years?"

"Yes."

"We have had the testimony of her coachman that her decision was sudden and unexpected. She did not tell her servants ahead of time that she was leaving. Did she tell you?"

"No, but—"

"Just a simple yes or no, please. She did not tell you that she was leaving?"

"No."

"And under ordinary circumstances you would have expected her to stay until the end of the Newport season?"

"Yes."

"How did you learn that she had returned to Boston?"

"Her housekeeper told me."

"Her housekeeper told you. Did you find that odd?"

Carefully, carefully—I walked a minefield, every step threatened disaster.

The judge leaned toward me. "The witness shall

answer the question."

"I—not really."

"Just yes or no, Mrs. Motley. Did you think it odd that the defendant left you in her house—without a word of parting? And you her oldest, her dearest friend?"

"No."

"No? No? Can you explain why?"

"I—she had been under the very great strain of her daughter's wedding preparations." Careful. Careful. "I knew that she was tired. I could understand that she wanted to get away—"

"To a hot, dusty, dirty city while all of her friends and family were still at Newport or Bar Harbor or Nahant?"

Silence.

"Yes, Mrs. Motley? What is your opinion of that?"

"I—I have no opinion. I accepted it."

"You accepted it. And yet you yourself returned the following day, did you not?"

"Yes."

"Why, Mrs. Motley?"

"I—I too was tired of Newport. I wanted to come home."

"To a city which for all practical purposes was deserted?"

"I thought—that it would be restful."

"You did not come back for your friend's sake?"

"No."

"You were not concerned for her? About what she might do?"

"I—no."

"Did you contact her?"

"Yes."

"And did you see her?"

"Yes."

"When?"

"The day after my arrival."

"And did she tell you where she had been, what she had been doing?"

"Yes."

"And what was that?"

"She had taken her son to be fitted for clothing. She had supervised the opening of her house for the winter season. She had visited her own dressmaker."

"Nothing else?"

"No."

And then it was the turn of Isabel's lawyers to get what help they could out of me:

"Mrs. Motley, do you remember Charlotte Kittredge Barnes's wedding?"

"Yes."

"There were many guests there?"

"Yes, about two hundred."

"All of them, of course, were people with whom Mrs. Kittredge was friendly?"

"Yes."

"She would not have invited anyone to her daughter's wedding with whom she was not on good terms?"

"No."

"Was the deceased at that wedding?"

"Yes."

"An invited guest like all the others?"

"Yes."

"And he mingled freely—well known, well liked?"

"Yes."

"Did you see Mrs. Kittredge speak to him?"

"Yes."

"She was friendly to him?"

"Yes."

"No—ah—hesitation, no constraint in her manner?"

"No."

"You would not have said that they were enemies?"

"No. Certainly not."

"In your opinion, Mrs. Motley, knowing Mrs. Kittredge as well as you do, would she have invited the deceased to her daughter's wedding if she knew that he had—ah—ruined that daughter?"

"No."

"Or if he had demanded money from her?"

"No. Never."

"Such a man would not have been allowed to attend?"

"He would not have been allowed on the grounds. much less at the wedding."

"Now, Mrs. Motley, can you tell us about the last time you saw Mrs. Kittredge before she left Newport? Do you remember it?"

"Yes."

"When was it?"

"It was the evening of the day of the wedding."

"Where?"

"At her house—in the garden, more exactly. We were very warm, and we walked out to get a breath of air."

"And how would you describe Mrs. Kittredge that evening?"

"She was tired, of course. She had been very busy for days—weeks."

"How would you describe her—ah—state of mind?"

"She was happy for Charlotte."

"Yes. Anything else?"

"Not particularly. She was looking forward to having some rest; she was talking a bit about the season just past in Newport and the winter season in Boston. Nothing struck me particularly."

"She was not distressed in any way, distraught?"

"No. Not at all."

"Did she mention the deceased?"

"No."

"Anyone else in particular?"

"No."

"So you had no reason to fear for her—ah—mental balance?"

"No, not at all. She seemed perfectly normal, well and happy."

Never once during this exchange did I look at Isabel. What I said in that witness stand I said deliberately, it was a matter for me and my conscience.

And then the defense presented their own witnesses, character witnesses for Isabel, and they attacked motive, and they reminded the jury that the murder weapon had not been found, and they emphasized the absence of any bloodstains on Isabel's clothing. They brought in three women unknown to any of us who admitted to having had affairs with Cushing, thus leaving the implication that any one of them might have had a motive stronger than Isabel's supposed one.

667

They did not put Isabel herself on the stand—a tactical decision, said Curtis, but one for which I was very grateful. She could not, I think, have withstood such battering as others did.

Motive, and again motive—they hammered at it in their summing up, they came back to it again and again— what motive? Would a woman of Mrs. Kittredge's position really do such a deed? Consider the stupidity of it, if nothing else—consider what she had to lose. Everything! Whereas if she had simply kept silent she could have brazened it out, for it would have been Cushing's word against hers and Charlotte's together. The man would have been banished from decent society for trying to spread such a tale. No one would have believed him—no one! Gentlemen, gentlemen, do you really believe that a lady born and bred, a lady as refined and gentle as Mrs. Kittredge—and you have heard much testimony as to the worthiness of her character, her charitable work, her faithful attendance at church, her devotion to her family—do you believe that a woman of the very highest type, which she unquestionably is, could have committed this terrible crime which even the basest, most degraded man would hesitate to commit? What woman, the repository of all goodness and gentleness in the world, could have done such a thing? What woman? Not Mrs. Kittredge—most assuredly, gentlemen of the jury, not Mrs. Kittredge.

At last they were done, and the jury went out and we were left to wait. A speedy return, Curtis had said, almost surely would mean acquittal.

Minutes passed. It was midafternoon. The sky beyond

the tall windows of the half-deserted courtroom was blank and dirty white; an icy snow had begun to fall and it spat against the glass and slid down it in rivulets. I sat on the bench, Carrie beside me, and drifted into a soothing reverie. The room was very warm; I was uncomfortable in my gray woolen suit, but I declined Carrie's invitation to go across the street for a cup of tea because I wanted to be sure of a seat when the jury returned. I felt a great lassitude: all my strength had been sapped and I wondered how I would ever find the energy to rise and go home when it came time to do so.

The minutes became hours. The sky beyond the windows were dark. People wandered in and out; reporters huddled together in a corner; we saw no sign of any of the lawyers.

At last, near six o'clock, Carrie persuaded me to leave. "We will know as soon as it is humanly possible," she said, "and meanwhile we do Isabel no good by sitting here." And, since there was no possibility that we could see Isabel before the verdict came in, I agreed. As I rose to follow Carrie out, I saw among the few remaining spectators a woman whom I realized I had seen there often. She sat alone, staring into space: a small, pretty woman, finely dressed in a sealskin cape and muff, a large gray hat with a spray of matching plumes. Suddenly, as I came opposite her, she turned to look at me. Our eyes met, and I felt my heart contract. What sadness in her eyes, what anguish! I had seen that look before, I thought: I had seen Isabel look so. All the sorrows of the world seemed concentrated there.

The moment passed; she looked away and we went out.

"Who was that?" I said when we were in the corridor.

"Mrs. Strafford Newhall."

"Really? I've been introduced to her at least once, but I didn't recognize her just now. But I've seen her here— she's been here nearly every day. Why, I wonder?"

"To see one of her betters brought down," said Carrie grimly. "Nasty little climber."

We had a solitary supper that night, Diana and I: and I, at least, had a sleepless night. Why was the jury out so long? Who among those twelve men was arguing Isabel's guilt? I pictured them in their deliberation, smoking no doubt, jackets off, voices raised perhaps in heated argument over her fate. It did not seem possible that her innocence was in question and yet—what was keeping them?

On the following day I called around at Isabel's for Carrie, who was staying with Avery and the children, and together we went downtown to the court. We found Curtis in the corridor. His face told us the bad news: still out! He advised us to go home; he would telephone the verdict to us at once, he said, and meanwhile we could do no good there. And so we obeyed him and retraced our steps through the dirty, slushy streets to the new underground at Park Street, which in due course delivered us to the Back Bay.

No word came that day, and none the next. I did not go out. The weather continued foul, and so I stayed indoors with Diana and helped her with her lessons, and brought out a new piece of petit point for her to begin, and half a dozen times I took up a new novel and half a dozen times I put it down again. I sat by the windows in the drawing room and looked out on the dreary expanse of Beacon Street, a few pedestrians making their precarious passage, the horses pulling carriages and delivery wagons slipping and sliding their way through the uncertain footing. Even if the day had been mild and sunny I would have stayed indoors, for I did not want to meet anyone, I did not want to have to tiptoe around the topic of Isabel's trial, I could not bear to speak of it to anyone except her family. All winter I had avoided society for just that reason. I had long since run out of polite responses to people's horror at Isabel's situation (mingled all too often with delight), and yet I could not afford to be blunt, to shut them off and antagonize them, for I felt that to do so would in some way endanger her.

On the evening of the second day Curtis told us in tones of outrage that the jury had come in, exhausted, to report that they could not agree on a verdict; the judge had sent them out again for further deliberation. For the first time in all the long weeks since Isabel's arrest we were forced to consider the possibility that she might, after all, be found guilty. No, I thought: it could not be. Never, never could they convict her!

On the third day Carrie and I returned to court, unable to stay away longer. Surely, I thought, we must have the verdict today. A few spectators had taken their seats but the lawyers' places were empty; I did not see Mrs. Strafford Newhall either in the courtroom or in the corridor outside. After we had waited for nearly an hour I was aware of a sudden activity. The clerk came in, followed by the district attorney; next the defense lawyers appeared. Curtis saw us, and though he recognized us with no more than a brief nod we understood the jury was coming in at last. In no more than a moment the news had spread through the courthouse, and now the seats filled rapidly and a low hum of voices filled the cavernous room. I heard Carrie's quick intake of breath and I looked to see Isabel being led into the dock.

"All rise!" cried the clerk as the judge appeared.

And then the jury filed in. They say that experienced lawyers can read the verdict on the jurors' faces, but these men were impassive, I did not see how anyone could read theirs. I had begun to tremble; to keep my hands still I clasped them tight together, and then I felt Carrie's hand on mine and I clung to her.

"Gentlemen of the jury, what say you: Is the defendant Isabel Kittredge guilty of the matter whereof she stands indicted, or not guilty?"

Their foreman spoke, a short, stout man with a pompous air and a stentorian voice that has echoed in my mind all the years: "We find the defendant, Isabel Kittredge, not guilty!"

Sometime in the small hours of that night Mrs. Strafford Newhall threw herself from the Massachusetts Avenue bridge into the icy waters of the Charles.

Twenty-Two

The news of Isabel's acquittal dominated the headlines for one day and then, suddenly, it was over and we were allowed to take up our lives again freed of the intrusions of the press.

The suicide of Mrs. Strafford Newhall received less attention, but some little interest was aroused by a letter that she left behind and which an enterprising reporter for the Boston *Post* got hold of. It was, according to his report, a pathetic, tearstained missive, nearly incoherent (thus attesting to the disordered state of mind which had led her to take her life). "I cannot live without him," she had written; "even when I told him so he laughed, he would not believe me, but it is true. I cannot. She walks free and alive and he is dead. God forgive me but I loved him. She had no right to him. Why did she do such a cruel thing?"

"What does it mean?" I said to Curtis. "'She had no right'—what is the woman talking about?"

"Damned scribblers!" he said. "Poking and prying—it is beyond my comprehension how they can be allowed to print this vicious nonsense!"

The matter of Mrs. Newhall's letter was never explained or even, so far as I know, investigated; it sank beneath the surface of our lives even as she herself, poor soul, had vanished into the Charles.

Nor was the murder of Lawrence Cushing ever solved. The police kept the case officially open, waiting, presumably, for someone to come forth with new information; but the active pursuit of evidence had ceased.

Isabel came home. The winter ended; April came, spring abounded. Diana returned to school, where she was welcomed by repentant playmates. Charlotte, older, wiser, returned to the West, where her husband awaited her. Leighton and his wife went back to New York. I no longer dreaded awakening each morning. Our lives picked up; we slipped into them smoothly, gratefully, finding rest and solace in them, mending our shattered privacy.

In the middle of April Victoria announced that she had completed her *oeuvre* and had sent it to a publisher in New York.

"Not Boston?" I said. "We have several good publishers here."

"No. They are—ah—too stuffy. On the other hand, I wouldn't want to think that they would publish my book merely for the sensational value of my name." For she was proud of her work; she had abandoned the idea of a pseudonym.

Poor child! I could not help but agree with her; the name Kittredge would have a certain notoriety clinging to it for years to come. She might have capitalized on that, of course, but it seemed that now she was after something different.

"It's not a bad job, you know, Aunt Marian," she said with a sprightly laugh. "Not bad at all if I do say so. I want people to judge it on its own merits."

I did not know whether to be amused or annoyed. Proper ladies did not, after all, brag about their accomplishments—especially when the accomplishment was a scandalous *roman à clef.*

Within a week she announced that her book had been accepted for publication, and by mid-June I had a copy in my hands. Appropriately enough, it had been bound in red; its gilt letters spelled out the title: *A Slave to Love.* It was an immediate sensation, for its story—innocence seduced, betrayed, and abandoned—is one that safe, proper women everywhere never tire of reading. I myself was alternately fascinated and repelled, and yet, strangely, I am sure that reading Victoria's uninhibited confessions helped me to write my own. I could hardly believe that she had dared to put on paper her most intimate moments with Fletcher, and yet there it was for all the world to see. And—oddly—when I had finished it I did not feel disgust, I did not feel contempt; rather, I came away with deep sympathy for her, and a feeling that there but for the grace of God went I, and that all women—and men too, for that matter—were subject to those same weaknesses, those same passions, and that none of us had the right to turn our backs on one whom the world would call sinner.

Thousands and thousands of copies of *A Slave to Love*

were sold during the summer after its publication, and hundreds of thousands more in the years since. It has never been out of print; I saw it in a bookshop only the other day. Not only did Victoria become wealthy; she became herself a figure of enormous interest—sometimes, I feared, in the manner of one of Barnum's freaks. She was invited to lecture everywhere save Boston, where the Watch and Ward, still energetic long after Perseus' death, succeeded in banning her. She was amused. "Let them!" she said, her small, perfect chin tilted in an attitude of defiance. "They can't stop me elsewhere, and someday I'll appear in Boston too." It was, in fact, a wonder that they did not ban her book as well as her person, but I suppose that even the Watch and Ward knew its limits; contraband copies would have flooded the city and would have made a mockery of the Society's vigilance.

Isabel went to Newport that summer, of course, and Diana and I were with her.

I say "of course"—but she might have withdrawn; she might, after such an ordeal, have never wanted to see Newport or her Newport circle again. Many women, even women of Isabel's station, have been ostracized for less—for nothing, compared to the scandal in which she had been enmeshed.

It was her pride that sustained her. I drove down with her on a brilliant day in June and walked through the Casa del Mare with her, the housekeeper in tow, as she prepared to open the house for another season. She was full of plans for her first reception, which was to be held the following week. It never occurred to her that people would refuse her invitations, and in fact they did not. They came from curiosity, perhaps, to see how she had survived; but they stayed, and came again, from admiration. She stood in the reception hall that night, resplendent in a new gown of pale yellow silk, a diamond stomacher at her waist, her eyes sparkling more brightly than any diamond, and greeted her guests as if she had never known an hour of scandal in her life. Victoria was at her side. She welcomed her mother's guests as if she were her namesake herself, with regal courtesy, conferring upon them the honor of being received in that house.

I look back on that summer, the last of the old century, through a golden mist of happiness, for that was Isabel's last great season at Newport. Day after perfect day she triumphed, night after night she was the center of attention. Whether as hostess or guest, she knew her part and played it magnificently: smiling, charming, gracious —and always sustained by that iron pride, that ramrod backbone bred into the ruling families of New England from the first Puritans.

The sun never shone so bright as it did that summer, the air never sparkled so clear; the sky was unsullied by a cloud, so it seemed, and at night the stars twinkled like diamonds hurled against the blackness by some wildly extravagant debutante. The champagne we drank in lively toasts enlivened us to dance all the more through the night, and the rich food that we consumed gave us only stamina, never dyspepsia. There may have been unhappiness—even sorrow, even tragedy—that summer at Newport, but we never saw it; it was as if we had stopped Time in his tracks, and once again we were young, and happy, and heedless of the years to come.

The magic of those weeks included Victoria. Of course everyone read her book at once; and no matter what headshaking occurred behind her back, people were quick to congratulate her, to give receptions for her, and dinners, and even a few afternoon readings.

It was at one of these events, an evening affair, that she met Count Ulrich von Bernstorff. I saw them meet, and the enchantment of that moment was simply a distillation of the enchantment of the summer. It was at a waltz evening at Oyster Point, a Venetian palazzo built several years previously by Mrs. Morton Chubb. As was the custom at such evenings, the ladies had their dance cards filled out in advance; the fourth place on Victoria's card bore the name of a young man who only that afternoon had slipped on a grass court at the Casino and broken his arm. Count von Bernstorff was his replacement. As the moment arrived for the gentlemen to find their partners and escort them onto the dance floor Count von Bernstorff came to Victoria, who was standing with her mother and me. She looked at him, amused, as he audibly clicked his heels and bowed and offered her his arm. Since she had not been informed of her partner's injury she had no idea who this young man was. And then, all in an instant as their eyes met, she saw him and recognized him; he was the man with whom she was going to fall in love. So simple it was, so sudden—as if she had been struck by the lightning that we never saw, that summer, in the sky.

"Miss Kittredge?" He smiled at her; and his smile was

as intimate as if they were lovers already. He was a man of only medium height but his proud, erect bearing made him seem tall. His delicate features, his dark, long-lashed eyes were more than handsome: they bespoke generations—centuries—of patrician ancestry (Prussian, as it turned out), which had produced fine character as well. You could not look at Count Ulrich von Bernstorff but that you saw a man of such goodness, such rectitude and decency that you would trust him with your life. Add to all of this an enormous charm—an absolutely devastating appeal—and it is not difficult to understand Victoria's immediate capitulation.

As he led her out onto the floor Isabel turned to me, astonished. "Did you see that?"

"I did."

"Am I dreaming?"

"No. We are all quite awake."

"Look, Marian—ah, *look.*"

The music had begun: the "Acceleration Waltz." They started slowly, two separate people, lightly touching, patterning their steps to the music: *one* two three, *one* two three, around and around, accelerating with the music until their bodies were no longer two but one, circling and swaying, faster and faster until they whirled in a race to keep up; they passed us in a blur of motion, obedient to the call of the rhythm. Their eyes were locked in an embrace; they were alone, they neither knew nor cared for the other dancers, for anyone else in the world. When they had finished, when the music stopped and he brought Victoria back to us, we saw at once that it was not only the dancing that had made her breathless.

And so, that night, Isabel snared a title at last. Fate has its ironies: just when she least expected it, this European nobleman—the real thing, the absolutely genuine article—dropped into her lap. Or, rather, into the palm of Victoria's dainty, ink-stained hand.

"I can't believe it," said Isabel some days later, "he is simply too good to be true, Marian. And he does not mind a bit that she is so celebrated—he delights in it, I think."

Nor did he mind, apparently, that Isabel herself was lately notorious; perhaps he did not know. He had come to America in the spring, starting at Charleston and working his way north. At each city he had been introduced to the cream of the debutante crop. Always he had moved on. Now, in Newport—and later in Boston— he would stay, for he had found what he sought.

In early September he returned to Boston when Isabel did, and by then it was an accepted fact, although not yet publicized, that he and Victoria would marry.

Isabel was quite blunt about Victoria's deficiencies as the bride of a Prussian count. "The affair with Fletcher, for one thing," she said, "would ordinarily rule her out completely. But von Bernstorff is the last of the line and no one can keep him from marrying whomever he pleases. And as for her gadding about—he goes with her, as if he were her adviser—her manager!" And indeed the two of them had become an accustomed sight as he accompanied her at her lectures, dancing attendance on her, ready to envelop her in a velvet or sable cloak as the weather grew cold, transporting her in his carriage or, to distant places, in the most expensive railway accommodations short of a private car. "And I imagine he'd have that for her if she'd consent to it," said Isabel. She seemed bemused—thunderstruck at the good fortune that had befallen her wayward child—her black sheep, as she must have thought of her.

They were to be married the day before New Year's— the last day of the old century. And so once again Isabel was plunged into the round of wedding preparations, and I along with her. No expense, apparently, was to be spared; money was never mentioned, certainly not by me. Avery came and went like a stranger; once in a while I passed him coming in or going out and we spoke like promenaders on the deck of an ocean liner. What he thought of Victoria's book, of her ceaseless round of activity, of her engagement, I did not know. From time to time—at a dinner, at a reception—I saw him in Isabel's presence. He hardly seemed to notice her. He spoke politely to me, to the others, but no smile ever crossed his large, grave face, and his eyes seemed to look through us, beyond us, as if they were focused on some more important vision.

The announcement of Victoria's impending wedding to Count von Bernstorff only added to her desirability as a lecturess, and all that fall, while her mother and I worked to prepare her wedding, she traveled hither and yon speechifying about her book and the true-life experiences upon which it was based. The newspapers could not get enough of her. Her comings and goings were chronicled as if she were royalty itself. Countless people came to see her, to hear her, to request her autograph; adoring crowds cheered her in lecture halls across New England and beyond; and more than once

Isabel's man opened the door to find a worshipful admirer on the front steps, hoping for a glimpse of Victoria, or perhaps a word with her, or an autograph.

She was married to Count von Bernstorff on New Year's Eve, and we raised our glasses to 1900 with her wedding. She was magnificent, and Isabel even more so. There might never have been a shadow of impropriety on the Kittredge name. Their heads high, their posture regal, their smiles perfection, they were the picture of proud gentility.

The crowd that watched the bride and groom depart for the railway station nearly rivaled the one that had mobbed Consuelo Vanderbilt a few years previously. Victoria was happy to see them; she waved at them, and blew kisses, and tore roses from her bouquet to throw into their midst. They cheered her, calling her name, adoring her—and there is no doubt that she loved them in return, she bloomed on their adulation. The wedding trip, in fact, was hardly that at all—a week on a yacht in the Southern waters, and then a transcontinental lecture tour. Surely Victoria was the only bride in the history of Eastern society to spend her honeymoon speaking coast to coast about the horrors of her aborted elopement with another man!

And so, suddenly, it was over; and for the first time in more than a year peace and quiet came to us again. A heavy snowstorm on January 2 only added to my desire to stay indoors, solitary, to recuperate from the exhausting months just passed. I telephoned Isabel once or twice, but I did not see her until more than a week after Victoria's wedding. Then I called the carriage one afternoon and drove through the snowy streets to Commonwealth Avenue. The house was quiet; only Isabel was at home. As she greeted me with a slow, tired smile I saw that suddenly she looked years older: she had aged ten—twenty—years in only a few days.

We sat in companionable silence by the fire in her sitting room and sipped hot tea. She smoked a cigarette and focused her eyes on the thin stream of smoke curling from its tip. Her small, plump hand trembled slightly. She was not laced; she wore a loose afternoon gown under which the soft lines of her body sank back comfortably into her velvet slipper chair.

"I wonder," she said suddenly, "if he went to heaven."

She did not look at me; she stared into the fire.

"Or perhaps," she went on, "perhaps he went to hell, as they say sinners do. Perhaps he burns like that coal in the grate."

So calm was she, so quiet—and yet, what was she saying? I had no idea how to reply to her, and so I waited, I held my breath and did not dare to move. The electric lamps on either side of the marble mantel dimmed and then brightened again as they often did, uncertain, undependable.

"I will burn too, I fear," she said. "Did you know that I am a great sinner, Marian? I have sinned every day of my life since I married Avery, and that is twenty-nine years come May."

Still she spoke in that tired, slurred way; and it occurred to me to wonder if she had taken laudanum. Despite the electric lamps the room was too dim to see

683

whether her pupils were constricted.

"Isabel—"

"No!" Suddenly her face came alive, her eyes sparkled with—what? The need to tell her secrets? "I know what you want to say, you want to help me, to send for the doctor, to ask me if I want to sleep. Sleep!" She laughed but it was not a pleasant sound. "I will sleep soon enough. Even as he sleeps, there in his grave in Mount Auburn. And who put him there, Marian? Who sent him to dance in those flames?" She reached out to me and I clasped her hand. She was there already, I thought: she lives in eternal torment, even as we are told the poor lost souls in hell suffer their damnation.

She clung to me and laughed in that agonizing way. "Do you know what I think, Marian? I think that the prosecutor was—"

A knock at the door came then, and she pulled back and instantly composed herself.

"Come!"

It was Mary, her youngest child, a sweet, quiet girl, not a beauty by any standard but pretty enough to find a husband when her time came. Dutifully, she was stopping in to see her mother after her return from school. We chatted for a time and then, in the manner of old friends, Isabel announced to me that she was tired and wanted to rest for a while. She had recovered her composure; I was sure that Mary sensed nothing wrong. Since I could hardly argue with Isabel, accordingly I took my leave and allowed Mary to see me out.

The lights were just coming on as Henry drove me home. The streets were banked with snow, and the sky, dark in the east, was pale rosy-tinged blue where the sun had gone down. Twilight is my favorite hour, a magical time suspended between day and dark, a time of anticipation: people hurrying home, preparing for the evening's pleasures, making safe against the night. Comfortably ensconced under my lap robe, borne safely through the streets in my carriage, I pondered Isabel's outburst. *"Do you know what I think?"* she had said. How I wished that Mary had come five minutes later! For I had no idea what Isabel thought, no notion of what went on inside her head. *"The prosecutor"*—what? What had she been about to say?

I telephoned her that evening, but the maid said that Mrs. Kittredge was sleeping and was not to be disturbed. On whose orders, I thought; and how did they know she was sleeping?

Again the next day I was put off. That evening I rang Curtis and told him of my concern: did she really not want to speak to me, or was she being prevented? Wait another day, he said, and if you are still unsuccessful, let me know and I will go to her.

The next morning, again, they would not let me speak to her. I put back the earpiece and stood in the hall, irresolute; then I went to the vestibule door and opened it and looked out through the sidelights at the sunny day. I opened the front door and stood on the stoop breathing in the soft, mild air. It was the thaw: melting snow dripped from the eaves, the sun shone brightly, even the horses in the street seemed invigorated, no longer braced against winter's iron cold.

The day called to me. I fetched my warmest cloak and

my galoshes and my hat and gloves and muff and began to walk toward Isabel's. I came to Commonwealth Avenue, passing the variegated and yet elegantly uniform housefronts, each with its prim flight of brownstone or limestone steps, each with its individual facade which the eye, scanning the length of the street, made into a pleasing architectural whole. The trees that lined the central mall formed a kind of screen through which I saw a similar facade opposite; their spare, bare branches, like trees in a Japanese painting, pointed to the soft blue sky as if they begged the warming sun to warm them into bud. But this was false warmth—false promise; we had many weeks of cold to endure before the mall bloomed again.

At last I came to Isabel's. A carriage that I did not recognize stood at the curb, its coachman seemingly asleep on his perch. As I went up the steps to the front door it was thrown open and a well-dressed, middle-aged man came out and hurried past me down the steps, barely nodding at me, touching his fingers to the brim of his top hat. I stared after him. I had seen him before; I knew him, but how? And, further, although I could not remember our meeting, I knew that it had not been a happy one. I watched him as he sprang into his carriage, and then I watched the driver, instantly awakened, as he flicked the reins and the coach pulled away.

Who—? The man's identity hovered at the edges of my recollection, but I could not place him.

More than a little uneasy now, I proceeded to pull the bellpull. At once the door was opened by the butler.

"Good morning, Vickers. Is Mrs. Kittredge in?"

"Good morning, madam. She is, but I have orders—" He stopped, embarrassed, his face faintly pink.

I stood on the step feeling like an unsuccessful encyclopedia peddler. I was too alarmed, now, to be annoyed.

"Vickers, what is it? What orders do you have?"

He stepped back and motioned me inside. "One moment, madam. If you could step into the reception room."

This man had been in Isabel's service for ten years at least. I knew him as well as one can ever know other people's servants, which is to say that I had seen him in good times and bad; but never had I seen him quite so constrained, so cautious. Why?

Alone in the small, ornate reception room, with its gilt chairs and brocaded walls hung with popular etchings, I was ridiculously ill at ease. This was the home of my oldest friend—a house that I knew almost as well as my own. Why, then, did I feel like a stranger—an interloper who had forced her way in?

I heard one sharp tap on the door. Immediately it opened to reveal a woman who came in and shut it behind her. She was of medium height, thin, dressed severely in black, her gray hair pulled into a tight knot on her neck. Her eyes were small and dark, bracketing her sharp little nose; her thin-lipped mouth turned down at the corners, giving her a contemptuous look.

"Yes?" she said abruptly, giving me a sweeping up-and-down look; what she saw did nothing to change her unpleasant expression.

Annoyance tickled my brain and quickened my

tongue, but I kept myself in check. "Good morning," I said as pleasantly as I could. "You are—?"

"Mrs. Briggs."

"And your position?"

"Nurse." She snapped out her words as if she were a miser, and they gold that she did not want to expend.

"I see. And you have been employed to care for—"

"Mrs. Kittredge."

"Yes. I have come to see her."

"No visitors, the doctor said."

"But—"

She was not quite a servant, and she took full advantage of that fact.

"Doctor's orders," she said; somewhere in the depths of those hostile eyes I saw grim amusement.

"Then let me leave her a note."

She made no response, and so I took a card from my handbag and bent over the small inlaid desk where pen and ink were kept for the convenience of callers who, like me, were denied admittance but still wished to leave a message. I wrote three words—"Please call me"—but I did not put the card into her outstretched hand. "I will just give this to her maid," I said.

"Her maid has gone." What satisfaction this woman had from giving bad news!

"Gone! You mean that she has left Mrs. Kittredge's employment?"

"I mean that Mr. Kittredge dismissed her."

As far as I knew, Avery had never involved himself in the management of the household's servants other than to complain now and then if something annoyed him—a bad meal, say, or a coachman who was perpetually tardy. For him to have dismissed Isabel's personal maid was an unprecedented breach of domestic etiquette.

"I will give it to Vickers then," I said.

"Mr. Kittredge has given me my orders," said Mrs. Briggs. "All communication with Mrs. Kittredge is to pass through me."

Without a further word I walked out of the room and into the front hall. It was empty, and for a moment I considered bolting up the broad oak staircase to Isabel's room. But of course my heavy skirts and tight lacing made such a scheme impossible, and even if I succeeded in reaching Isabel this time I would undoubtedly be banished from the house thereafter.

I heard Mrs. Briggs behind me as she came out from the reception room.

"I will have Vickers show you out," she said.

"He doesn't need—" I began, and then I caught myself. There was a slight commotion at the door, and then I saw Avery coming in, red-faced, slightly winded, undoubtedly having just walked home from his office downtown.

"Ah, Marian," he said by way of greeting; I was conscious of Mrs. Briggs's suspicious presence behind me and I was pleased that she could see at least that I was a friend of the family. Avery took my hand and held it for a moment and then glanced up at the nurse.

"You have met the newest member of our household, I see," he said.

"Yes. I just came by to see—"

"I know. Ah—just come with me for a moment into

the library. That is all right, Mrs. Briggs, I will see Mrs. Motley away."

I did not see the nurse's face as she left us, but I caught a glimpse of her ramrod back as she ascended the stairs.

Neither Avery nor I said a word further until we were alone in his library, the door shut against anyone who might care to listen. We seated ourselves on either side of the unlit fire, and without preliminary, he began to speak. "You should have told me you were coming," he said, and instantly I was in the wrong despite the fact that never once in all the years had I alerted Avery when I went to see Isabel.

"I didn't know— Why? Why should I?"

"Because, as you see, she is not—ah—competent." His face showed no emotion; he might have been discussing the illness of a stranger.

"But I do not see that, Avery. I do not see anything. I have not been permitted to. Why can I not see *her*, talk to her—"

He shook his head: a short, sharp no.

"Avery! Why? What is it? She is ill, isn't she, and you do not want to tell me—"

"She is physically well." He looked at me reprovingly as if I were an errant child. "But here"—he brushed his temple lightly with the fingers of his right hand—"she is not. She has after all been under rather a strain for the past year and more." He had never been given to sarcasm, but I heard it in his voice now.

"Yes, but—" But what? The reassurance that had sprung to my lips died before I could give it voice. What could I say to him? That everything had turned out for the best? That the nightmare of the trial had faded in the light of Victoria's triumph? That Isabel had survived in spite of everything, and that now she had only to live on, serene, triumphant, to a happy old age?

"Avery, let me see her. Please. You cannot deny me that—you cannot deny *her*. I am her dearest friend—"

"You do not need to remind me of your friendship. I sometimes wonder why— Well. Never mind. I know that you are faithful to her. And as soon as Dr. Gardner gives his permission I will send for you."

"Dr. Gardner!" Yes—that was the man I had passed, the man whom I could not place but whose face had had an unpleasant association. An image flashed into my mind: Isabel tied to her bed in a cell, Isabel begging for release. "Oh, Avery, is it as bad as that?"

"It is that bad and worse. He has ordered complete isolation. Mrs. Briggs is absolutely in charge. Isabel must be watched constantly. She is not—" He broke off, searching for the right word. After a moment he found it. "She is not responsible," he said.

Not responsible for what? I wondered. For her willful heart? For desires that she could not subdue? For the memory of the man that she carried with her always?

Tears rose to my eyes and I blinked them away. I felt a sudden stubborn pride; I did not want him to see what he was sure to interpret as foolish feminine weakness. I regained my composure; I stood up and held out to him the card upon which I had written my brief message.

"Give this to her, then," I said; but even as I spoke I was certain that he would not. "And tell her that I long to see her."

691

He looked up at me, and for a moment I thought that he would not—could not—rise to see me out. Then, slowly, as if he were exhausted unto death, he got to his feet.

"You understand," he said. "I must do for her as I see fit. She is not responsible."

I left him and went out. The sun had disappeared behind a bank of clouds and now the day was cold; we were in the grip of winter still, the thaw was Nature's jest to seduce us into surviving the weeks of cold yet to come. The freezing air stunned me; I walked rapidly toward home, my feet firm and steady on the pavement, but still I walked in a daze, I saw nothing of my surroundings, I might have passed a dozen people whom I knew and I would not have recognized them. My thoughts were with her—with Isabel, held captive there in her own home, as far from me as if she were with Captain Dreyfus on Devil's Island.

Why?

They say that Captain Dreyfus was innocent, that he was punished for a crime that he did not commit.

But what was Isabel's crime? And was she—could she have been—guilty?

I do not speak of the trial. There was some other, some larger crime—the crime of denying her heart's demands, perhaps: of living a life that was a lie.

But if she were guilty of that crime, then so were we all.

And if she were guilty, then surely Avery, now, was having his revenge.

Twenty-Three

The thaw left us the next day, and the day after that we were housebound by a blizzard that nearly rivaled that of '88. When the streets had been cleared and we were able to get around once more I called at Isabel's to inquire whether I could see her. Not surprisingly, the answer was no. A few days later I called again, and then again. The answer was the same.

In desperation I appealed to Curtis. "Surely they cannot be so cruel. Even if she is as badly off as they say it would do her good to see me. Speak to Avery—make him understand that I must see her!"

But Curtis only shook his head and shrugged his shoulders in defeat. "I can do nothing, Marian. She is legally in her husband's charge. If both he and Dr. Gardner agree that she is—"

"Not 'responsible.' That is what Avery said. 'Responsible'—what does it mean? Does it mean she cannot have the comfort of a visit from me?"

He gazed at me with his fine eyes, clouded now by sadness.

"It means, my dear, that they can do with her as they will. We must simply wait and hope for better days."

And so I waited; through February, through March, and still I could not see her, still I had no idea whether the messages I constantly sent were even delivered.

At the end of March I had a letter from Carrie in which she announced that she and Leighton were "going across," as she put it, in early May and would I care to join them? And Diana too, if she could be excused early from school. Their itinerary included Paris and a motor trip to the Riviera and thence to Switzerland, which I had never seen. They would return in late June, in time for the Newport season.

"Go," said Curtis. "What can you do here except worry? Go and take Diana with you. I will know where you are, and I will cable you at once if there is any need to have you here."

And so we went; and we had, if not a wonderful time— my concern for Isabel would not allow that—then at least a welcome change of scene. We returned on the last day of June, and instead of opening the Beacon Street house we went directly to Newport where I had taken rooms at the Ocean House Hotel. It seemed very odd indeed to be at Newport and not to have the comfort and freedom of Isabel's house, but we managed well enough, and in a few days we had recovered from the rigors of our journey.

Carrie, minus her husband and children, had come to Newport also to stay with a family whom I did not know—"although not for the entire season, my dear, it's far too stuffy for me to endure more than a few weeks. I shall go to Saratoga and let my hair down."

I did not inquire what, precisely, letting her hair down involved; Carrie's kind heart and blunt ways were sufficient unto themselves, and if she chose to mingle in circles which Newport and Boston held to be not quite proper it was no concern of mine or of Newport's or Boston's either.

Meanwhile, on a warm and brilliant day about a week after we arrived, Carrie, in her compassionate way, suggested that we go to see Isabel. Curtis had told us that she was in residence—although not, of course, going into society—apparently because her keepers had determined that the sea air would do her good.

"Perhaps with two of us going we can overpower her dragon," Carrie said (for I had told her how I had been prevented from seeing Isabel the previous winter). "Come on. I'd like to see her—the dragon, I mean—and see how easily she puts *me* off."

And so we went. We bowled down Bellevue Avenue in Carrie's maroon barouche, bowing and smiling as we went, looking, I suppose, as though we had not a care in the world, while I strengthened myself for what I knew would be an unpleasant encounter. For I had had no word from Avery, not the slightest indication that my presence was wanted, and so what lay in store for us at Casa del Mare was surely another rebuff.

We turned in at the high iron gate and proceeded down the drive. To my surprise the house and the surrounding lawns and gardens looked as beautiful as ever; I realized that I had somehow expected them to be unkempt, let go to ruin, the tall windows draped in black, perhaps, to signal what was to my mind at least the death of someone within! Was she not as good as dead, locked in a prison from which I could not help her to escape?

A boy came to take the horses and we climbed down and approached the ornately carved front door. Carrie glanced at me as she pulled the bellpull.

"Let me talk," she said. "You are always so polite, and I don't mind fighting a bit to get my way."

The door was opened by a maid whom I did not recognize, a temporary for the season, no doubt, whose frightened eyes and nervous stammer spoke of more than simply being new to the job. She was young, not more than twenty-one or -two, and as she hesitated, not knowing whether to admit us, we had a chance to look beyond her into the center court. There was a shallow pool there, and a small bronze fountain, dolphins cavorting with a naked boy. Seated on the tiled wall that surrounded the pool, staring into the water like Narcissus pining for his own image, was Isabel.

She was perhaps thirty feet away—within hearing, although she seemed not to have heard us. Carrie raised her voice and repeated her demand.

"Mrs. Kittredge, please. We have come to see Mrs. Kittredge."

"I—you—she cannot—we are—"

But, hot with the scent of victory, Carrie brushed her aside and strode into the courtyard, and I followed, caution to the winds, overcome by the sight of that one whom I had so longed to see all the months past.

At last she saw us, and she stood up. She was unlaced, dressed in a loose-fitting pale blue sacque. Precariously perched on her untidy hair was a golden tiara; several rings adorned her fingers, and a heavy gold and pearl brooch dragged at her bosom.

"There," she said to no one in particular. "You see I was right. People are beginning to arrive after all." She held out her hand to us, not in a gesture of greeting but palm down, fingers drooping, as if she were presenting it to be kissed. Carrie seized it nonetheless and clasped it for a moment before advancing to embrace her.

But Isabel suddenly stiffened and pushed her away, and Carrie did not persist.

"Excuse me," said Isabel. As her eyes swept over us I saw with a sinking heart and a kind of horrid fascination that she did not recognize us. "I am here to receive my guests," she went on. "Please excuse me—please stand to one side, stand over there where you will not interfere. Yes. Like that."

I was conscious of the maid hovering fearfully in the background, but I was too intent on Isabel to send her away.

Isabel peered at the entranceway. "There," she said; she was smiling. "Now they come, just as I said they would." She pressed her hands together in gleeful anticipation as she stared at forms and faces that only she could see. And then, as she watched the phantom figures come near, she began a litany of greeting such as no hostess had ever dared speak but which many surely had wished to:

"Mrs. Willingham. Delightful to see you." (An aside: "Mrs. Willingham has had a liaison with her son's tutor for the past two years.")

"Mrs. Furbush—*dear* Mrs. Furbush." (Aside: "Mrs.

Furbush has had three illegal operations that I know of, and possibly more.")

"Mrs. Pevey—how well you look! How prosperous!" (Aside: "Mrs. Pevey's husband engineered the Circle Affair, in which he swindled thousands of people's life savings.")

"Mrs. Kittredge!" The voice turned us all, including Isabel, to stone. Mrs. Briggs stood halfway down the staircase, staring at Isabel with an expression of what I can only call wrath. She did not seem to notice Carrie and me at first; then, looking for a servant, perhaps, she saw us as we hovered near a marble pillar. "Out!" she snapped. For a moment she did not move from her place on the stairs: she paused there as if she were a general considering what battle strategy to employ. Then, swiftly, in an oddly fluid motion (like a snake, I thought), she descended to where we stood transfixed. She confronted us in a paroxysm of controlled anger. "Who let you in?" she hissed. "You are forbidden! No one is to see her—no one!"

To my surprise (for I was dumbstruck) Carrie was able to reply. "We need to see her, Mrs. Briggs. We cannot be denied, we are her closest family—Mrs. Motley is like family as you know—and we must reassure ourselves—"

"It is forbidden! Dr. Gardner gave his orders. How dare you force your way in—"

"We did not do that. We simply asked the girl—"

"Who? Who was it let you in? Look at her—look and see the damage you do! She has gone off again, she has not had a spell like this in weeks, and now you bring it on—James!"

This was directed to the person of the butler, who, no doubt alerted to the crisis, had appeared from belowstairs and now came to Mrs. Briggs' bidding. He was new also; apparently Isabel was not to have even the comfort of familiar servants.

"Show them out," commanded Mrs. Briggs.

He glanced at us as if he were giving us a cue. Still we hesitated. Mrs. Briggs, having enlisted an ally, turned to Isabel. Her attitude changed suddenly from anger to that of the conscientious caretaker—a schoolmistressy attitude. She went to Isabel's side; gently, firmly, she took her arm. "Now, Mrs. Kittredge, just come along. You will tire yourself standing there."

Isabel stared at her. Her face was blank, but for an instant I thought I saw a flicker of contempt pass over it before blankness descended again. I struggled with my emotions; how I longed to rush to her, embrace her, tell her how I loved her and wanted her back safe with me again! Why could I not overcome my hesitation, why could I not defy these people who kept her from me, locked in the prison of her tormented mind? *Isabel!*

The moment passed. Mrs. Briggs took Isabel by the arm and steered her toward the stairs. Isabel did not resist. She walked slowly, as if she were sleepwalking, but her steps were unhesitating as she reached the stairs and climbed them. She did not look back. I am sure that she never knew, that day, that we had come. In a moment she had vanished into the upper reaches of the house.

The butler waited, implacable. Carrie touched my arm. "Come," she whispered; and, having no choice, I obeyed her.

We left the house with the heavy thud of the door echoing in our ears. The day was still bright, still warm, a day for Newport to pursue its pleasures—and yet I felt cold to the bone, I felt the deadly chill of that house and I thought that some part of me would never be warm again.

Although we had not summoned it, the carriage had been brought round. We climbed in; the coachman drove us away. I felt as though I left half my life behind, for Isabel had been my life and now I had lost her, so it seemed, for good.

Carrie left Newport a week or so later with a promise to demand a family conference in the fall to confront Avery with our request to see Isabel. "Curtis will help us," she said, giving me a reassuring hug. "We will simply insist. We will bring Charlotte and Victoria back to plead our case, if necessary. Somehow we will break through this—this impossible barrier they have thrown up!"

As good as her word, she came to Boston in September and arranged a meeting with Avery. He was unyielding: we could not visit Isabel until Dr. Gardner gave his permission. It struck me more forcefully than ever that Avery, and not Dr. Gardner, was the perpetrator of Isabel's isolation—that he had been storing up his anger against her all the years, and now, when she was most helpless, he had given it full rein.

Had he known of her love for Cushing all those years—did he ever even suspect?

We did not give up, of course. Intermittently in the months that followed we tried repeatedly to see her without success. She lived not a quarter of a mile away from me, and yet she was beyond my reach.

In the summer of '03, while Diana and I were in France, we received word that Mrs. January and Mrs. Roberts Reed, dear friends and sisters-in-law in life, had died within a week of each other. We missed their funerals, of course, unable to return in time, and when we came home and I wrote to Isabel I had no reply.

At last I accepted my defeat. I lived my life; I traveled; I watched Diana bloom. I had little to remind me of years gone by.

No; that is not true. I had many reminders of the past, had I chosen to acknowledge them. But I did not; I lived in the present, I looked forward to the future, and I tried for Diana's peace of mind if not for my own to put the past behind me—behind us both.

One day, more than two years after Mrs. January's death, the telephone rang and I answered it to hear Curtis' voice telling me that Avery had died. It was quite sudden: he had simply keeled over in his office the previous afternoon.

Isabel came to the funeral in Mrs. Briggs's charge, her children protectively near her. After the service I went to speak to her. She responded politely enough, but it seemed to me that she did not know who I was. Mrs. Briggs hovered hear; she made me uncomfortable, unable to speak freely.

"She *is* a dragon," murmured Carrie as we took our leave. "If she could have kept Isabel away I wager she'd have done so."

A few days later I presented myself, as I had done so many times before, at Isabel's house in Commonwealth Avenue. But I was turned away, and after that I did not try another time. One day, I thought, I will see her; for the time being, again, I gave up.

And so we resumed our separate lives, Isabel and I. Curtis, who had fallen into the habit of calling on me once or twice a week, told me that she was physically well at least; of her mental state he was not sure. "But she is quiet—no raving, no obvious breakdown. Avery's will provided for two trustees to oversee her welfare. Mrs. Briggs will continue to care for her under Dr. Gardner's guidance." All her children were grown now; Mason had gone to New York with Leighton, and Mary lived mostly in Germany with Victoria.

The following year was the year of Diana's debut. It was a great success—a splendid party and a triumphant debutante year. She showed no interest in an early marriage and, perhaps selfishly, I did not encourage it. I knew that one day she must go away from me, but I saw no reason to hurry her departure. Young men came and went. She was happy to see them, but none of them seemed to make a very deep impression.

"I have time, Mother," she would laugh. "And meanwhile I have more important things to do."

But sometimes the past reared its ugly head and would not be denied.

In the fall of '07, I was asked to take in a student—the nephew of a friend; he needed a home for the semester. He would, if he came, need to be put in what had been Perseus' room. I took it as a sign from fate; here was one memory—the memory of the man who had been my husband—that needed to be buried once for all. It would not be so very unpleasant, I told myself; he had been gone a long time, he could not come back now to torment me. His ghost, if he had one, had long since been laid. He could do me no more harm. What did I expect to find, after all? Nothing—there could be nothing. I should have done this years before.

Rejecting any help, I set about my task. I unlocked the door and went in. The air was stale, the light dim because the drapes were drawn. I pushed them back and opened the windows. I looked around, wondering where to begin. It might have been a room in a hotel: he had had almost no personal gewgaws of the kind that most people have. No photographs, no books, no souvenirs from travels, a favorite pipe from London, perhaps, or a framed Italian scene.

His desk was neat, holding only an inkwell and pen stand. There were three drawers. I expected that they would be locked but they were not. One held a stack of stationery; another was empty; in the third were two small volumes bound in marbled paper. I opened them. The pages were blank; they were diaries which he had not lived long enough to fill. Somewhere, then, were diaries which he had written in.

His clothing hung in the wardrobe, his shoes and boots in a straight row beneath. I took them out: suits, an overcoat, odd jackets and trousers. I laid them on the bed. Men's fashions did not change so frequently as women's; these would be welcomed by someone, they were of good quality and hardly looked worn at all. When I had emptied the wardrobe, fighting down my reluctance to touch his things, I paused for a moment, wondering whether to ring for the housekeeper at once to have her take them away.

The double doors of the wardrobe stood open. At the back, behind the shoes and boots, I saw a wooden box about a foot wide, two feet long. It was very ordinary-looking, not polished. It seemed to have no lock.

I did not want to touch it. I stared at it for a long moment. I could have the housekeeper come, I thought. I could simply ask her to put it in the rubbish, she would never open it without permission. . . .

I crouched in front of the wardrobe; I pulled out the shoes and boots—far more worn than the clothing, I noted—and reached for the box. I lifted it out. It was heavy. I set it on the floor; then I opened the hinged lid.

It was filled with volumes like those in the desk drawer. I opened one at random. Its pages were covered with a tiny, crabbed script—Perseus' handwriting. At the top of one page I saw a date: Oct. 3, '91. There were many books—twenty, perhaps. I began to take them out. At the bottom of the box I saw several other books—larger, printed books—and several packets wrapped in brown paper, tied with string. I slipped off the string and paper of one of them. They were photographs of women. All were unlcothed; some were in odd, awkward poses. I put them by; I opened one of the books: *My Life* by a Courtesan.

A patch of sun fell across the dark red patterned carpet. From the front hall I heard the shrill of the telephone. After a moment it stopped. All around me, outside this room, the world went on—my world, Diana's world. The world of the living. Suddenly I wanted to rush out to join it again, I was afraid that if I stayed here one moment more I would be trapped forever, I would never find my way back. I threw everything into the box and slammed shut the lid and lifted it into my arms. I pulled the bellpull and, carrying the box, went out into the hall. When the maid came I told her to finish cleaning Mr. Motley's room: throw away everything personal, I said, clean it, dust and polish it, fetch new bed linen, bundle the clothing for charity.

I carried the box to my room and put it in the back of my dress closet, behind a stack of hatboxes. Not now, I thought: later. Later I will do what I have to do, I will read what he wrote. I felt that I must: it was an obligation, something I needed to do, I did not understand why. And when I did, when I read the record left by that anguished, tortured soul who had been my husband, I felt that now, finally, his spirit had been put to rest and I need never fear him again. The student, as it happened, never came; but I was grateful to him nevertheless for doing me that service.

And then one day in the spring of '09 I saw Isabel again, and all our past, which I thought I had left safely behind, came rushing back to claim me once more.

Twenty-Four

We met, quite by chance, in the Mount Auburn Cemetery in Cambridge: a white marble wilderness of winding graveled paths and specimen shrubs and trees, a botanical showplace then, in April, just coming into bloom.

I saw her first from a distance: a short, plump figure clothed in black, standing before a chained-off family plot, head bowed in prayer or possibly contemplation. I paid her no notice, continuing on my leisurely way, enjoying the warmth of the sun upon my face, the satisfying crunch of gravel under my feet. I had a destination of my own: a small plot, a small stone weathered by two decades of the harsh New England climate. I often went there; and this day, too, I would get to it in time; there was no hurry. And when I arrived I would spend awhile with the memory of the child who once had been mine. I would feel no anger at his death, as once I had done; I would simply visit with him once again and come away soothed and refreshed, knowing that he waited there for me when my time came.

I never look at Perseus' stone.

Eventually I came near to her; I rounded the corner of the path where she stood, meaning to slip past this stranger without disturbing her meditation. But as I approached I saw the tilt of her head, the set of her small shoulders, the familiar slant of the nose beneath the veil. I hesitated; I would not have been more surprised had I seen a visitor from Percival Lowell's Martian landscape where, they say, strange small creatures live, stranger even than the inhabitants of earth.

She stood before the Cushing family plot. The wind fluttered the black-dyed plumes of her hat; the sunlight played on the diamond brooch at her throat. When she heard my footstep she looked up; and then, knowing surely who she was, I spoke.

"Isabel."

She turned to me, not surprised or startled; she smiled, she spoke as easily as if we had been talking all afternoon, as if there had never been a break in our friendship.

"I thought when they buried him that they might have given him some poetic inscription," she said, "but they did not."

She looked at the tombstone again: plain gray granite, a severe rectangle with only the name and dates upon it:

Lawrence Stearns Cushing
1847-1898

On all sides we were surrounded by winged angels, cherubim, representations from life—as varied a population of statues and bas-reliefs as that of any crowded,

ancient European plot. But Cushing's grave was unadorned—a kind of abandonment, I thought.

Suddenly she spoke again, not in a conversational
tone, this time, but in a voice thick and hoarse with rage.
"He was a terrible man," she said. "Terrible terrible
terrible. I am glad he is dead. I am glad he died as he did.
He deserved that."

I was too startled to reply at once, and then, before I
could, I was aware that a woman was approaching: my old
nemesis, Mrs. Briggs. To my surprise she nodded at me in
a civil way and then turned to Isabel.

"Now, Mrs. Kittredge, isn't it time to go?"

Isabel glanced at her with ill-concealed dislike. "No,"
she said. "I have met my friend, as you see—my oldest
and dearest friend. I will walk with her for a while, and
when I am ready to leave I will call you."

Remembering my former battles with Isabel's
"dragon," I half expected her to whisk Isabel away now.
But she did not; after a moment's scrutiny of me she
turned away and left us alone.

Isabel took my arm, leaning on me a little, and we
walked on. When we reached a marble bench overlooking
the little lake we sat down and settled our skirts and
stayed silent for a moment, enjoying the warmth of the
sun after the long winter. The trees were just coming into
leaf; yellow willows shimmered against the purple clouds
massed at the horizon, white birches with their pale green
tips clustered against a stand of dark pine. Clumps of
golden forsythia bloomed everywhere; soon pink and red
azaleas would burst their buds and overshadow the
crocus and daffodils now scattered in splotches of color

across the grass.

Isabel lifted her veil and stared frankly at me.

"This will be a pleasant place to sleep when our time comes," she said. She smiled. Her face looked as soft as underdone custard. Formerly she had the look of a warrior princess. Now she seemed old—far older than I, although there is not more than a year's difference in our ages. Time passes relentlessly, more relentless for women than for men.

"Yes," I said, humoring her. "The Kittredge plot is very pretty."

"So it is," she said. A note of malice crept into her voice. "And the Motleys' too. How good it is to know that we will lie next to our husbands for eternity." She took on a conspiratorial tone. "Perhaps," she murmured, "you can arrange it so that you do not have to lie next to him. Perhaps you can pick another place."

"No," I said. Why did she talk so? She must have known that she hurt me. "No—I will lie there. With the Motleys." With my child, I might have added; with *my* child. Not Perseus Motley's child, but mine.

She did not reply. She seemed to have fallen into a daydream—back into the past, perhaps, when we were young and full of hope, when life was, if not completely happy, at least not the tangle that it became. And then, abruptly, "I shall go to the trial tomorrow. Will you?"

"To the—what trial, Isabel?" But of course the moment I spoke I knew the answer, and I cursed my stupidity.

"I wouldn't miss it," she said. Her eyes gleamed; for a moment she was the warrior princess again, triumphant, vanquishing enemies left and right.

"Isabel—"

"I met her once," she said. "Mrs. Newhall. People say
she is dreadful, but she isn't, really. She only lacks
imagination. She was in love with him. And he betrayed
her. It was his nature. And she had no means to survive,
after that. And so—ah, but I mustn't say it. She is
innocent until they prove her guilt. I will go and watch
them try to do it."

I fought down my rising alarm. I will telephone to
Curtis, I thought. He will know what to do.

Mrs. Briggs approached then, and Isabel, having made
her small rebellion, rose docilely to go. I went with her. I
had no heart, now, to visit the small stone with my son's
name upon it. I will come another day, I thought, when I
can be tranquil and alone.

And so I walked with Isabel to the gate, Mrs. Briggs
following behind, and we said good-bye and climbed into
our waiting vehicles—hers, a closed trap; mine, a shining
Rolls-Royce Silver Ghost adorned with the emblem of the
flying lady. I had bought it the previous autumn in a fit of
extravagance which, I knew, I could well afford. Even
sober ladies rising sixty, as I am, are subject to such self-
indulgence; when Isabel saw it, in the moment before
Mrs. Briggs and the coachman helped her into her
carriage, she shot a glance of surprise at me as if to say:
"Is this what you do with Uncle James's money?" But
she made no comment. She and her companion—her
keeper, rather—nodded good-bye and drove away in the
cool, gathering twilight, leaving me to sort out what
significance our meeting had had.

Henry started the engine easily enough and we set off. We came out to the river and, shortly, to the bridge at Massachusetts Avenue. The sun had set; behind us the western sky glowed crimson, while before us, across the wide pale expanse of water, rising over the clustered rooftops of the city, rising over the church spires, over the golden dome on Beacon Hill, shone the new moon: that other Diana for whom my own girl had been named.

She waited for me at home; we had an early dinner because, as she so often did, she had an evening engagement. I debated whether to tell her my news; finally, when we had finished our soup and the girl had brought up the roast and left us alone again, I did.

"Isabel!" Diana had been cutting her meat; now she paused and stared at me. "How? Where?"

"Walking in Mount Auburn."

"Alone?"

"No. Mrs. Briggs was with her."

She grimaced. "How did she seem? Aunt Isabel, I mean."

Although I had confided some of my news, I was not prepared to tell all of it. "She was—calm, I should say."

Diana threw me a sharp glance. "You mean she is still—ah—disturbed. That's all right, Mother. I'm grown up now. I can hear unpleasant things without collapsing." (She was not yet twenty-one.) "But this is really very interesting. No one has seen her for years." She thought for a moment while she went on eating. Then: "Where, exactly, did you see her?"

"At the stone of—someone she once knew."

"Who?"

"A man named Lawrence Cushing."

"Lawrence Cushing!" Again she paused to stare at me. "Dreadful man."

I was taken aback. "How on earth do you know what he was? You were only a child when—"

"I remember him. I saw him once or twice—and at Cousin Charlotte's wedding, remember? I never liked him. His eyes were hypnotic. It made me uneasy just to look at him."

I was sure that she knew nothing of Isabel's infatuation with Cushing; certainly I did not intend to tell her.

Suddenly Diana said: "Why did she behave so?"

"Who? What do you mean?"

"Aunt Isabel, of course. Why did she struggle all those years to achieve her position and then simply abdicate, if you will? People have told me what a power she was. And then, after Cousin Vicky's wedding, she just seemed to give it up. I know there was that awful trial, but still. It was almost as if she deliberately became ill so that she would not have to go on with it."

Ah, she is a clever girl, my Diana! Beautiful, yes— large brown eyes, her mother's eyes, and Isabel's sweet heart-shaped face and a yard and more of shining thick brown hair, chestnut brown that glows like fire in the sun; and tall and willowy, as is the fashion, long slender hands, long slender bones, gliding like a swan as she moves. She would be a fitting adornment for any man, but she does not want to be that. I admire her independence, even as I fear it. If she joins the suffragists, as she has threatened to do, who will marry her then?

Later, as we finished our dinner, Curtis came. He stood waiting for us by the drawing-room fire. He kissed Diana, and we chatted for a moment before she went to join her friends at Symphony. When she had gone we sat opposite each other as we have done so many times. He sipped his coffee; he lit his cigar.

"Well," he said. "Here I am. Is anything wrong?"

"Not yet. But there may be." And I told him of how I met Isabel, and where, and of what she had said. He watched me closely as I spoke, his fine eyes never wavering. When I finished he pulled once more at his cigar and then waited for a moment more before he spoke.

"I think that nothing will come of it," he said at last.

"But if she—"

"Mrs. Briggs is very competent."

"I suppose she is. But what if Isabel actually tries to go, what if she runs out into the street—"

"She will not. And if she does, Mrs. Briggs can restrain her. Physically, if necessary."

I looked away, shuddering. I had seen her once, physically restrained, and the horror of that sight had never left me.

"Marian, do not worry about Isabel. She is my sister, after all. If she needed help, do you not think that I would help her? She is not unhappy. She wanders back and forth in time, she has lucid moments and moments when she does not know her own name. But she is not unhappy, I think."

I looked at him again, I watched him for a moment, and

713

then suddenly, impulsively, I said: "Tell me."

"About Cushing?"

"About everything."

"I don't know everything. You know as much as I, if not more. How he betrayed her—"

"No. No. There are blank spaces, times when I—when I had my own concerns."

"Yes." He smiled at me; he reached out and took my hand. His eyes were filled with compassion. "You were a good friend to her," he said gently. "Other women might not have been."

I did not want his pity. I knew what he was thinking: of my brother George's death, and how Isabel, some said, had caused it.

"I will go to her tomorrow," I said at last. "Surely now—now, after all these years—surely now she will speak to me, she will tell me what I long to know. I will ask her—I will implore her, if necessary. Even wandering as she is, she can tell me— It is not just idle curiosity, you know it is not. I want to understand her life."

"And yours?" he said softly.

"All our lives—yours, and hers, and Cushing's too, for that matter. Help me to do it."

He paused, thinking how to begin. In an attempt to leave him alone to collect his thoughts, I went to the sideboard where I kept a bottle of brandy. I poured two small snifters and carried them to the low table before the fire. I stood warming myself, waiting. Curtis struggled with it; he rose and paced to the windows and back; then he turned to me and put his hands on my shoulders. I am tall, nearly as tall as he, and so our eyes were almost level.

Suddenly he gathered me up into his arms, but without passion, without demand—we were, after all, well past middle age, past the time when our bodies betray us.

He was quiet for a long moment; then he released me, he took his brandy and sipped it, and then he began to speak. And when I heard what he had to say I understood that it was a relief to him to tell me, the lancing of a wound that had festered for nearly forty years.

He cried a little, at the end. Well he might.

The next day I presented myself at Isabel's door. I was admitted by a middle-aged maid who put me into the reception room. I remembered the previous times that I had waited there. How long ago!

When the tap on the door came at last it was not Mrs. Briggs as I had anticipated but the maid once more. She asked me to follow her upstairs, and I did so—an intruder into my own past. Up and up—into the broad paneled upper hall, past doors closed for how many years!

The maid rapped at Isabel's door and I entered upon her command. Her voice sounded reasonably firm. She was sitting on a chaise before the fire. She did not rise, but she held out her arms to me and we made an awkward embrace.

"There!" she said. "I knew you'd come. I told Mrs. Briggs so. How good—how good to see you, Marian! Come—sit—take your tea—ah, how many times have we done this, you and I?"

We had a happy hour, that day, reestablishing ourselves. She was calm, sometimes slow-spoken but not irrational as she had been the day before. When I left her I promised to return again soon. Before long we had a visit every afternoon. She knew nothing of my conversations with Curtis, of course (for when he came to me now, in the evenings, he talked even as she did); she knew nothing of the pile of notebooks on my desk growing higher with each passing week. She spoke to me with complete frankness—as if she knew that she had not long to live, as if she wanted to make her confession, as it were, before she went away forever.

In late September she began to fail, and our conversations ceased. I still called every day, but now I simply sat by her side and held her hand or read to her a bit. She was rational, fully conscious at the end, as if, having wandered in the wilderness for so many years, she was now determined to hold fast as long as she could.

She died at dawn of a mild October day. As she had foretold, we laid her to rest beside her husband in Mount Auburn. One day several weeks later Curtis and I went to visit her grave. When I told Bowditch where we were going he snorted his disapproval. "Let her be," he said. He shifted his weight in his chair. His arthritis pains him very much now; some days he cannot even hold his brush, and those are the worst days, the times when his black moods engulf him. "Why do you want to go traipsing about over there? Stay here and keep me company instead. I need you more than she does."

But I went, all the same. How could I not?

We walked slowly, as if we were reluctant to get to her. It was November now, a cold, cloudy day. The cemetery was deserted—of living people, that is; like all such places, it was crammed with a population that could not speak to us. The spiritualists would argue that point, but

I have never wanted to experiment with communication with the dead; communication with the living is difficult enough.

We came to the Kittredge plot. Curtis removed his hat. We stared at the marble stones, the statue of a winged angel over the graves of Avery's parents.

"We must believe that she is at rest," he said. "She never was while she lived."

"No. She always wanted—more than she had."

"She always wanted *him*." He nodded his head toward Cushing's grave, which lay not far distant.

"Yes."

"Did she tell you that?"

"Yes."

"Did she tell you everything, as you said you wanted her to do?"

"Yes. Well—no. Not everything."

He turned to look at me. "She never told you—about his death?"

"No."

"Do you think that she could have? Told you, I mean—told you more than any of us know."

"Or more than they were able to prove in court?" I paused. Even now, even after she was gone, I felt a sense of loyalty to her. "I don't know," I said at last.

He accepted it; he questioned me no further. After a few moments we left her. We walked back to the gate as Isabel and I had walked that April afternoon months before. We passed Cushing's grave, but we did not stop to look at it. All around us the world seemed held in suspense ready for the long winter's onslaught, leafless

717

trees, shriveled lawns, bare earth where flowers would bloom again. The statues stood watch; they kept their secrets, the secrets of the dead. They would not confide in us.

It was a bleak, brown landscape, very different from the spring—that New England spring, fickle lover whispering false promise to our willful hearts.

BESTSELLERS BY SYLVIE F. SOMMERFIELD
ARE BACK IN STOCK!